The Connoisseur's Guide to
ANTIQUE FURNITURE

PLATE I (overleaf)
(*frontispiece*) A vermilion lacquer cabinet on an elaborately carved gilt wood stand, *c*.1675.
Mallet and Son, London

The Connoisseur's Guide to
ANTIQUE FURNITURE

EDITED BY
L. G. G. RAMSEY AND HELEN COMSTOCK

THE CONNOISSEUR
LONDON

This book was designed and produced by
Rainbird Reference Books Ltd.,
Marble Arch House, 44 Edgware Road, London W2,
for The Connoisseur,
Chestergate House, Vauxhall Bridge Road, London SW1.

© The Connoisseur, 1957, 1959, 1961, 1962, 1969
© Hawthorn Books Inc., 1958
All Rights Reserved. No part of this publication
may be reproduced, stored in a retrieval system, or
transmitted, in any form or by any means, electronic,
mechanical, photocopying, recording or otherwise,
without prior permission of The Connoisseur.

The following previously published works have been
used to compile this book:

The Concise Encyclopaedia of Antiques, Vols 1–5
The Connoisseur, 1954–1961

The Concise Encyclopaedia of American Antiques, Vol 1
The Connoisseur, 1958

The Complete Encyclopaedia of Antiques
The Connoisseur, 1962

718   3062   8

Printed by Balding & Mansell Ltd., London and Wisbech,
and bound by Nevett, Key & Whiting, Ltd., London.

PRINTED IN GREAT BRITAIN

CONTENTS

		Page
On Collecting Antique Furniture by GEOFFREY WILLS		19
Oak Furniture by ANTHONY COLERIDGE	Plates 1–12	45
Walnut Furniture by E. T. JOY	Plates 13–24	48
Mahogany Furniture by E. T. JOY	Plates 25–36	76
Victorian Furniture by PETER FLOUD	Plates 37–44	89
American Furniture 1640–1840 by MARVIN D. SCHWARTZ	Plates 45–64	118
American Victorian Furniture by MARVIN D. SCHWARTZ	Plates 65–68	150
Windsor Chairs in America by MARVIN D. SCHWARTZ	Plates 69–72	171
Country Furniture in New England by FRANK O. SPINNEY	Plates 73–76	174
The Craftsmanship of The American Shakers by EDWARD DEMING ANDREWS	Plates 77–80	178
Italian Furniture by HUGH HONOUR	Plates 81–86	184
Viennese Furniture in the Eighteenth Century by DR FRANZ WINDISCH-GRAETZ	Plates 87–94	205
French Furniture from 1500 to the Revolution by R. A. CECIL	Plates 95–104	214
Chest Furniture by THERLE HUGHES	Plates 105–116	239
Smaller Furniture of all Periods by E. T. JOY	Plates 117–124	275

Contents continued

European Lacquer Furniture by HUGH HONOUR	*Plates* 125–132	276
Gothic Revival Furnishings by HUGH HONOUR	*Plates* 133–140	304
Furnishings in the Egyptian Taste by HUGH HONOUR	*Plates* 141–144	308
Glossary		313
List of Museums		357
Index		359

COLOUR PLATES

LIST OF COLOUR PLATES

    I (*frontispiece*) A vermilion lacquer cabinet on an elaborately carved gilt wood stand, *c*.1675. *Mallet and Son, London*

   II Cupboard. Ornamented with Italian terracotta. Gothic French, early fifteenth century. On it stand a pair of German kneeling figures in polychrome wood, from the early eighteenth century. *Mary Bellis Collection*

  III Corner Table. French, early eighteenth century. *Victoria and Albert Museum*

  IV Small Secrétaire. Mounted in ormulu. French, Louis XV period. |*Victoria and Albert Museum*

   V Bergère. One of a pair, giltwood covered with Beauvais tapestry. French, Louis XV, *c*.1750. *Wernher Collection*

  VI Secrétaire Book-case. Ornamented with insets of porcelain. Mid-eighteenth century.

 VII Armchair. From a design by the brothers Adam, *c*.1815. The coverings are Spitalfields silk, earlier than the furniture itself (probably *c*.1790). *Iveagh Bequest and the Baron Brabourne*

VIII Commode. Boulle corner commode, one of a pair, with marble top. Ormulu decoration on the drawer front and with canted corners. Early nineteenth century. *Iveagh Bequest, Kenwood House*

  IX Combined Games and Work Table. Made of fine rosewood, richly inlaid with brass. The top flap is painted in water colours. Regency period.

PLATE II

Cupboard. Ornamented with Italian terracotta. Gothic French, early fifteenth century. On it stand a pair of German kneeling figures in polychrome wood, from the early eighteenth century. *Mary Bellis Collection*

PLATE III
Corner Table. French, early eighteenth century. *Victoria and Albert Museum*

PLATE IV
Small Secrétaire. Mounted in ormulu. French, Louis XV period. *Victoria and Albert Museum*

PLATE V
Bergère. One of a pair, giltwood covered with Beauvais tapestry. French, Louis XV, c.1750.
Wernher Collection

PLATE VI
Secrétaire Book-case. Ornamented with insets of porcelain. Mid-eighteenth century.

PLATE VII

Armchair. From a design by the brothers Adam, *c*.1815. The coverings are Spitalfields silk, earlier than the furniture itself (probably *c*.1790). *Iveagh Bequest and the Baron Brabourne*

PLATE VIII

Commode. Boulle corner commode, one of a pair, with marble top. Ormolu decoration on the drawer front and with canted corners. Early nineteenth century. *Iveagh Bequest, Kenwood House*

ANTIQUE FURNITURE

PLATE IX

Combined Games and Work Table. Made of fine rosewood, richly inlaid with brass. The top flap is painted in water colours. Regency period.

ON COLLECTING ANTIQUE FURNITURE

By GEOFFREY WILLS

The word 'antique' was once synonymous with 'dry-as-dust', but this is no longer the case. Of all the relics of the past, furniture is the most useful and adaptable, and even the most modern decor can advantageously incorporate one or more pieces. The designers and makers of former times were highly competent men, who could not have anticipated that in so many instances their handiwork would have such lengthy functional and decorative lives.

While some may share the late Henry Ford's view that 'History is bunk', the majority have an inbuilt respect for the achievements of an earlier age. One of these, undoubtedly, was a remarkable degree of skill in the art of cabinet-making, which was not confined to any one country or era but was varied in its application. Whereas the craftsmen of one land expressed themselves in complicated inlaying, those of another specialised in elaborate carving, and those of a third emphasised the beauties of timber through the utter simplicity of the designs they followed. Each excelled at one or more of these skills, so today there is a wide choice available.

In the following pages the reader is presented with an extensive selection of furniture from many parts of the world. Some, like the English Georgian (Plates 25–36) will be widely known, but others, like the Italian (Plates 81–86) and the Viennese (Plates 87–94) are less familiar. These latter may suggest new fields for collectors to explore, and stimulate some of them to stray a little from the well-trodden paths pursued by so many.

The collector of today has advantages over his predecessors. Improved transport has made the globe a very small one, and methods of printing and reproduction, with the help of photography, enable the dedicated and wealthy collector not only to know all about a rarity in, say, Rome, but to get there from London or New York in a matter of hours. In an equal space of time he can be back in his home with the prize, and ready to seek the next one.

The 'father' of furniture-collecting is the Hon. Horace Walpole, who fortunately possessed the three attributes of money, time and taste: the order in which they are listed being no more than fortuitous and not indicating their comparative importance. He lived during the eighteenth century when it might be thought that contemporaneous styles and workmanship were good enough for anyone, and for the majority they certainly were. Although Walpole patronised many of the craftsmen of his day, his greater pleasure was to acquire objects from the past.

The happy days in which he lived are reflected in part of a letter he wrote to his friend, George Montagu, in August 1761:

> Dicky Bateman has picked up a whole cloister full of old chairs in Herefordshire – he bought them one by one, here and there in farm-houses, for three-and-sixpence and a crown apiece. They are of wood, the seats triangular, the backs, arms, and legs, loaded with turnery.

Four years later Walpole wrote to the Reverend William Cole, who was about to set out on a journey to Cheshire. He described the chairs found in Herefordshire and added:

> I have long envied and coveted them. There may be such in poor cottages in so neighbouring a county as Cheshire. I should not grudge any expense for purchase or carriage; and should be glad even of a couple such for my cloister here.

Finally, in 1773, Dicky Bateman died, much of the contents of his house at Old Windsor was sold by auction, and Walpole duly recorded in triumph – 'I have crammed my cloister with three cartloads of lumbering chairs from Mr Bateman's, and at last am surfeited with the immovable movables of our forefathers.'

Horace Walpole was most particular in placing his furniture, pictures and other objects in the rooms of his house, Strawberry Hill, which were decorated to receive them. Others took considerably less trouble in the matter, and concerned themselves more with acquisition than display. Of these, Elizabeth Chudleigh was an example: her untidy home reflecting her disorderly life. In the House of Lords she was found guilty of having bigamously married the Duke of Kingston when already the wife of the Earl of Bristol, while earlier it had been rumoured that she was the mistress for a time of George II. She had caused a furore by appearing at a masquerade in the royal presence wearing a minimum of clothing: 'so naked you would have taken her for Andromeda.'

ANTIQUE FURNITURE

Writing to Montagu, Walpole recorded a visit to Miss Chudleigh's London home in 1760, when she was secretly wife of the future Lord Bristol:

> I breakfasted the day before yesterday at Ælia Lælia Chudleigh's. There was a concert for Prince Edward's birthday, and at three a vast cold collation, and all the town. The house is not fine, nor in good taste, but loaded with finery. Execrable varnished pictures, chests, cabinets, commodes, tables, stands, boxes, riding on one another's backs, and loaded with tereens, philigree, figures, and everything upon earth. Every favour she has bestowed is registered by a bit of Dresden china. There is a glass case full of enamels, eggs, amber, lapislazulis, cameos, toothpick-cases, and all kinds of trinkets, things that she told me were her playthings; another cupboard full of the finest japan, and candlesticks and vases of rock crystal ready to be thrown down, in every corner. But of all curiosities, are the *conveniences* in every bedchamber: great mahogany projections, as big as her own bubbies, with the holes, brass handles, and cocks, etc.—I could not help saying, it was the *loosest* family I ever saw! Never was such an intimate union of love and a closestool!

In contrast, the Round Drawing Room at Strawberry Hill was hung with crimson damask, and a suite of French gilt chairs covered in Aubusson tapestry stood on a Moorfields carpet especially designed and woven for the room. The chimney-piece was adapted by Robert Adam from the tomb of Edward the Confessor in Westminster Abbey, and the ceiling copied from an engraving of a window in old St Paul's Cathedral which had been irreparably damaged in the Great Fire of London in 1666.

In this carefully-devised setting were some first-class oil paintings, a Boulle coffer and stand, some lacquered furniture, and a gilt table that had belonged to Sir Robert Walpole, father of Horace. China included Sèvres porcelain and Italian majolica, and on one of the lacquer pieces stood a pair of silver candelabra 'bought at Lady Vere's sale in 1783'.

Altogether the house personified a very catholic taste, although today we tend to consider that the Gothic style should be confined to ecclesiastical use, and few might care to entertain their friends beneath a ceiling designed after part of a cathedral. In 1765 its owner noted ironically: 'I believe in 20 years there will not be a convent left in Europe but this at Strawberry.'

Following Walpole's death, which occurred in 1797, six years after he had become fourth Earl of Orford, the collection remained intact. Eventually it became the property of his niece, the Countess of Waldegrave, whose son offered it for sale in 1842 and gave a fresh generation of collectors an opportunity to acquire what had been amassed with such care during the preceding century.

The sale was held at the mansion, situated at Twickenham, a few miles outside London, and occupied twenty four days. The auctioneer, George Robins, was known in his time for the flowery language in which his catalogues were compiled, and on this occasion he understandably gave himself full rein. The title-page announced that the contents 'may fearlessly be proclaimed the most distinguished gem that has ever adorned the annals of auctions . . . and within will be found a repast for the Lovers of Literature and the Fine Arts, of which bygone days furnish no previous example, and it would be in vain to contemplate it in time to come'.

The whole realised just short of £30,000, to which was added the proceeds of a sale of the prints and engravings. These were dispersed in London for about £4,000 and brought the total, according to the *Gentleman's Magazine* to £33,453 4s 3d. There can be little doubt that with the publicity it received it fetched what it was worth in 1842. Today's auctioneers are more sober in their descriptions, and only occasionally use more than one adjective with which to describe their lots. The best of them reserve extravagance of language until it is really merited, and then only bestow it after careful deliberation.

Equally with Horace Walpole in the line of great collectors was William Beckford, member of a family that owed its fortune to the sugar-plantations of Jamaica. Beckford built himself a vast house at Fonthill, Wiltshire, and filled it with all the fine works of art he could obtain. His taste ran to the exotic, and he favoured cabinets inset with plaques of amber, 'a rich cabinet of ebony, inlaid with lapis lazuli, designed by Bernini', a cabinet 'covered with a great variety of designs in silver', and 'two inestimable cabinets of the rarest old japan, enriched with bronzes by Vulliamy'.

The last-mentioned serves as a reminder that Beckford, like Walpole, appreciated Japanese lacquer, which had for long been valued by discerning Europeans. Beckford was fond, too, of having his possessions, porcelain as well as furniture mounted in gilt bronze in the French manner (Plate 102B). The Vulliamy who supplied mounts for his cabinet, noted above, was either Benjamin, or Benjamin Lewis, son of the former, who were clockmakers to the royal family, in particular to George IV. Recently, some of the firm's books have been brought to light; now it is known that they supplied their clients with many articles besides clocks, and these included gilt bronze ordered from a Parisian maker. Probably he was the source of the mounts on the 'two inestimable cabinets'.

Both Walpole and Beckford had a liking for historical relics, and while the former owned Cardinal Wolsey's red hat (bought in 1842 by Charles Kean, the actor), Beckford possessed six ebony chairs which were catalogued as having once been in the Cardinal's ownership at his Palace in Esher. The two men shared a liking for the Gothic style, which Walpole praised so energetically to his friends. Beckford's devotion to it was perhaps even more marked, for he named his house Fonthill Abbey and it was an outstanding example of the 'monastic gloomth' favoured by romantics of all periods. (See *Gothic Revival Furnishings* page 304.)

Beckford's expenditure on Fonthill has been estimated to have exceeded £250,000, and in 1822 he sold the property. In the year following, the contents came under the hammer of the London Auctioneer, Harry Phillips, and thirty-nine days were occupied in the dispersal which was held at the mansion. Twenty-five of the days were devoted to books, prints, pictures and miniatures, and the remaining fourteen to 'unique and splendid effects' and furnishings.

At the sale, many of the lots were bought-in by Beckford and duly passed to his elder daughter, who was married to the 10th Duke of Hamilton. The Duke was himself a keen collector, made purchases at Fonthill for himself, and in 1882 most of the accumulated riches of Hamilton Palace, Lanarkshire, were transported to London for auction by Christie's.

The event excited enormous interest on both sides of the Atlantic, and what were then sensationally high prices were realised. Two of the most important pieces of furniture were a commode and *secrétaire* inset with panels of Japanese lacquer and mounted in gilt bronze, which were the final items on the eleventh day. Both had been made in about 1787 by the royal cabinet-maker, Jean Henri Riesener for use by Queen Marie-Antoinette, and she had had them sent to the château de Saint-Cloud. (Also from Saint-Cloud is the *secrétaire* by Riesener illustrated in Plate 100A.)

At the time of the French Revolution it had been intended that the commode and *secrétaire* should be retained for the Louvre, but for some undiscovered reason they were sold and came into the possession of Beckford. As he was a frequent visitor to Paris it is not at all surprising that he should have acquired them, although it is not known when or for what amount of money. In 1882 they were sold for a total of £18,900 ($94,500 at the time), and in 1920 were presented by William K. Vanderbilt to the Metropolitan Museum, New York. At Fonthill the two pieces had realised £71 18s 6d (about $350).

So much for the past; what of the present? Nowadays, the results of research are quickly known to both dealers and auctioneers, indeed they should and do initiate advances in scholarship. Numerous magazines in every language print and re-print each discovery, and the twentieth-century collector is able to keep his knowledge up-to-date. In addition, there are groups of specialists, such as the Furniture History Society*, who have banded together in order to pursue inquiries into their particular interest.

The majority of buyers favour the personal contact between client and dealer, and only on special occasions do they venture into the open battle-field of the saleroom. The auctioneer is an agent, a go-between, and while he does his utmost for both seller and buyer he cannot be expected to favour the one party more than the other. Thus, his advice must be impartial and convey in words little more than his catalogue entry.

On the other hand, a dealer will have spent his own money on his wares, and while this may prejudice him in their favour it does mean that they represent an expenditure of his experience as well as his cash. A reputable shopkeeper willingly stakes his reputation on what he offers for sale, and will guide a client to the best of his ability. Not only will he select pieces he is pleased to recommend, but will ensure that, as far as possible, they represent good value.

A majority of collectors begin by buying a piece of furniture for use, with style and rarity as secondary considerations. It is then not long before they seek to buy what is fashionable and, usually, expensive. The rules of supply and demand affect antiques, and as soon as a certain type of article is sought after it is inevitable that its price rises. The supply of anything old is limited, and once costs are considered to have over-reached themselves, then demand falls off and something else takes its place to repeat the process.

In recent decades the heavily carved mid-eighteenth-century mahogany furniture, linked with the name of Thomas Chippendale because of his designs for such pieces in his *Director*, has become less sought after than it was earlier in the present century. Unsophisticated Elizabethan Jacobean oak pieces evince rather less interest than they did following the William Morris revival and its Arts and Crafts movement. The taste for veneered walnut of Queen Anne and George I is less widespread than it was before the discovery, in the late 'twenties, that a steam-heated atmosphere caused the veneers to peel off.

---

*Details can be obtained by writing to: The Assistant Secretary, Furniture History Society, c/o. Department of Furniture and Woodwork, Victoria and Albert Museum, London, S.W.7. The annual subscription (in 1969) is £2 2s (U.S. $6.00).

In the place of these, at the moment of writing, demand is concentrated on the inlaid and painted satinwood pieces, popularised in the design-books of Thomas Sheraton. Their straight lines relieved by gentle curves have suddenly attracted the interest of those who failed to notice their charm only a few years ago. Yellow satinwood completely replaces the red-brown and brown of mahogany and walnut in the affections of up-to-the-minute collectors, and the femininity of the 1790s has ousted, at least for the time being, the rococo and *chinoiserie* of thirty years earlier.

Like most other changes in taste this is only a revolution of the wheel, for the very same furnishings had been popular in the last quarter of the 19th century and the first years of the present one. Few smart late Victorian or Edwardian homes were complete without at least a bow-fronted satinwood commode with painted panels after Angelica Kauffmann and a set of frail-looking chairs in the same style. Much of the finest and costliest of this furniture was bought by Sir William Lever (later, 1st Viscount Leverhulme), some of whose collection of such pieces is displayed at the Lady Lever Art Gallery, Port Sunlight.

Today, interest is focussed also on the individual cabinet-makers of the eighteenth and nineteenth centuries. A start has been made in gathering information about them and their productions; a task made difficult by the fact that only very exceptionally did they sign their work. Unlike the French craftsmen, who were required to do so by means of a metal stamp (see pages 235 to 238), English, American and many other makers can only be traced from the fortuitous preservations of documents. These take the form of bills, account-books, mentions in contemporary letters and memoirs, and similar papers that are all too liable to suffer destruction over the years.

Argument sometimes centres on the amount of repair a piece of furniture can suffer before it ceases to be an antique and becomes more new than old. There is no short answer, as it must vary with the article in question. Most repairs are slight in nature, such as replacing missing veneer or making good a small piece of carving. The replacement by bracket feet of the original, and usually very worn, ball feet of early Queen Anne cabinets and chests is so commonplace as to go largely unremarked. So much so, that a piece retaining the old turned ones is almost an exception. Replacement of turned wood knob handles by brass ones is equally a normal practice. In most instances the piece looks no worse, if not better, for the change, and it can be commended provided the new handles are in the correct style. Nowadays, is it rarely difficult to obtain brass hardware in a range of period patterns, but apparently in the past this was less easy and some unsightly mistakes were made. It was not unusual to find a late eighteenth-century mahogany chest of drawers painstakingly equipped with brasses of Queen Anne design, or of a straightforward Edwardian pattern that did not echo any other age.

Repairs and what may be termed minor substitutions are, therefore, not unacceptable, but major work involves careful consideration. The exchange of a damaged chair-leg or the stand of a cabinet by completely new ones, however well done, does materially affect authenticity and value. Such instances should be brought to the buyer's notice, and the price adjusted downwards as compared with a perfect article.

Copies of antique furniture are not infrequently met with, and should be judged on their merits. When of high quality workmanship they command a high price that is commensurate with their making. Many of the most renowned eighteenth-century French pieces have been reproduced at various times, and a hundred years or so ago it was not unusual for famous examples to be loaned especially for the purpose.

In the mid-nineteenth century Napoleon III granted permission for the sumptuous *bureau-du-roi* made for Louis XV by Riesener and Oeben, to be copied. The copy was made for the Marquis of Hertford, who was acquainted with the Emperor and therefore probably had little trouble in obtaining the necessary sanction, and is now displayed in the Wallace Collection, London. While it is a close replica as regards outline, overall measurements and so forth, it does vary slightly in some details. When it was made the faded veneers of the original were matched for colour as closely as possible, but the passage of time has resulted in a marked difference in the appearance of the two.

The Hertford *bureau* was made by the Paris cabinet-maker, Pierre Dasson, and the Marquis is supposed to have paid the sum of 90,000 francs for it (roughly £3,600 or $17,000.00). Other copies of the piece are known to exist, and while Dasson's work of this nature is well-known he was not alone in its production. On both sides of the Channel similar reproductions of varying quality have been made for many decades.

It is apposite to conclude with a few brief notes on the care of old furniture. General maintenance in the way of occasional polishing is best done by using

(continued on page 43)

Oak hutch, demonstrating perforated work of a type in vogue early sixteenth century. *S. W. Wolsey.*

PLATE I

(A) Box-stool, early sixteenth century, showing typical 'slab' construction akin to that of the Boarded Chest. *Mary Bellis.*

(B) Child's Table (square joined stool), first half seventeenth century, with unusual dentil ornament. *Private collection.*

(C) Falling-table, with one flap and single gate, early seventeenth century. A type ancestral to the characteristic Gate-leg. *Mary Bellis.*

(D) Joined Stool, first half seventeenth century. *S. W. Wolsey.*

(A) Windsor-type Chair of very unusual design in that category. *Mary Bellis*.

(B) Caryatid and Atlanta on bedhead, *temp.* James I. *Private Collection*.

(C) Detail of foot of late sixteenth-century half-headed bed. *Private Collection*.

(D) Chair of so-called 'Farthingale' type, early seventeenth century. *S. W. Wolsey*.

PLATE 3

OAK FURNITURE

(B) Wainscot chair, carved with thistles. Early seventeenth century. *S. W. Wolsey.*

(A) Derbyshire or Yorkshire 'Mortuary' chair, mid-seventeenth century, the seat recessed for a loose squab (cushion). *S.W. Wolsey.*

PLATE 4

OAK FURNITURE

Oak settle, with lozenge or 'diamond' carving, seventeenth century. *S. W. Wolsey.*

PLATE 5

OAK FURNITURE

(A) 'Welsh' oak dresser of fine colour and quality. Deriving from the junction of the seventeenth and eighteenth centuries, the type has features which became traditional (e.g. arched-top, raised-centre panels). *H. W. Keil Ltd.* (B) Welsh Tridarn, dated 1705. *Leonard Wyburd Ltd.*

PLATE 6

OAK FURNITURE

(A) Press-cupboard demonstrating various ornamental motifs in vogue in the first half of the seventeenth century. *H. W. Keil Ltd.* (B) Break-front bookcase, junction of seventeenth and eighteenth centuries. The wing cupboards are filled with divisions and drawers. *H. W. Keil Ltd.*

PLATE 7

(A) Table-chair, or Chair-table, the top dated 1668. *S. W. Wolsey.*

(B) Child's chair, mid-seventeenth century. *Private Collection.*

(C) Box-stool, or 'Stoole with a Lock', seventeenth century. *Mary Bellis.*

(D) Gate-leg table, with twist-turned ('barley sugar') legs, second half seventeenth century. *Mary Bellis.*

Cane-chair of so-called "Restoration" type, in oak, carved with Royal Arms and 'boys and crowns' and dated 1687–8. *S. W. Wolsey*.

OAK FURNITURE

(A) Side table, early seventeenth century. *H. W. Keil Ltd.*

(B) Joined form, seventeenth century. *S. W. Wolsey*

PLATE 10

OAK FURNITURE

(A) Long table and set of joined stools in oak, seventeenth century. *Mary Bellis.*

(B) Oak dresser, *temp.* Charles II, showing use of mitred mouldings. *Mary Bellis.*

PLATE II

Oak trestle-table of *c.* 1660, its traditional type preserving medieval characteristics. *H. W. Keil Ltd.*

WALNUT FURNITURE

A Queen Anne walnut bureau with bracket feet and matched veneers. The drawers and flap have ovolo moulding, crossbanding and herring-bone borders. *Mallett and Son.*

PLATE 13

A Queen Anne walnut bureau-bookcase, showing burr veneers on the drawer fronts and fine quartered veneers on the doors. The bureau has double half-round mouldings. *Leonard Wyburd.*

WALNUT FURNITURE

A William and Mary chest of drawers, with oyster veneers, cross-banding and half-round mouldings.
Frank Partridge.

PLATE 15

WALNUT FURNITURE

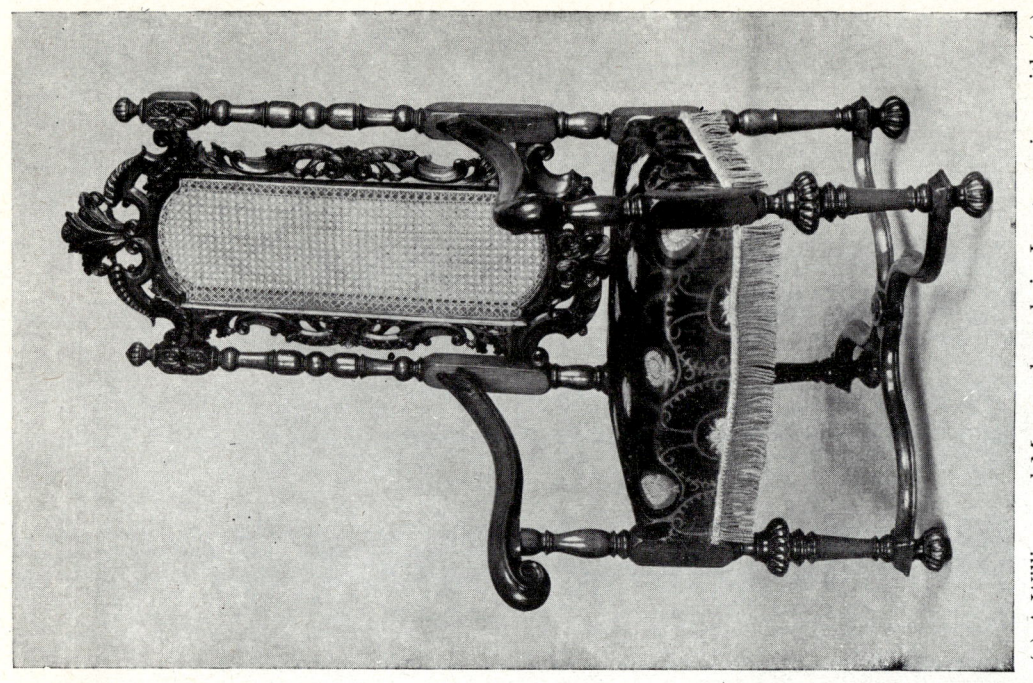

(B) A William and Mary walnut chair. In comparison with (A) note the turned front legs (with mushroom swell), the curved stretchers and the upward lift of the cresting rail. *Mallett and Son.*

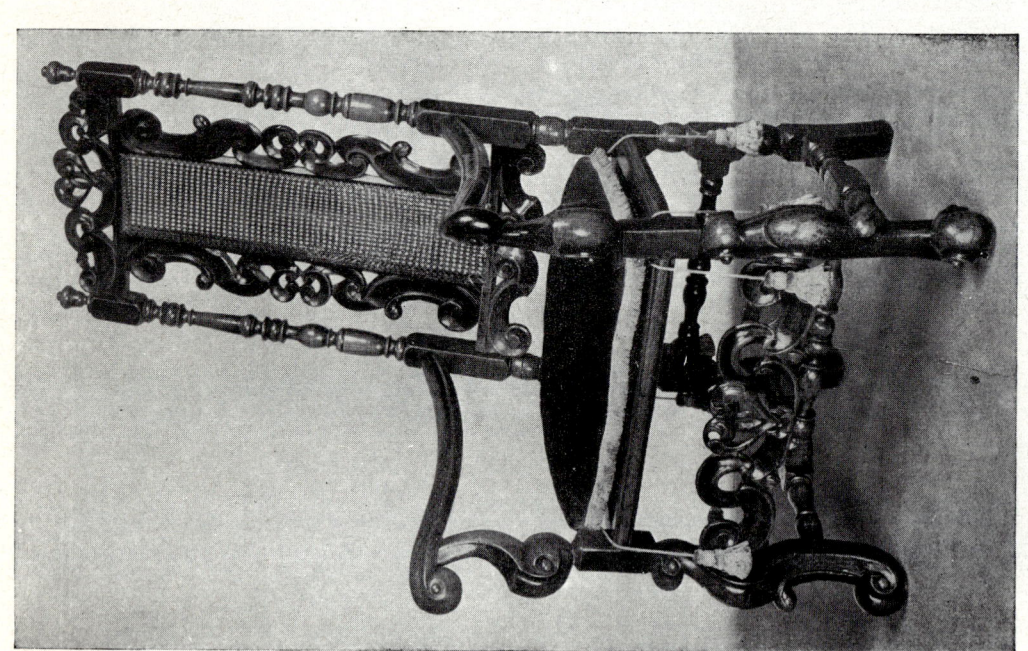

(A) A late Charles II walnut chair. The front legs and arm supports have the scroll design popular after 1675. Other chairs of this type had twist-turned uprights (cf. Plate 21). *Mallett and Son.*

PLATE 16

one of the special polishes on the market; several are recommended by their makers for antique pieces. Gilt bronze mounts should never, ever, be touched with any kind of metal-polish or their thin coating of gold will be spoiled, and replacement of it is costly. If such mounts are discoloured, they usually require removal and professional treatment, and all that should be attempted by the amateur is dusting.

Attacks of wood-worm, which are unsightly as well as likely to cause damage, can be treated successfully by applications of a proprietary liquid. It is either liberally painted on the affected area, or squirted into the holes by hand-pressure or with an aerosol. Action should be taken whenever the tell-tale dust is seen, and unless the infestation is a big one it should respond to it.

Where damage has been suffered it is unquestionably best to have it repaired by an expert who is skilled in doing the type of work needed. It is most important to save detached fragments of veneer or carving, as their replacement can be not only tiresome and expensive but can sometimes adversely affect the value of the article.

Like other examples of good craftmanship, old furniture demands and repays respectful treatment. However commonplace a piece may be, its life can certainly be lengthened by exercising care in handling and using it. The guilt felt after damaging a rarity is seldom completely effaced, and the article bears the scars forever.

A study of the examples of old furniture described and illustrated in the present volume can be usefully augmented by seeing actual examples. There can be no better and more pleasant way of increasing knowledge of the subject than by so doing. Present-day display methods in both museums and houses permit incomparably closer access to pieces than in the past, and a serious request for more detailed examination than is normally possible is usually granted without demur. Many of the houses with contents of particular importance have what they term a 'Connoisseurs' Day', on which there is more freedom to make close inspections.

The list of museums open to the public on pages 357 and 358 should prove helpful in arranging either a brief visit or a protracted tour. A large number of both publicly and privately owned houses, castles, châteaux etc, are also open to the public. Details of their situation, hours of opening and admission fees can generally be obtained from regional guide books or the local tourist offices. It is within grasp to confirm whether Walpole was correct, in one's own opinion, in describing the tapestry-hung drawing-room at Osterley as 'the most superb and beautiful that can be conceived', or echo him in saying loftily that the interior of Chatsworth 'is most sumptuous, but did not please me'. Equally one might visit Kedleston to see if it really merited Dr Johnson's verdict that 'the state bedchamber was very richly furnished,' but that the whole mansion 'would do excellently for a town hall'.

Horace Walpole's words are quoted from *Letters of Horace Walpole*, edited by Mrs Paget Toynbee, 16 vols., 1903–5, and *Supplement*, edited by Paget Toynbee, 3 vols., 1918–25.

OAK FURNITURE

By ANTHONY COLERIDGE

ENGLISH furniture from the Middle Ages to the Restoration in 1660 was made almost entirely of oak. William Harrison, writing late in the sixteenth century in his *Historical Description of the Island of Britaine*, said that "nothing but oak was any whit regarded".

The oak, which is the most common species of tree in this country, is hard and heavy, the colour varying from white to brown. Evelyn, in 1663, writes that it was "of much esteem in former times till the finer grain's Norway timber came amongst us which is likewise of a whiter colour". Although the oak is a very tough tree, it was discovered at an early date that there was little difficulty in splitting it along the lines of the medullary rays, provided that this were done before the fibres hardened. However, it must always have been necessary to use a saw for wood of a great age, or for wood that had been allowed to harden after felling. These saw-cut logs were immersed in flowing water for a period of up to two years and were then stored for a further ten to twenty years, after they had been converted into planks.

CONSTRUCTIONS

Furniture of the oak period is generally rectangular in construction and is very strongly built. Its component parts are put together with mortise and tenon, which in turn are held in position by wooden dowels. Evelyn, describing the furniture of the early seventeenth century, writes "they had cupboards of ancient, useful plate, whole chests of damask for table ... and the sturdy oaken bedstead and furniture of the house lasted the whole century". Much of this oak furniture has, of course, lasted far longer than a century, and on account of its strength has come down to us in almost pristine condition.

SURFACE DECORATION

Early Gothic furniture, which is extremely rare, was of relatively plain form and relied on colour for its decoration. Its surface was often lime-whitened, and to this ground was added a polychrome scheme of decoration executed in oils or tempera. By the middle of the sixteenth century the surface was frequently left in its natural state, and by the seventeenth century some kind of preservative such as beeswax was rubbed in, which now gives to the oak its deep and rich patination. The use of gilt and gesso, so dear to the Italians during the Renaissance, was seldom if ever used in England during the period under review.

CARVING

The Gothic style of carving and ornamentation, which had grown very flamboyant by the end of the fifteenth century, was gradually superseded during the reigns of the Early Tudors by Renaissance motifs. These were introduced from the Continent by Italian, French, and Flemish craftsmen. The earlier linen-fold panelling was often combined with the new forms of decoration, such as grotesque masks, arabesques, and carved caryatids. During the Elizabethan period every kind of carved motif was employed and we find strapwork, terminal figures, bulbous supports, festoons, swags, geometric and medallion panels, lozenges, arcading, and pilasters.

There was a marked reaction against this flamboyant style by the early seventeenth century, and carving began to give way to applied decoration. Bosses, demi-balusters, and other forms of pendant decoration, often stained black in imitation of ebony, were applied to the plain or panelled surfaces, and moulded geometric panels were a favourite form of ornamentation. The sober spirit of the Commonwealth was reflected in its furniture, which was simple to an almost monotonous degree, as every form of decoration was frowned upon. The Restoration of the Monarchy, which heralded the walnut period, was a complete antithesis to the austerity of the Interregnum, and the exuberance and vivacity of the Court of Charles II were immediately attracted to the International Baroque.

INLAY

The use of an elaborate pictorial marquetry of many exotic woods was a feature of Renaissance decoration and entire rooms were panelled in this extravagant form of ornamentation. It was greatly favoured on the Continent, as the panelled rooms at the Escurial outside Madrid and the Ducal Palace at Urbino bear witness, and it was also popular in the North of England. The finest extant example in this country is the room from Sizergh Castle which has now been reassembled in the Victoria and Albert Museum.

Pieces of Elizabethan and Jacobean oak furniture were often inlaid with a chequered design of marquetry – or parquetry, as a geometric, mosaic, or cube design inlay of woods is called – in boxwood, holly, poplar, and bog oak. The last-named was obtained from portions of trees which were found submerged in peat bogs – hence the black hue. The most elaborate form of marquetry found in oak furniture is in the so-called "Nonsuch Chests". The term is derived from the name of the celebrated palace which was built by Henry VIII at Cheam, and representations of it were inlaid into the front panels of coffers or chests, and occasionally smaller objects. Chests of similar design were made in Scandinavia and southern Germany, and it is probable that chests of this type originated in one of these countries, the design then being copied by craftsmen in England. Burnt poker-work, which is employed in conjunction with floral marquetry, is another form of decoration which is sometimes found in this country. It is usually used on chests which are of a distinctly Italian appearance. However, there is evidence enough to show that some were made in this country, and the style of dress worn by the figures which are portrayed is definitely of British origin.

Shaped slivers of wood about the thickness of a piece of paper are laid on the ground which is to be inlaid, and the required design is then marked round them. This is in turn cut out from the surface and the prepared pieces of wood are inlaid and glued down. A distinctive style of inlay was evolved during the latter half of the seventeenth century in which pieces of engraved bone and mother of pearl were inset as a form of surface decoration. The Portuguese in India and the Moors in southern Spain both used this form of inlay, and it was probably introduced to this country from one of these two centres.

CHIEF PERIODS AND STYLES

The history of early furniture is in many cases affiliated to the architectural styles. Oak furniture can therefore be readily divided into the Gothic, the Renaissance, and the Jacobean and Commonwealth periods. The Gothic forms of design and ornamentation, although they were firmly established, offered little resistance to the new influences of the Renaissance. The wealth which was suddenly acquired by Henry VIII and his friends from the Dissolution of the Monasteries, the stability of the country at large, and the King's and Wolsey's personal taste for grandiose building schemes were all important factors which helped towards the adoption of the new designs.

During Queen Elizabeth's reign wealth and prosperity were even more abundant, and this new gracious form of living was not reserved for the nobility and gentry alone, as is shown by Harrison's reference to yeomen farmers who were able to "live wealthie, keep good houses, and travell to get riches". They also bought "costlie furniture", and they had learnt to "garnish their cupboards with plate, their joined beds with tapestrie and silk hangings, and their tables with carpets".

By the mid-sixteenth century the High Renaissance style had percolated through to England via Flanders and Northern Europe. It had become rather vulgar and over-elaborate and the true decorative motifs were considerably coarsened. The style was introduced by Continental craftsmen, who were either invited over to carry out special commissions or who were attracted by the general prosperity of the country. Pattern books were also being published in Italy, France, and Germany, and these had a wide influence on the embryonic Elizabethan style.

Many ambitious building schemes were put in train during the early years of the seventeenth century, and of course the necessary furniture and furnishings had to be produced to decorate these new rooms and apartments. "No kingdom in the World spent so much on building as we did in his time," writes a diarist of James I's time. Most of the oak furniture which survives today was made in the early seventeenth century, and it must be borne in mind that much of the extant furniture of Elizabethan design was actually produced in the reigns of James I and Charles II. Craftsmen were conservative to a degree, and new ideas and designs travelled slowly to the provinces.

BOOKS FOR FURTHER READING

FRANCIS BOND. *Misericords* (1910); *Stalls and Tabernacle Work, etc.* (1910).

E. H. B. BOULTON and B. ALWYN JAY. *British Timbers* (ed. 1946). (For insect infestation, etc.)

OLIVER BRACKETT. *English Furniture Illustrated* (ed. rev. by H. Clifford Smith, 1950).

IRIS BROOKE. *Four Walls Adorned* (1952).

HERBERT CESCINSKY. *The Gentle Art of Faking Furniture* (1931).

J. CHARLES COX. *English Church Fittings, Furniture and Accessories* (ed. 1933).

J. CHARLES COX and ALFRED HARVEY. *English Church Furniture* (1907).

JOHN GLOAG. *A Short Dictionary of Furniture* (1952).

M. HARRIS and SONS. *The English Chair* (1946).

ARTHUR HAYDEN. *Chats on Cottage and Farmhouse Furniture* (ed. rev. by Cyril G. E. Bunt, 1950).

CHARLES H. HAYWARD. *English Period Furniture* (ed. 1947).

PHILIP MAINWARING JOHNSTON. *Church Chests of the Twelfth and Thirteenth Centuries in England* (Arch. Jnl., Vol. LXIV, 1908).

MARGARET JOURDAIN. *Decoration and Furniture of the Early Renaissance* (1924).

H. W. LEWER and J. C. WALL. *The Church Chests of Essex* (1913).

PERCY MACQUOID. *A History of English Furniture* (1904-1908).

PERCY MACQUOID and RALPH EDWARDS. *The Dictionary of English Furniture* (1954).

PHILIP NELSON. *Some Heraldic Wood-Carvings* (repr. from *Trans. Hist. Soc. Lancs. and Cheshire*, 1916).

EDWARD H. PINTO. *Treen* (1949).

FRED ROE. *Ancient Coffers and Cupboards* (1902); *Old Oak Furniture* (ed. 1908); *A History of Oak Furniture* (1920); *Ancient Church Chests and Chairs in the Home Counties round Greater London* (1929).

F. GORDON ROE. *English Period Furniture: An Introductory Guide* (1946); *Old English Furniture from Tudor to Regency* (Connoisseur Booklet, 1948); *English Cottage Furniture* (ed. 1950); *Windsor Chairs* (1953).

JOHN C. ROGERS. *English Furniture* (ed. rev. by Margaret Jourdain, 1950).

DONALD SMITH. *Old Furniture and Woodwork* (ed. 1947).

FRANCIS W. STEER. *Farm and Cottage Inventories of Mid-Essex* (1950).

R. W. SYMONDS. Articles in *The Connoisseur*, specified in Glossary of this Section; *Modern Research and Old English Furniture* (Jnl. Royal Society of Arts, No. 4829, 1950); *English Furniture from Charles II to George II* (1929).

L. TWISTON-DAVIES and H. J. LLOYD-JOHNES. *Welsh Furniture: An Introduction* (1950).

VICTORIA & ALBERT MUSEUM. *Catalogue of English Furniture and Woodwork*—By H. Clifford Smith, Vol. I, *Gothic and Early Tudor* (ed. 1929); Vol. II, *Late Tudor and Early Stuart* (1930); by Oliver Brackett, Vol. III, *Late Stuart to Queen Anne* (1927); —, *Catalogue: Exhibition of English Medieval Art* (1930); by Ralph Edwards, *A History of the English Chair* (1951).

WALNUT FURNITURE

By E. T. JOY

THERE is some doubt about the exact date when the walnut tree was introduced into England, but it is certain that it was being used for furniture in the Tudor period, especially for beds. One of Henry VIII's great beds had a headpiece of walnut, and in 1587 we read of 'a bedsteed of wallnuttrye in Ladies chamber'. But as the chief wood of fashionable furniture the great period of walnut can be considered to cover the best part of the century beginning at 1660. Two main kinds of walnut were used, the European (*Juglans regia*) and the North American (*Juglans nigra*, the black or Virginia walnut). The former had many good qualities for furniture. Its attractive colouring, with beautiful figure and uniform texture, made it very suitable as a veneer, on a carcase of yellow deal. When properly seasoned (a process which might take seven to ten years) it was a solid and compact wood, hard enough to carve into delicate shapes, and, unlike oak, comparatively free from shrinkage or swelling. The burr and curl woods were particularly beautiful, the former being cut from the burrs or abnormal excrescences which grew at the base of the trunk and produced a finely mottled grain, and the latter from just below a fork in the tree. The timber's one great defect was that it was liable to worm, especially in the sap wood. In this respect the Virginia walnut was much better, as the well-seasoned timber was largely immune from worm.

The *Juglans regia* grew throughout most of Europe and was the chief kind used until about 1720. The English variety was considered to be somewhat coarse and featureless for high-quality work, though at times it produced some good varieties of figure. Italian walnut was rated very highly, for the timber which grew in the mountainous regions had a close-grained texture with dark streaks, ideal for decorative work. French walnut was also greatly esteemed; it was straight-grained with a lighter, quiet grey colour. The Grenoble area produced timber which became a hall-mark of distinction in furniture. Spanish walnut was similar to the French, but it was liable to have more faults. The superiority of these foreign timbers over the English led to considerable imports of walnut into England, especially from France. In the three years 1700–2 inclusive, just before the Spanish Succession War (1702–1713), imports of 'wallnut tree plank' from France amounted to £534 8s, £1,009 4s and £339 respectively, and just after the outbreak of war, in 1704, walnut worth £1,330 was registered among the prize goods captured from the enemy.

There are indications that English walnut was relatively scarce in the seventeenth century. John Evelyn, in his *Sylva* (first published in 1664), wrote: 'In truth, were this timber in greater plenty amongst us, we should have far better utensils of all sorts for our houses, as chairs, stools, bedsteads, tables, wainscot, cabinets, etc., instead of the more vulgar Beech'. He praised the black walnut highly: 'The timber is much to be preferred, and we might propagate more of them if we were careful to procure them out of Virginia . . . yet those of Grenoble come in the next place and are much prized by our cabinet-makers'. Some of the black variety was grown in England in the seventeenth century, but there is little doubt that the shortage of English walnut and the cost of imported walnut had much to do with the great use of veneers. After the Spanish Succession War, during which the severe winter of 1709 had killed off many trees, the French Government prohibited the export of walnut in 1720, with the result that from that date, though supplies continued to come in from Holland and Spain, much more of the North American variety was imported. Virginia walnut was darker and of a more uniform colour than European (it is the only walnut with traces of purple), and its strength and excellent working qualities explain the bolder designs in the solid after the Queen Anne period. But after the first quarter of the eighteenth century walnut was beginning to feel the effects of competition from mahogany, and was entering on its last phase as the fashionable timber. In 1803 Sheraton wrote in his *Cabinet Dictionary* that 'the black Virginia was much in use for cabinet work about forty or fifty years since in England, but is now quite laid aside since the introduction of mahogany'.

CHIEF PERIODS AND STYLES

In the walnut period the styles take their names from the reigning monarchs – Charles II (1660–85, and including the short reign of James II, 1685–8); William and Mary (1689–1702); Anne (1702–14); and the early Georgian (George I, 1714–27, and George II, 1727–60). The furniture of the whole period reflected the growing standards of wealth and comfort; many new pieces were produced to satisfy social needs, and adapted to conform with improving standards of design. Two factors which helped to make the knowledge and use of good furniture widespread were the increased skill of the craftsmen and the development of London as the chief furniture-making centre of the country. This was the period when the joiner was being replaced by the cabinet-maker as the supreme furniture craftsman. It will be noted that Evelyn, in the passage quoted above, was already referring to cabinet-makers as early as 1664, and he frequently used this term in his various works. The English craftsmen had to learn many new techniques at first from foreigners, but on the whole it can be said that they assimilated them and interpreted them with good sense and balance; and by the end of the seventeenth century they were not only supplying the home market but had also built up a flourishing export trade in furniture to all parts of the world. London's size was meanwhile making it a focal point for the whole kingdom. By 1700 the capital had half a million inhabitants; the next largest towns had no more than 30,000. Though there were other notable furniture centres – Lancaster, for instance – there was no doubt about London's leadership in styles. The social convention of the seasonal migration of the landed gentry to London helped to spread furniture fashions throughout the country, as Defoe noted early in the eighteenth century, and for the first time it was possible to distinguish town and country pieces.

The reign of Charles II was marked by an exuberance and flamboyancy which was reflected in such things as costume and plays, as well as in furniture. The reaction to the Puritanism of Cromwell's regime and the return of Charles and the aristocracy from exile abroad opened the country to a flood of Continental fashions – French, Spanish, Portuguese, Italian, Dutch and Flemish. Increased trade and colonization brought riches to the upper and middle classes. The Great Fire of 1666 both led to a greater output of furniture and brought it under the influence of architects like Sir Christopher Wren and of craftsmen like GRINLING GIBBONS. New ideas, or new twists to older ideas, were apparent in the use of glass, cane, turning, veneering, marquetry, gesso and japan. The reign of William and Mary saw, in general, a sobering down in furniture styles, due to William and his Dutch background, and the work of his great craftsman DANIEL MAROT, a Huguenot refugee, who in his furniture for his royal patron interpreted Louis XIV fashions in a quieter Dutch idiom. But there was no decrease in output. The revocation of the Edict of Nantes by Louis in 1685 sent many Huguenot refugees to England, and one result was the flourishing Spitalfields silk industry and improvements in upholstery. There were developments in such things as writing furniture (in which increased letter-writing, due to improved postal services, was a major

WALNUT FURNITURE

factor), card and tea tables, bookcases, chests of drawers and cabinets, the last-named due to the upper-class fashion for collecting 'rarities' or curiosities of all kinds. It was in the Queen Anne period that walnut furniture reached its best phase. With its emphasis on graceful curves, and a return to veneers to bring out the beauty of figure, compared with the previous Dutch fashion of marquetry, this reign is distinguished by its simple elegance, shown in such details as the hooped-back chair, the cabriole leg, the bracket foot and a general stress on good design. The earlier Georgian period produced a heavier and more florid style, partly perhaps as a reaction to simpler fashions, but mainly due to the Palladianism of WILLIAM KENT, the architect (1684–1748), who affected much elaborate gilt ornament with classical motifs, carried out in softwoods or gesso.

OTHER TIMBERS

Though walnut put the seal on fashionable furniture, many other timbers were important during the same period. The great popularity of veneers, inlay and marquetry led to a demand for a wide range of coloured woods. Among the native timbers used for these purposes, lighter shades, white or yellow, could be obtained from apple, holly, dogwood, boxwood, maple, laburnum, sycamore and plane, and darker colouring from olive, pear and yew. Elm and mulberry were also prized for their burr veneers. Timbers imported from the East, South America and the West Indies included ebony (black), fustic (yellow, turning to a dead brown), and kingwood, lignum vitae, partridge wood, rosewood and snakewood (all giving various shades of brown and red). For carcase work, and as a ground for veneers, yellow deal was almost always used. But for clock cases wainscot oak was used. Great quantities of deal were imported from Baltic countries in the late seventeenth century. Oak and ash were used for drawer linings.

DECORATION

Gesso: gesso work came into fashion in England just before 1700 and was a popular form of decoration until about 1740. It was a mixture of whiting and parchment size which was applied coat after coat and allowed to dry. When there was sufficient, a pattern was formed in relief by the background being cut away. The former was burnished and the latter left mat. Furniture was given a brilliant and highly ornate effect when gold leaf was used, but there was also much cheap colouring which tended to fade. Gesso lent itself to the Kent style of decoration, and it had the same appearance as the work on the carved and gilt table in Plate 24.

Japan work: japanned or lacquered furniture enjoyed a considerable vogue in the walnut period. As early as 1661 Pepys recorded seeing 'two very fine chests covered with gold and Indian varnish'. Lacquer work was originally imported from the East, and was known variously as Indian, Chinese or Japanese, but the best kind was made in Japan, and was called 'fine' or 'right' Japan, to distinguish it from substitutes. Most of the genuine Japanese work was brought to England by the Dutch, but the English East India Company handled Chinese and Indian varieties, which had a ready sale in the home market and went under the general name of 'Indian' goods (and were sold in 'Indian' shops). So great was the demand for these goods that some English merchants exported patterns and models of all kinds of furniture to be copied and lacquered by native workmen, who could thus manufacture English-style furniture. The completed goods were reimported and sold at home. But meanwhile an English japan industry had sprung up. In 1688 STALKER and PARKER published their *Treatise of Japanning and Varnishing*, and in 1693 a company was formed with the title of 'The Patentees for Lacquering after the Manner of Japan'. Naturally, the home producers of japan disliked the practice of sending goods abroad to be lacquered, and so did other cabinet-makers, who looked upon it as unfair competition. In 1701 the London cabinet-makers, joiners and japanners petitioned Parliament to put a stop to it, and an Act was passed imposing heavier duties on all imported lacquer (12 & 13

William III, c. 11). Thus from that date nearly all japan work was home made. It was very popular until about 1740, and much of it was exported. The colours used were bright ones, often scarlet, yellow, etc, and carried out Eastern designs (Fig. 1), but English work lacked the high quality of

Fig. 1

the true Oriental variety. In fact, inferior work was merely varnished. It was usually applied on a background of deal for carcases, or of beech for chairs. Good-class work often had a smooth-grained, veneered surface as a basis. Normally, designs were raised on the surface, but a rare form of lacquer work, known as Bantam work, used incised designs. Cabinets, chairs, bureaux, screens, clock cases and mirrors were among the more usual pieces for japanning. There was a revival of this fashion in the later eighteenth century.

Mouldings: mouldings, the contours given to projecting members, were an important part of the decorative treatment of walnut furniture. On tall pieces – cabinets, tallboys, clock cases, etc – the profiles of the straight cornices, which were popular until the Queen Anne period, were built up in architectural style, usually in layers of cross-grained wood. One characteristic feature of the later seventeenth century was the convex (torus or swell) frieze (Plate 18). This was not universal, however, for the concave (cavetto) frieze was used at the same time, and superseded it early in the next century. Mouldings also accentuated the arched curves and the varieties of broken pediments when these came into fashion. Towards the end of the walnut period dentil mouldings (tooth-like cubes) were often found on straight-line cornices or angular pediments.

Another moulding of convex profile, the ovolo (or lip), was applied to the top edges of chests of drawers (Plate 15), stands (Plate 18) and tables (Plates 21 and 22), and on the upper sections of bureaux (Plate 13). Chests of drawers and bureaux also had plinth mouldings, above ball, bun or bracket feet (Plates 13 and 14). The general development of drawer furniture produced several kinds of smaller mouldings (sometimes called reeds) around the drawer fronts, to offset the otherwise flat surface. These were normally cross-banded veneers of walnut glued to a back of deal, and applied at first to the carcase, and later to the drawer edge. From 1660 to about 1700 the most usual kind was a half-round moulding on the rails between the drawers (Plates 15, 18 and 22), but just before the end of the century two smaller half-round mouldings (Plate 14), or sometimes three reeds together, were applied to the rails, and this vogue lasted until about the end of Anne's reign. From 1710 a distinct change in method was beginning; the mouldings were now applied to the edge of the drawer, in ovolo section, and projected sufficiently (about a quarter of an inch) to hide the join between opening and drawer when the latter was shut (Plates 13 and 19A). From about 1730 cock-beading, a half-round bead projecting outwards from the edge of the drawer, was introduced, and became the chief drawer moulding for mahogany furniture. Mouldings also edged the doors on clock cases (Plate 19B) and surrounded mirrors or panels on cabinet doors (Plate 14). On the latter broader types of moulding were common, in astragal section, semicircular with the addition of a fillet at each side.

Turning: until about 1700 turning was one of the outstanding features of the legs on chairs, tables and stands, and of the uprights on chairs. It was carried out on the foot-operated pole lathe which rotated the wood while the turner's chisel cut the required shape. Twist turning, which came to England from the Continent shortly after the Restoration, and replaced the earlier bobbin turning, resulted from a mechanical device which moved the chisel continuously to produce the oblique curves. For this walnut was a much better medium than the more brittle oak. At first the Flemish 'single rope' style was used, but this was followed by the English double rope or 'barley sugar' twist, finished by hand and sometimes pierced. The design was working itself out on chairs by 1685, but it persisted on tables for some time longer. Another form, baluster turning, was produced by the turner holding the chisel himself and varying the pressure to get a number of diverse shapes. This type is connected with William and Mary furniture. There was an almost bewildering variety of such designs, but among the more popular can be distinguished the Portuguese swell, a bulb-like shape, followed by the mushroom, and, later still, by the inverted cup. Some legs were squared off by hand to octagonal and other patterns. (Plate 21 illustrates twist turning, and Plates 18 and 22 the inverted cup, *see also* Chairs).

Veneers, Marquetry and Parquetry: veneering was the chief decorative feature of walnut furniture. It originated on the Continent, and gave opportunity for flat decoration, which showed to the full the beauties of the grain. Veneers were thin layers of wood cut by hand-saw, perhaps one-eighth of an inch thick, and glued to a carefully-prepared surface, which was nearly always of imported yellow deal, a variety of pine or fir which was better able to take glue than oak. Not only did the veneers preserve and strengthen the wood underneath, but they were found to be the only practical way to use the rare woods like walnut burrs, which would twist if worked in the solid. The chief patterns were the 'curl' or 'crotch', a plume effect taken from the junction of a side branch with the main trunk (Plate 13), the 'oyster', cut from branches to show the rings (Plates 15 and 21) and the 'burr', an intricate figuring from abnormal growths at the base of the trunk (bureau section of Plate 14). Successive veneers from the same piece of wood, showing duplicated patterns, were often quartered, or glued in sections of four, on suitable surfaces (Plates 13 and 14). Besides walnut, yew, elm and mulberry made high-quality veneers, and laburnum and olive produced excellent oyster figures.

Marquetry was an advanced form of veneering which first came into prominence in English furniture from Holland about 1675. With infinite patience and skill veneers of various coloured woods were cut into delicate patterns and fitted together like a jigsaw puzzle. For this process walnut could be changed in colour by dyeing, scorching with hot sand, staining, bleaching and fading, but, naturally, many other timbers of suitable colour, both native and foreign, were used (as indicated under 'Other Timbers' above). At first English marquetry followed the Flemish mode and concentrated on bird, flower and foliage designs (Fig. 2), sometimes with the aid of

FIG. 2

other materials than wood, such as bone and ivory. The colours tended to tone down to quieter dark or golden shades about 1690. By 1700 arabesques were popular, together with the most intricate form of all, the seaweed or endive marquetry, which was shown to great effect on clock cases (Plate 19B), cabinets and table tops. Early in the eighteenth century the marquetry phase was running out, and there was a return to the plainer veneering. Parquetry was a form of marquetry which emphasized geometrical patterns, with the same skilful use of contrasting colours.

Veneered surfaces had two characteristic decorations, cross-banding, or cross-grain, veneered strips bordering other veneers, and herring-bone banding, two smaller rows of tiny strips of veneer applied diagonally, often in contrasting colours. Each could be used singly, or together, on drawer fronts, table tops, bureau flaps and similar fields. (Plate 15 shows cross-banding, Plate 18 herring-bone banding, and Plate 13 both together.) The popularity of veneering introduced distinct changes in the construction of furniture as well as in its appearance. The panelling technique of oak was unable to provide the flat, smooth surfaces necessary for taking veneers. For angles on carcases and drawers the old method of dovetailing (the through or common dovetail), though the strongest form, had the great disadvantage of showing the end grain on both sides of the angle, and this was unsatisfactory for holding veneers (Fig. 3). Shortly before 1700 it was replaced by the lap or stopped dovetail, which had the end grain on the side only, leaving the front quite clear for veneering (Fig. 4).

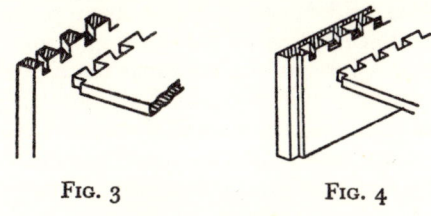

FIG. 3   FIG. 4

Bureaux, Cabinets, Bookcases, etc

The bureau was one of the pieces of furniture which met the demands of the new habit of letter-writing in the Restoration period. Early bureaux were mounted on stands and were nearly always of narrow width, with one or two rows of drawers under the sloping writing fall. The stands were gradually discarded and bureaux became wider and more solid. Most were now three feet six inches wide, though narrower ones (for standing between the windows of a room) continued to be made. The legs of the early stands followed contemporary side-table developments, while the more solid bureau followed the chest of drawers (*see* separate sections below). Plate 13 illustrates the fine proportions and appearance of the Queen Anne bureau. It has bracket feet, slides for the flap, and ovolo lip moulding round the drawers, which also have cross-banding and herringbone inlay. The veneers are good, and the matching on the flap, and on the drawers (both across and upwards), are worth close attention.

Another piece was the writing cabinet, which developed in two main stages. The first stage was the scrutoire, a box-like structure consisting of an upper part of drawers and pigeon-holes, enclosed by a let-down front which made a large writing surface, and a lower part formed by either a chest of drawers or a stand with legs and stretchers. The disadvantage of having to clear away all papers before the front could be closed led to the second stage, the bureau writing cabinet or the bureau-bookcase as it is now termed. This had a shallow cupboard enclosed by two doors for the upper part and a bureau for the lower. The space in the bureau top for papers made this a more convenient piece than the scrutoire; it was also more elegant. Plate 14 illustrates a Queen Anne bureau-bookcase. Here the cornice balances the arched mouldings, which contain quartered veneers on the doors. The bureau drawer fronts have burr veneers and reeded mouldings. The opened flap displays the neat arrangement of the bureau top. The bureau-bookcase became fashionable in William III's reign and was either veneered with walnut or japanned.

Meanwhile, the cabinet was assuming the forms which had long been known on the Continent, and from the increasing skill required in making it was producing the first English cabinet-makers. It developed from the chest, acquired a number of drawers (many of them 'secret'), cupboards and pigeon-holes, and was mounted on tall stands or chest of drawers. At first the tops were straight, with rather heavy cornices, and two doors enclosed the front. Later the frieze was developed; the swell variety became more common, and a shorter stand was used. One type of cabinet that was mounted on a chest of drawers was copied from Chinese cabinets, and had engraved hinges and lock-plate, and finely figured walnut veneers to vie with japanned pieces. Other cabinets were excellent show pieces for decorating with marquetry and parquetry, applied to the many small drawers as well as to the doors inside and out.

There was, however, from 1600 onwards considerable diversity of decoration and design in these pieces, as the cabinet could be used for various purposes. With glazed front and shelves, it was used as a bookcase or display cabinet. It now seems clear, contrary to former belief, that cabinets were not used to display china but held small curios like medals and miniatures. Other cabinet fronts had mirror-plates instead of clear glazing, or no glass at all, relying upon panels of finely figured walnut for effect; mirrors and panels were often enclosed in mouldings which had a graceful curving form at the top. These shapely curves were a predominant feature in the late seventeenth century and in Anne's reign, and were applied to the tops of cabinets in various

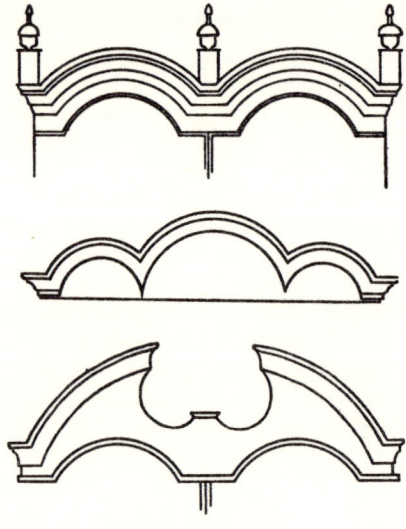

FIGS. 5, 6 and 7

ways – double, and occasionally, triple arches and broken circular pediments (Figs. 5, 6 and 7). They showed the application of architectural principles to these larger pieces of furniture. But there was still a strong liking for the simple straight cornice, as shown in Plate 14. It is not always certain now for what purpose some cabinets were intended. Many which resemble bureaux-bookcases, with the bureau replaced by a chest of drawers, have survived. They have been used for storing clothes in the bedroom or as a cupboard in the parlour.

For larger bookcases, such as those which Pepys bought from SIMPSON the joiner in 1666, the doors were glazed in rectangular panes like windows. The growing popularity of glass fronts made glazing bars important.

At first they were usually semicircular, veneered with cross-grained walnut, or astragal, a half-round moulding worked on the edge. In the eighteenth century another form of astragal, with a small fillet at the top of the curve, came into use. These astragals, often larger in shape, framed the mirrors or veneers on doors which did not have clear glazing.

Chairs, Day-beds, Stools and Settees

Plate 16A illustrates the type of chair that was produced in the Charles II period. These chairs were distinguished for their elaborate carving and turning. Twist turning was at first often applied to the back and front legs and uprights, and carving was the treatment for the top rail between the uprights and for the wide stretcher set half-way up between the front legs. Another novelty, canework, was found on the seat and back, framed in a carved panel, rectangular or oval in shape, separated from the uprights and seat. After the middle of the century carving improved considerably. At first it was heavy looking, emphasizing scrolls, foliage and crowns; later it became much lighter and pierced, and top rail and stretchers curved upwards, often ending in a crown (Fig. 8) supported

 FIG. 8

by amorini. From about 1675 S-shaped scroll designs (the 'Flemish' scroll) were popular for front legs, and on arm-chairs this shape was continued in the arms which curved downwards in the centre and formed deep scrolls over the supports. By the end of Charles's reign twist turning was being replaced by baluster turning. Canework was also becoming finer in texture, and many specialist craftsmen were making large numbers of cane chairs for export as well as for home use. The back legs were splayed for steadiness. There was also a fashion for some chairs to be entirely upholstered with over-stuffing, carried out in fine materials, damask, velvet, embroidery or Mortlake tapestry.

The lightness of cane helped to popularize

a pre-Restoration piece, the day-bed, or couch. This had a chair-back (sometimes one at each end) and a long seat carried on six or more legs joined by richly carved stretchers. It was used in the living-room (which no longer had a bed in it), and had to be easily movable. Some day-beds were ornately japanned.

William and Mary chairs saw distinct changes in design. The flamboyancy of the previous period tended to give way to a simpler style, though there was still much rich carving. Backs (Plate 16B) had a tall and narrow appearance, due to the fashion in women's hair styles, and took on a pronounced backward tilt. Chair legs either kept the scroll form or were decoratively turned in one of the many baluster or geometrical shapes. Prominent among these were the Portuguese bulb (Fig. 9), mushroom (Fig. 10), inverted cup and square (Fig. 11).

All these changes were nothing to the revolution in chair design in the early eighteenth century (of which Plate 17A represents a somewhat later development). Straight lines gave way to curves, turned legs and stretchers to cabriole legs without stretchers, and overstuffing to the drop-in seat. The back uprights took a graceful hoop form, and the centre of the back was occupied by a single solid splat, often veneered, showing a variety of smooth curves. For the first time the chair back was shaped for the sitter, giving the aptly-named 'bended' back. The cabriole leg came from France about 1700. Taking its shape from an animal's leg, it had various endings, a hoof, a pad or club (Figs. 12 and 13), or the celebrated ball-and-claw foot which came in about 1720.

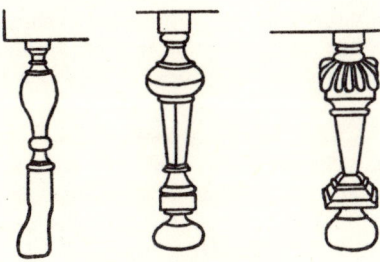

FIGS. 9, 10 and 11

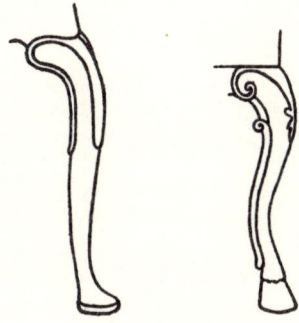

FIGS. 12 and 13

Feet were ball or bun shape, or else carved in the Spanish foot design. Another novelty was the introduction of curved stretchers under the chair, going diagonally from squares just above the feet, and either crossing directly, tied in the centre with a finial, or fixed into a central platform. Front stretchers in the older form still persisted, but the fashion now was to set them back from the front legs and fit them to the side stretchers. The upright aspect of the backs, very characteristic of this time, was accentuated by the arching of the cresting rail above the back uprights. Usually seats were upholstered, with a tasselled fringe, but backs were treated in various ways – pierced carving, canework (in thinner panels), or upholstery.

These legs, worked from the solid by hand, were strong enough to hold the chair without stretchers. The general emphasis on curves was continued in the frame of the seat. Carved decoration was usually limited to the knees of the cabriole legs, cresting rail and seat rail, in the form of shell or acanthus designs, or, later, as in Plate 17A, a mask on the rail. A new treatment of chair arms was to set them back in a curve from the front of the chair, to allow room for the wide-hooped dresses of the time.

Another pleasant type of chair which had made its appearance by about 1700 was the upholstered wing variety (see Plate 17B). The wings at the shoulders curved down to well-padded arms which scrolled outwards. The legs often had cabriole shape, but the size and weight of the chair required stretchers, of the simple turned kind.

Towards the end of the walnut period some of the simple grace of the Queen Anne chairs was lost. In the early Georgian era they tended to become heavier and more squat in appearance, and carving was more ornate. The splat was not left plain, but was carved and later pierced with strapwork designs (Fig. 14).

From 1660 stools closely followed the prevailing chair designs. They had an importance which today may be easily overlooked. In general, their form was that of chairs without backs, except that all four legs were the same shape. They were often richly upholstered. A later development was the settee, which sprang from the fusion of two arm-chairs, with double backs, outer arms and five legs. In their earlier forms – later seventeenth century – they were often two cane chairs together.

FIG. 14

Chests of Drawers and Tallboys

The time-honoured chest, long distinguished for its frame construction and carving in the oak period, became the more useful chest of drawers after the Restoration. Already in 1661 Pepys bought 'a fair chest of drawers' in London. The chest itself did not disappear quickly; it persisted well into the next century, made in the traditional oak, then walnut and, later, mahogany, or japanned, when that form of decoration was popular. But long before 1660 its future development was indicated when the bottom drawer was added to it, to form the mule chest. The chest of drawers developed along three lines: the familiar solid type, from the chest; the chest on stand; and the chest on chest, or tallboy.

The solid type was still being made in oak in Charles II's reign, but it was gradually replaced by walnut and incorporated all the refinements and techniques due to the new wood. Larger chests of drawers stood up to three and a half feet high, usually with five drawers, three long ones at the bottom and two smaller ones at the top. But many fine smaller ones were also made. They were admirably suited for veneers (applied to the top and sides of good pieces, as well as to drawer fronts, with cross-banding and herring-bone patterns), marquetry and japan. Besides walnut, or used with it, other woods, particularly yew, fruit woods and burr elm, made good veneers. To overcome the straight-line effect of the drawers, various mouldings, at first on the frame and then on the drawer edges, were applied to give decorative effect. The tops also had larger ovolo mouldings jutting out over the edges, and similar mouldings at the bottom of the carcase, above the feet. The development of the feet showed a constant search for good design. At first they were of the turned ball or bun type, but as this did not harmonize with the general appearance of the chest, they gave way to the square bracket feet, flanked by small curved pieces. These details appear in Plate 15, a smaller chest of drawers of the William and Mary period, which shows, besides bracket feet, the top and bottom mouldings, half-round mouldings on the carcase and cross-banding on the drawers. It is also an excellent example of oyster veneers.

The use of stands for mounting chests of drawers was common after the Restoration, and lasted until the early eighteenth century. The chest of drawers developed on the same lines as the solid type, and the stand bore very close relationship to contemporary side tables (*see* Tables). At first the stand was low in appearance, on thick turned legs linked by a succession of arches, but by the 1690s it was higher, with twist-turned and later baluster-shaped legs joined together by curling stretchers. Drawers were added to the stand, usually a shallower central one and a deeper one at each side. The apron piece, an important decorative feature, took the form of smooth-flowing curves, which balanced the severer lines of the upper work. In the William and Mary period (Plate 18) two other characteristics were the inverted cup legs and the pronounced swell frieze below the cornice. The drawers in the stand tended to shorten the legs once more, and they took cabriole form by Anne's reign. From about 1710 there was a natural transition to the tallboy, in which the stand was replaced by another chest of drawers. Tallboys reached monumental proportions, and came in for a great deal of architectural treatment. The frieze lost its swell outline and became concave. Plate 19A shows the stage of development which had been reached by about 1730. The drawers throughout are cross-banded and have ovolo mouldings. The corners of the upper section have been canted to take partly fluted and partly reeded pilasters, and the feet have gone from the plain bracket to ogee form, resembling cabrioles. The tallboy had a long vogue in the eighteenth century as a cabinet-maker's show-piece, until the awkward height of its top drawers led to its gradual disuse in England. It persisted longer in America, where some very fine examples were produced.

Clock Cases

The long clock case (or grandfather clock) was another new piece of furniture which appeared at the time of the Restoration. Two major factors in its development were Robert Hooke's invention of the anchor escapement (which made the long pendulum possible) about 1670, and the outstanding work of great English clockmakers like Thomas Tompion and Joseph Knibb. From its beginning the case took on the familiar design of a hood for the dial and movement, a long, narrow body for the pendulum, and a pedestal base. The body became wider as the clock dial increased in size but retained its slender waist appearance until mahogany was extensively used. Naturally, the size of the cases (up to seven feet in even the earliest examples) and their prominent position in the house brought out all the case-maker's skill, and the large space available was ideal for the best decorative work in veneers, marquetry and japan. At first – about 1660 – the cornice of the hood was surmounted by a classical pediment which was followed after 1670 by a carved and pierced cresting. The glass face of the dial was usually flanked by two columns, which were either twist-turned or plain-turned with tiny capitals and bases. Oak was the usual carcase wood, veneered with ebony and walnut and often finely decorated with the various kinds of fashionable marquetry. The door on the body was edged with half-round moulding in rectangular lines. Many of these features can be seen in Plate 19B, a late William and Mary clock case with a movement made by Samuel Stokes of London about 1699. It is veneered with seaweed marquetry, and there is a narrow fret-carved frieze below the cornice. By 1700 the hood had begun to change its appearance. A flat dome (Fig. 15) was added to the top, which was sometimes ornamented with brass or gilt wood finials at the corners and centre. From about 1715 the clock dial

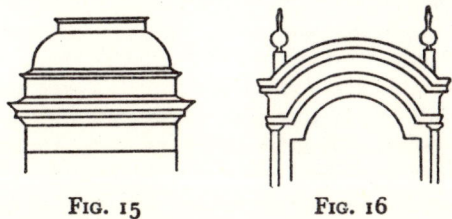

FIG. 15   FIG. 16

was arched (Fig. 16), and the cornice above it took the same curving shape, as did the moulding over the door in the body. The clock case, in other words, underwent the same treatment of arched curves as cabinets and mirrors. English japanners had a partiality for clock cases, and hundreds were exported during this period; but walnut enjoyed a considerable vogue for cases, and retained its popularity until after 1750.

Mirrors

Mirrors began to play an important part in interior decoration in late Stuart times, and an indication of their growing use is that while in 1660 they were still being imported (particularly Venetian glasses), by 1700 English-made glasses were being sent abroad. Between those two dates progress was largely explained by the establishment of the Duke of Buckingham's famous glass works at Vauxhall in 1665 and the emergence, some twenty years later, of the

WALNUT FURNITURE

specialist looking-glass makers. Mirror plate was expensive for some time to come, but wealthy people used it in many ways, for wall mirrors, toilet mirrors, tall ornamental glasses and on cabinet doors. Until about 1690 wall mirrors were square in shape and the glass, with bevelled edges, was enclosed in frames up to six inches in width, topped by a semicircular crest in the Italian manner. They were naturally picked out for fine (especially oyster) veneers and marquetry work. By 1700 taller mirrors were becoming fashionable (of large Vauxhall plates, or smaller mirrors joined together with a moulding to cover the join) and the influence of Wren and Gibbons was shown in architectural features like pediments and pilasters, or in intricately carved lime-wood frames. Colourful decoration was emphasized and took several forms, bright gilding, marquetry, japan, gesso and even silver. These forms continued into Anne's reign, but there was also a return to simpler styles. Three main trends can be distinguished among the many varieties. One attractive type of wall mirror (Plate 20B) had a narrow frame, the glass itself surrounded by a thin gilt gesso moulding, and wide flat crest and base, both carved in graceful flowing curves, veneered with walnut and holding two circular inset pieces with the shell motif. Another kind had an inch-wide frame all the way round following the top of the scalloped glass in simple arched curves. It was this design which was often found on cabinet doors, the mouldings surrounding the mirror plate taking the same curves as the top of the cabinet (similar to Plate 14). A third kind was the pier glass, tall and narrow in shape, usually made in pairs to stand between windows, in elaborately carved and gilded frames, often with another mirror in the arching crest, and with pilasters at the sides. John Gumley, who opened his glass works at Lambeth in 1705, specialized in these. Towards the end of the walnut period gilded mirrors were common, and came under architectural influence. Plate 20A shows a typical example; the frame enriched with gadrooning, drapery and foliage; the shell decoration in the base; and the broken pediment with a central cartouche (other finials were a plume, shell, mask or eagle). There were, however, other examples carried out with burr walnut veneers and gilt gesso ornament.

The early eighteenth century also saw the introduction of the 'chimney glass', a wide mirror above a chimney-piece, consisting of three plates, two smaller ones flanking a larger one, and all topped by flowing curves, framed in walnut or following the other decorative fashions. Another development, the toilet mirror, had the same curved top and was mounted on two uprights resting on a miniature chest of drawers (Fig. 17).

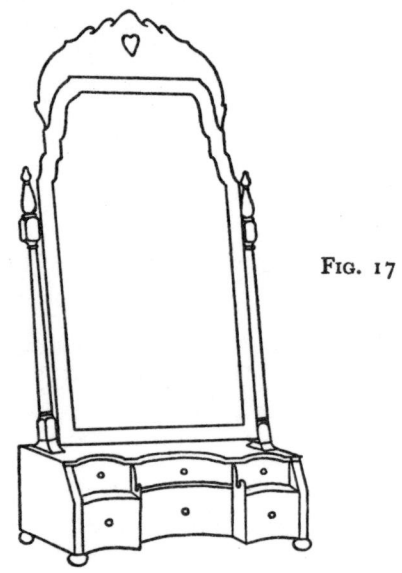

FIG. 17

Some of these, in walnut or japan, were beautifully made and were designed for the slender dressing-tables of the period.

Tables

The walnut period inherited the gate-leg tables introduced during the preceding oak period, and these continued in use for dining, with modifications due to the new timber. Gate-leg tables retained their popularity for a long time, and in larger houses several were used together, when required. Their legs gradually took on cabriole form. But a new feature from 1660 was the variety of small tables, many of them multi-purpose, the more formal side and occasional tables,

WALNUT FURNITURE

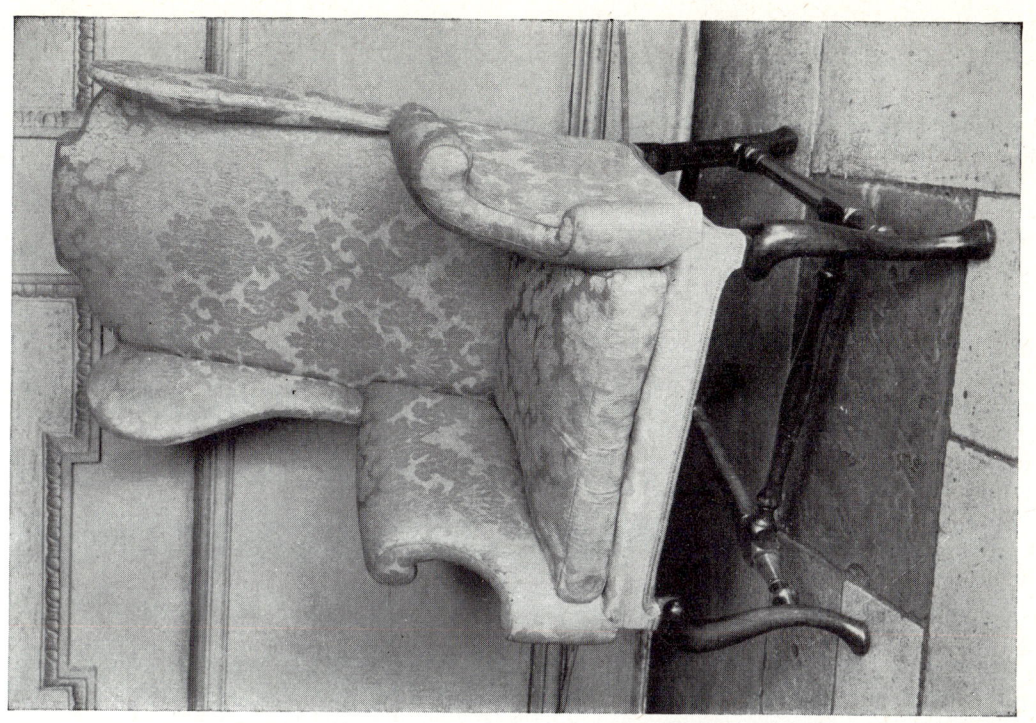

(B) A Queen Anne upholstered wing chair. The front legs are in cabriole form and have turned stretchers. *Jetley.*

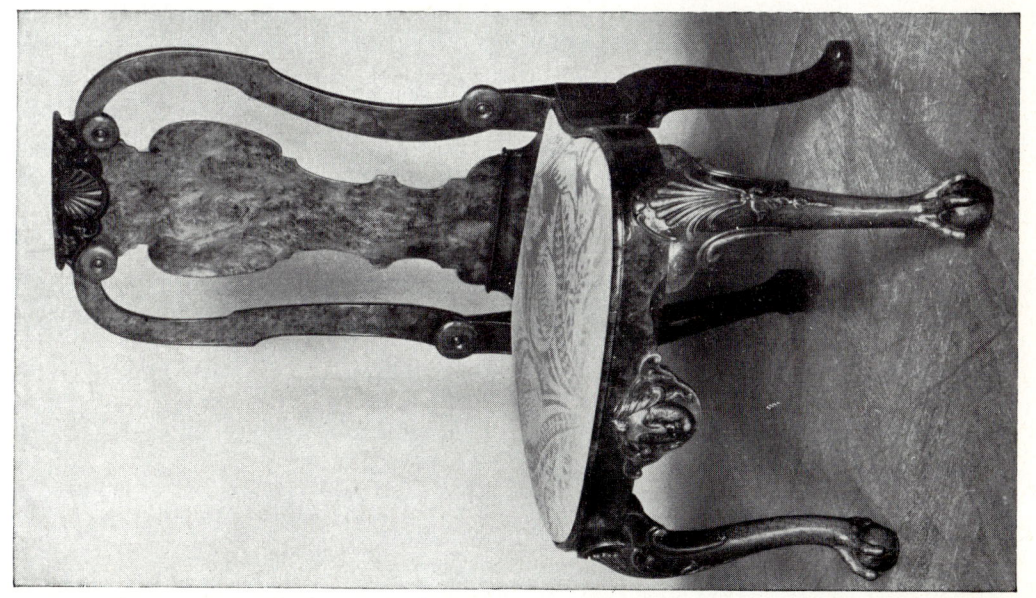

(A) An early eighteenth-century walnut bended-back chair with solid splat, cabriole legs and ball-and-claw feet. *Hotspur.*

PLATE 17

A William and Mary walnut chest on stand, with characteristic swell frieze, inverted cup legs, curving apron piece and waved stretchers (c. 1690). *Hotspur*.

PLATE 18

WALNUT FURNITURE

(A) An early Georgian walnut tallboy. Note the canted corners, partly fluted and reeded, the cabriole form of the feet, and the ovolo mouldings on the drawers (c. 1730). *Mrs L. G. G. Ramsey Collection.*

(B) A William and Mary walnut clock case with the front veneered in seaweed marquetry; c. 1699. *Frank Partridge.*

WALNUT FURNITURE

(A) An early Georgian gilded mirror, with broken pediment and central cartouche. Note the ornate decoration compared with (B). *Jetley.*

(B) A Queen Anne walnut mirror with carved crest and base. *Jetley.*

WALNUT FURNITURE

A late Charles II walnut table, with twist-turned legs, waved stretchers and oyster veneers.
Mallett.

WALNUT FURNITURE

A William and Mary walnut side table illustrating the development from Plate 21, i.e. inverted cup legs, narrow X-shape stretcher with central finial, and curved apron piece; *c.* 1690. *Hotspur*.

WALNUT FURNITURE

A Queen Anne walnut card table with cabriole legs and ball-and-claw feet. *Mallet & Son.*

PLATE 23

WALNUT FURNITURE

A carved and gilt side table in the William Kent style, with marble top. *Jetley.*

A mahogany clothes press, *c.* 1760, showing effective use of figure and carving. *H. W. Keil.*

Late eighteenth-century mahogany bureau-bookcase, with Hepplewhite-style feet and apron piece. *Stuart & Turner.*

MAHOGANY FURNITURE

Late eighteenth-century mahogany break-front bookcase with fine matched veneers and Gothic glazing bars. *Mallet & Son.*

PLATE 27

A Chippendale period mahogany desk with cock-beaded drawers and carved gilt handles. *Frank Partridge & Sons.*

PLATE 28

MAHOGANY FURNITURE

(A) A mahogany chair in the Chinese style, *c.* 1755. *Hotspur.*

(B) An Adam period mahogany upholstered armchair in the French style, showing a late version of the cabriole leg, and scroll feet. *M. Harris.*

(C) A shield-back mahogany elbow chair of the Hepplewhite period, with a wheat-ear design. *M. Harris.*

(D) A mahogany Sheraton chair, showing the wide cresting rail and forward-splaying front legs. *M. Harris.*

PLATE 29

A serpentine-fronted mahogany commode of the Chippendale period showing French influence in the carving on the canted corners and feet. *Frank Partridge & Sons.*

MAHOGANY FURNITURE

An Adam style mahogany side table with classical treatment. This kind of table with a classical pedestal at each end was the forerunner of the sideboard. *Leonard Knight.*

A mahogany table cabinet, c. 1760, with Chinese fret gallery, curved stiles on the doors, and cock-beaded drawer. *Hotspur*.

and others used for specific requirements like writing, tea-drinking, dressing and card-playing. At first solid walnut was usual, but later table tops (and drawer fronts, wherever these were found) were decorated with veneer or marquetry, with cross-banded or herring-bone borders and ovolo-moulded edges. Plates 21–24 show four well-defined stages in small-table design between the Restoration and early Georgian periods.

The side table in Plate 21, with its oyster veneers, single drawer, twist-turned legs and wide flat stretcher was very characteristic of the later part of Charles II's reign. The legs ended on ball or bun feet, immediately above which the stretcher terminated in small square platforms. The stretcher was noted for its curves and central shelf. Twist-turning persisted on tables for some time after it had passed out of fashion on chairs. But by the William and Mary period varieties of baluster turning, or the more elaborate scroll form, were coming into use. Plate 22, a side table of about 1690, shows the inverted cup legs and bun feet. The stretcher has become more slender and has a pronounced X-shape. The finial on the shelf is matched by similar finials, inverted, on the apron piece, which has become an important part of late seventeenth-century work (*see also* Plate 18). Tables like Plate 22, fitted with drawers and a knee-hole, could be used as dressing or writing tables. The marked change in design by the early eighteenth century is well illustrated by the Queen Anne card table (Plate 23). The slender cabriole legs and ball-and-claw feet did not require stretchers and gave the table a shapely line. The tops of these card tables unfolded and were supported by swinging out one of the legs; or else in some cases the whole top was pivoted sideways and opened to rest on the frame. The surface was covered with cloth or veneered. To protect it the corners were rounded to hold candlesticks (later small movable trays, hinged to the top, were used for this) and small circular depressions were made for money or counters. The wide ovolo mouldings found at the edges of the earlier table tops were now replaced by flatter, vertical mouldings. Decoration was usually limited to a carved shell or leaf on the outside of the knee and a scroll on the inside, and to a curve on the frieze. These tables emphasized the beautiful figure of walnut. Despite subsequent changes, this simple design was never entirely lost, for small tables were made in walnut, even when mahogany was becoming fashionable. But, by contrast, from about 1725 pier tables (standing between mirrors and windows) and console tables (permanently standing against the wall with bracket-shape legs) had a florid magnificence, in the Kent tradition, as shown in Plate 24. Made of gilded softwoods, or with the addition of gesso, they relied for effect on masks, scrolls, foliage and classical designs, and heavy marble tops.

Small tripod tables also appeared after 1660 for use as candle-stands, in the form of a tray held by a turned pillar standing on jutting-out feet. As can be expected, the upright at first was often twist-turned, and the feet had scroll shapes. From about 1685 the feet began to show sharper angles where the various curves met. By the Queen Anne period the feet were beginning to show cabriole form and the ball-and-claw ending. This type of table was to have a long vogue, as candle-stands were in great demand when large plate mirrors came into use and as much light as possible was called for to add brilliance to large rooms.

BOOKS FOR FURTHER READING

The Diaries of JOHN EVELYN and SAMUEL PEPYS give the social background to the walnut period in the later seventeenth century, and make interesting references to furniture. Evelyn's *Sylva* is invaluable for its accounts of timbers (especially the late eighteenth-century edition, with many footnotes by Dr A. Hunter). Much information of the period is contained in *A History of English Furniture*, by P. MACQUOID (Vol. 2, *The Age of Walnut*), though parts of this work now need revision. Detailed accounts are to be found in *The Dictionary of English Furniture*, by P. MACQUOID and R. EDWARDS (3 vols.), and in two works by R. W. SYMONDS, *English Furniture from Charles II to George II*, and *Old English Walnut and Lacquer Furniture*, and *The London Furniture Makers* (1660–1840), by Sir AMBROSE HEAL (Batsford 1953).

MAHOGANY FURNITURE

By E. T. JOY

MAHOGANY was competing with walnut after the first quarter of the eighteenth century and had supplanted it for the highest quality work about 1750. From then on its many virtues made it the premier wood in cabinet-making. It had a beautiful patina which improved with age; a metallic strength which led to remarkable advances in carving and outlines; a fine figure which made it equally suitable for veneers; a range of colour from light-reddish to a rich dark shade; and a natural durability which was resistant to decay. It also seasoned readily, and the great size of the trees produced excellent timber for table tops, wardrobe doors and similar pieces. Altogether, for furniture of every kind, for work in the solid, for carving, inlay or veneer, it was an excellent medium for the great cabinet-makers of the Georgian era. Two main varieties of mahogany were used. One kind (*Swietenia mahogani*) came from the West Indies, mainly San Domingo, Jamaica and Cuba. The San Domingo timber (usually known as 'Spanish', or sometimes as 'Jamaican') was prized more highly at first. It was a dense, hard wood, with little figure, and was used mainly in the solid. Then the Cuban mahogany became more popular, as it had two outstanding qualities; it was easier to work and had a fine figure for veneers. The other species (*Swietenia macrophylla*) came from Central America, particularly from Honduras (whence it obtained its other name of 'baywood'). It was lighter and softer than the Cuban, and was often used as carcases to take Cuban veneers. There was considerable overlapping in the periods when these various kinds were most in use, but it can be said that San Domingo mahogany was popular until about 1750, when it was replaced by Cuban for best work, while Honduras was found in later eighteenth-century carcase construction.

Mahogany had been used for shipbuilding since the sixteenth century, and for inlay and panelling since the seventeenth. It was known at first as cedar or cedrala. Evelyn referred to its worm-resisting qualities in his *Sylva* under its French name of *acajou* from 'the Western Indies'. The date when it came into use for furniture cannot be given exactly. The story of Dr Gibbons of Covent Garden, who is said to have had some mahogany made into furniture by his cabinet-maker Wollaston about 1700, and to have thus popularized this wood, has now become a tradition. Its use was no doubt encouraged by the shortage of European walnut after the Spanish Succession War, though supplies of Virginia walnut were to be had. Probably mahogany advertised itself well enough. An Act of 1721 allowed timber from any British plantation in America to be duty free. Another Act in 1724 mentioned mahogany by name; it had a special rate imposed upon it instead of the declared value by the importer, but if it were from British possessions it was included in the terms of the 1721 Act and allowed in duty free. From the 1720s, therefore, Jamaican mahogany had preferential treatment. This not only assured supplies from British sources but also encouraged timber dealers in the West Indies to send the popular Spanish wood to England via Jamaica and other colonies to avoid the duty. This practice went on throughout the century. In fact, the British Government connived at it, for it allowed, and later legalized, the entrepôt trade with the Spanish settlements. There was thus no lack of mahogany, once trade had got under way, as there had been with European walnut. Mahogany was certainly competing strongly with walnut for fashionable furniture by the 1730s. In 1733 the poet James Bramston, in his *Man of Taste*, written to defend the modes of his day against those who complained of lost hospitality, asked: 'Say thou that dost thy father's table praise, Was there Mahogena in former days?' By that time, also, British logwood cutters in Campeche Bay, Central America, were leaving that area to cut the more valuable mahogany in the Belize district of Honduras, thus provoking a long-drawn-out dispute with Spain. The ever-growing demand for mahogany can be judged in the rise of import values from £276 in 1722 to £77,744 in 1800. In the early nineteenth century import duties which had been imposed on mahogany during the French Wars began to affect trade figures, but Crosby's Pocket Dictionary of 1810 still described cabinet-makers as 'workers in mahogany and other fine woods'.

CHIEF PERIODS AND STYLES

The furniture styles of the eighteenth century take their names not from the reigning monarchs but from outstanding designers, both craftsmen and architects. In the case of the craftsmen like Chippendale, Hepplewhite and Sheraton this distinction must be recognized as doing less than justice to many contemporary cabinet-makers whose work equalled or even in some cases excelled theirs. Indeed, it is not certain that Sheraton had a workshop or produced furniture of his own. Their claim to fame rests on their famous design books, which interpreted prevailing styles with a high degree of skill, and thus their names serve as a very convenient label for particular phases of development. The whole period showed a ceaseless spirit of experiment and a constant demand for novelties from the upper classes, whose needs were supplied by a succession of great cabinet-makers and upholsterers; some of these cabinet-makers' shops, like that of GEORGE SEDDON (1727–1801), were large-scale businesses. Their products displayed a technical excellence fully equal to the work of the best Continental craftsmen. Their patrons, with wealth from land, trade and industry, showed, in general, a high standard of taste. Much furniture was designed for the many new town and country houses, and this explains the importance of architects like Robert Adam, whose planning of a house covered every detail, inside and out.

The earlier Georgian period, to the mid-forties, when mahogany was beginning to come in, was dominated by the Palladian revival, largely inspired by Lord Burlington, and interpreted by WILLIAM KENT (1684–1748) and another contemporary architect, HENRY FLITCROFT. Kent was the first architect to include furniture in his schemes of work. He used mainly softwoods to take carving and gilding, but some of his pieces were in mahogany parcel (i.e. partly) gilt. His designs, somewhat modified, appeared in one of the earliest design books, *The City and Country Workmen's Treasury* by BATTY and THOMAS LANGLEY (1739). But it is noteworthy that a prominent contemporary cabinet-maker, GILES GRENDEY, produced mahogany furniture in a simpler style, reminiscent of the Queen Anne period.

Palladianism went out of fashion in the mid-century, and was replaced by a diversity of styles, the rococo from France (then called the 'modern' taste), Chinese and Gothic. This was the period of THOMAS CHIPPENDALE (1718–79), whose *Gentleman and Cabinet Maker's Director* first appeared in 1754. No mention of mahogany appeared in the first edition, and only a passing reference (to six designs for hall chairs) in the third, in 1762. But much first-class furniture was made in this wood by Chippendale himself and the best contemporary craftsmen, such as JOHN BRADBURN, WILLIAM VILE and JOHN COBB (these two in partnership) and BENJAMIN GOODISON. Chippendale's great service was to apply the rococo style of decoration to a wide range of furniture and generally to curb its more excessive forms. He is now known to have employed on the 'Director's' plates two artists, MATTHIAS LOCK and HENRY COPLAND, who were pioneers of the rococo in England. The taste for Chinese and Gothic furniture, the former largely inspired by the works of Sir William Chambers, and the latter by Horace Walpole, was cultivated by sections of the upper classes. While rococo relied for its effect on the use of flowing lines, Chinese work was seen in the popularity of geometrical fretwork patterns and Oriental figures and designs, and Gothic in the use of the pointed arch.

The neo-classical revival began in the sixties, inspired by ROBERT ADAM (1728–92). His furniture, beautifully designed and made, was decorated with delicate classical motifs, paterae, pendant husks, urns, fluting, etc (Figs. 1–3). His liking for furniture of a

FIGS. 1–3

more elegant appearance led to a revival of fine inlaid work, and much use of satinwood and other timbers. But mahogany, used as a veneer by itself, or with other woods, or for carving the classical motifs, was well adapted to the new mode, shown in the work of Chippendale (who worked for Adam) and Cobb in their later periods, JOHN LINNELL, WILLIAM FRANCE and others. In 1788 appeared GEORGE HEPPLEWHITE's *Cabinet-makers' and Upholsterers' Guide*, two years after the author's death. The great merit of this work was to interpret the new classical styles very skilfully for all kinds of furniture. The explanations of the designs in the Guide constantly stress the suitability of mahogany both for small work like cellarets and knife-boxes, and for larger pieces like tables and bookcases.

THOMAS SHERATON (1751–1806) produced the *Cabinet Makers' and Upholsterers' Drawing Book* between 1791 and 1794 and bridged the gap between the neo-classical and the Regency periods. Sheraton favoured light, delicate furniture, including painted work, and for his finest pieces he recommended satinwood. He also used other tropical woods, popular about 1800, for the best apartments of the house, such as the drawing-room and boudoir. His period is distinguished for the dainty, almost fragile, appearance of some of his furniture. This cannot be said of the final period, the Regency, ending about 1830. There was a renewal of classical forms inspired by the Directoire styles in France, but these were carried out in a strict and narrow fashion, a 'chaste' and literal interpretation of Greek, Roman and Egyptian examples. The designer THOMAS HOPE in his *Household Furniture* (1807) heralded this stress on an archaeological approach. Furniture took on a heavier appearance. One result was to re-emphasize dark, lustrous or heavily-figured woods, especially to show brightly gilt mounts in the prevailing mode. This explains the popularity of rosewood after 1800, but there was also a great demand for mahogany because of its suitable colour and grain.

OTHER TIMBERS

The popularity of satinwood from 1770 has already been mentioned, paving the way for a lighter, more delicate, aspect of furniture design. This trend, emphasized by a revival of veneers and fine inlaid work, led the cabinet-makers to experiment with a wide range of exotic timbers, brought to them from all parts of the world, especially from tropical areas, by enterprising merchants. Satinwood itself, from both the East and West Indies, was yellowish in tone; so was fustic, from the West Indies, but this faded to a dead brown and was decried by Sheraton. Other woods, which showed rich shades of brown and red, varying from light to deep, included calamander, snakewood, coromandel and rosewood from India and Ceylon, thuya from Africa, ebony from the East, kingwood, partridge wood, purple wood and tulip wood from Central and South America, and amboyna from the West Indies. Camphor from the East Indies was also used for boxes and trunks, and red cedar from North and Central America for drawer linings, trays and boxes. Native woods were not neglected: holly, pear, maple and laburnum were used for inlays on first-rate pieces, and there was a demand for sycamore, which was stained a greenish-grey colour, and known as harewood, for veneers. Mahogany was used with these woods, which led to a closer study of its beautiful figure and fine range of colour, and made it appreciated more than ever. Figure and lustre were fashionable qualities after 1800, hence the importance of rosewood, large fresh supplies of which were now available from the opening-up of trade with South America (particularly Brazil), calamander, coromandel, snakewood, tulip wood and zebra wood: the last, as its name implies, having an effective dark stripe. Imported deal continued to be the favourite wood for carcase work during this period, but from 1750 red deal from North America largely replaced the former yellow variety.

DECORATION

Fret-work: this form of decorative work was popular in Chippendale's time, particularly to show Chinese patterns. Fret designs could be either open or applied. The open fret was seen on table and cabinet tops and the applied fret was found on the flat surfaces of chairs, tables, cabinets, etc (Plates 25 and 29A for applied fret, Plate 32 for open fret-work).

Inlay: Robert Adam revived fine inlaid work, which in technique resembled seventeenth-century marquetry (*see* Walnut) but differed from it in the use of classical designs and figures, and of new, lighter-coloured woods. An effective form of inlay much favoured by Sheraton was stringing, or lines of inlay in contrasting woods or brass, some of the work being of extreme delicacy (Plates 35 and 36).

Metal Mounts: these were made of brass and were fine gilt, which gave them a rich and golden appearance. They were used for work in the rococo style (Plate 28) and decorative effect in the Regency period.

Veneers: mahogany had a variety of beautiful figures or mottles. Some of the early San Domingo wood had 'roe' mottles, dark flakes running with the grain (as on the drawer fronts, Plate 25), giving attractive effects of light and shade, and at their best when the lines of figures were broken, they then varied in appearance according to the angle from which they were viewed. Cuban and Honduras mahogany, however, had a wider range of figures and were in great demand for veneers after 1750. Cuban 'curls' (giving the effect shown in Plates 25, 26, 27, 35 and 36) were highly prized. Their feather was obtained by cutting the tree where a large branch joined the trunk. This limited their size, and made them expensive and somewhat brittle ('Cross and unpliable' – Sheraton), unlike most mahogany veneers. The 'fiddle-back' came from the outer edge of the trunk and had even streaks running across the grain. The 'rain' mottle was similar but had wider and longer streaks. The 'stopped' or 'broken' mottle had irregular but brilliant flame-like markings. Dark and oval spots in the wood produced the 'plum' mottle. All these veneers were saw-cut and thick enough by modern standards to be considered more as facings than veneers.

Bureaux, Cabinets, Desks, Bookcases, etc

Endless varieties of writing, display and cupboard furniture were produced in the mahogany period, many of them being directly descended from the walnut prototypes. Bureaux followed very much the same development as contemporary chests of drawers. Mahogany was a favourite medium for these until Sheraton's time, as the figure of the wood, especially Cuban curls, made a fine show on the flaps and drawers (Plate 26). A newer development was the desk, which had taken its place in the rich man's library by 1750. This was usually solid in appearance, with side drawers or cupboards of similar proportions to the classical pedestals of early sideboards (*see* Tables). Plate 28 shows a desk of about 1760. Other kinds were serpentine-fronted and often had canted corners with rococo carving like the commode (Plate 30). Mahogany was particularly suitable for all kinds of library furniture, and both Hepplewhite and Sheraton stressed this in their design books. Sheraton, however, gave his bureaux a lighter appearance.

Many of them were intended for ladies' use, and he favoured the employment of satinwood. He also preferred the tambour or cylinder front instead of the flap.

But what specially exercised the best Georgian cabinet-makers were the combined pieces – the bureau-bookcase, cabinet, press and their variations – which demanded the highest skill in design and decoration. Their size encouraged an architectural treatment. Such pieces in the walnut period had been topped by arched curves, but these were replaced in early Georgian times by forms of broken pediments, angular or swan-neck. The open space in the centre was filled with a carved piece, or left free. Kent emphasized his pediments, and used classical pilasters on the corners of the doors, with much gilding. Many cabinet-makers, however, preferred a simple straight cornice, and one effect of the wider use of mahogany was the return to a general lighter style. Pediments were retained but often their only decoration was carved dentil mouldings, also found on the cornice (Plate 25). Towards 1750 mirror plates on cabinet doors were going out of fashion. They gave way either to clear glazing or to panels of carefully-chosen mahogany framed in applied mouldings or in stiles (Plate 32) with curved inner edges.

The mid-century Gothic and Chinese fashions affected these pieces in several ways. The glazing bars of glass-fronted cabinets formed geometrical patterns or pointed arches. Carving or fret-work with similar designs was applied to the frieze and bottom edge of the cabinet, and to the frieze and feet of the bureau. A pagoda roof was sometimes added, and the pediment was pierced with fret-cut outlines. Rococo treatment might be found in ornate carving or fine gilt mounts. Some of these designs were used with extravagance, but Plate 25, a mahogany clothes press of about 1760, is an excellent example of balance and restraint. The angular broken pediment has a dentil moulding on one edge, repeated on the cornice and plain central platform. The doors have crossbanded borders and incorporate two fine curl panels within applied astragal mouldings. A fretted frieze in Chinese style and carved paterae at the corners of the doors complete the upper decoration. The drawers have cock beading and the whole is supported on feet of cabriole shape. Loop handles without back plates were popular in the 1730s.

Plate 26 shows a bureau-bookcase of the late eighteenth century. Below the plain cornice is a 'pear-drop' moulding, popular after 1770. There is a delicate key pattern at the central edge of the doors, along the top and bottom edges of the bureau, and on the uprights separating the small drawers within the flap. The curved apron piece and slender outward-pointing feet are characteristic of this particular period. The bureau drawers have notable matched curl veneers. Equally simple, despite its size, is the bookcase illustrated in Plate 27. This is an example of break-front design. The glazing bars show the pointed Gothic arch. The whole piece is finely-proportioned and is built to bring out the beauties of the figure on the drawer fronts and cupboard panels. The octagonal handles in Plates 26 and 27 dated from about 1785. In the Regency period a feature of the bookcases, apart from the new forms of decoration, was their low height, to leave the walls above them free for pictures.

Chairs

In the transitional period between walnut and mahogany the graceful Queen Anne hooped-back chair had become more ponderous in appearance, with an emphasis on the carving of ornament. At the same time Kent was designing his elaborate chairs for wealthy clients, making use of walnut or mahogany partly gilt, or of softwoods entirely gilt, for scroll-shaped legs, or versions of the cabriole, and a great deal of flower, fruit and mask ornament. This vogue was passing about 1745, when mahogany really came into its own in chair design. The general effect was to re-emphasize form and proportion, and to initiate an era in which much ambitious splat-work became the fashion. Chippendale used the rococo, Chinese and Gothic motifs in a great variety of chair backs. The typical rococo chair consisted of a back framed by two outward curving siderails meeting in a Cupid's-bow top (which had made its appearance some little time before Chippendale), usually with scrollwork on the corners, and the splat pierced with interlaced strapwork. The back legs tended to curve away noticeably. The cabriole leg was lighter in treatment than the Queen Anne variety and the ball-and-claw foot, though it was found on many chairs, was sometimes replaced by the French knurl or scroll toes. (The scroll foot can be seen in Plate 29B.) The famous 'ribband-back' chairs showed mahogany carving and rococo decoration in perhaps their most dazzling forms, the ribbons and bows forming intricate patterns which in some chairs joined up with the side-rails (Fig. 4). This was an extreme form. In general, Chippendale avoided the excessive ornament of the Continental rococo. In some of his chairs he showed the craftsman's eye for a well-balanced design. These had carefully restrained rococo carving in the splat, which tended to be narrower in shape, and straight legs, sometimes fluted, joined by plain stretchers, which were now being re-introduced on chairs of this type. The contrast between straight legs and curved backs and the use of carefully-chosen upholstery for the seat (including plain leather) was pleasing. Plate 29A shows a Chinese chair, about 1755. The characteristic features are the pagoda cresting-rail, the splat pierced and carved with geometric patterns, the fretted work in similar designs on the back uprights, legs and feet, the cluster column legs, and the bracket between legs and seat.

Other chairs of this type had stretchers which, together with the front legs and brackets, might be pierced and fretted with patterns, or, alternatively, applied ornament might be found on legs, stretchers and seat front. In the case of Chinese armchairs, lattice work also filled the space between arms and seat. Gothic chairs showed interlacing pointed arches in the splats, or covering the whole of the back. Another attractive chair design was the 'ladder-back', taken from a traditional country style. At its best it showed undulating curves on the cross- and cresting-rails, which were pierced and carved and often had a small carved emblem in the centre (Figs. 5 and 6 for Gothic and ladder-back).

The interest of the Adam brothers in classical art influenced chair design by introducing a lighter type of chair, emphasizing oval lines in the backs and using straight legs tapering from square knee blocks to feet set upon small plinths. The construction of chair backs changed, as the splat gradually lost its link with the back rail of the seat and became enclosed within the uprights. In this, again, the strength of mahogany was a definite factor. There was a sympathy for delicate fluting and channelling on the back, arms and legs, and the addition of classical ornaments on the seat-rail and (especially carved paterae) at the top of the front legs. But another kind of chair which enjoyed a long vogue was the 'French Adam' type illustrated in Plate 29B. Dating from about

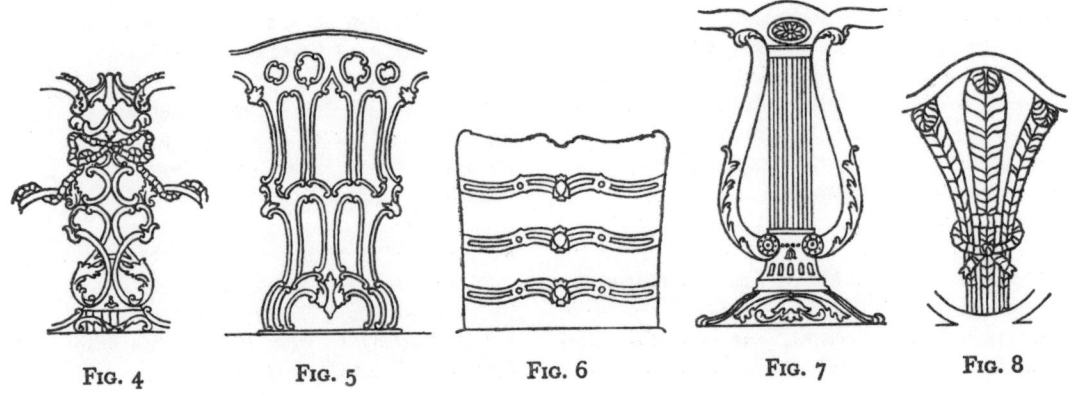

FIG. 4   FIG. 5   FIG. 6   FIG. 7   FIG. 8

the mid-1770s, it shows the cabriole leg in its final form, ending on scrolled feet. This chair is distinguished by the use of gentle curves, of gadrooning on the edges of the legs, arms, seat and back, and of beautiful upholstery, all treated with the utmost refinement. Other French-style chairs had straight, tapering legs, usually fluted, and some of the backs were square in shape, with a lyre, including brass strings, for the splat (Fig. 7). The versatility of form cannot be over-stressed. Adam liked both painting and gilding; beech was used if chairs were to be gilded, and satinwood was becoming popular for fragile-looking drawing-room chairs. He also reintroduced cane seats.

As Hepplewhite's chairs are famous, it is worth noting his own directions for making them: 'Chairs in general are made of mahogany, with bars and frame sunk in hollow, or rising in a round projection, with a band or list on the inner and outer edges. Many of these designs are enriched with ornaments proper to be carved in mahogany.' Plate 29C shows one of his shield backs, his most celebrated form (which he varied with heart or oval shapes). The top rail rises in the centre over a splat consisting of narrow curving bars which terminate in a carved wheat-ear design. The bottom of the shield is just above the back of the seat. The arms add distinction to the chair, with the pronounced backward-sweeping curve from the top of the front legs straightening out at the arm-rests which join the shield about half-way up. The tapering legs and plinth feet, the carefully limited carving on legs and arms, the channelling throughout, the serpentine front to the seat, overstuffed, are all typical of Hepplewhite's work. Other carved ornaments in the back included the Prince of Wales's feathers (Fig. 8), leaves, vases and drapery. He also used satinwood inlay on a mahogany background and, like Adam, designed some lyre-backs.

The refinement in chair design reached its peak with Sheraton, and Plate 29D shows some of his features. He preferred rectangular shapes to emphasize lightness. The wide cresting-rail overrunning the uprights and shaped for the sitter's back is particularly worth noting, as this was a novelty in chairs and was found in wide use after 1800. The back has merely a single rail, and the legs are forward splaying, with little attempt at foot design. Carving is replaced by clear, straight-lined inlay, in a contrasting coloured wood, on the cresting-rail. For upholstery a striped material was popular, in keeping with the general rectangular effect of the rest of the chair. Like other designers, Sheraton did not confine himself to one pattern. On the whole he preferred to leave the back of his chairs as open as possible, and broke away from the vertical splat designs of his predecessors. He brought in a revival of painted chairs (of beech), usually decorated with bright floral devices on a black background and having plain cane seats and turned legs. He did not neglect carving by any means, but he is particularly noted for his employment of stringing as decoration. Basically, this was the same as the inlay on the cresting-rail in Plate 29D, but he carried it to extreme delicacy by using very thin lines of wood or brass. Chair arms often took a wide sweep upwards immediately above the legs, and another at the back to join the uprights at the cresting-rail.

Sheraton's work already reflected many features of the so-called French Empire style, which blossomed out fully in the Regency period. Painted chairs remained popular, and the sweeping forward of the front legs, balanced by a similar outward curve on the back legs, was accentuated because of its resemblance to the chair figured on classical Greek vases. The cresting-rail, in a variety of shapes, was a prominent feature, and the whole back was often given a very pronounced rake. Much of Sheraton's lightness disappeared with the extended use of lion's-paw designs for legs and arms (Fig. 9), and the addition of gilding and novelties like Egyptian motifs. A throne-like arm-chair, in which the whole sides—front and back legs, uprights and arms—were made in units, into which the back and seat fitted, tended to give this type a somewhat heavy and ornate appearance.

FIG. 9

Chests of Drawers, Commodes and Tallboys

Until about 1750 chests of drawers were still straight-fronted, with, normally, four or five drawers, bracket or cabriole-shape feet, and ovolo or cock-bead moulding on the drawer edges. Not much change had been made in the Queen Anne design except that the front corners were usually canted and carved, as were the top edges. Classical pilaster designs were popular on the corners. From 1740 chests of drawers began to be designed with their shape serpentine after the French style. Such chests of drawers were called commodes (though these in France had perhaps special reference to drawing-room pieces). A commode made completely in the French taste had pronounced outward-curving front corners, short legs, curved bottom framing, rococo carving or fine gilt mounts on the sides and legs, and often doors on the front to enclose the drawers. Plate 30 shows a more restrained use of French decoration. This serpentine-fronted commode has on each canted corner a carved console and *cabochon* (at the top and bottom respectively) linked by foliage, acanthus leaves on the bracket feet, gadrooning on the top edge (which is squared at the corners) and beading on the bottom rail. Gothic and Chinese motifs might appear in the same parts of other chests of drawers, Chinese fretted ornament, for example, on the corners, or along the top and bottom front edges.

Adam's work expressed itself principally in two ways. Where solid work persisted, the carving naturally became classical in treatment, emphasizing the corner pilasters, and making use of dentil and key patterns on the cornice moulding. On the other hand, fine inlay, in all the fashionable woods, was used eagerly by designers when drawing-room commodes were in great demand and their doors were ideal for showing first-rate work. Great patience was expended in devising ovals and circles to show figures or scenes from classical mythology, surrounded by inlaid designs. This set the taste for a lighter appearance in chests of drawers, in satinwood especially, or for painted decoration. Sheraton is connected with the bow-fronted chest of drawers, which was now used with the serpentine and straight-fronted types. He by no means emphasized the new style, however. He designed in all shapes, including a return to the simple straight lines of early pieces. Two other innovations were the stringing (in wood or brass) on the drawer fronts and the use of an exceptionally deep frieze above the top drawer, which gave the chest of drawers a characteristic tallness. In the Regency period the decline of marquetry decoration gradually led to the replacement of the drawing-room commode by the chiffonier, a low cupboard with shelves. Bedroom chests of drawers, tall, and either bow- or straight-fronted, had turned feet, and a distinctive feature on many were the quarter columns, spiral-shaped or reeded, on the front corners (Figs. 10 and 11). By this time tallboys were going out of fashion, after a long vogue; they followed closely the designs for chests of drawers, and in their final period a few bow-fronted ones were made. These pieces do not require any separate description, therefore, except to stress that their great size led to special care being taken over their proportions and decoration.

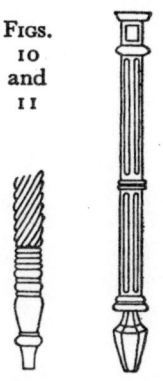

Figs. 10 and 11

Clock Cases

Mahogany affected clock-case design somewhat later than other pieces of furniture, for japanning and walnut veneers enjoyed a long vogue; indeed, figured walnut cases continued to be made until late in the eighteenth century. But by about 1760 mahogany was sufficiently in use to begin to give cases a heavier and broader appearance. At first veneering on an oak carcase was normal, followed by solid mahogany carcases for the best work, and carving. Hoods came in for elaborate treatment. As the arched dial was usual, the cornice was also strongly arched and moulded above it, and surmounted by a broken pediment, usually swan-neck, with finials as in the earlier fashion, or a simple plain pedestal in the centre. Naturally, full advantage was taken of the high case front to show the fine figure of the wood, and some very beautiful Cuban curls are found on outstandingly good work. In the mixture of styles of the Chippendale period detailed decoration was carried out in various ways; Chinese pagoda hoods (Fig. 12) and japanned

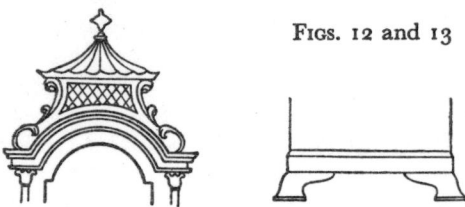

FIGS. 12 and 13

cases, Gothic arches in the mouldings above the door, ornate rococo motifs; or fretwork in the frieze, across the top of the body below the hood, and around the bottom edge and sides of the base. The classicism of the latter part of the century emphasized the proportions of the case, used capitals at the sides of the hood (sometimes two at each side) and showed fluted pilasters worked in the canted front corners of the body, as on chests of drawers. The base was mounted on a solid plinth at first, but later acquired small bracket (Fig. 13) or cabriole-shape feet. Later work also included fine inlay such as satinwood inlays in classical designs on a background of mahogany. By Sheraton's time the tall clock case was going out of fashion. His period produced some fine inlaid and veneered work in many woods, but such pieces were now comparatively rare.

Mirrors

Mirrors were no longer a novelty in the eighteenth century. Improved methods of production led to a greater output of glass and to larger plates. Very large mirrors were still expensive, but small wall and toilet mirrors in simple styles were cheap enough for tradesmen's houses. In larger houses mirrors of all kinds adorned the best rooms, from smaller wall mirrors to pier and chimney glasses, often combined with wall-lights (sconces and girandoles), and their conspicuous position singled them out for highly decorative treatment, especially gilding. For this reason it cannot be said that mahogany played any decisive part in their development. In the Kent period pier glasses, already reaching a height of six or seven feet by the 1730s, were given brightly gilded frames and broken pediment tops, and this design affected wall mirrors in general. The pediments sometimes ended in a graceful acanthus leaf, and there was a prominent central motif in the form of a spread eagle, cartouche or shell. The gilding was carried out on softwoods. On the other hand, the simpler kind of Queen Anne mirror with carved flowing curves on crest and apron piece continued to be made. These had mahogany frames, sometimes partly gilt, and incorporated a dominating centre-piece in the prevailing fashion.

There was a distinct change after the mid-century, when mirrors provided perhaps the best examples of the almost fantastic limits to which the new styles could go. Several designers, including Lock, Copland and Johnson, paid particular attention to applying rococo and Chinese ornament to mirrors, and these trends were made fashionable by Chippendale, who employed the first two to produce designs for the 'Director'. Mirror frames now avoided a symmetrical appearance and were carved and gilded in an intricate pattern of scrolls and foliage in the rococo mode (Fig. 14), and to these were added numerous Chinese designs like exotic birds, pagodas, mandarins and bells, or even Gothic elements. Nowhere else were these styles so intimately united. This vogue did not last long, for Adam, and after him Hepplewhite, designed beautiful and delicately proportioned mirrors, oval or rectangular in shape, surrounded by much simpler scrollwork picked out with paterae, husks and honeysuckle and leading up to a vase or similar classical motif. Adam favoured gilt work, usually on carved pine, and he used the mirror frames to show fluting, the key pattern and Vitruvian scrolls.

Typical of the Sheraton and Regency periods was the circular gilt mirror, one to three feet in diameter. The gilt frame usually had a fillet on the inside edge and a reeded band on the outside; between the two was a pronounced hollow filled with small circular patterns of flowers or plain spheres. Above the frame was foliage, usually the acanthus leaf, supporting an eagle, one of the most popular designs for mirror crests during the whole of this period, or a winged creature (Fig. 15).

Mahogany played a much more important part in the evolution of the toilet mirror. From early in the eighteenth century many dressing-tables were designed with collapsible mirrors which fitted into the tops of the tables, and the latter usually followed the design of chests of drawers, with a knee recess. But there was a great demand for the separate toilet glasses, the rectangular swing mirrors above minute drawers, made in mahogany. They preserved their simple, attractive shapes and avoided excessive decoration. In the Hepplewhite period the mahogany frames followed the design of the shield-back chair (Fig. 16); later still, about 1800, they became flat rectangles. The tiny chests of drawers were often veneered and had serpentine or bow fronts. Sheraton devoted much skill to incorporating mirrors in dressing-tables. He also popularized cheval glasses, known for some time before. These tall glasses stood between two uprights ending in outward curving feet connected by a stretcher, and had decorative headpieces often painted, inlaid or fretted (Fig. 17).

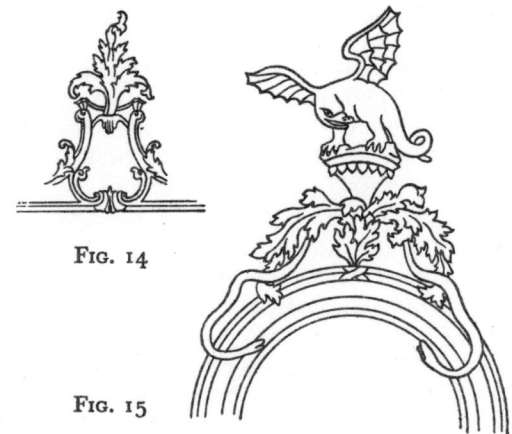

Fig. 14

Fig. 15

Tables and Sideboards

Small Tables: as mahogany came into general use and the heavy side-table of the Kent period (Plate 24, Walnut Section) went out of fashion, there was a return to the simpler style of small and occasional table which had been produced in Anne's reign. By the time of Chippendale's 'Director' the constantly changing needs of the upper classes were reflected in endless varieties of tea-, breakfast-, card-, writing- and dressing-tables, as well as the more formal side- and pier-tables. One very characteristic piece of the mid-century was the Chinese tea-table. This had Chinese patterns on the frieze (usually in applied work), on tiny fretted galleries which ran round the edge of the top, and on the straight legs which were fretted or perhaps carved in the solid. Some of these tables had fretted stretchers which crossed diagonally between the legs. Breakfast-tables, made for the convenience of fashionable people who rose late and had their first meal in their bedrooms, had the same kind of decoration but a different form; they usually included flaps and drawers and a shelf, which was enclosed on three sides by trellis-work in mahogany or brass wire. A restrained French taste showed itself in slender curved legs, sometimes with metal mounts, and curved friezes edged with gadrooning. Plates 32 and 33 are examples of two small tables of about 1760. Plate 32, a table cabinet which could be used for writing, has a Chinese fret gallery at the top. The

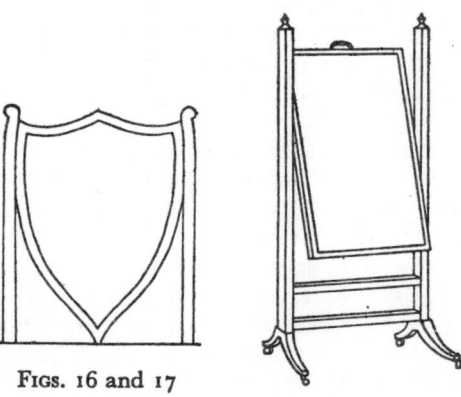

Figs. 16 and 17

cabinet doors, displaying good figuring, are framed in curved stiles (a fashion which dated back some time before 1750), and are finished off with small foliage carving at the corners. Plate 33 is a tea-table with hinged top, and has traces of Gothic work in the legs, which are fluted in ogee section and have a tiny trefoil arch at the top. The delicate carving on the table edge and at the bottom of the frieze, and the curved bracket, as well as the veneers, show the many admirable uses to which mahogany could be put. The Adam period introduced two distinctly new trends. Besides rectangular shapes, others were appearing – oval, semicircular, kidney-shaped and serpentine – with tapering and fluted legs or, as on some contemporary chairs, slender cabriole legs ending on knurl or scroll toes. For the daintier kinds of tables, satinwood and other exotic woods, inlays and gilding, and the choicest figured mahogany were all used, and in some of the best examples the tops were painted by Angelica Kauffmann, Pergolesi and others. On the other hand, for the large rooms of the new town and country houses were produced many long side-tables in mahogany, as illustrated in Plate 31. In this table straight lines were emphasized. The legs are fluted, and taper to plinth feet. Carved decoration appears on the frieze in the classical moulding and the typical paterae over the legs and on the small central panel, where they are linked by husks. This kind of table represented the midway design between the dining- and side-table, and from it developed the sideboard, as is indicated below, as a separate piece of furniture.

This development of the sideboard seemed to re-direct the designers' attention to small tables. Hepplewhite continued on Adam lines, but Sheraton designed a number of extraordinarily delicate tables, some, like his ladies' work-tables, with an ingenious arrangement of drawers and sliding tops, being specially made for carrying from room to room. Neatness was indeed Sheraton's own word for this kind of work: 'These tables should be finished neat, either in satinwood or mahogany'. He also popularized the Pembroke table (though it had been known for some time before), with two semi-circular flaps hinging on a rectangular centre. Usually the legs on his tables were unmistakable for their long, fragile-looking, tapering forms, but on some he showed a radical change in treatment which was to last through the Regency period. He used two solid end uprights, in the old trestle style (Fig. 18), resting on short outward-curving legs; or else a lighter version, with a central stretcher joining the ends.

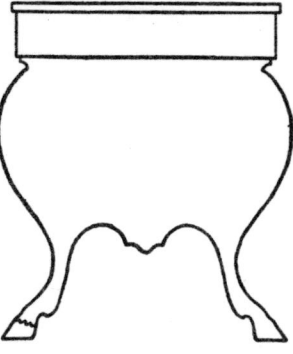

FIG. 18

Plate 34A shows another kind of table which was common in the early nineteenth century. This is the drum or capstan kind, with a deep frieze for drawers (or sometimes this was left open for books) and a central support in tripod style, the legs having the pronounced curve typical of the period. Some of these tables had a solid three-sided pedestal base or monopodium mounted on claw feet. Rosewood or mahogany was usually the wood; some had light-coloured mahogany veneers and classical designs inlaid on the top and pedestal sides, in a contrasting colour.

Tripod Tables: the application of the tripod construction to tables in general, from about 1800, indicates how popular this feature had become during the previous century. The small tripod tables developed from the candle-stands of the walnut period, but by Chippendale's time they were being used for other purposes, as occasional and tea-tables. Mahogany led to a considerable increase in them as the tops could be made from one piece of wood, and, naturally, they became show-pieces for the various fashionable enrichments. Plate 34B shows one of the celebrated 'pie-crust' tables, named after the scalloped and slightly raised edge of the top, which is hinged so that it can stand against the wall when not in use. The legs show cabriole treatment with the ball-and-claw feet, but in this case the ball has been modified to increase stability. The knees are decorated with carved acanthus leaves and the upright has been given contrasting forms of mouldings. Other tripod tables had elaborate carving on the top as a border to the edges. On others, again, a small fretted gallery appeared, like those on contemporary Chinese tables. Feet might be hoofs, paws or dolphins (the latter copied from French tables). Later in the century the tops had often fine inlaid work when this fashion revived under Adam. About 1800 the legs had tended to become very delicate in appearance, with definite concave or convex curves finishing on thin, pointed feet. Sheraton used these on screens as well as tables. But even in Hepplewhite's work the three legs had sometimes been replaced by a solid base, and the extension of this practice, and the many varied leg forms, meant the loss of the original 'pillar and claw' principle.

Dining Tables: for the better part of two centuries it has been almost a convention to associate mahogany with good dining-room tables. One of the chief uses to which the early imports of San Domingo mahogany were put was to make the spacious tops of these tables. They had remarkable weight and strength and yet the mahogany legs were able to support them without stretchers. This gave clean lines to even the biggest tables and led to many developments in flaps and pivoted legs. In the second half of the eighteenth century large dining tables were made up of two smaller ones which were joined, when necessary, by flaps supported on gate legs. These legs at first either had cabriole form or were turned. The same construction continued in the Adam period, but very effective use was made of the size of the tables to give them figured veneers instead of solid mahogany, straight, tapering legs and the classical ornament typified in Plate 31. The side-table in this illustration in every way resembled the contemporary dining table, except that the latter had ten legs, four each for the two end-tables and an extra two for the flaps. The tops were of varied shapes – rectangular, semicircular, or D-shaped – but, naturally, the central flaps were rectangular. Cabinet-makers produced, and in some cases patented, many ingenious devices for extending tops. From about 1800 changes in design became marked. The circular table for dining – an enlarged version of the drum table referred to above – and long tables supported on two or three tripods or similar stands were Regency features. Sheraton also designed a 'universal table' with the old-fashioned draw-leaf top on four tapering legs. 'This', he wrote, 'should be made of particularly good and well-seasoned mahogany, as a great deal depends on its not being liable to cast' – a reminder that dining tables had missed much of the changing fashions in new woods and applied decoration.

Sideboards: the sideboard was a late eighteenth-century development and sprang from the table. It is said to have been originated by Adam, who introduced the custom of standing a classical pedestal mounting an urn at each end of a side-table, of the kind in Plate 31. The obvious advantage of having this storage space so close to the table led to pedestals and tables becoming one unit, and later to the replacement of the pedestals by either smaller cupboards or drawers. The cupboards were used for many purposes; some were lined with metal to keep plates warm, or to hold water or wine-bottles. At first the urns which stood on the pedestals contained the cutlery, but this was transferred to a drawer when urns went out of use. Both Hepplewhite and Sheraton designed light and elegant sideboards. The former is credited with serpentine- and bow-fronted shapes and the latter paid special attention to the brass rail which often stood at the back of the table to hold plates. The fine proportions of the sideboard in Hepplewhite's time are well demonstrated in the serpentine-fronted example in Plate 36. This has the usual arrangement of legs, four in front and two at the rear, found on longer sideboards, and of a single central drawer flanked by two others (or in some cases single deep ones) on each side. The central arch (an important feature on these sideboards) has delicate inlay work, like the drawer fronts and apron piece, and there is also line inlay on the legs. The curving front makes a very effective display of figuring. So does the serpentine, break-front example in Plate 35, which is typical of the smaller Sheraton sideboard.

It has two side cupboards, a sharper curve to the arch, and stringing decoration. The four legs on this piece are turned and reeded, a style for which Sheraton showed a preference in his later work (and which also appeared on his chairs). In the Regency period there was a return to the pedestal type of the early sideboards. Other versions discarded the side drawers or cupboards altogether and replaced them with two or four legs, often carved in animal forms. The deepening of the table frieze, and the elaboration of the brass gallery in classical designs on these pieces deprived them of the graceful symmetry of previous examples.

BOOKS FOR FURTHER READING

For further reading a good introduction is *Georgian Furniture* by R. EDWARDS (Victoria & Albert Museum). More detail can be found in *A History of English Furniture* by P. MACQUOID (*The Age of Mahogany*, Vol. 3, and *The Age of Satinwood*, Vol. 4), though parts of this work are out of date, and in *The Dictionary of English Furniture* by P. MACQUOID and R. EDWARDS. For the later mahogany period the best account is in *Regency Furniture* by M. JOURDAIN. Eighteenth-century furniture, including Irish examples, is also dealt with in *The Present State of English Furniture* by R. W. SYMONDS.

For eighteenth-century furniture-making the reader is referred to the design books of CHIPPENDALE, HEPPLEWHITE and SHERATON, mentioned above, and also to Sheraton's *Cabinet Dictionary* (1803). Modern works on this subject include *Georgian Cabinet Makers* by R. EDWARDS and M. JOURDAIN and *Thomas Chippendale* by O. BRACKETT.

An interesting account of the trade in mahogany is *The Mahogany Tree* by CHALONER and FLEMING (1851).

A further recommendation is *The London Furniture Makers* (1660–1840) by Sir AMBROSE HEAL (Batsford 1953), with a chapter by R. W. SYMONDS on the problem of identification of furniture.

VICTORIAN FURNITURE

By PETER FLOUD

Introduction

IN the history of the decorative arts Victorian furniture occupies a strange position. Although it is probable that fifty per cent of all the furniture ever made in this country was made during the sixty-four years of Victoria's reign, and that even today perhaps twenty per cent of all surviving furniture dates from those years, it is almost a closed field to serious scholarship or collecting. All standard works on the history of furniture stop at 1830, and the same terminal date is recognized, for example, by the Antique Dealers' Fair. In the last few years some dealers and collectors have begun tentatively to edge their way into the 1840s, usually with a limited interest in one line only (e.g. papier-mâché), and a few books have skated over the surface. The main course of Victorian furniture remains, however, totally uncharted, with the result that whereas there are thousands who can confidently date a fifteenth-century brass-rubbing to within thirty years, there is no one in this country who can be equally certain about a Victorian sideboard.

The normal justification given for this curious position is that after about 1830 there was such a disastrous deterioration in standards of taste and craftsmanship that Victorian furniture does not merit the attention legitimately bestowed on earlier periods, and that in particular the eclectic enthusiasm of Victorian designers for copying the historic styles of the past deprives their productions of that degree of originality which is essential to serious connoisseurship. These arguments are not convincing. Firstly, the deterioration can only be established if the evidence is studied rather than ignored. Secondly, ugliness in the products of earlier periods has never proved a bar to serious research or enthusiasm on the part of either antiquarians or collectors. Thirdly, the accusation of unoriginal eclecticism can equally be brought against the furniture designers of the eighteenth century, and was indeed used by many nineteenth-century writers to dismiss the works of Chippendale and the Adams brothers, for example, as debased rehashes of Chinese, classical and renaissance elements. Finally, it is surely absurd to suppose that the vast amount of earnest and informed effort put into the design of furniture by leading architects and others, especially after 1850, could have produced nothing whatever of interest.

The real explanation for the neglect must be sought elsewhere, namely in the totally different research techniques which are required to investigate Victorian furniture by comparison with that of earlier periods. The difference arises mainly from the change in the nature of the documentary evidence available after about 1840. Research into earlier furniture has always taken actual examples as its starting-point, and has, where possible, worked back from the furniture to surviving documents (family records and the like) as supporting evidence for attributions and dating. For these earlier periods the tangible evidence of the furniture itself far outweighs that of the fragmentary documentary references, and even after the appearance of pattern books in the eighteenth century the majority of surviving examples must be assessed without the aid of any contemporary visual or even verbal sources. After about 1845 the development of illustrated periodicals, trade catalogues and exhibition catalogues rapidly transformed the situation, so that for the Victorian era the bulk of systematic contemporary day-by-day visual evidence far outweighs the quantity of authentic surviving furniture, with the result that research must necessarily take the documents as the starting-point and work from them to the furniture instead of vice versa. This necessarily places collectors at a disadvantage, for it means that those who might hope to pick up interesting Victorian items at country auctions will probably find their time wasted unless they have first spent many tedious hours ploughing through trade periodicals in Shoreditch Public Library.

The clearest proof of the significance of this change in research requirements after about 1840 is the fact that the small amount of systematic research into Victorian furniture that has hitherto been undertaken has appeared in journals such as the *Architectural Review* rather than the *Connoisseur*, and has been the work of experts on twentieth-century taste (who take the bulk of contemporary visual evidence for granted) pushing their researches backwards, rather than of eighteenth-century experts (who are trained in the opposite technique) pushing forwards. It is equally significant that the only substantial collection of Victorian furniture in existence – that of the Victoria & Albert Museum – has been mainly built up as a result of a systematic search for particular pieces, the original existence of which had first been established from a study of contemporary periodicals and catalogues.

It is as well that this watershed which divides pre-1840 from post-1840 research and collecting should be widely recognized as soon as possible, for otherwise there is a serious danger that the established practice of collecting without prior documentation will itself produce a cumulative distortion in the public assessment – even in informed circles – of Victorian design, by fostering a process of 'selective survival'. For example, in the absence of a study of the contemporary records, there is a general but erroneous belief that Early Victorian furniture (in contrast to mid-Victorian) retained some of the lightness and elegance of the Regency. Once such a stereotype is established, collectors tend to be interested only in pieces whose authenticity seems to be attested by their conformity to it, and dealers will come to prefer such pieces and reject others as untypical, until in the long run the only pieces which survive in quantity are those which fit into the mistaken picture, while the examples whose survival would establish its falsity are weeded out. By that time it will be too late to redress the balance and all the really interesting pieces will have disappeared.

However, even after it is recognized that the prior research into and the subsequent collecting of Victorian furniture is a legitimate, indeed a praiseworthy, pastime, there still remains the problem of the type of furniture to be sought, for so much has survived, and there is documentary evidence of so many parallel levels of taste, that some choice is inevitable. The problem is aggravated by the appearance for the first time after 1850 of two separate streams: namely the *avant-garde* (what would today be called the 'contemporary') furniture, consciously produced by designers from outside the ranks of the trade – often inspired by a missionary zeal to reform public taste – and appealing to a very small educated clientele; and the enormously larger bulk of trade productions designed anonymously in the studios of the large manufacturers on conservative and traditionalist lines. At first sight these two streams appear to be not only separate but entirely opposed, each contemptuous of the other; the former believed by the latter to be constantly changing in a feverish search after novelty at the whim of each individual designer, the latter believed by the former to be stolidly unchanging and impervious to any progressive influence. Both pictures are distorted, for the evidence shows that a clear logical development can be traced through the apparently unrelated twists and turns of the *avant-garde* designs, and that this in its turn, and with a long time-lag, is reflected in a modified form by changes in the trade designs. The length of the time-lag naturally varies between London and the provinces and according to such factors as the price of the furniture and the nature of the firm, so that a comparison of trade catalogues demonstrates at any one time the whole gamut between the most advanced and the most conservative in current production

MAHOGANY FURNITURE

A Chippendale period mahogany tea table. The legs are fluted in ogee section, and the frieze has matched curl veneers. *Stuart & Turner.*

PLATE 33

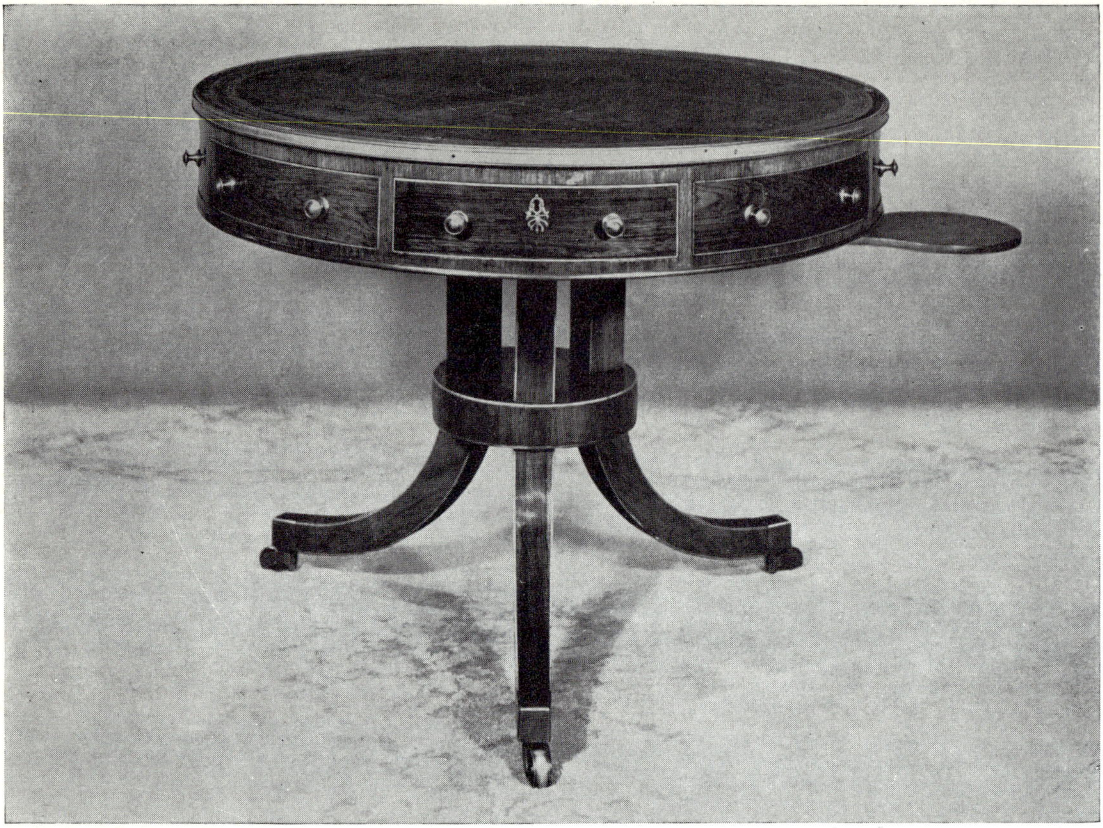

MAHOGANY FURNITURE

(A) A mahogany drum table associated with the Sheraton and Regency periods, with characteristic jutting handles. *H. Blairman & Sons, Ltd.*

(B) A Chippendale period mahogany tripod table with hinged 'pie-crust' top, cabriole legs and ball-and-claw feet. *Leonard Knight.*

PLATE 34

MAHOGANY FURNITURE

An example of the smaller serpentine- and break-front mahogany sideboard of the Sheraton period. The turned and reeded legs are characteristic Sheraton designs. *Frank Partridge & Sons*.

PLATE 35

MAHOGANY FURNITURE

A serpentine-fronted mahogany sideboard c. 1780, showing stringing decoration and brilliant curl figures. *Jetley.*

VICTORIAN FURNITURE

(A) Wood settle with painted panels and encrusted decoration, *c.* 1845. *Victoria and Albert Museum, London.*

(B) Oak table, designed by Philip Webb, 1859. *Dr D. C. Wren, Kelmscott Manor.*

PLATE 37

VICTORIAN FURNITURE

(A) Oak cabinet, designed by A. W. N. Pugin, and made by J. G. Crace, 1851. *Victoria and Albert Museum, London.*

(B) Satinwood cabinet inlaid with Wedgwood plaques; Wright and Mansfield, 1867. *Victoria and Albert Museum, London.*

VICTORIAN FURNITURE

(A) Oak sideboard decorated with carving and enamel, designed by Bruce Talbert, 1867. *Victoria & Albert Museum.*

(B) 'The Backgammon Players', cabinet, designed by Philip Webb, painted by Edward Burne-Jones, 1862. *Metropolitan Museum of Art, New York.*

PLATE 39

VICTORIAN FURNITURE

(A) Ebonized wood cabinet with metal fittings, designed by E. W. Godwin, made by William Watt, c. 1877. *Victoria and Albert Museum, London.*

(B) Adjustable chair, made by Morris, Marshall, Faulkner and Co., c. 1866. *Mrs Tozer.*

(C) Painted and ebonized mahogany cabinet, designed by T. E. Collcutt, made by Collinson and Lock, 1871. *Victoria and Albert Museum, London.*

Carved and painted wood washstand with marble and silver fittings, designed by William Burges, 1880. *Victoria and Albert Museum, London.*

(A) Satinwood cabinet, designed by A. H. Mackmurdo for the Century Guild, made by E. Goodall and Co., Manchester, 1886. *William Morris Gallery, Walthamstow.*

(B) Painted oak cabinet, designed by C. R. Ashbee, 1889. *Abbotsholme School, Rocester, Staffs.*

(C) Escritoire decorated with sycamore marquetry, designed by George Jack for Morris and Co., 1893. *Victoria and Albert Museum, London.*

VICTORIAN FURNITURE

(A) Oak dresser inlaid with ebony and bleached mahogany, designed by W. R. Lethaby, 1900. *Victoria and Albert Museum, London.*

(B) Oak chair, designed by C. F. A. Voysey, made by Story and Co., 1899. *Victoria and Albert Museum, London.*

(C) Cabinet inlaid with ivory, designed by Ernest Gimson for Kenton and Co., 1890.

(D) Oak chair, designed by Charles Rennie Mackintosh, *c.* 1900. *Glasgow School of Art.*

PLATE 43

Oak wardrobe inlaid with pewter and ebony, designed by Ambrose Heal, made by Heal and Son, 1900.
Lt-Col. C. G. Price.

AMERICAN FURNITURE 1640–1840

(A) Press cupboard of oak, pine and maple; New England, 1660–80. *Metropolitan Museum of Art, New York.*

(B) Arm-chair with Carver type back and rush seat; New York, late seventeenth century. *Metropolitan Museum of Art, New York.*

(C) American wainscot chair, oak, c. 1650. *Brooklyn Museum.*

PLATE 45

AMERICAN FURNITURE 1640–1840

(A) Carved oak chest of Thomas Dennis type; Ipswich, Massachusetts, 1660–80. *Israel Sack, New York*.

(B) American Brewster-type chair, actually belonged to Governor William Bradford, d. 1657. *Pilgrim Hall, Plymouth, Massachusetts*.

(C) The American 'Hartford', 'Connecticut' or 'Sunflower' chest; late seventeenth century. *Formerly Collection of Luke Vincent Lockwood; courtesy Parke-Bernet Galleries*.

PLATE 46

AMERICAN FURNITURE 1640–1840

(A) Court cupboard of oak, pine and maple; Massachusetts, about 1675. *Metropolitan Museum of Art, New York.*

(B) Hadley chest marked IP for Joanna Porter (1687–1714) who married John Marsh, representative to the General Court in 1704. (*Luther, The Hadley Chest,* No. 65.) *C. Sanford Bull collection, Yale University Art Gallery.*

(C) Joint stool, maple; Ipswich, Massachusetts. 1660–80. *Israel Sack.*

PLATE 47

AMERICAN FURNITURE 1640–1840

(A) Oak table; Plymouth, Massachusetts, c. 1650. *Greenwood collection, Smithsonian Institution.*

(B) Bible box, painted green. *Brooklyn Museum.*

(C) Hooded pine panel-back settle, seventeenth century. *Israel Sack.*

side by side. Any systematic charting of the history of Victorian furniture – at least after 1850 – must therefore take constant account of this overlapping of styles, though necessarily giving prior attention to those pioneer, and indeed often rebel, designers upon whose inspiration the entire development ultimately depends. Collectors have the choice of furniture at every level of taste, though for obvious reasons it is usually only the more 'advanced' pieces, in so far as they survive, which can provide the additional interest of exact dating and documentation.

In the absence of an accepted body of doctrine on Victorian furniture, the opinions expressed in the survey which follows are necessarily personal and tentative. Moreover, they are unavoidably based as much on an examination of contemporary documents as of actual surviving furniture. The survey concentrates on cabinet-makers' furniture, and excludes upholstered furniture and those sidelines, such as metal furniture, wicker, cane and bent-wood furniture and garden furniture, which require separate study.

Early Victorian Furniture: 1837-51

The first fifteen years of Victoria's reign mark the lowest ebb ever reached in the whole history of English furniture design. Indeed, the most severe strictures so often applied indiscriminately to Victorian taste as a whole are entirely justified if only directed against the products of this initial period. It would, however, be absurd to suggest that a sudden deterioration set in as soon as the new reign had begun; the most that can be said is that a debasement which was already evident as early as the late 1820s gained steady impetus during the 1830s and 1840s. The Great Exhibition of 1851 is always taken to mark the culmination of this debasement. In a sense this is true; although it is only right to remember that by stimulating competitive ostentation among manufacturers it tended to exaggerate the most vulgar elements in Early Victorian design, while the fact that, for the first time, the various illustrated catalogues of the exhibition provide a permanent record of its horrors, unfairly weighs the evidence against the Early Victorians. Had a similar exhibition been held in 1837 instead of 1851, it would hardly have demonstrated a higher average standard.

As always in such debased periods, it is impossible in retrospect to discern any logical development of design, to distinguish the personal styles and influences of the leading designers and manufacturers or even to specify any criteria enabling one to date a surviving piece in default of documentary evidence. The pattern books of this period, such as those of R. Bridgens, R. Brown, Thomas King and Henry Whitaker, throw no light on the matter, for each exhibits the same tepid eclecticism in which a slavish copying of past styles is accompanied by a straining after novelty in trivial details. Judgment is made more difficult by reason of the fact that no surviving examples have so far been precisely related to these patterns, with the exception of a few commonplace pieces designed by Whitaker for Osborne House in about 1845, and still there.

Two characteristics stand out in the general confusion: an emphasis on rich and elaborate carving, preferably with a narrative or anecdotal interest, and a delight in the numerous new substitute materials which technical progress was making available. Lacking any accepted architectural framework, the shape and outline of such items as cabinets and sideboards was frequently entirely subordinated to an overall covering of carving, often worked not by hand carving but by new methods such as the burning techniques of the Burnwood Carving Company's 'Xylopyrography' and Harrison's Wood Carving Company (Pimlico), or the machine stamping of Jordan's Patent Wood Carving, or even produced from materials such as gutta-percha, Jackson's 'carton-pierre', Bielefeld's 'Patent Siliceous Fibre', White and Parlby's 'furniture composition', or Leake's sculptured leather.

Elaborate carving became so established as the hall-mark of fine furniture during this period that the furniture section of Wornum's Report on the Great Exhibition is actually headed 'Carving and Modelling', and the only artists known to have been commissioned during the years 1837-51 to design funiture from outside the trade (with the exception of Pugin, to be mentioned below) were not architects as one would expect, but sculptors, such as Sir Francis Chantrey (1781-1841), John Thomas (1813-62) and Baron Marochetti (1805-67). Inevitably the most popular examples of English furniture at the Great Exhibition were the elaborately carved cradle presented to Queen Victoria by W. G. Rogers (1792-1875) – known as the 'Victorian Grinling Gibbons'; the monstrous 'Kenilworth' buffet (now at Warwick Castle), the *chef-d'oeuvre* of the Warwick school of wood carvers which flourished throughout the nineteenth century; and Arthur J. Jones's ludicrous patriotic carved furniture in Irish bog-oak.

The only one of the new materials which may be said to have produced something new and attractive was papier-mâché, enriched after 1842 with Jennens's and Bettridge's patent jewelled effects. This plastic material, though suitable for trays, caskets and the like, is, however, basically unsuitable for load-bearing furniture, and has no real place in the development of Victorian furniture. Owing to the natural attraction of the smaller items for collectors, it has, nevertheless, received disproportionate attention, and has helped to spread the myth that Early Victorian furniture is lighter and less clumsy than mid-Victorian. In a few cases, of which the settle illustrated in Plate 37A is a good example, the techniques for decorating papier-mâché (e.g. lacquer painting and encrustation with shell and mother-of-pearl) were applied to a normal wooden framework, thus producing a legitimate piece of furniture; but such examples are rare.

Mid-Victorian Furniture: 1851-67

The furniture of the period 1851 to 1867 differed very markedly from that of the preceding period. In particular the wild eclecticism and confusion of styles was rapidly replaced after 1851 by a surprising uniformity, and a single consistent style soon imposed itself on the great bulk of fashionable productions. Victorians themselves gave no name to this style, but usually described examples of it with generalized phrases such as 'following the purest taste of the Italian Renaissance'. Twentieth-century writers have hitherto ignored its existence, although a careful analysis of, for example, the copious records which have survived from the vast Modern Furniture Court of the 1862 Exhibition makes its existence perfectly clear.

Its main characteristics were the use of solid wood, usually walnut or mahogany, rather than veneers or inlay, a repudiation of baroque or rococo curves in favour of more severe outlines, and a continuing emphasis on carving. The latter, however, was now no longer allowed to sprawl over the whole surface with a profusion of unrelated motifs, as in the 1840s, but was concentrated into carefully disposed and deeply cut masks, swags and trophies (usually of 'appropriate' objects, such as dead game birds on sideboards), and almost invariably incorporated human figures in the form of caryatids or brackets. Indeed, this emphasis on human figures became something of an obsession with designers during this period, so that no fashionable sideboard or cabinet was considered complete without them – as large as possible and preferably free-standing. Equally indispensable was an enormous mirror, backing, and usually dwarfing, the whole piece – a direct consequence of the technical developments in mirror making first displayed in the industrial section of the 1851 Exhibition.

It cannot be doubted that the best examples in this manner – however unacceptable to present-day taste – show a sense of style and consistency that had been completely lost in the 1840s, and certainly justify the enthusiasm with which all writers in the 1860s refer to the great improvement in the stylistic purity of English furniture since the nadir of 1851. The improvement must be mainly attributed to the influx of French designers imported from Paris by all the leading firms after the 1851 Exhibition had so clearly exposed the general superiority of French design. Some, such as Eugène Prignot and Alfred Lormier, who acted as chief designers to Jackson and Graham throughout the 1850s and 1860s, were brought over permanently, while in other cases designs were commissioned from artists in Paris, such as Ernest Vandale and Hugues Protat. In either case, the manufacturers always emphasized that 'the piece has been entirely executed by English workers'.

Although this dominant style was pervasive enough to influence not only the productions of all the leading London houses (i.e. Gillow, Trollope, Howard, Thomas Fox and Johnstone and Jeanes) but also the cheaper mass-production manufacturers such as Lucraft, Smee and Snell, and the leading provincial firms (i.e. Henry Ogden, Henry Lamb and Bird and Hull in Manchester, John Taylor, Whytocks, and Purdie, Bonnar and Carfrae in Edinburgh, and C. and W. Trapnell in Bristol), some furniture was, of course, produced in other manners. Thus, a few firms (Charles Hindley, William Fry of Dublin and J. G. Crace) worked in the 'Gothic taste' (see next section); Wright and Mansfield produced an entirely untypical series of copies of original Adams designs; and Dyer and Watts had considerable success with cheap, stained bedroom furniture, an example of which was even purchased by the Empress Eugénie from the Paris Exhibition of 1867.

This nameless mid-Victorian style must be regarded as the last style to have originated within the trade. Thereafter all further developments took place under the shadow of the individual reformist artist-designers and architect-designers whose appearance on the scene so decisively changed the whole trend of English furniture design.

The Gothic Revival

The first conscious reformers of Victorian furniture design – A. W. N. Pugin (1812–52) and William Burges (1827–81) – cannot be said to have had a direct or decisive influence on the general trend of trade design. Nevertheless, the developments of the late 1860s cannot be explained without a reference to their role. Though they both worked within the orbit of the Gothic Revival, their actual designs differed very radically.

The influence of Pugin on English furniture design has usually been overrated. His general influence as a propagandist, his key position in the mid-century transition from a sentimental to a scientific medievalism and the significance of his teachings on church furnishings have tended to obscure the fact that his own domestic furniture had little influence and that his following among furniture designers was always small. He himself designed a good deal of furniture in an extremely plain and unromantic Gothic style for the numerous houses which he erected in the 1840s, but as this was never published, it had no effect on the trade.

By contrast, the much more ornate and monumental furniture which he designed for the Houses of Parliament, and in particular the elaborate display piece which he designed for J. G. Crace for the Medieval Court of the 1851 Exhibition, and which was purchased by the Museum of Ornamental Art in 1852 (illustrated in Plate 38A), were much publicized and copied. Consequently the trade furniture of the 1850s which was claimed by its manufacturers to be 'in the purest Gothic taste, after recognized authorities', and dismissed by its detractors as 'Puginesque', tended to repeat all those faults of over-elaboration with architectural conceits in the way of finials, crockets and the like, which Pugin himself had so trenchantly attacked in his *Contrasts* and which his own domestic work so skilfully avoided. In fact, this type of architectural Gothic furniture was far too closely associated in the public mind with Pugin's catholicism to have any wide vogue, and soon came to be the exclusive preserve of a number of specialized houses – of which the most prominent were Hardman and Cox – dealing mainly in church fittings, and generally referred to by contemporary writers as the 'Wardour Street ecclesiastical upholsterers'. It is true that in 1862 the young Norman Shaw (1831–1912) designed an elaborate bookcase in this style, which has often been quoted since, merely by virtue of having been illustrated in the official catalogue of the Exhibition, but it typified no general trend and was produced not by a furniture firm but by James Forsyth, a specialist in stone carving.

The Gothic furniture of William Burges occupies a somewhat different position. The main body of his furniture – designed largely for his own use or as part of the huge schemes of interior rebuilding which he undertook for the Marquis of Bute at Cardiff Castle and Castell Coch – involved a far too personal interpretation of thirteenth-century Gothic to have any wide influence (a typical example is illustrated in Plate 41). Its fanciful – even facetious – adaptation of medieval forms to present-day needs, and its garish polychromatic decoration, made its incorporation into a normal domestic interior quite impractical. However, two particular pieces in a rather more restrained style, which were shown in the Medieval Court – not (significantly) in the Modern Furniture Court – of the 1862 Exhibition, received a great deal of favourable attention and publicity and deserve separate consideration. They were a huge bookcase, admittedly castellated but otherwise severely unelaborated, painted by no fewer than eleven leading artists, and now in the possession of the Ashmolean Museum, Oxford, and a celebrated plain rectangular cabinet painted to Burges's specifications by E. J. Poynter (1836–1919) with scenes representing 'the Battle of the Wines and the Beers' (bought for the South Kensington Museum from the Exhibition). The main significance of these pieces is that they are both in the plainest possible shape, entirely unlike the Wardour Street architectural Gothic, and depend entirely for their appeal on the painting of their surfaces. A subsidiary significance lies in the fact that their message to the trade was simultaneously endorsed at the 1862 Medieval Court by the furniture here displayed to the public for the first time by the newly created association of Morris, Marshall, Faulkner and Co.

Morris Furniture

Several pieces exhibited by the Morris firm in the 1862 Court have survived (the least known but most attractive example is illustrated in Plate 39B), and all are similar to Burges's exhibits in being solidly constructed, supposedly Gothic, carcases, used as surfaces for painting. They belong by rights to the history of painting rather than of furniture. However, the Morris firm also produced (though it did not exhibit in 1862) several other types of non-Gothic furniture each of which had an influence on the general trend of furniture design. So many misconceptions are current about Morris furniture that it is necessary to examine these in some detail.

Morris himself (despite frequent statements to the contrary) never designed any furniture, nor do his writings indicate much interest in it. All the furniture produced by the firm was the work of his various collaborators. Four different types were manufactured in these early years. Firstly, Philip Webb (1831–1915), the architect, designed a number of large tables depending for their effect entirely on the use of unstained oak and on the interest of their unconcealed joinery construction, thus marking a conscious revolt against the debasement of mid-Victorian cabinet making. Though they were exaggeratedly massive and monumental (one of the most interesting is illustrated in Plate 37B), their proportions and their simple chamfered decoration reveal the hand of a sensitive architect. Their importance lies not in any immediate influence on the trade but in their delayed influence on the Arts and Crafts furniture designers of the 1890s, and they can be legitimately regarded as the original prototypes of the whole Cotswold school of joinery.

Secondly, Ford Madox Brown designed a set of cheap bedroom furniture, produced by the Morris firm in large quantities, usually in a green-stained version, of which a few examples have survived. These appealed particularly to those mid-Victorians who felt that the introduction of examples of good plain design into servants' bedrooms could not but help raise the taste, and even the morals, of the lower classes. Their success led to plagiarism by many firms in the 1880s.

Thirdly, the firm produced and sold right up to the 1920s a set of cheap rush-bottomed chairs and settle in turned ebonized wood, including seven alternative shapes, which quickly became immensely popular with middle-class families anxious to escape from the general philistinism of contemporary decoration. These also were copied with minor modifications by numerous other firms. This set was not originally designed by the firm, but was adapted from a traditional-type country chair seen by William Morris in Sussex.

Fourthly, the firm produced with equal success a drawing-room easy chair with an adjustable bar at the back, which became so popular that in the United States the type is still known as a 'Morris chair' (one is illustrated in Plate 40B). Though often spoken of as designed by Morris himself, it was in fact copied directly from a chair seen in 1866 by Warington Taylor, the young manager of the firm, at the workshop of a Herstmonceux furniture maker named Ephraim Coleman.

Later in the century the firm evolved several entirely different types of furniture, which are referred to below in connexion with the Arts and Crafts movement.

Bruce J. Talbert and C. L. Eastlake

Although neither the architectural Gothic of Pugin nor the painted-plank Gothic of Burges and the Morris firm had much direct influence on trade design, they were nevertheless responsible for providing the point of departure for the development of what ultimately became the most widespread and original of all Victorian styles – a development that was so rapid that in the decade 1868 to 1878 it transformed the whole course of Victorian furniture design. Two stages – or rather two overlapping strands – can be traced in it: the first associated with Bruce J. Talbert (1838–81) and C. L. Eastlake (1836–1906), the second with T. E. Collcutt (1840–1924). Once again the usual Victorian confusion about labels has served to obscure the significance of these changes and the originality of the furniture which developed from them, for contemporary writers gave the style no name and referred to its products as simply Gothic, Early English, Old English or even Jacobean.

The first stage dates from 1867, when Talbert, a prolific and neglected designer, won a silver medal for Holland and Sons at the Paris Exhibition with a so-called 'Gothic dressoir' and several smaller cabinets. The influence of this success was consolidated by the publication in the same year of Talbert's *Gothic Forms, applied to Furniture, Metalwork, etc. for Interior Purposes*, and in 1868 of Eastlake's *Hints on Household Taste*, a book which exerted an enormous influence in sophisticated middle-class circles – especially in America, where it gave rise to a so-called 'Eastlake style'.

Although Talbert's Paris Exhibition pieces were still in a heavy semi-Gothic style, not so far removed from the 'Puginesque', the more unpretentious examples in both his book and in Eastlake's, which were of course, those which had most influence on trade production, marked a definite step away from the Gothic of both Pugin and Burges towards a style more practical and three-dimensional. Its main characteristics were a rigid avoidance of curves or florid carving, a concentration on straight lines and an elaboration of surface colour and texture (but always in the lowest possible relief) by the use of a great variety of different techniques and materials, including the insertion of painted and stained panels, tiles, stamped leather, embroidery, enamels and chased metal. Talbert produced large quantities of this furniture, not only for Hollands, but also for Gillow, and for Marsh, Jones and Cribb of Leeds. However, only two authenticated examples of his work have so far been traced (both are now in the Victoria & Albert Museum, and one is illustrated in Plate 39A). They are both in this modified Gothic style, and demonstrate the particular flavour of rich sobriety which characterized his work. Other examples must certainly survive, along with pieces by Eastlake himself (he designed for Heaton, Butler and Bayne), and those designers who closely followed this style in the 1870s, such as E. J. Tarver (working for Morant Boyd) and Owen Davis, the eclectic assistant of Sir Matthew Digby Wyatt and author of *Art and Life* (1885) (working for Shoolbred).

Despite the acclaim with which Talbert's book was received and the designs in it copied, he himself quickly abandoned the style, and already in the early 1870s turned towards a dull and unoriginal rehash of

Jacobean motifs, with a tedious elaboration of carved strap-work and a generally baronial air. This change can be clearly traced in the designs which he exhibited at the Royal Academy over these years, and in his second book of designs, *Examples of Ancient and Modern Furniture*, published in 1876. Its influence was slight, for it merely provided additional models for the large firms of traditionalist decorators, such as Gillow and Trollope, who had in any case always found in late Elizabethan and early seventeenth-century oak carving a ready-made source of inspiration for their more pretentious schemes.

T. E. Collcutt

The second stage in these developments, though it stemmed directly from the first and rapidly followed on its heels, was due neither to Talbert nor Eastlake, but to Thomas Edward Collcutt. Though remembered as the architect of the Imperial Institute, his role as a furniture designer has been entirely forgotten. It opens in 1871, when Collcutt exhibited at the South Kensington International Exhibition a cabinet designed for Collinson and Lock (illustrated in Plate 40c), which was bought by the Commissioners of the Great Exhibition and finally found its way into the South Kensington Museum. The publication in 1872 of a large catalogue of designs by Collinson and Lock (mostly the work of Collcutt, although J. Moyr Smith, the author of *Ornamental Interiors* (1887) later claimed some credit for them) gave the style a wide currency in the trade, so that already by the time of the Paris Exhibition of 1878 firms such as Cooper and Holt, and Bell and Roper of London, and Henry Ogden of Manchester were copying it precisely. By 1880 its influence appears in the catalogues of mass-production firms such as Hewetson and Milner, Smee, and Lucraft.

In Collcutt's hands the style, though following Talbert in the emphasis on straight lines and the use of coved cornices and painted panels, was elaborated in a far more fanciful and light-hearted spirit, which marked a further stage in the evolution away from the medieval. A simultaneous emphasis on both verticals and horizontals, and a proliferation of shelves and divisions, diversifies the façade and provides variety by giving space for the display of knick-knacks. As always, the rapid spread of the style was accompanied by an equally rapid debasement, so that by the early 1880s it was responsible for a mass of elaborate but gimcrack cabinets, whatnots, corner-cupboards (a particular favourite) and the like, with spindly supports, a profusion of small pigeon-holes, often divided off by little railings of turned balusters or embroidered curtains, and panels painted with floral sprays or willowy female figures, usually on a gold ground. A persistent cliché which became almost a trade-mark for the style was a double panel in which an inner oblong or hexagon is joined to an outer frame by ties at the four cardinal points.

At its best, the style must be regarded as the Victorian era's most individual contribution in the whole field of furniture design. Quantities of its cheaper manifestations have survived, particularly in country rectories. Overmantels, usually backed with numerous small mirrors, have tended to survive as being fixtures, and examples of a drawing-room version of the style, decorated in black and gold, can also be found. Authentic pieces from the Collinson and Lock 1872 catalogue are, however, very difficult to come by.

The surprisingly rapid spread of Talbert's original style, and Collcutt's later version of it, can only be explained if account is taken of the way in which Eastlake and the many publicists who followed him supported their influence with arguments which seemed to provide would-be connoisseurs and purchasers with certain easily remembered maxims for judging furniture, and which buttressed their own uncertain taste with apparently authoritative criteria. These all derived ultimately from the teachings of Pugin, Owen Jones and Ruskin on 'honesty in design'. The most telling was the proposition that because wood has a straight grain it should always be used in the plank and never debased by being carved or curved into twisted shapes more appropriate to plastic or ductile materials. This argument was strengthened by simultaneous appeal to economic and nationalist considerations, for philosophical views than did Jack's expensive projects. In 1890 he exhibited a 'Cheap Chest of Drawers for a Workman or Cottager' which created a great deal of interest. Judging from a contemporary photograph, the piece was so far in advance of its times that it could easily have passed for an example of utility design in the Second World War – even to the use of sunk finger-holes instead of drawer handles.

The furniture of the short-lived association of architect-designers known as Kenton and Co. (named after a street near its Bloomsbury workshop), which lasted for eighteen months in 1890–1 and exhibited at the Arts and Crafts Exhibition of 1890, throws these contradictory tendencies within the movement into even sharper relief. Reginald Blomfield (1856–1942) and Mervyn Macartney (1853–1932) used the workshop to produce eclectic walnut and mahogany pieces in adaptations of eighteenth-century styles. (R. S. Lorimer produced some similar designs at the very end of the century.) Ernest Gimson's designs (apart from some turned ash chairs which he made himself by the traditional methods which he had learnt from a Herefordshire chair-turner in 1888, and one or two Windsor-type examples) were entirely original, and clearly adumbrated that combination of angularity and elegance and of austere outlines and elaborate surface decoration which he later developed so successfully in the Cotswolds (one of his Kenton pieces is illustrated in Plate 43c). On the other hand, Sidney Barnsley's solid pieces in unstained oak acknowledge a direct debt to Philip Webb and clearly anticipated the more unsophisticated and rustic side of the Cotswold movement. The same is true of W. R. Lethaby's (1857–1931) essays in the use of a coarse type of floral marquetry using unstained woods (an example dating from a few years later than the Kenton experiment is illustrated in Plate 43A), though, as if to emphasize the confusion of styles, Lethaby was simultaneously designing in 1890 some entirely dissimilar rosewood and mahogany drawing-room furniture in a modified Chippendale manner, executed by Marsh, Jones and Cribb of Leeds.

When we come to consider the furniture designed by other pioneers of the Arts and Crafts movement, the picture is even more complex. On the one hand, each tended to strike out in his own individual direction, uninhibited by the existence of any accepted norms. On the other hand, the very frequency of the Arts and Crafts exhibitions, and in particular the extent to which the illustrated journals immediately published photographs of every interesting piece as it appeared, made it quite impossible to design in isolation. As a result, the years between 1888 and 1901 witnessed a most complicated pooling of ideas and interplay of influence and counter-influence which would require a large volume to unravel. For example, a characteristic square-cut tapering leg with an enlarged foot, first used by Mackmurdo in the 1880s, was taken up and exploited by Voysey in the 1890s; the latter's weakness for fanciful spreading hinges was immediately copied by C. R. Ashbee; Ashbee's use of thonged leather was plagiarized by Baillie Scott and Wickham Jarvis – and so the list could continue. In fact, so interwoven are the various strands that it is difficult to date precisely, and to pin down initial responsibility for, the introduction of even the most emphatic mannerisms of the period, such as the addition of elongated finials to the corners of cupboards and sideboards (probably first used by Walter Cave on a piano exhibited in 1893) or the decoration of chair backs with cut-out heart shapes (almost certainly due to Voysey).

Although a painstaking examination of the huge mass of contemporary periodical literature of these years is an indispensable prerequisite to any definitive unravelling of these developments, the story must equally remain obscure until more of the key-pieces of the period are unearthed. Many have unhappily disappeared for ever, but others undoubtedly survive, as yet unrecognized and awaiting discovery by enterprising collectors. Century Guild furniture, for example, which was designed by A. H. Mackmurdo (1851–1942), is known only by a small group of pieces in the William Morris Gallery at Walthamstow (one of which is illustrated in Plate 42A), and yet much more must surely survive, for a good deal was sold by Wilkinson's of Old Bond Street in the late 1880s. Examples of the work of C. R. Ashbee's (1863–1942) Guild of Handicraft are even scarcer, for only three have so far been traced (one is illustrated in Plate 42B). Contemporary photographs exist, however, of many more examples, and it is inconceivable that they have all disappeared.

C. F. A. Voysey (1857–1941) is rather easier, and a fair amount of his furniture has already been located. It is unlikely that many more of his elaborate – and often eccentric – individual pieces have survived untraced, but many examples of the several styles of chair which he designed for standard production (one of which is illustrated in Plate 43B) must still be in use. Furniture by Charles Rennie Mackintosh (1868–1928), the Glasgow architect, is in a different category, for although considerable quantities of it survive (a typical example is illustrated in Plate 43D), it is almost all concentrated in the hands of the Glasgow School of Art and the Glasgow City Corporation, and therefore unavailable to the private collector. It also differs from all other Victorian furniture in that it has already been fully catalogued and documented.* There should be considerable scope for pioneer collecting in the early furniture of M. H. Baillie Scott (1865–1945), for though a number of his Edwardian pieces have survived, notably in Switzerland, nothing of his work in the Isle of Man (1887–1900) has been traced. Minor figures of the movement, such as Edgar Wood, Charles Spooner, Wickham Jarvis and Walter Cave, all of whom designed interesting if not startlingly original furniture in the last years of the century, await the attention of both research workers and collectors. Many photographs of their work exist in contemporary periodicals, but nothing has so far been traced.

If so many different cross-currents are discernible among the furniture of the leading Late Victorian designers, it is not surprising that the changes of fashion in the run-of-the-mill trade furniture produced during the 1890s should be even more difficult to chart. The days when the trade could afford to ignore the existence of the reformers were now long past, and Arts and Crafts developments were recorded as a matter of course – and usually respectfully – in the various trade periodicals. Indeed, in 1893 the firms of Gillow, Howard and Sons and Collinson and Lock participated in force at the Arts and Crafts Exhibition, though for some reason this experiment was not repeated.

The direct influence of the movement on the trade seems to have operated at two quite different levels. In the first place, a certain number of hack designers simply added to their repertory of styles some of the more obvious mannerisms of the Arts and Crafts designers and evolved from them a bastard concoction which they christened the 'Quaint Style'. This first appeared in 1891, and became more monstrous as the century ended, especially after 1893 when the so easily aped and misunderstood extravagances of Parisian 'Art Nouveau' were added to the mixture. This so-called style is too debased and spurious to merit serious attention, though the student of the bizarre can trace its ramifications week by week by simply following the so-called 'original' designs by A. Jonquet and H. Pringuet published for the use of manufacturers in the *Furniture Gazette* and the *Cabinet-maker* respectively. Its existence need hardly be drawn to the attention of collectors were it not that in the early stages of collecting, before the field has become familiar, there is always a danger that the most extreme and fantastic specimens will be given undue prominence, both because they are the most easily identifiable and because their very extravagance exercises a certain ludicrous charm. It would, however, be a great pity if, for these reasons, the attention of collectors was diverted from the serious work of the real pioneers of the movement to the entirely derivative corner cupboards and ingle-nooks of the 'Quaint Style' with their shoddy stained glass and machine-stamped repoussé tulips.

On an entirely different level was the furniture produced at the very turn of the century by a few firms, such as Heal and

---

*See Thomas Howarth: *Charles Rennie Mackintosh and the Modern Movement* (London, 1952).

Son, the Bath Cabinet Makers, J. S. Henry, and Wylie and Lockhead, which had taken the trouble to assimilate the basic principles of the Arts and Crafts movement. Though the full fruits of this most important development fall properly outside the Victorian era, some of the exhibits at the Paris Exhibition of 1900 and the Glasgow Exhibition of 1901 (the most striking of which is illustrated in Plate 44) already herald the change.

AMERICAN FURNITURE 1640–1840

By MARVIN D. SCHWARTZ

From the beginning of colonization in America there was some conflict of interest between the settlers and the nations that nurtured the new colonies. Although colonization was undertaken by the mother countries for the dual purpose of acquiring raw materials and a market for manufactures, it was impractical for the settlers to depend entirely upon the homeland for manufactured goods. There were craftsmen available to produce some of what was required, so that in spite of prohibitions by the governing companies and nations, pewter, silver and furniture were made locally before the end of the seventeenth century.

Seventeenth century: one of the remarkable features of American furniture from the very beginning is its distinctiveness from the provincial styles of the British Isles. It has qualities that place it apart because of its consistent simplicity. The first style to be encountered is a late version of the Tudor style, which was current in the English provinces all through the seventeenth century. It is a style in which there are few furniture forms. Chests for storage and cupboards for display and storage were the only large case pieces. Several kinds of decoration are found on American chests of the seventeenth century. One is an arcade carved in the panels across the front of the chest with foliate pattern on the arches and the columns (Plates 45A, 46A). Another kind of decoration consists of the application of strips of molding which divide the panels across the front of the chest into patterns such as a modified cross or a hexagon. Turned wooden spindles and bosses are often applied between the panels. A number of related pieces have been traced to the Ipswich, Massachusetts, area, where the joiner, Thomas Dennis, made furniture in the seventeenth century. A variation of the type has been associated with Connecticut; in these the applied decoration is combined with flat carving in a floral pattern interpreted as a sunflower surrounded by tulips. This has been called the Hartford or Sunflower chest (Plate 46c). In rare instances, seventeenth-century chests have been found with the floral decoration painted on (Plate 49A). One variation of the form has drawers added below the usual chest which adds height to the piece.

Small boxes for the storage of books and for the storage of toilet articles are also known. The box for books, more popularly known as the Bible box (Plate 48B), usually has a slanting lid which may have been used to hold books while they were being read, or as a surface for writing.

The same decoration is encountered on the small forms as on the larger ones. The seventeenth-century cupboard was used for storage and display. Two important variations exist, the court (Plate 47A) and the press cupboard (Plate 45A), which vary in the degree they provide for each of the two functions. The court cupboard was designed mainly for showing off objects. It consists of three shelves with a recessed cabinet between the middle and upper shelf. There are shallow drawers making a skirt below each shelf. The cabinet frequently has canted sides to increase the display area. The decoration on this form is elaborate. The shelves are supported by heavy baluster-like columns decorated with turned rings or carving. The flat areas are decorated either by the application of turned spindles and bosses or carving. The turnings are generally painted black to simulate ebony. Motifs in carving are floral or foliate. The black turnings on the rich dark brown stain of the oak were made even richer by the addition of brightly colored carpets and cushions which are mentioned in seventeenth-century inventories as being on such pieces.

The chair was not as common in middle-class homes of the seventeenth century as it became later. The inventories of Plymouth, Massachusetts, between 1633 and 1654, and those of Boston for relatively the same period, reveal that most homes had only a few chairs. The chair had special significance and was reserved for the master of the household or an important guest. Others sat on chests, benches or small joint stools. These stools (Plate 47c) had wooden seats, rectangular in shape, on turned legs joined by low stretchers.

Several varieties of seventeenth-century American chairs are known: the wainscot; the chair of turned posts and spindles; or slats; and the so-called Cromwellian or Farthingale chair. The wainscot chair (Plate 45c) has a back and seat of solid panels, with curving arms on turned supports and turned legs joined by straight stretchers. The back is decorated with flat incised carving in foliate, floral or geometric patterns. Occasionally a curving crest tops the back. This chair, which had been fashionable in the sixteenth century Elizabethan court, actually was one variation of a type that existed at least as early as the fourteenth century, but by the seventeenth century was found only in the provinces. Its heaviness makes it impressive, and the characteristic decoration reflects the Renaissance taste, which affected English culture rather late.

Chairs of turned posts and spindles or slats fall into three categories: the Carver, the Brewster and the slat-back. The Carver and Brewster both use spindles. Each is named for a founding father of Massachusetts because of a resemblance to chairs these men owned (now in the Pilgrim Society in Plymouth). The Carver (Plate 45B) is an armchair with a single tier of spindles making up the back. The turned decoration on the spindles and posts is simple. The seat is of rush. The Brewster (Plate 46B) is basically the same type of chair; the back has two tiers of small spindles across it, however, and under the arms and between the seat and the stretchers there are also rows of spindles. The origin of this type is unclear. There are thirteenth-century Scandinavian examples related vaguely, and in the sixteenth century in England a three-legged version is encountered. The chair brought to the New World which became the President's Chair at Harvard is an example of this later group.

The table varied greatly in size and type. The trestle table might have a top as large as eight feet in length resting loosely on two or more trestles joined by a brace. Another type of rectangular table has four turned legs joined by low stretchers (Plate 48A). The skirt below the top often has a drawer. These vary in length, and the tops are square or oblong. Occasionally the skirt is molded. The gateleg table is a type that generally dates quite late in the period (Plate 49c). It is a narrow table with large drop leaves which are supported on a leg and stretchers that swing out. The top is round, oval, square or oblong when opened. Still another type is the chair table. Similar in construction to the wainscot chair, its back was made so that it could be pivoted down and rested on the arms of the chair to serve as a table top.

The furniture of the seventeenth century in America was made predominantly of oak, although pine and other soft woods were used where there was no great threat of heavy wear. Construction was simple and heavy; the mortise and tenon was used to join sides of large pieces of furniture as well as drawers, a continuation of a technique that goes back to medieval times. Painting and staining furniture in black, blue, red and green to emphasize flat carving or to bring out moldings on chests is common in this early furniture. This also is a technique that dates back to medieval times; however, the motifs and the decoration in this furniture are classical in source.

William and Mary style: toward the end of the seventeenth century a change of style can be discerned in American furniture. This was a late manifestation of tendencies occurring all through the century in England and the rest of Europe. These changes were in part the result of the economic development in Europe, which made it possible for the middle and upper classes to seek new and greater luxuries. One factor was the expansion of trade, with each nation reaching out for new markets, which resulted in a growing trade with the Far East and the importation of all kinds of exotic merchandise.

In America the style named for William and Mary lasted from 1690 to 1725. It combines elements of the English William and Mary style with tendencies that began earlier in the century in England.

The style very clearly reflects the taste for the luxurious and relates to the baroque; as in the baroque, classical motifs are interpreted with inventiveness which is most obvious in the designs of the legs as scrolls, spirals and columns. Another facet of the new taste is an interest in attractive surfaces. Walnut, with its fine grains, replaced oak as the predominant wood, and other woods were also chosen for the pattern of the grain. To obtain the best patterns, veneers were employed. Beautiful effects were achieved by cutting sections of the tree near the root into thin strips, for application as veneer. The burl of the walnut was favored for veneering case pieces. Inlaid strips of contrasting wood were used as borders, and occasionally larger designs were inlaid.

Oriental lacquered furniture inspired imitations in Europe, England and America. Since true lacquering is long and laborious, some of the processes were greatly simplified. In 1688 an English publication, *Treatise of Japanning and Varnishing*, by John Stalker and George Parker, was published with instructions on how to imitate lacquer work with Western varnishes. These were probably followed almost as avidly in America as in England. The results vary from close copies of the Oriental design to some fairly different designs. Japanners advertised in Boston in the early eighteenth century. Surviving examples of their work are rare, and the best are of the Queen Anne period, such as the highboy illustrated (Plate 52A).

One of the most important changes that came with the new style was the introduction of greater variety in furniture form. New forms for special purposes, such as the desk and the dressing table, were developed. In the seventeenth-century American home the simple box-like chest served as storage for everything, but toward the end of the century the chest of drawers evolved, finally raised on a stand or frame (Plate 51C). The earliest examples occurred before the transition to William and Mary, and there are examples in oak with panelled decoration, but the form is more typical of the later style.

Another variation is the chest of drawers on tall legs, correctly called the high chest, but popularly named the highboy during the nineteenth century. The high chest lends itself more readily to elegant design. In some William and Mary examples (Plate 50A) the chest has four legs across the front and two in the back. The legs are elaborately shaped and are joined just above the foot by a curving stretcher that goes around the piece. The upper part is rectangular with a flat top; occasionally a bolection molding is used at the top, as in the example illustrated, to conceal a narrow secret drawer that was probably designed for papers.

The low chest was made at table height and seems to have been devised to serve as a dressing table. On tall legs, like the high chest, it has one or two tiers of small drawers. In later periods, more often than in the William and Mary period, it was made to match the high chest. The mixing table is very similar in form. More often it has four legs, joined by crossed stretchers, than six, and to replace the center front legs there are turned ornaments attached to the skirt. Rare examples have tops of imported slate framed in marquetry (Plate 50B).

The desk evolves as a large form in this period by the addition to a chest of drawers of an upper section enclosed by a slant-top which contains pigeon holes, small drawers and a writing area. Occasionally a cupboard is added above for book storage. This has been called a scrutoire or escritoire; it is known as a bureau in England, or bureau-cabinet; the modern term is secretary. In another type of desk the slant-top enclosure is used on a frame of turned legs joined by stretchers, the desk-on-frame.

In the category of tables, gateleg tables (Plate 49C) seem to have been the most popular type in the period. They appear in a great variety of sizes, so that they evidently served many different purposes.

Chair design was affected quite radically by the change of style. The wainscot chair all but disappeared, Carvers and Brewsters became rare, and the slat-back was retired to the country. Taller, thinner proportions were characteristic of the new style in chairs (Plate 51B). There are relatively more side chairs than in the earlier period. Frequently a material from the Orient, cane, was used to make the seat and the back (Plate 51A). Most of the American examples are simplified versions of a type that was introduced in England after being popular in Portugal and the Netherlands. The typical American example has an elaborately carved cresting-rail, turned stiles and front legs carved in scroll or vase shapes.

The wing chair (Plate 49B), with back and arms completely upholstered, and a flanking, curving 'wing' coming out from the back over the arms, was introduced in this period as a bedroom chair.

The William and Mary style marked the beginning of variety in furniture form in America. It possessed a new lightness and elaborate decoration, such as fine carving and the application of rich veneers and inlays, being the American version of the baroque.

Queen Anne style: the Queen Anne style was at its height from 1725 to 1750 but persisted longer in rural areas. It combines influences from the style of the reign of Queen Anne, 1702–14, with later influences from the period of the early Georgian rulers. Naming the style in America after Queen Anne is unfortunate, because her reign was short and its style was not significant. The American counterpart marks the beginning of an eighteenth-century style that lasted until the Revolution. It developed at a time when the larger towns in the American colonies were becoming more prosperous and taste more sophisticated. Importation of expensive textiles, porcelains and other objects became increasingly important and the demand for more skilled work by local craftsmen was augmented. The furniture of the larger American towns reflected this greater sophistication in the technical improvement shown by cabinet-makers. Fine details in construction, and finesse in carving became more evident than in earlier work.

A comparison of the Queen Anne style with contemporary movements in the arts reveals at once that it includes elements of the rococo. There is restraint and balance in line and ornament typical of the style which, however, is more classical than truly rococo. American Queen Anne furniture is characterized by a lightness in line and delicate symmetrical ornamentation. The favored wood was walnut, but mahogany, imported from the West Indies, was used to some degree. Veneers and inlay became less fashionable than fine solid wood with carved decoration. In the important centers, where walnut and mahogany were used, furniture occasionally continued to be japanned in imitation of Oriental lacquer (Plate 52A). Curves take a particularly prominent place in the shapes encountered during the Queen Anne period. The cabriole leg, a simple curving support inspired by the design of an animal leg, which had occurred on rare occasions in the William and Mary style, became quite important. There were few new furniture forms in the Queen Anne period, and most of those introduced in the previous period were employed.

The high chest underwent certain changes in the transition to the Queen Anne style. The top is less frequently flat than pedimented with a broken arch flanked by finials on either side (Plate 53B). Often the center drawers at the top and the bottom have shell decoration and occasionally pilasters flank either side of the upper section. The cabriole legs on which it stands terminate in a variety of ways: a simple round pad; a curving three-section design called the trifid (Plates 53A, 53C), or a pointed type called the slipper foot (Plate 54B), shown here with a carved tongue. Very rarely the Spanish foot (*see* Glossary), a variation of the scroll foot, is used with the cabriole leg. On the more elaborate pieces, the knees of the cabriole legs are decorated with shells (Plate 53C), or, in what appear to be late examples, the acanthus leaf. The typical examples of the period have a skirt that is scalloped, although frequently there are vestigial remains of the two center legs of the

William and Mary period in the form of drops attached to the skirt. Matching low chests were more common in this period. Apparently the chest of drawers became a little less popular.

There was a great increase in the variety of tables. Tables for tea and for china, of small dimensions and with fine detail, occur in a variety of shapes. The simplest type is rectangular (Plate 52c) with a top surrounded by an enclosing molding that makes it seem like a tray (the tray-top, or dished top). The corners of such tables are apt to be curved and the legs are sometimes decorated with a shell on the knee. On rare occasions the top is of marble rather than wood. For serving tea, a round table which could have its top tilted up to save space when it was not in use, was also introduced in the Queen Anne period. The top rests on a turned baluster terminating in a tripod of cabriole legs. A smaller version was used as a candlestand.

The gaming, or card table, is another small table that was developed in this period. This table has a folding top whose two hinged halves rest in layers when not being used. One or two legs swing out as supports when the table is opened for games. Occasionally there is a fifth leg or both rear legs can be extended. When the top is opened, a surface covered with baize or felt, with oval depressions for counters and a wooden area at each corner for a candlestick is exposed.

Although there is evidence to show that dining rooms were not common in the American Queen Anne period, a few special forms relating to dining developed. A table that would appear to have been a serving table appears. It is rectangular, or roughly so, with the back unfinished and the front usually curving. The tops are marble and there is a plain, thick skirt in several of the examples known. The most frequent top of dining tables is the kind with drop leaves supported by swinging cabriole legs. The tops are rectangular, oval or round.

The chair is a form that clearly reflects style, because it can be changed easily. The Queen Anne chair is light and graceful and made up of a series of curves (Plates 52B, 54B). It is quite different from the stiff, but elegant, William and Mary type. The back of a Queen Anne chair consists of a curving top rail, which in the center provides space for a shell. This rail is joined to stiles that often curve also, and from the center of the toprail to the seat there is a solid splat shaped like a vase or violin. The seat is horseshoe-shaped (also called compass seat), and the front legs are cabriole. The rear legs are generally plain and round, the stump-leg. In some examples stretchers brace the legs. The curving lines are emphasized by the curving of the individual wooden members. The back is often shaped to accommodate the human form.

Sofas or settees of this period have straight upholstered backs, which are sometimes plain across the top (Plate 54c) and sometimes scalloped (Plate 55A). Occasionally a settee is made up of two or three chair backs joined together.

Regional differences in American furniture become more apparent in the Queen Anne period than they had been earlier. These are summarized at the conclusion of the sections on the Chippendale and classical styles.

The curve is the most important element of Queen Anne furniture design, with simplicity and restraint significant characteristics. The forms are relatively the same as in the William and Mary style, but there is greater variety in size and greater lightness in line. Veneers became less important than fine solid woods. Walnut, a local wood that is hard and handsome, was gradually replaced by imported mahogany. The Queen Anne style is a restrained version of the rococo.

Chippendale style: the American Chippendale style, in many ways a continuation of the Queen Anne, may be dated from 1750 to 1780, the period in which the colonies came of age, culturally as well as politically. Thriving American towns kept as much in fashion as any in provincial England by following the latest trends in London. In spite of this similarity, it is interesting to see that the style of colonial America is as different from that of the provinces of the mother country in furniture as in the different accents of speech, which were also recognizable by that time.

AMERICAN FURNITURE 1640–1840

(A) Painted chest, oak, pine, and maple; graining on body, with panels, red, black, and white; Massachusetts, c. 1700. *Brooklyn Museum.*

(B) American wing chair with rudimentary Spanish foot; c. 1700. Blair Collection, *Metropolitan Museum of Art, New York.*

(C) Walnut double gate-leg table; New England, 1690–1725. *Metropolitan Museum of Art, New York.*

PLATE 49

AMERICAN FURNITURE 1640–1840

(B) Mixing table, slate and marquetry top, burl veneer and herringbone cross-banding; New England, 1690–1710. *Coll. of C. K. Davis.*

(A) William and Mary high chest; burl maple; bolection moulding; has drawer; 1700–25. *Henry Ford Museum, Dearborn, Michigan.*

PLATE 50

AMERICAN FURNITURE 1640–1840

(B) Leather upholstered side chair of maple and oak; Massachusetts, 1685–1700. *Metropolitan Museum of Art, New York.*

(A) William and Mary American caned maple side chair, c. 1700. *Metropolitan Museum of Art, New York.*

(C) William and Mary high chest on rope-twist turned legs; late seventeenth century. *Metropolitan Museum of Art, New York.*

PLATE 51

AMERICAN FURNITURE 1640–1840

(A) Japanned Queen Anne highboy, maple and white pine; Boston, c. 1735. *Metropolitan Museum of Art, New York.*

(B) Queen Anne walnut side chair; Rhode Island, c. 1740. *Israel Sack.*

(C) Tea table, dished top with incurved corners; New England, Queen Anne period, 1725–50. Downs's *American Furniture*, No. 365. *Henry Francis du Pont Winterthur Museum, Winterthur, Delaware.*

AMERICAN FURNITURE 1640–1840

(A) Philadelphia Queen Anne walnut side chair; 1725–50. *Antiques*, xlix, 49.

(B) Cherry bonnet top high chest; Rhode Island, c. 1745. *Ginsbury and Levy*.

(C) Walnut dressing table or lowboy; probably Maryland, 1745–60 Downs's *American Furniture*, No. 324, Winterthur Museum.

PLATE 53

AMERICAN FURNITURE 1640–1840

(A) New England Queen Anne wing chair, 1725–50. *Blair Collection; Metropolitan Museum of Art, New York.*

(B) Philadelphia Queen Anne walnut arm-chair, *c.* 1730–50. *Former Haskell Collection; courtesy Parke-Bernet.*

(C) Queen Anne walnut leather-covered sofa, arrow-shape stretchers, carved web feet, and scrolled knee blocks; Philadelphia 1740–50. Downs's *American Furniture, No. 269, Winterthur Museum, Delaware.*

AMERICAN FURNITURE 1640–1840

(A) Chippendale upholstered settee of mahogany and maple; Massachusetts, c. 1765–75. *Metropolitan Museum of Art, New York.*

(B) New York mahogany oval drop-leaf dining-table, c. 1770. *Metropolitan Museum of Art, New York.*

(C) Philadelphia mahogany pier or side table with top of black and white marble; carved fret on rounded frieze; c. 1760–75. *Metropolitan Museum of Art, New York.*

PLATE 55

AMERICAN FURNITURE 1640–1840

(A) Blockfront mahogany chest-on-chest, Townsend-Goddard, cabinet-makers; Newport, 1765–70. Downs' *American Furniture*, No. *183*, Winterthur Museum, Delaware.

(B) Tripod tea-table with piecrust edge and birdcage attachment; Philadelphia, 1765–80. *Karolik Collection; Museum of Fine Arts, Boston.*

(C) Tea-table made by John Goddard, Newport, 1763, for Jabez Bowen. Downs' *American Furniture*, No. *373*, Winterthur Museum, Delaware.

PLATE 56

AMERICAN FURNITURE 1640–1840

A

B

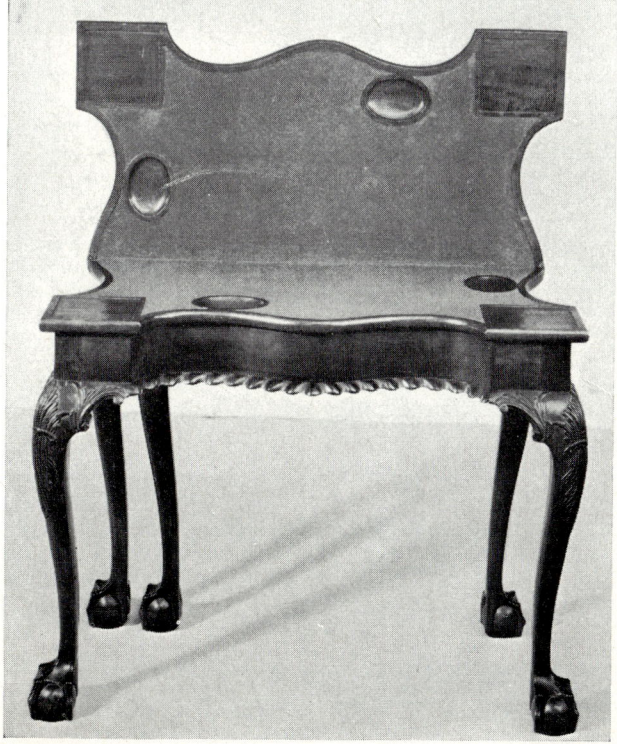

C

(A) Philadelphia mahogany ribbon-back side chair; design of back from Chippendale's *Director*, c. 1760. Brooklyn Museum.

(B) Massachusetts desk and bookcase in rococo style; with bombé base; possibly by John Cogswell, Boston, c. 1765–80. Downs's *American Furniture*, No. 227, Winterthur Museum.

(C) New York gaming table, serpentine form, with gadrooning on skirt; c. 1760–80. Ex-Norvin Green collection; courtesy of Parke-Bernet.

PLATE 57

AMERICAN FURNITURE 1640–1840

A

B

C

(A) Philadelphia high chest; the Van Pelt highboy, formerly in the Reifsnyder collection; c. 1765–80. Downs' *American Furniture*, No. 195, Winterthur Museum, Delaware.

(B) One of the six so-called "sample chairs" of Benjamin Randolph; design of back from Chippendale's *Director*, Plate IX, 1762 ed. Downs' *American Furniture*, No. 137, Winterthur Museum, Delaware.

(C) Philadelphia dressing-table or lowboy with fine rococo ornament; made for the Gratz family, 1769; companion to the high chest also at Winterthur. Downs' *American Furniture*, No. 33, Winterthur Museum, Delaware.

PLATE 58

AMERICAN FURNITURE 1640–1840

(A) Connecticut blockfront cherry desk signed by Benjamin Burnham of Norwich (U.S.A.); dated 1769. *Metropolitan Museum of Art, New York.*

(B) Chippendale arm-chair with Marlborough leg; Boston (U.S.A.), 1765–70. *Metropolitan Museum of Art, New York.*

(C) Charleston chest-on-chest with fret on frieze; of type attributed to Thomas Elfe, *c.* 1775. *Heyward-Washington House, Charleston Museum.*

A

B

C

PLATE 59

AMERICAN FURNITURE 1640–1840

(A) Baltimore inlaid sideboard showing use of contrasting woods emphasizing ovals; panels with mitred corners; c. 1800. *Ginsburg and Levy.*

(B) New York Hepplewhite side chair with drapery and feather carved in splat; 1790–1800. *Karolik collection, Museum of Fine Arts, Boston.*

(C) New England Hepplewhite mahogany and satinwood bowfront chest of drawers on French bracket foot; 1790 *Coll. of Mrs Francis P. Garvan.*

AMERICAN FURNITURE 1640–1840

A

B

(A) Mahogany commode with cupboard ends; Duncan Phyfe, c. 1810–15. *Ginsburg & Levy, New York.*

(B) Philadelphia Sheraton drapery back arm-chair with inlay on legs; c. 1800–10. *Ginsburg & Levy, New York.*

(C) Duncan Phyfe mahogany dressing-table with curule legs; c. 1810–15. *Ginsburg & Levy, New York.*

C

PLATE 61

AMERICAN FURNITURE 1640–1840

(A) New England Sheraton tambour secretary; attributed to John Seymour, Boston, c. 1810. *Ginsburg and Levy.*

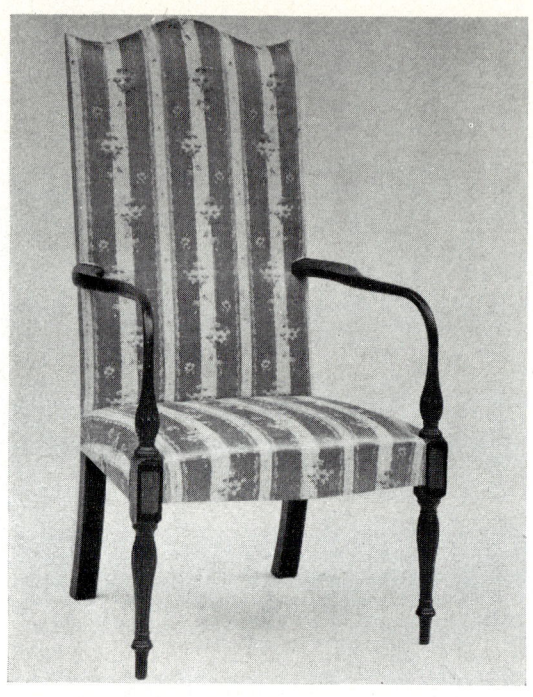

(B) Martha Washington armchair, mahogany, c. 1790–1800. *Metropolitan Museum of Art, New York.*

(C) New York sewing table, mahogany and birdseye maple; c. 1815. *Coll. of Mrs Giles Whiting.*

(D) Mahogany sewing table. Salem, 1800–10. *Ginsburg and Levy.*

PLATE 62

AMERICAN FURNITURE 1640–1840

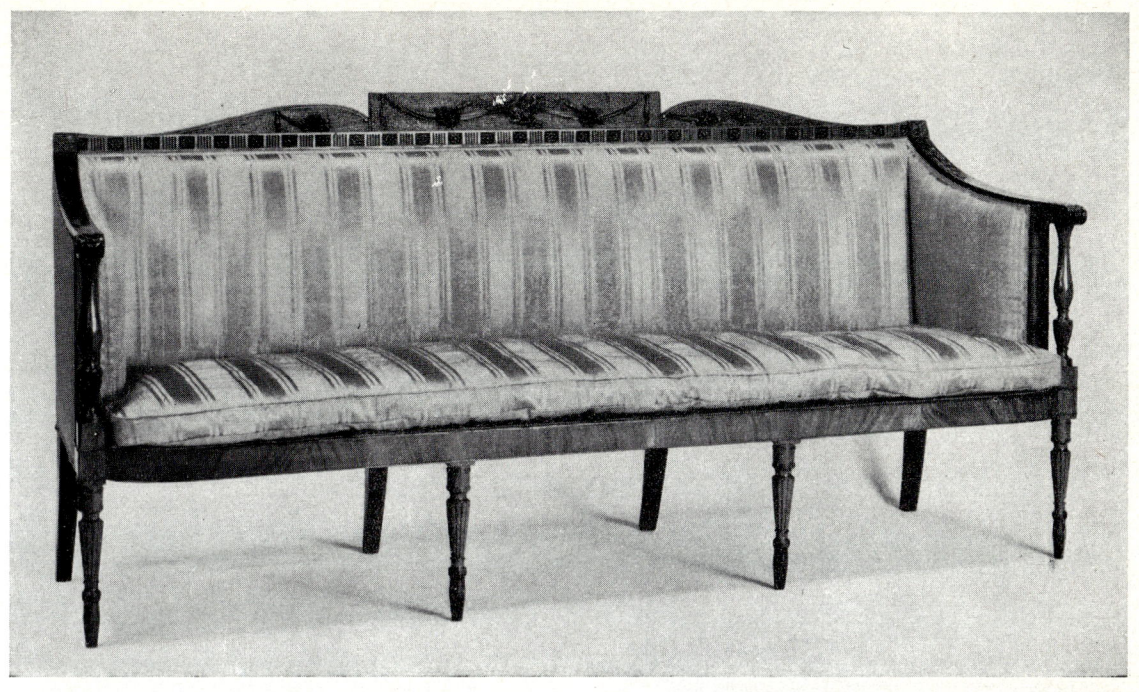

(A) Salem sofa with carving attributed to Samuel McIntire, c. 1800. *Metropolitan Museum of Art, New York.*

(B) Baltimore Hepplewhite inlaid mahogany card table, 1790–1800. *Karolik Collection, Museum of Fine Arts, Boston.*

(C) Duncan Phyfe medallion back side chair; reeded stiles are one with the seat rail; c. 1800–10. *Ginsburg & Levy, New York.*

PLATE 63

AMERICAN FURNITURE 1640–1840

(A) Salem desk and bookcase with ivory finials and knobs; white and gold glass panels in bookcase section; *c.* 1800–10. *Ginsburg and Levy.*

(B) Mahogany armchair; attributed to Henry Connelly, Philadelphia, *c.* 1800. *Ginsburg and Levy.*

(C) Inlaid Pembroke with reeded legs; attributed to Duncan Phyfe, New York, 1790. *Ginsburg and Levy.*

The style is named after the English cabinetmaker, Thomas Chippendale, who published a volume of furniture designs in 1754. This book, *The Gentlemen and Cabinetmaker's Director*, published in three editions and translated into several languages, was known all over Europe and in some of the European colonies. The designs epitomized the rococo in England, when this style was at its height, with admittedly French inspiration. On the title page the reader is advised that the designs are in the Gothic, Chinese and Modern (meaning French) taste. Each of the tastes is basically French, the differences are in motif rather than spirit or source.

The American Chippendale style is more conservative than its name implies. Besides Chippendale's designs, earlier English styles serve as a source of inspiration, so that while it brings the incipient rococo tendencies of Queen Anne into a more prominent position, it is more restrained than English Chippendale. In general, the furniture forms of American Chippendale are likely to be somewhat more elaborately decorated continuations of Queen Anne forms rather than innovations.

Forms that started in the William and Mary period changed in design in the Queen Anne, and really only became more ornamented in American Chippendale furniture. The simple shell and the plain architectural detail with limited carving so popular in the Queen Anne period were replaced by more complicated foliate patterns on pieces that are relatively alike in line and function.

The curving cabriole leg continued to be common, but rather than terminating in such a simple form as the pad foot, the claw and ball, which had been introduced late on American Queen Anne furniture, became the usual solution. This type of foot was too old-fashioned in England to appear in the *Director*, where cabriole legs generally terminate in the scroll foot which appears in America only on rare occasions. Still another type of foot, and one that is more elaborate than the claw and ball, but less rococo than the scroll, the hairy paw, appears once in the *Director* and on some very fine American furniture (Plate 58B). It had been used in English furniture earlier.

One type of leg introduced for tables and chairs in the main is straight and in the Chinese taste. This is sometimes called the Marlborough leg, a term of uncertain origin, but known to have been in use in the eighteenth century. The leg is sometimes plain, sometimes fluted or molded, and occasionally cut-out frets are applied (Plate 59B).

The high chest is handled with relative conservatism. Not mentioned in the *Director*, it is a form that had grown unpopular in England. In America it found particular favor in Philadelphia. The form was a continuation of an earlier tradition, repeating the same general characteristics. In a few of the more outstanding examples, however, the decoration is in the latest fashion (Plate 58A). Strips of asymmetrical foliate patterns are applied across the skirt and in the area just below the broken arch pediment. Asymmetrically carved shells are on the top and bottom center drawers. Finials in the shape of flaming urns, a classical motif, flank the pediment, with the center finial a rococo scroll device called a cabochon. The knees of the cabriole legs are carved in an acanthus leaf pattern.

In England the high chest had been replaced by the chest-on-chest, and by a chest combined with an upper section that is a cupboard. These were introduced in the American colonies shortly after they were known in England. They were used everywhere, but some of the outstanding examples were made in New England, New York and Charleston, South Carolina (Plate 56A). Several Connecticut examples show simple ornamentation and are quite plain. In New York there are a few examples of the second type, sometimes called a linen press. These have features typical of the area, such as a fret frieze applied just under the cornice.

The chest of drawers, important in the William and Mary period, was almost forgotten in the Queen Anne period, but it was revived in Chippendale furniture. Some chests were straight fronted with chamfered front corners, or with engaged quarter columns at the front corners. These usually rested on claw and ball feet. This is a design followed in New York. More often, in keeping with the tendency toward greater elaboration in decoration, the fronts of these chests were curved. The curve varied between oxbow and serpentine. Occasionally the corners were chamfered. Each variation was popular for a time, and the shapes varied from region to region. In Massachusetts the curving front is occasionally accompanied by sides that swell toward the bottom in a kettle or bombé shape, seen in the desk section of the exceptionally graceful desk-bookcase at Winterthur (Plate 57B). This form was occasionally found in Connecticut. A variation of the curving front is the blockfront in which flattened curves in three vertical sections are either applied or cut from solid wood. In some outstanding examples made in Newport (Plate 56A) and Connecticut, these sections are topped by shells that are finely carved.

The desk remained a form that is a variation of the chest of drawers (Plate 59A). Its development is the same with similar enrichment of detail. The form with the bookcase added (Plate 57B) is better known as a Chippendale piece than earlier. Details of dentil molding on the doors of the bookcase, mirrored doors, fluted chamfered corners, architectural elements such as pilasters with richly carved Corinthian capitals are among the many devices used for enrichment.

Although little new development is seen in the forms of tables, there is greater variety in size and decoration in the Chippendale style. Oval, round or rectangular drop-leaf tables with cabriole legs continued in use as dining tables with subtle changes (Plate 55B). Acanthus leaf carving on the knees and claw and ball foot terminals were favored over the ordinarily plain legs of Queen Anne examples.

China or tea tables, rectangular in shape, seem to have been made in greater numbers. Again, it is the character of the decoration that changes. Carved ornament becomes more ostentatious, with elaborate acanthus leaf decoration on the legs and the skirt. The shape of the top is more often curved as a further concession to the new taste (Plate 56C). The tilt-top baluster base table, which serves as a candlestand when very small and a tea table when larger, was introduced as a form in which the baluster was plain, but Chippendale examples have elaborately carved balusters and legs, and in some cases the top is scalloped and fitted with a molding around the edge. The scalloped top inspired the name 'piecrust' for these elaborate tables (Plate 56B). A feature making the top turn is the 'bird-cage', a cube of approximately six inches, with solid top and bottom and sides consisting of small baluster or columnar pegs. The base fits into the 'cage' and the table top rests on it, connected by a hinge so that it can be tilted. The 'cage' can be turned on the base. The baluster on a tripod is also used as the base for firescreens. The baluster is tall and thin and often elaborately carved. The screen is ordinarily needlework.

Another type of small table, the card or gaming table (Plate 57C), also becomes more elaborate in carved decoration without any significant changes in form. The serpentine front becomes more popular since it is so suitable to a form with carving. The outstanding new form is the Pembroke table, a rectangular breakfast table with short drop leaves. The name is not used in the *Director*, but it is found on bills of the time. Usually the legs of these tables are in the 'Chinese taste' and reinforced by crossed stretchers.

A larger form devised for use in serving a meal is the side table, the predecessor of the sideboard. The Chippendale examples often have marble tops (Plate 55C). There again, the form is one known in Queen Anne examples but now decorated with more elaborate carving. Occasionally the cabriole leg is replaced by the Marlborough.

Chairs changed radically in line, although the proportions remained virtually the same. The back is much more intricate, the curving top rail turns up at the ends in a 'cupid's bow' shape, and the center back support, the splat, is cut out and carved in a pattern often borrowed from the *Director* (Plates 57A, 58B). The rails and stiles frequently are carved in foliate patterns. This is all in contrast to the rich but simply curving Queen Anne back with its solid splat. The seat, which had been curved in a horseshoe shape, becomes straight sided. Besides the usual cabriole leg, the straight leg is also employed as a support (Plate 59B).

In the choice of designs for the back, there is a variety of pattern which often can be traced back to inspiration from one of the 'tastes' suggested by Chippendale. The use of a Gothic arcade, however, can not readily be distinguished from a Chinese or French pattern in all cases because of the liberties taken with the various motives. The objective was whimsical design rather than archeological precision. There were other designers besides Chippendale who provided designs in a very closely related spirit. Although entire books of designs might not be available, groups of engraved designs were. Another source was the actual furniture, which was at times imported. The advertisements are confusing on this score, because the allusions to importations tend to give us an exaggerated idea of their importance.

The curving lines of the rococo are aptly used in the backs of upholstered pieces. Sofas and settees have curving frames which were covered by rich imported fabrics (Plate 55A). In rare pieces a part of the upper frame is exposed and carved as in English examples of late rococo design.

Regional characteristics summarized: the differences in taste that developed in the various American colonies as an attribute of location are very complex. By the Queen Anne period they could be distinguished, and in Chippendale furniture the characteristics are perhaps even more apparent. In Massachusetts one finds very thin cabriole legs with the knees coming to a point in the center (Plate 55A). The skirts of tables and chairs of such pieces are narrow and there is a general tightness of line. The claw and ball foot, characteristic of the area, has claws that are turned back so that they appear to be grasping the ball tightly (Plate 55A). The ball is high in an almost oval shape. Almost completely contradictory is another trend in which elaborate carving and shapes are important. The bombé (Plate 57B), the serpentine and other types of shaped fronts are employed. In some cases finely carved details are added to make the form even more elaborate. The work of a Boston cabinetmaker, John Cogswell, is outstanding in its rich detail, while just across the river in Charlestown, Benjamin Frothingham produced furniture in which elegance is achieved through delicacy and simplicity.

Newport was the center of a very special style in this period. As a rich port town and already a summer resort, it had many wealthy residents, and its cabinetmakers were able to produce some masterpieces of technique and fine design. Since designs are quite conservative, hardly any truly rococo details are used. The finest and most typical work is in the blockfront pieces where shells are used to top the section of blocking (Plate 56A). These shells are superbly carved with great restraint. A group of tables made in Newport has carving on the cabriole legs in a design that combines leaf and shell in a simple intaglio pattern (Plate 56C). A concession to the rococo is seen in some tables where the Marlborough leg is used with rich classical detail in the form of fluting and reeding rather than Chinese ornament.

Another sign of the virtuosity of the Newport craftsmen is the way claw and ball feet are carved. The claws on the finest Newport examples are joined to the ball at the nails of the claw, with the rest of the claw raised above the ball so that light is seen between the ball and claw (Plate 56C). This is a minor but significant detail.

Newport and Boston influence can be seen along with New York and Philadelphia influence in Connecticut furniture. Connecticut developed a particular style in which various influences remained easily recognizable.

New York made heaviness a virtue in design. Rich New York carving always lacked delicacy, but rarely finesse. The skirts of New York tables and chests often have a molding of gadrooning (Plate 57C) and carving on the knees is cut deep, with an area of cross hatching frequently in a triangular shape at the center of the top of the knee. New York case pieces tend to be straight across the front with corners chamfered and fluted. The double chest often has a frieze of fretwork applied below the cornice. As in the Queen Anne period, New York chairs retain a closeness to English furniture in details such as the footed rear leg. The claw and ball typical of New York (Plate 57c) has the three front claws quite straight, with the two on the side appearing perpendicular to the center claw. The rear claw is often a continuation of the rear of the cabriole leg without any break or turn of line to distinguish the foot from the leg.

Philadelphia was the largest city in America for decades before the Revolution, and the center of fine craftsmanship. Philadelphia furniture tends to be elaborately carved and generally ornate. There is a squatness in proportion that emphasizes the richness of the ornament (Plate 58c). Forms, such as the high chest, may be conservative, but frequently the ornament is in the latest fashion and directly from an engraving (Plate 58A). The most elaborately carved and wonderfully shaped American chairs are of Philadelphia workmanship, and are closely related to the most ornate English examples (Plate 57A). The claw and ball foot in Philadelphia is squat and proportionately smaller than that of other centers.

One center of fashion south of Philadelphia was Charleston, where furniture was made in high style and fairly close to English design. Significantly, the high chest, out of fashion in London, was a form not used for Chippendale furniture in Charleston but the chest-on-chest was favored (Plate 59c). Ornamentation is used freely, with fretwork added to many plain surfaces.

In short, each of the centers of fashion in the American colonies developed a particular way of interpreting style. Within bounds of variety there are factors of similarity. No matter how ornate American furniture is, there remains an element of clear line. The American Chippendale style is a conservative, almost classical, version of the English rococo, with enough consistency and quality to be accepted as an integral style rather than as a provincial echo.

Classical style: about 1780 the classical style was introduced in America as a reaction to the rococo. This style is sometimes named for two English cabinetmakers who published books of furniture design, George Hepplewhite and Thomas Sheraton. Although neither of these men was responsible for original ideas, both provided neo-classical designs which America followed. The notion that American furniture can be separated into a Sheraton and a Hepplewhite style, however, presupposes basic differences which do not exist between the two.

The interest which began in the fifteenth century received in the classical art of Rome new vigor in the eighteenth. In 1738 excavations began near Rome at Herculaneum, and a decade later work on the most romantic of sites, Pompeii, was begun and continues to this day. This interest in the antique was reflected in the architectural design of Robert Adam, who introduced the new style in England shortly before 1760. Adam's innovation was in going to the antique for sources, whereas earlier eighteenth-century attempts at employing the classical usually sought inspiration from Renaissance and baroque models.

Besides designing houses, Adam frequently undertook furnishing their interiors. For this he commissioned important cabinetmakers to execute his furniture designs. Thomas Chippendale executed some of Adam's furniture at the time his *Director* was in vogue. Adam attempted to establish a vocabulary of design dominated by simplicity and straight lines. He used oval, round and straight motives in clear linear patterns that were entirely unlike the complicated floral, shell and foliate designs of the rococo.

Adam's new style was very quickly taken up by other architects. It was more than something personal, rather an expression of the mood of the era. The reaction to rococo exuberance is to be found elsewhere in Europe at the same time. In France the same kind of reaction occurred so that the style of Louis XVI in many ways is a parallel expression.

The books of furniture designs in the style came later. In 1788 two books of designs were published. One was by Thomas Shearer, who contributed illustrations for *The Cabinet-Maker's London Book of Prices*. The other, *The Cabinet-Maker and Upholsterer's Guide*, was by George Hepplewhite and was published by his widow, Alice. Hepplewhite's book was a really comprehensive view of the style. It included 300 items for the use of cabinetmakers. None of the designs was original, rather they were practical modifications of the more elaborate designs by Adam. Even the shield-back chair was not really his invention.

Three years later Thomas Sheraton began the publication of *The Cabinet-Maker's and Upholsterer's Drawing Book*. Both Sheraton and Hepplewhite were adaptors of the Adam style in which neo-classical ornament was applied to variations of furniture form that normally evolved from what went before. The ornament was antique but the basic lines of the furniture were not. Early in the nineteenth century a more faithfully classical style developed with the design of furniture based at least in part on ancient furniture forms, a contrast to earlier efforts. A design book influential in the spread of this second phase of the classical style was *Household Furniture and Decoration* by Thomas Hope, published in 1807. Hope was a scholar and architect, a friend of the French architect Percier, whose influence was important in the formation of the Directoire style in France. Hope owned a large collection of antiquities and had studied in Greece and Egypt. He attempted to recreate ancient forms. For chairs, couches and a few other types he was on safe ground, but more frequently adaptation was required to make the style fit forms that had not existed in ancient times. The year after Hope's work appeared, a less scholarly and more practical work was published by a cabinetmaker and upholsterer, George Smith. It was entitled *A Collection of Designs for Household Furniture and Interior Decoration*, and contained furniture in the Greek, Egyptian and Roman styles. This more archeologically correct style continued in fashion until Victorian times. Smith published a volume of designs in the same classical spirit in 1826 in which he offered designs to replace those that had become obsolete in his 1808 book. The new work combined Greek and Gothic in heavy forms. In the earlier part of the period the designs of Sheraton and Hepplewhite were important, and in the later Hope and Smith were influential. The presence of French craftsmen who worked in America after the Revolution was another factor.

The classical style brought about many changes in design and form. It is basically a style in which delicacy is important. Straight line and uncomplicated curves are the basis of design. The straight leg, tapering to a narrow foot, either round or rectangular in cross-section, is the most common. Veneer and inlay, which were not used in the Chippendale period, regained a place of importance. The most popular classical motives are: the patera, husk, generally called bellflower, and eagle in inlay; the thunderbolt, sheaf of wheat, drapery, baskets of fruit and vines in carving. Besides mahogany, lighter colored woods such as satinwood were used in contrasting veneers.

Changes in furniture forms include the replacement of the high chest and low chest by chests of drawers and wardrobe-like presses. The dining room, as a separate room, became more common and furniture specifically for it was developed. The sideboard (Plate 60A), the most notable example, is a form invented by Robert Adam and developed by Thomas Shearer. American cabinetmakers commonly borrowed from designs of Sheraton or Hepplewhite. Many smaller forms were employed in this period, either as variations or as innovations. The sewing table, or lady's work table, is an example of such innovation (Plate 62c).

The chest of drawers, a form revived in the Chippendale period, became more common after 1780, with very few changes to transform it into an expression of the new style. Both Hepplewhite and Sheraton suggested a number of designs. A popular simple design offered in the Hepplewhite *Guide* and again in the Sheraton *Drawing Book* with only minor variations was a curving swell or bow-front chest supported on French bracket feet, a kind of curving high bracket foot (Plate 60c). The front and sides are generally veneered in contrasting light and dark woods. Occasionally there is an inlaid design on the front in an oval either on the skirt or across a drawer, and a border.

A design specifically attributed to Thomas Sheraton is the chest on round legs which extend through the entire piece as columns projecting at the corners as on the sewing table

(Plate 62D). These columns are reeded or have turned decoration.

The dressing table, with fewer tiers of drawers than the chest, and a mirror attached above, is a form introduced in the classical period. It is a transformation of the low chest. In some examples it is closely related to the Sheraton chests, but its lines vary. The form continues through the entire period and in some late examples one finds the curule leg, an ancient Roman type where two legs on each side roughly form an X (Plate 61C).

The slant-top desk popular in the Chippendale period and earlier continued to be common in the classical style. Hepplewhite suggested the rather moderate changes to the slant-top which American cabinetmakers followed. The surface is veneered with decoration inlaid on occasion instead of being solid wood with carved decoration. The claw and ball or bracket feet are replaced by the curving high French bracket feet, which make the lines lighter and more graceful. There are more complicated variations introduced. The folding lid of the slant-top was replaced by a rolling cylinder top made of a solid piece or of a tambour consisting of strips of wood on canvas. The new top is often found as a development of the desk-on-frame, supported on tall legs rather than being combined with the chest of drawers.

A new type of desk has a tambour enclosing the pigeon holes and small drawers. In this case the strips are vertical and are moved horizontally in two sections from the center (Plate 62A). The writing area is made by opening a hinged lid that rests flat before the tambour.

Each type of desk is occasionally topped by a bookcase with glass doors (Plate 64A), and in a wider variation the sideboard and secretary are combined.

The bookcase as a separate piece of furniture is extremely rare before 1780. Afterwards it is less rare, but not common. Usually it consists of a glass enclosed upper section and a lower part with wooden doors.

In the category of tables there is great variety of form. Small types for various uses were introduced. The dining table underwent several changes. In the early nineteenth century the dining room became a more common phenomenon and tables seating large groups were developed. An extension table was worked out which could be dismantled into several smaller tables. Shapes vary and the legs are round or square in cross-section. Inlay decoration was used on the legs of some of the finer examples. Late examples occasionally have a series of balusters on curving legs to support the top. Often balusters have heavy carving.

The sofa table was made for a position near the sofa and is described in Sheraton's *Cabinet Dictionary* as a 'sofa writing table'. It is long and narrow with short drop leaves at either end. The table usually has legs at either end joined by simple stretchers. The position back of a sofa is a modern arrangement.

The Pembroke table was known first in the Chippendale period, and the classical version has the expected modifications in design (Plate 64C). A larger variation, with the four legs replaced by a central baluster, or its equivalent, is called a library table. It seems to have been used in the middle of a room.

Tables designed to be used against a wall, side tables, were designed relatively high. A few examples of earlier styles are known, but in the classical period they seem to have been more numerous. These only occasionally have marble tops, and they may very well have been more than serving tables in a dining room. Some probably were used in halls and parlors.

The wardrobe is a form that was known in America from the seventeenth century, but it was fairly uncommon among English colonists, who favored chests of drawers of various kinds. During the classical period, marked by the disappearance of the chest, there was an increase in the popularity of the wardrobe. There are several types, some including a lower section of drawers.

Chair design changed in line and decoration during the transition from Chippendale to the classical. Although there was little change in proportion, the new vocabulary of motives suggests greater lightness. There is some variety among the early examples, with the shield back (Plate 60B), the oval back and a rectangular back (Plate 61B) competing. American cabinetmakers theoretically followed Hepplewhite when they used the shield or oval back and Sheraton for the rectangular form. The differences from the designs in the book and the fact that both designers used these shapes make it difficult to trace the specific source of inspiration. The early classical style chairs generally have straight, tapering legs and frequently the seat is curved. One aspect of American conservatism in design is manifested in the fact that there are chairs in which the back is a compromise between the shield shape and the Chippendale 'cupid's bow'. There the top rail is curved almost like a shield and the side stiles are straight.

In both the conservative and more stylish examples there is either a center splat decorated in a classical motif or a series of columns curving in toward the bottom. Popular motifs for decoration of the splat are the urn, and feathers. The second type, with columns, is sometimes called a baluster back. Inlay is used less frequently than carved decoration on American chairs, with small garlands of flowers on the tapering legs and intricate festoons surrounding the urns or feathers.

On the rectangular or square back the same motifs are used. Generally columns flank a center splat, or an arcade goes all the way across. Urns and feathers are equally popular. The straight round leg with reeding and a straight seat are used. Carving, or carving combined with inlay, is usual.

A different approach to the use of antique sources is seen in chair design after 1800, when the general design was based on actual classical chairs. The back has a solid, thick curving top rail with thin stiles that are often of one piece with the seat rail and the splat is generally horizontal when used (Plate 63c). Occasionally a lyre, harp or simple X-shape serves as a back support.

The seats of these pieces are often curved and cane was revived as a substitute for upholstery on side chairs. These designs began as suggestions of Sheraton, but after 1807 the more accurate interpretations of classical chairs by Hope gradually came to the fore.

Sofa designs are lighter and simpler in the classical style. The camel back of Chippendale is replaced by a straight lined back or one with a simpler curve. In a number of designs wooden arm supports were used projecting from the upholstered portion (Plate 63A). Legs were in the usual classical shapes. In later examples a curving leg, called the saber leg, is frequently used. This is simple in 1810 and is reeded, but by 1830 the curve became an elaborately carved lion's paw or cornucopia. The line is virtually the same, although much heavier.

The day-bed was revived in the classical period, a favorite variation being the 'Récamier', named for the famous subject of David's portrait, who is portrayed on a similar French example. Another name was 'Grecian sofa'. This has a curving back and extended seat with a long arm rest on one side.

Regional traits in the classic period: after the Revolution the newly established states continued to vary their interpretations of furniture styles. The same dependence on English inspiration held, but a French influence was discernible after 1800. In some centers independence brought with it a closer relationship to English furniture, possibly because of the renewed migration.

Salem took over Boston's position of preeminence as a center of fine craftsmanship in Massachusetts during the Revolution. Afterwards its cabinetmakers provided furniture not only for the region but for export. Carving on Salem furniture is an important feature. Elaborately carved motifs such as a basket of fruit, the cornucopia, garlands of fruit or grapes are found with punch-marked backgrounds. The finest of this carving was executed by Samuel McIntire (Plate 63A) for the various cabinetmakers.

Boston, although less active after the Revolution, remained the scene of fine craftsmanship. The work of John Seymour is outstanding. His labeled tambour secretaries are among the finest examples of American furniture. The tambour is made of thin strips of wood with a delicate garland inlay. Inlays of ivory are used around the keyholes. The pilaster, the herringbone and the lunette inlays seen on his work may have been used by other Boston craftsmen also, so attribution on stylistic grounds is difficult. The bellflower inlay of three petals which Seymour used is easily confused with the bellflower of Baltimore, another very sophisticated center.

Rhode Island, which had been most important before the Revolution, was less influential after it. Fine cabinetmaking continued to be important, and in the work of such men as Holmes Weaver we find really elaborate inlays handled with great skill.

In New York the early classical style had the local characteristic of simplicity and strength. Most famous is the later cabinetmaker, Duncan Phyfe, who worked in New York from 1795 until his retirement in 1847. His early work often follows Sheraton's suggestions (Plates 61A, 64c). His characteristic chair has a thick top rail and stiles joined in one piece with the seat rail (Plate 63c). The carving on the top rail was executed in a few specific motifs. The thunderbolt, the sheaf of wheat and a festoon of drapery make up almost the whole repertoire. The lyre and the harp are motifs used as splats and as a substitute for a baluster on tables with a center support.

New York was a city in which French influence was strong. After the Revolutions in France and the French West Indies there was an influx of French immigrants. They were probably responsible for the abnormally strong French influence there. Charles Honoré Lannuier, an émigré who worked in New York, produced certain pieces of furniture with a strong French quality, in others repeating Sheraton designs.

Philadelphia elegance was manifested in works of four cabinetmakers, Daniel Trotter, Ephraim Haines, Joseph Barry and Henry Connelly (Plate 64B). Haines and Connelly worked in a style that suggested their use of Sheraton designs. Reeded legs with delicately carved Corinthian capitals and round spade feet are often encountered. The work of Barry reflects Sheraton influence also. On his label are designs borrowed from the *Drawing Book*, but his work reflects later influences as well. Philadelphia was not as significant in classical furniture design as it had been earlier.

Baltimore came into its own during the Revolution and afterwards as a quickly growing, prosperous community and was a center of fine cabinetmaking. Baltimore's elegance is at times confusingly close to English style but goes to extremes, as in the use of painted glass panels, and gilt decoration on light wood inlays, which is typical of the exuberance of 'nouveau riche' ornament in any period. The small desks with elaborate ornamentation that follow Sheraton's suggestions are more elaborate than any other American classical example. Inlay on panels showing contrasting woods is typical (Plates 60A, 63B).

The classical style in America had its primary influences from England and secondary ones from France. It reflected various phases of the neo-classical revival. Early neo-classical influence was restricted to ornament, later it spread to the choice of furniture forms. In the last years there was a change in proportions, although the same basic forms and motifs continued to be used. The last phase, which is heavy, is the most difficult to understand, since it is very easily thought of as the result of a decline in taste, but it must be seen in its own context as a counterpart of the architecture of the Greek Revival.

AMERICAN CABINETMAKERS

AFFLECK, Thomas
Arrived from London in Philadelphia 1763, died 1795; most famous for his elaborate Chippendale pieces.

ALLEN, Josiah
Worked in Charleston and appears in the *Directory* between 1809 and 1813.

ALLISON, Michael
Worked in New York between about 1800 and 1810 in a style that has been occasionally confused with Duncan Phyfe's.

APPLETON, Nathaniel
Early nineteenth-century Salem cabinetmaker working in the classical style.

ASH, Gilbert
Born 1717, died 1785; New York chair and cabinetmaker of importance. Evidently he studied in Philadelphia, because his chairs are constructed like Philadelphia examples. Several labeled and one signed piece make his work distinguishable.

AMERICAN FURNITURE 1640–1840

Ash, Thomas
Died 1815; New York chairmaker, son of Gilbert. Succeeded by son, Thomas. (New York City Directory, 1815.)

Axson, William, Jr.
Worked in Charleston between about 1763 and his death in 1800. He did interior woodwork as well as furniture.

Backman, John
Lancaster County, Pennsylvania, cabinetmaker, leading member of a family of furniture makers; best-known work in the Chippendale style executed in the last quarter of the eighteenth century.

Badlam, Stephen
Born 1751, died 1815. Worked in classical style. His name is stamped on several fine chairs. His masterpiece is the chest-on-chest for Elias Hasket Derby of Salem, 1791.

Barry, Joseph B.
Cabinetmaker in Philadelphia who worked in an elaborate style. His label of c. 1810 illustrates a group of Thomas Sheraton designs of 1793.

Belter, John
Active 1844 to 1863. New York cabinetmaker of German birth. Famous for heavily carved Louis XV style Victorian furniture. He invented a technique of bending wood, lamination.

Beman, Reuben, Jr.
Active 1785 to 1800. Worked in Kent, Connecticut in a *retardataire* Chippendale style.

Burling, Thomas
Active before 1774 to 1801; worked in New York in a style more often derived from Chippendale than classical.

Burnham, Benjamin
Connecticut cabinetmaker active around 1769; his blockfront desk in American Wing, Metropolitan Museum, has an inscription.

Calder, Alexander
Cabinetmaker from Scotland, active between 1796 and 1807 in Charleston, S.C.

Chapin, Aaron
Worked in East Windsor and Hartford, Connecticut in the 1780s. A cousin of Eliphalet Chapin.

Chapin, Eliphalet
Born 1741, died after 1807; born in East Windsor, Connecticut; worked for a time in Philadelphia before returning to Connecticut. Made fine case pieces in a modification of Philadelphia style.

Cheney, Silas E.
Active in Litchfield, Connecticut, after the Revolution. Several sideboards are attributed to him.

Cogswell, John
Active from 1769 to 1782 in Boston where his most important work is in bombé-shaped case pieces with rich carving.

Connelly, Henry
Made fine classical style furniture in Philadelphia between 1800 and 1810. Worked with Ephraim Haines. A turned section with acanthus carving above reeded leg is characteristic.

Courtenay, Hercules
Active around 1762; he advertised as a carver and gilder from London, and worked for Philadelphia cabinetmakers including Benjamin Randolph.

Dennis, Thomas
Seventeenth-century Ipswich joiner to whom the key pieces of early New England furniture are attributed.

Disbrowe, Nicholas
Born in England around 1612, the son of a joiner. Was in Hartford before 1639. Perhaps 'Hartford' and 'Sunflower' chests were developed by his apprentices and followers.

Dunlap, Samuel, II
The best-known member of a family of New Hampshire joiners who did paneling and furniture. His distinctive style included an interlaced cornice design and shells carved deeply. Most of his furniture is in maple.

Egerton, Matthew
Brunswick, New Jersey cabinetmaker probably active in both Chippendale and classical styles.

Elfe, Thomas
Charleston, South Carolina cabinetmaker active between 1747 and 1776. Many elaborately carved case pieces are attributed to him through references to Charleston families in his account books.

Elliott, John
Philadelphia cabinetmaker known particularly for looking glasses. He was active from about 1756 until his death in 1791, when his business was carried on by his son.

Folwell, John
Philadelphia cabinet-maker most famous for making the case for the orrery by David Rittenhouse. Folwell solicited subscriptions for an American counterpart of Chippendale's *Director*, to be called *The Gentlemen and Cabinet-maker's Assistant*, which was never published.

Frothingham, Benjamin
Charlestown, Massachusetts cabinetmaker working from about 1756 to 1809. He was a Revolutionary major and a friend of George Washington. He is known best for Chippendale furniture of restrained design and used blockfront and serpentine fronts for chests and desks.

Gaines, John
A cabinetmaker born in Ipswich, Massachusetts, 1704,

who worked in Portsmouth, New Hampshire, between about 1724 and 1743. Known for chairs that combine William and Mary straight back with a Queen Anne violin-shaped splat.

GILLINGHAM, James
Philadelphia cabinetmaker in the Chippendale style responsible for work of fine quality.

GODDARD, John
1723–85; son-in-law of Job Townsend of Newport, Rhode Island, and active as a cabinetmaker from the 1740s on. Three pieces contain original inscriptions stating that he made them. Other members of the family include Thomas Goddard, 1765–1858, and Stephen, 1764–1804, sons of John, who carried on their father's business, and Townsend Goddard, 1750–90, their older brother.

GOSTELOWE, Jonathan
Lived c. 1744–95; Philadelphia cabinetmaker who produced elaborate Chippendale furniture. A labeled piece is in the Philadelphia Museum.

HAINES, Ephraim
Worked with Henry Connelly in production of superior classical style furniture in Philadelphia.

HAINS, Adam
Born 1768, active until at least 1815; this Philadelphia cabinetmaker worked in the Chippendale style after the Revolution.

HOSMER, Joseph
Concord, Massachusetts cabinetmaker, active around the time of the Revolution. He worked in a provincial style. His activity in the Revolution included leading an attack on the Concord bridge as a captain of the Minute Men at the outbreak of hostilities.

LANNUIER, Charles Honoré
New York cabinetmaker who emigrated from France. He was active at the beginning of the nineteenth century in a style close to the French.

LAWTON, Robert, Jr.
Active in Newport in the 1790s. Several labeled examples of his work are known.

LEHMAN, Benjamin
A Philadelphia carpenter most famous for the compilation of a price list for cabinetwork, 1786, the manuscript for which, in the Pennsylvania Historical Society, gives an indication of the types and styles available at the time.

LEMON, William
Salem cabinetmaker flourishing around 1796.

MCINTIRE, Samuel
1757–1811; a carver active after the Revolution until 1811; his work on Salem furniture as well as in architecture is quite important. He supplied Salem cabinetmakers with carved details; basket of fruit, cornucopia and grape patterns are most characteristic.

MILLS & DEMING
Classical style cabinet-makers in New York around 1790.

PHYFE, Duncan
1768–1854; New York's most famous cabinetmaker; worked from the late 1780s to 1846 in successive versions of the classical style.

PIMM, John
Boston cabinetmaker working around 1740. He is known from an inscribed high chest with lacquer and gilt decoration in the Winterthur Museum.

PRINCE, Samuel
New York cabinetmaker who worked in the Chippendale style.

RANDOLPH, Benjamin
Philadelphia cabinetmaker active from 1762 to around 1792, working in the Chippendale style. A group of 'sample' chairs with the most elaborate carving known on American furniture is attributed to him.

SANDERSON, Elijah
Active from 1771 to 1825 in Salem, Massachusetts. His furniture was exported to the south. He worked with his brother, Jacob; the two employed McIntire as a carver for their finest work.

SASS, Jacob
Active in Charleston from 1774 to about 1828. A desk and bookcase exist with the ink inscription: *Made by Jacob Sass, October 1794.*

SAVERY, William
A Philadelphia cabinetmaker active from the 1740s to his death in 1787. Both simple and elaborate furniture have turned up with his label.

SEYMOUR, John
A Boston cabinetmaker who worked in the classical style. Tambour doors, elaborate inlays, a liberal use of satinwood and an odd locking device are characteristics that make his furniture outstanding.

SHAW, John
Annapolis cabinetmaker advertising between 1773 and 1794, but living until after 1828. Several labeled pieces of his work are known.

SHORT, Joseph
Newburyport, Massachusetts cabinetmaker active from 1771 through 1819. He produced Chippendale and classical style furniture.

SKILLIN, John and Simeon
Listed as carvers in the Boston Directory, 1798; ship-carvers; worked also for Elias Hasket Derby; were responsible for pediment figures on Badlam's chest-on-chest in the Garvan collection.

STITCHER & CLEMMENS
Cabinetmakers who appear in the Baltimore City Directory in 1804. A labeled secretary is known.

AMERICAN FURNITURE 1640–1840

TOPPAN, Abner
1764–1836; Newbury, Massachusetts cabinetmaker who worked first in a belated Chippendale style, and then in the classical style.

TOWNSEND
A family of cabinetmakers active in Newport, Rhode Island for about a century from before 1750 to the middle of the nineteenth. Most famous for elaborate shell decoration on blockfront pieces.

TOWNSEND, Edmund
1736–1811; son of Job Townsend, working in the family style. A kneehole bureau with his label shows him to be equal to the best of the family.

TOWNSEND, Job
1699–1765; earliest of the Newport, Rhode Island family of cabinetmakers; worked for important families of Newport and Providence.

TOWNSEND, Stephen
Active in Charleston, South Carolina between 1763 and after 1768. A partner of William Axson, Jr., for several years.

TROTTER, Daniel
Philadelphia cabinetmaker in the Chippendale and classical styles; known for ladder-back chairs.

TUFFT, Thomas
Philadelphia cabinetmaker active during the Chippendale period.

WALKER, Robert
Active around 1799 to 1833 and the only Charleston craftsman whose labeled pieces survive. Two are known, one of which is at the Charleston Museum.

WAYNE, Jacob
Philadelphia cabinetmaker active after 1785; worked in the Chippendale style first, then in the classical.

WEAVER, Holmes
1769–1848; Newport, Rhode Island cabinetmaker in the classical style. He used elaborate inlays in a continuation of the Newport tradition of fine craftsmanship.

WILLET, Marinus
1740–1830; worked as a cabinetmaker in New York and distinguished himself as a colonel in the Revolution; advertised as a cabinetmaker in 1773 and 1774.

BOOKS FOR FURTHER READING

BURTON, E. MILBY: *Charleston Furniture, 1700–1825*, Charleston, S.C. (1956).
DOWNS, JOSEPH: *American Furniture, Queen Anne and Chippendale Periods*, New York (1952).
HORNER, W.M., JR.: *Blue Book of Philadelphia Furniture*, Philadelphia (1935).
KETTELL, RUSSELL H.: *Pine Furniture of Early New England*, Garden City (1929, re-issued 1952).
LOCKWOOD, LUKE VINCENT: *Colonial Furniture in America*, third edition 1926, reissued New York (1951), 2 vols.
MCCLELLAND, NANCY: *Duncan Phyfe and the English Regency*, New York (1939).
MILLER, E. G.: *American Antique Furniture*, Baltimore (1937), 2 vols. (re-issued 1948).
NUTTING, WALLACE: *Furniture Treasury*, vols. 1 and 2, Cambridge (1928); vol. 3, Framingham (1933); vols. 1 and 2 re-issued 1954 as one volume.
Southern Furniture, catalogue of the loan exhibition at Richmond, Va., 1952, *Antiques*, Jan., 1952.
Handbook of the American Wing, Metropolitan Museum of Art, New York (2nd ed. 1942). Revised edition in preparation.
Concise Encyclopedia of Antiques, vol. 1, pages 50–74. Hawthorn Books, New York, 1955.
Second Treasury of Early American Homes, Richard Pratt. Hawthorn Books, New York, 1954.

The illustrations on Plates 52, 53, 54, 56, 57, 58 from Joseph Down's *American Furniture, Queen Anne and Chippendale Periods*, Macmillan, 1952, are used by permission of The Macmillan Company, New York.

AMERICAN VICTORIAN FURNITURE

By MARVIN D. SCHWARTZ

THE American Victorian style, in existence from 1840 until about 1910, displays strong English influence, as the name implies. Designs and design books were simultaneously published in London and New York. Basically the Victorian is an eclectic style. Many different sources were used for inspiration with innovations introduced in construction and proportion. Most of the misunderstanding of this style comes from the fact that its originality is not accepted as anything more than lack of ability at imitating. Actually, the Victorian designers tried to remain close to their models but also wanted to create practical furniture and they changed the scale and some of the details to suit the rooms for which the furniture was intended.

The style has been referred to by Carol Meeks as one of 'Picturesque Eclecticism'. The emphasis is on visual elements. Covering and screening new types of construction with traditional motifs is general.

New designs were always based on previous periods. At times the sources were close at hand in the various eighteenth-century styles, but occasionally the more exotic and distant models such as Jacobean and Near Eastern were employed.

Very important to the development of furniture production was the partial industrialization that became typical of the craft in the United States. The large workshop, with the bare beginnings of mass-production and specialization, gradually became common in the centers where furniture was made. This was responsible, in part, for some of the changes in what might be considered traditional forms.

By 1840 many manufacturers in American cities were known to employ from forty to one hundred men, most of whom were unskilled workers. Furniture designs were created by the shop owner and a minimal number of skilled men were required to follow the designs. The larger shops produced inexpensive furniture that could be shipped easily. John of Cincinnati supplied many small Mississippi river towns with stylish furniture. The furniture of Hennesy of Boston was available in many smaller towns along the seacoast.

We can get some idea of the Victorian conception of styles from the writings of the American architect, A. J. Downing. In *Cottage Residences*, published in New York in 1842, he implies the use of more than one furniture style when he says, 'A person of correct architectural taste will ... confer on each apartment by expression of purpose, a kind of individuality. Thus in a complete cottage-villa, the hall will be grave and simple in character, a few plain seats its principal furniture; the library sober and dignified ...; the drawing room lively or brilliant, adorned with pictures. ...'

He continues in the same vein in another book, *The Architecture of Country Houses*, one edition of which was published in 1861 (others earlier): 'Furniture in *correct taste* is characterized by its being designed in accordance with certain recognized styles and intended to accord with apartments in the same style.' Downing goes on to describe the various styles and he includes Grecian (or French), Gothic, Elizabethan, Romanesque, and a version of the Renaissance style. Each has its place. The idea of using the different styles was criticized later by Charles Eastlake, an English architect who was influential in America. In 1872 he said, 'In the early part of the present century a fashionable conceit prevailed of fitting up separate apartments in large mansions each after a style of its own. Thus we had Gothic halls, Elizabethan chambers, Louis-Quatorze drawing rooms, etc. ...'

These various styles of the Victorian period were used at about the same time, but fashion determined when they were replaced and none lasted throughout the period.

The earliest significant style was a continuation of American Empire. This furniture was heavy in proportion and differed from the earlier models only in a few details. The wavy molding was a border introduced late; medallions and other small details of applied carving in leaf or floral motifs reduced the simplicity and classicism characteristic of earlier furniture. In the Victorian versions, drawers rarely have borders of molding but rather are flush with the front surface. Marble tops for small tables and bedroom chests are common. Bracket feet are a frequent support for heavy case pieces. On tall legs turning as well as heavy carving was employed. Popular as finer woods were mahogany, black walnut and rosewood. Simpler, less expensive pieces were made of maple, butternut or other hard woods which often are stained quite dark in red or brown. Veneers in prominent grains were used on case pieces as well as on the skirts of sofas and chairs.

In general there were few new forms developed. Among the new were such peculiarities as the Lazy Susan and the ottoman; however, the wardrobe and the bookcase, which were known only infrequently before, were better known in the Victorian period.

With the factory replacing the craftsman's workshop, techniques requiring less skill developed. Machine sawing and planing were used with hand-fitting and finishing. The lines were planned by someone higher in rank than the man who operated the saw or did the finishing. The larger scale operations made competition a more important factor than ever before with price more important than workmanship.

A Baltimore cabinetmaker, John Hall, published a book of furniture designs in 1840. One of the objectives of his book he describes by saying, 'Throughout the whole of the designs in this work, particular attention has been bestowed in an economical arrangement to save labor, which being an important point, is presumed will render the collection exceedingly useful to the cabinetmaker.' The designs are Grecian, he says in his commentary and '... the style of the United States is blended with European taste ...'. This is the style that A.J.Downing refers to as Greek, modern and French and 'the furniture most generally used in private houses'. Contemporary cartoons and illustrations confirm his remark by usually including this kind of furniture. A popular woman's magazine of the time, Godey's *Lady's Book*, consistently presented suggestions for furniture in the style from the late 'forties to the 'sixties which was called 'cottage furniture'.

The Gothic style in Victorian furniture has two aspects. As a variation of the classical, it involves only the use of the pointed arch (Plate 66A) and related motifs in what is basically the classical style. As a more ambitious innovation, it involves the use of Gothic ornament in a more serious attempt to create a special style. The first approach was used by Chippendale, who included Gothic motifs in his rococo suggestions. Later, Sheraton included Gothic arcades in suggestions of designs, primarily neo-classical. This continued in early Victorian furniture in the Greek style. The other aspect was connected with the Gothic revival in architecture which, although begun in the eighteenth century, had an important effect on home building after 1830. Suitable to houses in the Gothic style was furniture repeating the motifs. Large bookcases, which seem almost like architectural elements, and hall chairs, high-backed side chairs carved elaborately, are often the most spectacular examples of the style.

Some of the finest examples were designed by architects for use in their buildings. Occasionally spiral turned columns, seventeenth century in inspiration, are combined with elements of earlier inspiration. The characteristic feature of the style is the pointed arch of simple or complicated form used with incised or pierced spandrels and bold raised moldings. The Gothic style is one favored for hall decoration and used less frequently in the parlor. Sets of bedroom furniture in the style are known. Tables are extremely rare in this style.

When referring to furniture of various kinds Downing says in *The Architecture of Country Houses*, 'There is, at the present moment, almost a mania in the cities for expensive French furniture and decorations. The style of royal palaces abroad is imitated in town houses of fifty foot front....' This style was often called Louis XIV, although it is a combination of various French styles from Louis XIV to Louis XVI (Plates 66B, C).

Revival of rococo style had started in France as a reaction to its classicism which was dominant shortly before the Revolution. With the Restoration came a desire for the good old days and a style related to them. Napoleon's Romanism was as distasteful as his political upsets. From France the revival spread to the rest of the Continent, England and the United States. In the Victorian home, where each room varied in style to suit its proper mood, the French style was most popular in the parlor, although bedroom furniture in the style is known.

The American Victorian pieces were smaller in proportion than the eighteenth-century models. The curving lines of the back stiles are often exaggerated so that the back is balloon-shaped. Cabriole legs are restrained in their curve. Console tables with marble tops come in scallop shapes. Curving fronts are typical for case pieces. Carving in rose, grape or leaf motifs with elaborate details in high relief is seen on chairs and sofas. On other forms this carving is flatter. Elaborate carving was frequently used on cabriole legs.

The curve becomes all important as a contrast to the straightness of the classical. Small boudoir pieces were made in this style as well as whole matching parlor sets which include a sofa or love seat, gentleman's armchair, lady's chair, four side chairs, an ottoman and center table (Plate 65). In a drawing room set there are additional pieces such as an extra sofa, more side chairs and possibly a matching *étagère*. There seem to be no dining-room pieces in this style. Introduced in America about 1840, it was important until some time in the 1870s. One of the most important cabinetmakers working in this manner was John Belter of New York (Plates 67A, B). Born in Germany, he opened a shop in the city of New York in 1844 and continued in business until his death in 1863. Belter's work was a distinctive variation of the Louis XV style. He invented a laminating process for curving wood that he used in making the sides of case pieces and chair and sofa backs. He destroyed the means of doing this laminating shortly before his death, so that it was never used later. Solid curving pieces are characteristic of Belter's shop, as is elaborate carving in high relief and balloon-shaped chair backs. Belter's parlor sets are best known, but he also made bedroom furniture.

The Louis XVI style was more specifically popular after 1865 when there was some reaction to the exuberance of the rococo revival evident in the Louis XV-inspired examples. The straight line and the fine detail are distinctly opposed to the heavier curving style.

Other revivals of interest occur in the early period, but to no great extent. Downing's suggestions include pieces in what he refers to as the Flemish style, but actually of William and Mary origin.

After 1870 there were several other adaptations of eighteenth-century models. The Adam and Sheraton styles served as inspiration for dining-room and parlor pieces done with greater faithfulness to the model and less of a re-interpretation for modern requirements.

The Renaissance style was introduced at the Crystal Palace exhibitions of 1851 (London) and 1853 (New York). It is a style heavy in proportion and generally straight in line. Decoration is elaborate and frequently inspired by architectural rather than furniture design. The pediment is used to top many of the forms, from chairs to large case pieces. Bold moldings, raised cartouches, raised and shaped panels, incised linear decoration and applied carving in garlands and medallions are all characteristic. Occasionally animal heads and sporting trophies appear on dining-room pieces. The style was used primarily for bedroom, library and dining-room pieces, but there are examples of parlor furniture also. This style continued to be important until about 1880.

Factory production inspired spool-turned

furniture, a particular type easy to produce for the lower-priced furniture market. In the main, designs were simple and the sizes were right for easy handling in lower middle class interiors. This furniture was decorated by turning on a lathe the legs, arms and supports and obtaining identical units repeated in any of a variety of motifs that include the bobbin, knob, button, sausage and vase and ring. The lines are generally rectangular and simple. This furniture did not include every form, but rather emphasized beds and tables.

The first seeds of modernism can be traced from the reactions against bad craftsmanship in the Victorian period. As a period of mass-production and keen competition, the Victorian period saw the development of truly bad design as well as some very good design that has been misunderstood. By attempting to make things cheaply without simplifying the design and method of production, some makers produced surprisingly unsuccessful results.

One of the first important reactions was the book, *Hints on Household Taste*, which had an American edition in 1872. The author was the English architect, Charles Lock Eastlake, who decried bad craftsmanship and the shams it involved. He sought to inspire simple honest work in solid woods. He disliked shoddy veneer and overly elaborate work. His argument was: 'I recommend the re-adoption of no specific type of ancient furniture which is unsuited, whether in detail or general design, to the habits of modern life. It is the spirit and principles of early manufacture which I desire to see revived and not the absolute forms in which they found embodiment.'

Eastlake proposed that craftsmen follow appropriate models that would not be difficult to execute. He disliked the overly ambitious attempts of the 'fifties in which the rococo was used to excess. The resultant style was simple and rectangular (Plate 68A). Most of what he suggested was to be executed in oak, a durable but inexpensive wood. Carving could be simple and turnings were to play an important role. This style was gradually more and more important on the American scene. Related suggestions follow in ensuing decades and the oak furniture of the turn of the century by Gustav Stickley is probably basically of the same inspiration.

Attempts to find new and more appropriate sources of design resulted in furniture of exotic inspiration such as that of the so-called Turkish style, seen in overstuffed pieces for parlor use.

The Victorian period is marked by variety of inspiration, stimulated by the use of different styles to suggest different moods. In the first half of the period the changes from the original to the Victorian interpretation were probably greater. After 1880 there was a more faithful adherence to the lines of the models, although the results always differed from the originals. About the same time attempts to make furniture only vaguely connected with earlier styles were evident, and there was also a search for new sources of inspiration.

In the Victorian age mass-production was a key factor in the development of the kind of competition which made bad craftsmanship profitable. This resulted from cutting costs without considering the need for simplification in design. The contrast between good and bad craftsmanship was probably greater after the beginning of factory production.

CAST IRON FURNITURE

The manufacture of cast iron furniture in the United States began in the 1840s and continued until the first decade of the twentieth century. The manufacturers were firms making grille work, architectural ornaments and building fronts. Both indoor and outdoor furniture was produced, although, with few exceptions, the indoor furniture was popular for a much shorter time than the outdoor furniture. Cast-iron furniture for interiors was introduced in the 1850s, a little later than the garden furniture. It was designed as an imitation of wooden furniture in the various Victorian styles and was painted to simulate wood. The exceptions to this characterization were the beds and hatracks in which imaginative forms were developed. These two forms continued to be popular after cast-iron furniture for interiors had become unfashionable.

Garden furniture of cast iron was used for a longer period and the designs became standardized. The dominant influence was the romantic garden which had come into fashion at the end of the eighteenth century. It was created to appear wild, as if man had not had a hand in it. The furniture was designed to have a rustic look, to appear to be made of unhewn logs, or boughs of trees, vines or flowers (Plates 68B, C). The various patterns used seem to have been followed by many manufacturers. The same designs appear in early and late examples. The earliest catalogue known to contain an illustration of cast-iron garden furniture appeared in the 1840s in Philadelphia, but almost every American city of any size produced it some time during the nineteenth century. Often the mold contained the name of the manufacturer, and the piece can be dated by consulting city directories.

BOOKS FOR FURTHER READING

DREPPERD, CARL: *Handbook of Antique Chairs*, Garden City (1948).
LICHTEN, FRANCES: *Decorative Art of Victoria's Era*, New York (1950).
ORMSBEE, THOMAS H.: *Field Guide to American Victorian Furniture*, Boston (1952).
PRATT, RICHARD: *Second Treasury of Early American Homes*, Hawthorn Books, New York, 1954.
Concise Encyclopedia of Antiques, Vol. III, pages 17–29. Hawthorn Books, New York, 1957.

Victorian parlour from the Milligan house, Saratoga, New York; mid-nineteenth century. *Brooklyn Museum*.

PLATE 65

AMERICAN VICTORIAN FURNITURE

(A) American rosewood side chair; neo-gothic back designed by A. J. Davis, c. 1830. *Museum of The City of New York.*

(B) Carved walnut side chair inlaid with crotch walnut; by Thomas Brooks, Brooklyn, c. 1856–76. *Brooklyn Museum.*

(C) American rosewood table with marble top, inside frame inscription *J. H. Belter and Co. Antiques*, September 1848. *Photograph, courtesy of Metropolitan Museum of Art.*

AMERICAN VICTORIAN FURNITURE

(A) Dresser by John Belter, New York, c. 1850.
Brooklyn Museum.

(B) Bed by John Belter, New York, showing laminated construction; c. 1850. *Brooklyn Museum.*

PLATE 67

AMERICAN VICTORIAN FURNITURE

(A) Design for 'drawing-room cheffonier', from Eastlake's *Hints on Household Taste*, first American Edition, Boston, 1872.

(B) (C) Cast-iron garden furniture, James and Kirkland, New York, *c.* 1850. (Plate marked Janes, Beebe and Co., 356, Broadway, New York.) *New York Public Library.*

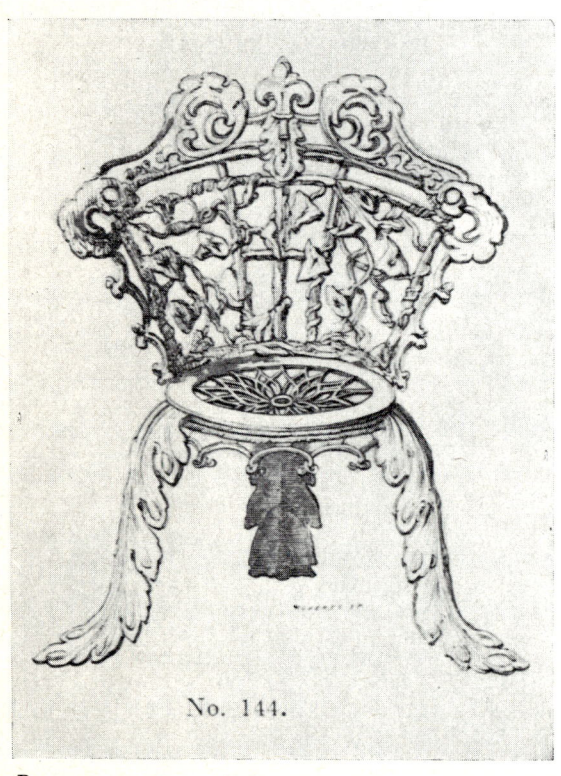

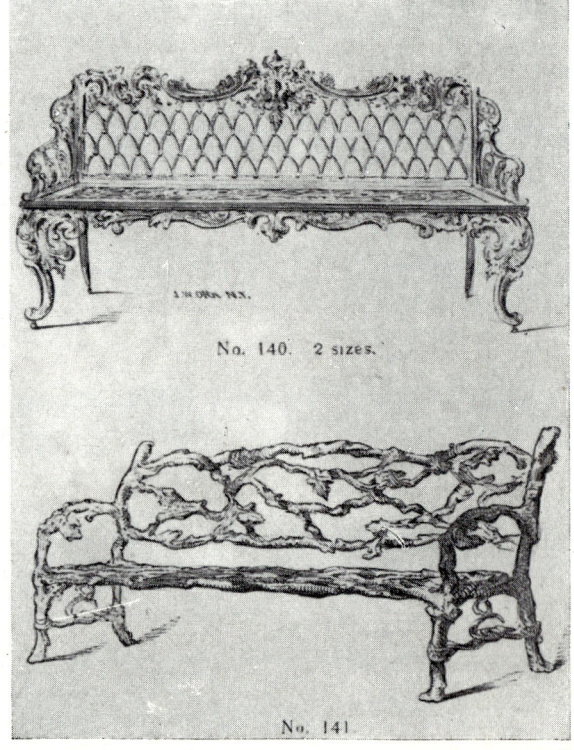

AMERICAN WINDSOR CHAIRS

(A) Three of the six basic American Windsor types: low back; comb-back; fan-back. From *The American Windsor* by J. Stogdell Stokes, *Antiques*, April 1926.

(B) Hoop-back; New England arm-chair; loop-back. From *The American Windsor*, J. Stogdell Stokes, *Antiques*, April 1926.

PLATE 69

AMERICAN WINDSOR CHAIRS

(A) New England writing arm Windsor showing old green paint; 1790–1800. *Shelburne Museum, Shelburne, Vermont.*

(B) A fine example of Philadelphia comb-back. *Coll. of C. K. Davis.*

(C) New York; *c.* 1797; label of John Dewitt; original leather seat. *Joe Kindig, Jr., and Son.*

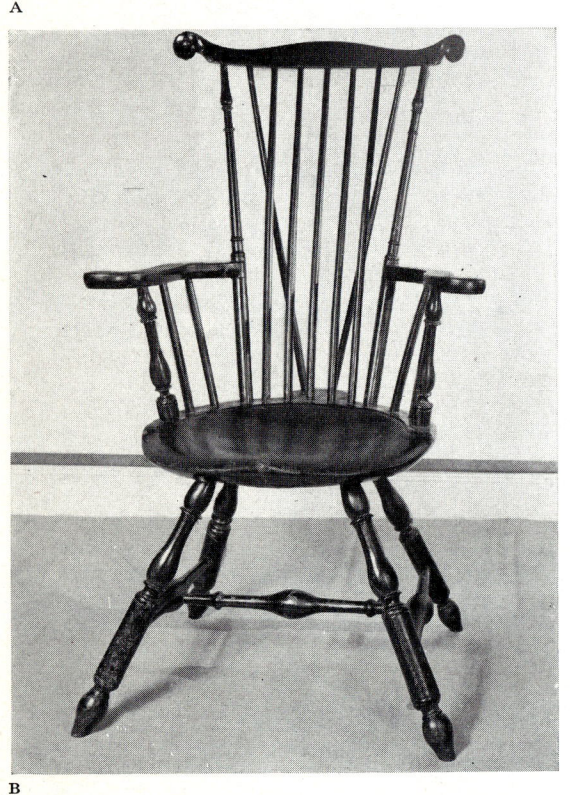

AMERICAN WINDSOR CHAIRS

(A) Connecticut low-back settee with knuckle arm; refashioned from a seven-foot straight settee as a result of a fire. *Davenport collection, Williams College, Williamstown, Massachusetts.*

(B) New England writing arm Windsor with bamboo turning; c. 1770. *Davenport collection, Williams College, Williamstown, Massachusetts.*

AMERICAN WINDSOR CHAIRS

(A) New England armchair with braced, one-piece back and arms; fine knuckle ends; *c.* 1760. *Davenport collection, Williams College, Williamstown, Massachusetts.*

(B) Triple-back armchair with comb; arms have three-finger ends. *Davenport collection, Williams College, Williamstown, Massachusetts.*

(C) New England braced fan-back side chair; *c.* 1770. *Davenport collection, Williams College, Williamstown, Massachusetts.*

(D) Comb-back armchair with double curbed arm; New England, *c.* 1760. *Davenport collection, Williams College, Williamstown, Massachusetts.*

PLATE 72

Unpainted pine cupboard; late-eighteenth or early-nineteenth century. *Plates 73-76 are from Old Sturbridge Village, Sturbridge, Massachusetts.*

PLATE 73

(A) Sunflower chest, taking its name from the rayed, aster-like flower in the carved oak centre panel; vicinity of Hartford, seventeenth century.

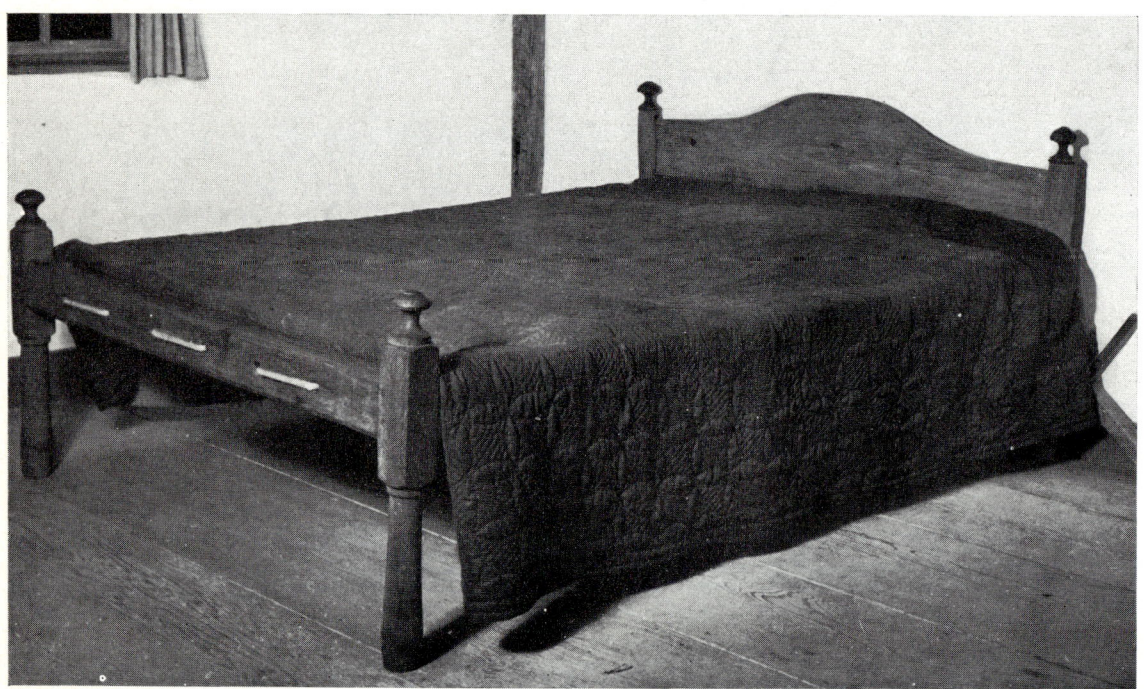

(B) This New England bed, probably eighteenth century, reflects an earlier tradition in the choice of oak for the posts and rails; headboards were usually pine.

COUNTRY FURNITURE IN NEW ENGLAND

A

B

C

(A) Slat back New England chair; three, four and five slats, turned members and finials, rush or splint seats, arms and rockers gave variety to a basic form.

(B) Country Chippendale chair of curly maple. Often made in sets; local cabinet-makers made numerous interpretations for almost a century.

(C) Painted pine New England settle, narrowed to a single seat; settles were made for two centuries.

COUNTRY FURNITURE IN NEW ENGLAND

(B) The hutch table with storage space in the seat was made in America in the seventeenth, eighteenth and nineteenth centuries; this one is pine, painted red; mid-eighteenth century.

(A) New England tavern table, maple with marbleized top; pine bottle chest has grooved and painted decoration; the pipe box is decorated in green and grey.

SHAKER CRAFTSMANSHIP

(A) Watervliet tailoress counter with drop leaf; drawer fronts and top curly maple stained red; pine panelled sides darker red; curly maple in mirror, also in posts and 'ladle' arms of rocking chair; high-seated chair for shop or counter use.
(B) Built-in drawers and cupboards in a room in the South family dwelling, New Lebanon; brethren's chair with foot-stool; on the table is a two-drawer lap or table desk.

PLATE 77

SHAKER CRAFTSMANSHIP

Simplicity of Shaker craftsmanship is seen in this 'round' stand from the Second family, New Lebanon, and matched side chairs from Enfield. Both are tilting chairs with finials identifying their origin. The stand is cherry, the hanging cupboard pine.

PLATE 78

Armed rocking-chairs with mushroom arms and cushion rails for Shaker eldresses at Hancock; for comfort a shag mat was sometimes hung from top rail. Tape seats were woven in various colour patterns. Cherry and maple table has typical turnings, braces, and long drawer.

SHAKER CRAFTSMANSHIP

(A) New Lebanon shaker trestle table 20 ft long; four-board pine top 34 ins wide; birch trestles; c. 1810.

(B) Sabbathday Lake sewing table has cutting board in drawer to be used also for writing. New Lebanon 'Shaker red' stand; swivel sewing stools.

WINDSOR CHAIRS IN AMERICA

By MARVIN D. SCHWARTZ

THE Windsor chair was introduced into the American colonies about 1725. The form originated in England and was particularly popular in Berkshire, where the town of Windsor is an important trading center. The chair developed from seventeenth-century country chairs and is unlike any Continental European chair. The American version, although obviously dependent on the English, developed individual characteristics.

The Windsor chair has a back of spindles, a solid wooden seat and turned splayed legs set right through the seat. There is a great deal of variety in the form of the back, the shape of the seat and the shape of the legs so that it is possible to name six categories of variation. These chairs originally were painted and generally they are made of several kinds of wood. The heavy plank seat is made of pine, the spindles are often hickory, with ash, white oak and maple used occasionally. Many colors are mentioned, but a dark green seems to have been favored. Indian red appears frequently, sometimes yellow and black, and white rarely (in spite of Wallace Nutting's abhorrence of white as a Windsor color).

Windsors are simple chairs that were primarily for garden and porch use, but they were reasonably priced and probably were used indoors by some. The variety and the place of use is suggested in an advertisement that Andrew Gauteir placed in the New York *Gazette or Weekly Post-boy*, April 18, 1765, which includes this statement: 'A large and neat assortment of Windsor chairs made in the best and neatest manner and well painted. Viz. Highback'd, low back'd and Sackback'd Chairs and Settees, or double seated, fit for Piazza or Gardens. ...'

The six categories (Plates 69A, B) that are generally distinguished today do not retain the names Gauteir used. They are:

1. *Low-back*: a chair with short spindles topped by a semi-circular rail that serves as top rail and arms (*a*).
2. *Comb-back*: the same as the low-back with a center addition of spindles on the rail topped by a curving thin cupid's-bow shaped rail (*b*).
3. *Fan-back*: a relatively high-backed chair with the top rail cupid's-bow shaped and spindles going from the seat to the top rail. It is most often a side chair and is closely related to the comb-back (*c*).
4. *Hoop-back (or bow-backed)*: a low-backed chair with a curving addition topping the center portion (*d*).
5. *New England armchair*: another version of the hoop-back. In this chair the hoop includes the arms so that one continuous binding encloses all the spindles of the chair back (*e*).
6. *Loop-back*: a variation of the hoop-back with spindles going from seat to top rail. It is the counterpart of the fan-back and bears the same relation to the hoop-back as the fan-back bears to the comb-back. Most often this is a side chair (*f*).

These are not all the variations possible. Comb pieces are added to the curving loop-backs on occasion (Plate 72B), and at times there are other variations in shape such as the braced-back (Plate 72C).

One important type is the *writing arm Windsor* (Plates 70A, 71B) in which one arm has a curving shelf added as a small writing area. Often a drawer was included under it and also under the seat. Thomas Jefferson developed one variation of this type in which the seat revolves.

The technique of making the Windsor chair explains its sturdiness. The chairs were made with green wood that shrank later, making joints firmer and tighter than any obtained when seasoned wood is used. Woods were chosen for their ability to withstand wear, and, since the piece was to be painted, the differences would not show. Pine and whitewood were used for seats because they were soft and, therefore, easily modeled. Frequently the seat is saddle-shaped.

Legs are turned in a variety of designs and for turning maple, birch, ash and chestnut are good woods. Although some chairs have all lathed parts of the same wood, there are also examples in which different woods are employed for the upper parts. Ash, white oak and hickory do not tend to fracture when steamed and bent so that spindles and hoops frequently were made of one of these woods. Wedges and small wooden pins found in Windsors were made of seasoned wood. In any case, the Windsor was constructed as a chair that could withstand hard wear.

In Colonial America, Philadelphia was apparently the first place where Windsors were made, and it was a popular place for their manufacture. In New York Thomas Ash, advertising in 1775 as a Windsor chair-maker complained, 'As several hundred pounds have been sent out of this province for this article, he hopes the public will encourage the business. ...' The money probably went to Philadelphia, because the year before the New York *Gazette and Weekly Mercury* carried the announcement that 'John Kelso Windsor Chair-maker from Philadelphia ... Makes and sells all kinds of Windsor Chairs ... and as he served a regular apprenticeship in Philadelphia he is persuaded he can supply those who may be kind enough to favour him with their custom with as well-finished, strong, and neat work as ever appeared in this city. ...'

Five of the six types of chairs were made in Philadelphia and the fifth on the list, the New England armchair, is thought to have had its origin in the latter locality (Plate 72D). The Windsor chair developed in the various colonies with distinguishing characteristics that can be separated into two general types, the Philadelphia and the New England. The geographical differences are logical with one exception, New York chairmakers followed Philadelphia before the Revolution and New England later (Plate 70C).

Characteristic of the Philadelphia examples are legs in a blunt-arrow design (Plate 70B). This leg starts with a ball foot, then there is a narrow ring and bun division, a straight cylindrical section follows, and after another narrowing an almost vase-shaped section makes up the rest of the leg. The New England leg has no foot; generally the lower part is cone-shaped, and after a narrow division a vase-shaped section follows (Plate 72A). The Rhode Island and Connecticut chairs have greater differentiation between the parts. The Connecticut leg is heavier and the curve is simpler (Plate 71A). The Rhode Island leg has a curve in the lower part of the cone-shaped section and a more exaggerated curve in the vase. Philadelphia stretchers have large balls in the center, occasionally flanked by ring turnings. In New England the center of the stretchers bulge but not to a ball shape.

The seats of Philadelphia chairs are usually straight across the front and cut out in a deep saddle shape. In New England chair seats are more often curved across the front and relatively shallow. They are oval-shaped rather than U-shaped. In the spindles the Philadelphians employed tapering shapes which New Englanders most often ignored in favor of a spindle with bulbous enlargements about one-third of the way up from the seat.

Legs and spindles were turned in bamboo shapes on some examples as early as the late-eighteenth century (Plate 71B), but this style developed popularity in the nineteenth century. One unusual type of Windsor, the rod-back, has rail and stiles of the back, legs and stretchers in the same bamboo turned pattern. In some examples the top rail is wide and in a shape inspired by Sheraton, with a raised rectangular area in the center.

Windsor chairs also appear extended, as settees (Plate 71A) and 'double seats', a term that probably referred to what today is called a love seat. The same turned construction sometimes was used to make simple small tables.

From the advertisements of the eighteenth century, it becomes evident that Windsors were often made in the large coastal towns and exported. There were, however, some made in rural areas for local use.

The American Windsor was used in many different homes, from those of the simple farmer to those of country gentlemen such as George Washington. The back porch of Mount Vernon had a group of Windsors; and chairs for some bedrooms ordered in 1757 were very likely of the same type. As well as in homes, the chair was used in public buildings. In Philadelphia, the members of the Continental Congress sat on Windsors. The American type differs from the English version in being simpler. The English had more variety and allowed passing fads to influence the form. In English examples a center splat reflecting the Georgian style is frequently used. Cabriole legs are sometimes substituted for the turned legs. The American seat is most frequently made of pine and is thicker than the English seat. Because it might easily be split, the holes for the legs are placed closer to the center and the legs are splayed more than the English examples.

The American Windsor is a strong chair, of simple construction, that served many uses. It was important in the American colonies possibly as early as 1725, although most known examples should be dated from the late-eighteenth century to about the middle of the nineteenth. It is interesting to note, on the subject of dating, that the English author, F. Gordon Roe, finds American dates early in comparison to English dates.

BOOKS FOR FURTHER READING

DREPPERD, CARL: *Handbook of Antique Chairs*, Garden City, New York (1948).

KINDIG III, JOE: 'Upholstered Windsors', in *Antiques*, July, 1952.

NUTTING, WALLACE.: *American Windsors*, Framingham and Boston (1917).

PRATT, RICHARD: *Second Treasury of Early American Homes*, Hawthorn Books, New York, 1954.

STOKES, J.STOGDELL: 'The American Windsor', in *Antiques*, April, 1926.

WESTON, KARL E.: 'Windsor Chairs at Williams College', in *Antiques*, November, 1944.

Plates 69–72 are from photographs lent by *Antiques* Magazine.

COUNTRY FURNITURE IN NEW ENGLAND

By FRANK O. SPINNEY

THE term *country furniture* derives from the observation that there developed in rural New England in the seventeenth, eighteenth and early-nineteenth centuries a kind of furniture different enough in character and spirit from sophisticated urban styles to be classed as a type in itself.

Such a development was, of course, not unique to New England nor to this period. In many places and in many times there has developed a country, even a 'folk' style of furniture. In like manner there have frequently coexisted twin streams of popular and classical music, academic and non-academic art, and formal and cottage architecture.

The characteristics of New England's country furniture tell the story of a simple, self-sufficient life, with its conservatism, thriftiness, individualism, isolation, and dependence on local resources of materials and skills.

To understand the development of New England country furniture as a distinct style, it may be helpful to recall the pattern of that region's growth from its earliest settlements to the time in the nineteenth century when craftsmen were superseded by machines and factory-made furniture replaced the product of local artisans.

During the first uncertain years of colonization, life in the newly established settlements was rugged indeed. Theirs was truly a pioneering venture. With their backs to the sea, new arrivals faced an unexplored wild territory, a virtually unrelieved expanse of dense primeval forest out of which they were literally to hew their livelihoods, their homes and much of their furnishings. Clearing fields, lumbering and building was heavy work. Settlements were planted and succeeded only because this work was performed. The homes of the men and women who did it were furnished with the barest necessities and sometimes not even those. Simple benches, a table, perhaps a chest brought with them on the voyage from England, a bed or a pallet thrown on the floor were about all the average household possessed. Some few pieces were brought by those able to afford it, but the ordinary settler had only what the housewright, the joiner or his own practical skill could make. From those first decades we have few physical survivals either of architecture or furnishings. Pieces of furniture that have come down to our day are usually the more elaborate and important ones, press and court cupboards, the Carver, Brewster and wainscot chairs, carved chests and an occasional table. All these are essentially country furniture, provincial versions of provincial pieces in the homeland. While most of the more elaborate New England pieces followed so closely their English prototypes that frequently their attribution hinges on the matter of the wood out of which they were made, there are certain ones, in which New Englanders take great pride, that have a definite stamp of local individuality. The Sunflower (Plate 74A) and Hadley Chests made along the Connecticut River, the Ipswich pieces of Thomas Dennis, and a few others are examples of New England's first native-born country furniture.

In the eighteenth century population grew rapidly. From a total of between 75,000 and 100,000 inhabitants in 1700, a doubling every two or three decades took place for nearly a hundred years. On the eve of the

Revolution, New England held close to three-quarters of a million people. The first Federal census in 1790 showed more than a million residents.

This growth of population, partly normal increase and partly immigration, meant a tremendous development of the interior parts of the region. Most of the increase went inland to set up homes in newly-granted towns back from the coast, in western Connecticut, central and western Massachusetts, Vermont and New Hampshire. The lure was land, virtually free acreage to those whose capital might be small but whose muscles and determination were large. It was this promise of land ownership that filled many ships from England and made New England a region where eight out of every ten persons were farmers.

The furniture needs of this growing population were nowhere near fully supplied by importations from England and elsewhere. In fact, purchases abroad declined not only relatively in respect to the growing number of people, but absolutely in terms of the amount of furniture brought in. Moreover, most imported furniture was undoubtedly of the more elegant type destined for the homes of wealthy city merchants and traders whose economic position and cultural ties enabled them to keep up with the latest English fashions. Even the importations were insufficient for these latter. Thus there arose in urban centers such as Boston, Salem, Providence, Newport and perhaps a dozen smaller places, groups of craftsmen who strove to meet the demand for silver, pewter, clocks, fabrics, art and furniture by the well-to-do and cultivated whose tastes were sophisticated and whose pocketbooks could afford the best. From these city craft shops came the Townsends, the Goddards, the Frothinghams, the Seymours, and others who created the masterpieces of New England cabinetwork.

It is easy to forget that even by 1810 there were only three cities in southern New England with over 10,000 population. These three with eleven smaller centers between 5,000 and 10,000 accounted for less than 15 percent of the total. In Maine, New Hampshire and Vermont, the proportion of rural population was even greater. Thus throughout the region close to 90 percent were farm and village people spread out in almost 600 small communities. In these areas, too, flourished craftsmen. Along with land, equally inviting to the newly-arrived immigrant or resident of the older coastal settlements, was the opportunity to ply a trade, housebuilding, blacksmithing, milling, tanning, potting and furniture-making to supply the needs of this vast and growing group.

The New England farmer was not a commercial farmer. With so small a part of the population living in the tiny urban areas, there was no real market for his products. Thus he raised his crops not to sell but for his own use. Small surpluses were traded for necessities he could not produce – spices, tea, coffee, powder and shot, iron, sugar, rum – and for the services of his neighbor craftsmen who accepted lumber, wool, tallow, beef and work for the product of their special skills. This money-poor, self-sufficient economy of the New England farmer is reflected in his simple farmhouse architecture, the interior decoration of his house and his furniture.

In such a milieu, isolated from the urban centers with their ties abroad, it is not strange that there developed a style of furniture that had a flavor of its own, reminiscent of but more vital than a mere country-cousin version of 'big city' fashions. It was created by artisans who shared and understood their customers' need for utility and economy, who were, with their neighbors, conservative and slow to take up new ideas, and who were dependent on local resources.

The men who made the tables, chairs, chests, stands, beds and coffins for their local customers were often only part-time craftsmen. In common with rural ministers, lawyers, doctors and other professional or craft workers, the cabinetmakers were frequently farmers who employed their special skill to supplement their return from the land. Their account books show them devoting perhaps a tenth or a quarter of their time to their trade. Pieces were produced on order, not for stock. They were jacks-of-all-trades in the field of woodwork, hewing out the frame of a house, constructing a workbench, making a window sash, turning a dish on a lathe, framing a picture or map, as well as constructing grain chests, dough troughs, candlestands, kitchen tables, desks, beds, bureaus, cupboards, settles, chairs and clock cases.

The materials used in their work were usually local in source. Often the pine, maple, birch, cherry and other woods were supplied by the customer from his own timber lot. Payment for the craftsman's work was frequently in the form of well-seasoned planks. To a certain degree the woods used varied somewhat from section to section (Plate 74B). Abundance or lack were factors as well as a local predilection. Thus what the Massachusetts cabinetmaker made in maple, the southern Maine or eastern New Hampshire craftsman often fabricated in birch. Poplar is a hallmark of a type of southern Connecticut piece. Cherry was the rural mahogany for many workers, while apple and pear wood were occasionally used. Unusual and unpredictable in source and supply was curly maple (Plate 75B). It was considered especially desirable and reserved for larger, more impressive pieces. Pine was the most common wood (Plate 73). It was used not only for concealed structural parts but for entire pieces. Oak, chestnut, walnut and other indigenous trees supplied materials on occasion.

The tools and techniques of the rural cabinetmaker were similar to those of his urban contemporaries. Perhaps the country worker had a smaller assortment of molding planes. Working alone, he may have had to use a pole or treadle lathe since he rarely had apprentices to turn the great wheel found in larger establishments. His techniques were the same, although perhaps he was not quite so careful when fitting a dovetail or cutting a tenon.

Workmanship was not usually of the highest quality. Experience, training and the intense continuous discipline of a large city shop where one's work was carefully scrutinized by the master-owner were not always a part of the rural craftsman's background. Today's eyes should not mistakenly glorify what is actually inability, carelessness or ignorance. Allowing for all of this, however, it is remarkable how consistently good was most of the work produced.

The cost of this kind of work to the purchaser was modest. In searching the ledgers and account books of the obscure rural cabinetmaker, one senses that he commonly took his labor into account at approximately the same daily rate prevailing for general work in the locality. To this basic cost was added the value of materials. Bookkeeping practices of the day did not expose the profit involved, if any. Possibly the net result was more in the direction of full employment. One doubts that country furniture makers accumulated substantial estates.

The finishes applied to country furniture were varied, ranging from varnish and shellac surfacing to oil and wax, or commonly to no finish at all, leaving the piece to the customer's taste and energy. Paint was used widely (Plate 76B), strong earth colors, red, yellow, brown, put on sometimes almost as a stain and then again in a heavy coat whose vehicle, tradition and early recipes assert, was skimmed milk which hardened in casein fashion into a nearly impenetrable plating. In addition to solid blacks, greens, blues and grays, multicolored decorations were popular at times. Astonishing abstract designs, simulated graining and marbleizing, and decorative freehand or stenciled patterns were common paint finishes in the later periods (Plate 76A). Whether this can be properly considered as part of the furniture itself or not, it contributed to the distinctive character of much country furniture.

While the style of country furniture followed changes that occurred in fashionable circles, often there was a time lag due to isolation, conservatism and the feeling that a form that had proved its usefulness was still useful even though fashion had decreed otherwise. Thus the familiar hearthside settle (Plate 75C), popular in England in the seventeenth century, was made in New England in the 1820s long after it had become obsolete elsewhere. The country version of the Chippendale style (Plate 75B) was a rural favorite for decades after urban tastes had passed on to newer delights. To try to date tables and chairs of this type is hazardous, for they were made practically unaltered for the greater part of a century.

While the elements of each style change are recognizable in country furniture, there is often as well an overlapping of fashions in a single piece. Whether this was due to the hazily understood design, the experimentation of the maker, or the iron whim of a customer, it sometimes produced the appealing friendly quality that a mongrel dog possesses and a highly-bred canine may lack.

Starting with a current style, well defined and highly developed in fashionable circles by talented master-craftsmen, the country furniture equivalent, worked out, modified, simplified or added to, became in the shop of the rural cabinetmaker a new thing with its own individual qualities and its own character, reflecting the period and place of its creators and users. Retrieved now from the past, it tells a story of rural New England.

BOOKS FOR FURTHER READING

BRIDENBAUGH, CARL: *The Colonial Craftsman*, New York and London (1950).
CORNELIUS, CHARLES O.: *Early American Furniture*, New York (1926).
KETTELL, RUSSELL HAWES: *The Pine Furniture of Early New England*, New York (1929).
PRATT, RICHARD: *Second Treasury of Early American Homes*, Hawthorn Books, New York (1954).
SPINNEY, FRANK O.: 'Country Furniture', *Antiques*, August, 1953.
Concise Encyclopedia of Antiques, Vol. 1, pp. 50–74, Hawthorn Books (1955).

THE CRAFTSMANSHIP OF THE AMERICAN SHAKERS

By EDWARD DEMING ANDREWS

The 'world's people' could adapt forms; the Shakers could create them. More than one generation would pass in America before this conception of logic with beauty would come into its own.

OLIVER W. LARKIN, *Art and Life in America*

For the sheer beauty of the direct solution, elemental but not primitive, there is little in America to surpass their designs.

JOSEPH ARONSON, *Book of Furniture and Decoration*

SHAKER furniture is religion in wood. It was made by craftsmen working in the spirit and holding the beliefs of a communitarian sect which had separated from the 'world' to seek a more spiritual way of life. The Shakers were separatists in a fundamental sense: dissenters from Anglicanism, Puritanism, even Quakerism – a people who, in their attempt to restore the primitive Christian church, repudiated private property, marriage, the bearing of arms, all worldliness. Joining in protest against what they considered the evils of the time, they affirmed new socio-religious principles, to ensure the development of which they established, in the late-eighteenth and early-nineteenth centuries, a system of semi-monastic communities largely insulated from the world around them.[1] It is within this framework, that of a separatist religious order, that its craftsmanship, as a distinctive American art form, must be considered.

Current in the Society was the saying that 'every force evolves a form'. What then, we must ask, *were* the forces that conditioned workmanship, that imbued the furniture and architecture of the Believers with a recognizable character? The answer can best be given in terms of five Shaker principles, closely interrelated to be sure, but each having a special bearing as a direct or indirect cause: the doctrines, namely, of order and use; separation from the world; separation of the sexes; community of goods, or 'united inheritance'; and perfectionism, or purity of life.

The earliest evidence of a standard of workmanship is found in the *Way Marks* of Joseph Meacham (1742–1796), the organizer of the Shaker Church and Ann Lee's successor as its head. In this guide to conduct and organization (*c.* 1790) 'Father' Joseph ruled that 'all things must be made ... according to their order and use', and that 'all work done, or things made in the church, ought to be faithfully and well done, but plain and without superfluity – neither too high nor too low'. In separating from a world of evil and disorder, in elevating themselves above the 'carnal' plane of existence, Meacham and other leaders considered the mission of 'Believers' to be the application, in social practice, of the Christian virtues of justice, peace and brotherhood. Organization was essential to the realization of such an ideal. 'Order,' the Shakers were constantly enjoined, 'is Heaven's first law.' And by order they meant not only the careful planning of the social, economic and religious structure, but the use of human and material resources for given ends. Order involved co-operative effort and specific responsibilities on the part of each member. It was equated, in the Shaker mind, with neatness and cleanliness, with Mother Ann's saying that 'there is no dirt in Heaven'. It meant, specifically, that labor, including the work of builders, joiners and other 'mechanics', should be directed to foreseen uses, should serve, as perfectly as possible, its appointed purposes. Meacham's injunction was an early statement of what today we call functionalism. In practice it meant that the use to which a building, or a piece of furniture, or a tool was to be put, predetermined its design. As a guiding precept, it had far-reaching implications.

The doctrine of 'united inheritance', or 'joint interest', has relevance here, for labor was consecrated to communal – and millennial-uses. The craftsman worked not to please his own fancy or the passing tastes of the world, but for the good of his brothers and sisters, the whole society, an order he believed would last a thousand years. Consecration of talent and possessions, 'the right use of property', was one of the seven moral principles of the church:[2] 'the true followers of Christ [an official statement reads] are one with him, as he is one with the Father. This oneness includes all they possess; for he who has devoted himself to Christ, soul, body and spirit, can by no means withhold his property.'[3] Since property, therefore, was a trust, not a personal possession – 'the earth is the Lord's and the fullness thereof' – it was the duty, the privilege indeed, of all Believers to be faithful stewards of their heritage, accountable to God for the improvement of their time and talents in this life. Laboring in such a spirit, the craftsman employed his skill, like a medieval artisan, to glorify a church eternal. The product, in turn, was part of the United Inheritance, to be held in perpetuity and used with scrupulous care.

Its communal function influenced craftsmanship in other ways. Meeting-houses, dwellings, barns, shops and furniture were designed for the convenience of societies divided into family groups of thirty to a hundred members. Such an organization necessitated commodious buildings, shops adapted to diverse occupational needs and furniture suited to group use – long trestle-tables and benches, built-in drawers, large cupboard-chests and tailoring counters, multiple-use kitchen and office furniture, spacious rooms. Group requirements, however, did not exclude the need for smaller, or specialized, cabinet work. Chairs were designed with given individuals in mind; small stands adapted to specific uses were consigned to the sewing and 'retiring' rooms; clocks promoted punctuality, and looking glasses neatness of person; desks of various types were needed by the family deacons and deaconesses, the eldership and the ministry. Joinery of all kinds was furnished on call from, and on specifications by, those entrusted with the 'temporal care'.

As a result, Shaker furniture presents a diversity of forms, within a general uniformity of style, which gives it lasting interest. Every piece has an unmistakable Shaker look, yet an individuality of its own. One explanation of the seeming paradox lies in the fact that the United Society was a decentralized organization, with each of its eighteen branches, and each family unit within the colony, semi-independent in its economy. At the outset the central order, or church family, at New Lebanon set up certain patterns and standards, in industry and the crafts, which other families in other societies were encouraged to follow. But in practice this did not result in outright copying or duplication. The distance separating communities was one factor making for differentiation. Another was the diversity in skills, methods and training of those 'mechanics' who, as converts, happened to be drawn into one community rather than another. There are peculiarities in Maine Shaker furniture, for instance – the turnings of table legs and chair finials, the high, narrow cupboards, etc. – which distinguish it from that of other New England colonies. One can recognize, by their finial turnings, the chairs made in Hancock from those, say, in New Lebanon, Enfield, New Hampshire or the Ohio communes. The size of a family, its financial status, the part played by furniture-making in its economy, all affected the crafts. Families bought from and sold to one another, and even engaged in friendly competition, a practice militating against standardization.

The multiplicity of patterns in Shaker craftsmanship derives from another source: the concept of 'use' mentioned above. If there was to be continual 'increase' in the gospel, individual as well as group potential must be utilized, with a concern, therefore, for the well-being of members as persons. This recognition of the worth of the individual is not unrelated to our central theme of craftsmanship. Take chairs, for instance. Chairs made for the 'world', an early industry dating back to the 1790s, eventually conformed to standardized designs. But the chairs intended for domestic use often have marked individuality. Armed rocking-chairs were made for the comfort of the aged and infirm, in sizes adapted to given users. Chairs for invalids had special characteristics. Children's chairs, weaving and tailoring chairs, footstools, settees for visitors to the novitiate order, etc., bear the stamp of particular intent. It was not unusual, also, for a craftsman, with the approval of the family 'Lead', to make a special piece, as a token of esteem or affection for some beloved brother or sister, elder or eldress. In the domestic economy of the sect, a sister was often assigned to look after the temporal needs of a given brother – his room, his clothes – in appreciation for which service some article of manufacture might be fashioned, as a symbol of gospel love, for the sister's comfort and convenience. A certain type of round-topped candle-stand, designed especially for the ministry, was called a 'ministry stand'. A color applied to the cots used by the 'Lead' was known as 'ministry green'. A sister or brother might take a fancy to a particular piece of furniture, which the family eldress or elder would thereupon consign to his, or her, use. Visiting the rooms of a unitary household, one is aware, by their appointments, that though, in theory, 'there was little importance in the individual', in practice the human personality was not lost.

Still another factor affecting both architecture and furniture design was the dual nature of their organization. The Shakers believed in a dual Deity – a Father-Mother God, Power and Holy Mother Wisdom – and a dual messiahship, Christ and Mother Ann. They believed in separation of the sexes, but also in their equality, with elders and eldresses, deacons and deaconesses, brethren and sisters sharing both privileges and obligations. Men and women lived together, but in opposite parts of the dwelling; they worshipped together, in song and dance, but in patterns which kept them apart; they worked for a common end, but in separate shops. The boys and girls received into the society under indenture agreements with their parents or guardians, lived with their caretakers in the Children's Order. The presiding ministry, two elders and two eldresses, engaged in manual labor with the rest, but in their own 'ministry's shop', a building adjacent to the meeting-house in which they had their private quarters. Churches, therefore, were built with at least three doors – one each for the brethren, sisters and ministry – and sometimes, as at New Lebanon, with two others for the males and females who often attended public meetings from the 'world'. Dwellings had separate doorways, stairs, halls and retiring rooms. Furniture, too, was differentiated on the basis of sex. Tables, chairs, desks, etc., consigned to the sisterhood were of lower height, and sometimes of more delicate construction, than those designed for the brethren.

Meacham's principle of 'plainness' derived from the Shaker belief that man could be purified, by degrees, from all his imperfections. The great imperfection was selfishness, the ego – 'Great I'. Man could rise above self, above his 'carnal' nature, only by devoting himself whole-heartedly, and with all his strength, to the love of God. Humility, honesty, innocence, charity, simplicity – these were the marks of the regenerate spirit. And of these 'foundations of the New Jerusalem' none had greater meaning, in the Shaker mind, than simplicity, a concept which Seth Wells, the author of *The Millennial Church*, defines in these words, that 'its thoughts, words and works are plain and simple. ... It is without ostentation, parade or any vain show, and naturally leads to plainness in all things.'[4] In the field of craftsmanship, which deliberately abjured the superfluous and useless, the concept had direct application. Carvings, inlays, veneers, moldings, excess turnings and surface 'embellishment' added nothing, the Shakers held, to the usefulness, the comfort, the 'goodness' of a piece of furniture or a building. Why obscure the beauty of the natural grain of woods with varnish? Why complicate the gentle curve with unnecessary turning, the broad plane with distracting ornament? That was what 'Father' Joseph meant by 'too high'. On the other hand, materials should be of 'substantial' quality and put to 'truly virtuous' use. According to the Gospel Orders, there was 'no room for half-way work, either in things inward or outward'. That was the inference of 'too low'. There is nothing somber, stilted or stereotyped about Shaker furniture. It has a harmony of proportion and refinement of line which give it a quiet, unassuming dignity. In perfect keeping with its setting, it makes a chaste contribution to the atmosphere of sanctity pervading the rooms of every Shaker dwelling.

Though the Believers were indeed seeking perfection, in works as in conduct, they did not contemplate a state in which there could be 'no increase for the better'. As in their covenants and relations with the world, their psalmody and mode of worship, their dress, their language and deportment, their theories regarding health and education – so in their architecture, industry and craftsmanship, they were constantly striving for 'improvement'. As regards their 'manner of building', a New Lebanon Shaker historian, citing the early handicaps of poverty and inexperience, explains that at first they had to build 'for the present, on a small scale, and in a cheap style ... with a rough way of building foundations ... little hall room ... crowded and steep stairs ... no jets to the eaves or ends of the roof,' etc. Therefore the structures were 'very inferior, and poorly adapted to the purpose for which they were needed'. He then records, by five-year intervals, the manifold advances: the door-caps or hoods, the recesses to the outside doors, the provisions for ventilation and sanitation, the tin roofs, the stone paths, the marble gate-posts and horse-blocks, the cisterns and aqueducts, the chimney caps, the improvements in tools (buzz-saws and planing, mortising and boring machines, etc.) and the shops, sheds, barns and mills constructed for the 'convenience' of various trades.

In their industrial practices, likewise, the Shakers were alert to the more useful method, the tool better adapted to its purpose, the mechanism which would save time and labor – ready, if necessary, to adopt worldly inventions, but always ingenious in their own right, as proved by the many inventions or improvements credited to the order. A partial list would include the metal pen, the common clothespin, cut nails, the one-horse wagon, the flat broom (and machinery for turning broom handles and sizing broom-corn brush), a loom for weaving palm-leaf for bonnets, a silk-reeling machine, a revolving oven, a pea-sheller, a butter-worker and 'self-acting' cheese-press, a machine for twisting whip handles, an improved washing-machine and mangle, a turbine water-wheel and a screw propeller, the original 'Babbitt metal', the circular saw, threshing and fertilizing machines, a side-hill plow, an improved corn-drying kiln, machinery for planing and matching boards, a device for making basket splints, a sash balance, a chimney-cap and 'stoves of the Shaker improvement'. They were pioneers in the medicinal herb industry, constantly experimenting with processes to ensure the highest quality of product. They were probably the first people in America to distribute garden seeds in small packages, priced at three cents each and appropriately labeled or printed. Seldom did they patent any invention, believing that patent money savored of monopoly.

The instinct – if such it may be called – for experimentation, for finding a better, the more logical solution, is also exemplified by many functional details of construction: by the lappers or 'fingers' of oval boxes, for instance, which gave them strength and held the form; by the ball-and-socket device at the base of the rear posts of side-chairs, enabling the sitter to rock or tilt without wearing the carpet; by the large wooden casters applied to bed-posts so the cots could be rolled forward and back without effort; and by the clever contrivances for locking drawers, raising window-shades, and raising or lowering desks to a desired height. The arrangement of drawers and cupboards, in moveable pieces of furniture, to utilize fully a given space; the application of drop leaves to tables, counters and walls; the practice of building drawers and cupboards into the walls, and lining the walls with peg-boards – all testify to a love of economy and order.[5]

To introduce our theme we have quoted from two commentators, both of whom, in their evaluations, use the word 'beauty'. In the Shaker vocabulary, however, the term had minor importance. 'The divine man has no right to waste money upon what you would call beauty, in his house or his daily life, while there are people living in misery.' Such was the stand of Elder Frederick Evans, one of the chief spokesmen of the sect. The society was concerned, as we have noted, chiefly with order, use, the avoidance of superfluities – a subject to which its Millennial Laws devote an entire section. From the first the emphasis was on neatness, good economy and industry. To labor was to pray. 'Put your hands to work,' Mother Ann had taught, 'and your hearts to God.' Even at a later period in their history, as the Shakers attempted to explain their philosophy, they talked in terms of the early values:

'Order is the creation of beauty.'

'Love of beauty has a wider field of action in association with Moral Force.'

'All beauty that has not a foundation in use soon grows distasteful, and needs continual replacement with something new.'

'That which has in itself the highest use possesses the greatest beauty.'

Yet one cannot say that the Believers neglected, or consciously repudiated, the beautiful. Evidence to the contrary is abundant: in their 'gift' for song and the painstaking calligraphy of their hymnals; in the soft reds, yellows and greens applied to furniture; in the yellow-greens of floors, and the warm browns or blue-greens of peg-racks, doors and window-frames; in their colored silk kerchiefs, and the natural dyes used in rugs and clothing; in their exquisite poplar basketry; in their finely wrought ironware; in their neat fences, paths and 'smooth-shaven greens'; and most conspicuously, in the inspirational designs accompanying the 'era of manifestations', beginning in 1837, when they drew or painted their trees of life and other 'emblems of the heavenly sphere'.

It is a matter of definition. Visitors were always impressed by the *neatness* of the Shaker villages. Harriet Martineau commented on the 'frame dwellings ... finished with the last degree of nicety, even to the springs of the windows and the hinges of the doors'. John Finch testified that 'the neatness, cleanliness and order which you everywhere observe in their persons and their premises, and the cheerfulness and contented looks of the people afford the reflective mind continual pleasure'. For another English traveler, Hepworth Dixon, 'no Dutch town [had] a neater aspect ... the paint is all fresh; the planks are all bright; the windows are all clean. A white sheen is on everything, a happy quiet reigns around'. It was the opinion of Robert Wickliffe, a prominent American lawyer, that 'in architecture and neatness they are exceeded by no people upon the earth'. To these persons, order was indeed 'the creation of beauty'.

Whatever the medium – the village unit, the individual structure, the furnishings of the buildings, even to the slightest accessory – Shaker workmanship achieved the status of an art, art in the sense employed by Emerson as 'the spirit's voluntary use and combination of things to serve its end'. When the sage of Concord wrote, in another connection, that 'in the construction of any fabric or organism, any real increase of fitness to its end, is an increase in beauty'; or when Walt Whitman, in the preface to *Leaves of Grass*, asserted that whatever 'distorts honest shapes ... is a nuisance' – they were expressing Shaker doctrine. Long before the American sculptor, Horatio Greenough, was proclaiming that 'beauty is the promise of function', that embellishment is 'false beauty', and that when the essential is found the product is complete, his principles had been exemplified in Shaker practice. In England, Ruskin, Morris and Charles Eastlake, had they known, would surely have found, in the craftsmanship of these overseas communities, an application of their ideals.

In one of his *Kindergarten Chats*, Louis H. Sullivan, the American architect, observed that 'Behind every form we see there is a vital something or other which we do not see yet which makes itself visible to us in that very form'. In the case of Shaker craftsmanship that 'something' was the spirit of a people laboring to create a heaven on earth – a people with an end to serve.

(Edward Deming Andrews and his wife, Faith Andrews, have given to Yale University (1956) their Shaker collection in order to ensure not only its preservation but its maximal educational use. Assembled over a period of thirty years, the collection represents the finest in the craftsmanship and arts of an indigenous religious order. A comprehensive library of books, pamphlets, manuscripts, etc., and a selection of artifacts illustrative of the industrial pursuits of the United Society, contribute to its unique historical value. – EDITOR).

[1] The movement had its origin in Manchester, England. In 1758 its founder, Ann Lee, a youthful worker in the textile mills of the manor, had joined a Quaker society which had come under the influence of the French Prophets, and which, in turn, was to accept 'Mother' Ann's revelations regarding celibacy, the millennium and Christ's Second Appearing. Persecuted for their 'heretical' beliefs and such practices as dancing as a mode of worship, eight of these 'Shaking Quakers', led by the prophetess, emigrated to America in 1774. Ann died ten years later, but not before the struggling movement had been revitalized by the fires of revivalism in various parts of New York and New England. The first colony was founded at Niskeyuna, or Watervliet, near Albany, in 1780. The first community to be fully organized was at New Lebanon, New York, in 1788. Eventually eighteen societies, divided into some fifty-eight 'family' units, were established: at New Lebanon, Watervliet and Groveland in New York; Hancock, Tyringham, Shirley and Harvard, in Massachusetts; Enfield, Connecticut; Alfred and Sabbathday Lake, in Maine; Enfield and Canterbury, in New Hampshire; Union Village, Watervliet, Whitewater and North Union in Ohio; and Pleasant Hill and South Union in Kentucky. A few other societies existed for short periods. The movement reached its zenith about the time of the Civil War when membership totalled about six thousand. Today only three colonies survive, at Hancock, Canterbury and Sabbathday Lake, with less than fifty members.

[2] The other principles were duty to God, duty to man, separation from the world, practical peace, simplicity of language and a virgin life.

[3] *Summary View of the Millennial Church*, Albany, 1823, p. 269.

[4] *Summary View, op. cit., p.* 249.

[5] A pine wash-stand recently added to the author's collection provides an apt illustration of Shaker functionalism. Parallel to one of the front legs is an inner post to which is attached, about two-thirds of the way down, a wooden plate – the post swivelling to allow the plate or disc to be swung freely forward. The plate was used to hold a slop pail, into which water from the wash basin could be emptied without the hazard of reaching underneath the top of the stand. A logical solution to a problem, entailing, to be sure, extra thought, extra effort – but that was the Shaker way.

BOOKS FOR FURTHER READING

ANDREWS, EDWARD DEMING, and ANDREWS, FAITH: *Shaker Furniture. The Craftsmanship of an American Communal Sect*, Yale University Press, New Haven, Connecticut (1937). (Reprinted by Dover Publications, Inc., New York, 1950.)

ANDREWS, EDWARD DEMING: 'Designed for Use: The Nature of Function in Shaker Craftsmanship', in *New York History*, July, 1950, Vol. XXXI, No. 3, Cooperstown, New York.

ANDREWS, EDWARD DEMING: 'Shaker Furniture', in *Interior Design*, May, 1954, Vol. 25, No. 5, New York.

ANDREWS, EDWARD DEMING, and ANDREWS, FAITH: 'Notes on Shaker Furniture', in *The Antiques Book* (ed. Alice Winchester), New York (1950). (A condensation of articles in the August, 1928, and April, 1929, issues of *Antiques*.)

ANDREWS, EDWARD DEMING: *The People Called Shakers: A Search for the Perfect Society*, Oxford University Press, New York (1953).

ANDREWS, EDWARD DEMING: 'The Communal Architecture of the Shakers', in *Magazine of Art*, No. 12, December, 1937, Vol. XXX, Washington, D.C. (1937).

ANDREWS, EDWARD DEMING: *The Community Industries of the Shakers*, Handbook No. 15, New York State Museum, Albany, New York (1932).

MCCAUSLAND, ELIZABETH: 'The Shaker Legacy', in *The Magazine of Art*, December, 1944, Vol. XXXVII, Washington, D.C.

'Shaker Furniture in a Little Red Farmhouse', in *Living with Antiques* (ed. Alice Winchester), New York (1941).

All the illustrations to this article, Plates 77–80, are from photographs by William F. Winter, from *Shaker Furniture; The Craftsmanship of an American Communal Sect*, by Edward Deming and Faith Andrews, Yale University Press, New Haven, Connecticut, 1937.

ITALIAN FURNITURE

By HUGH HONOUR

WHEN collectors turn their attention to Italian furniture they must be prepared to look for qualities different from those they see in the work of the great French and English cabinet makers. At first they may well be disappointed to find that relatively few pieces show the delicacy and lightness or the superb standards of finished craftsmanship of a Riesener or a Chippendale. Charming boudoir pieces were made in northern Italy, and especially in Venice, during the late eighteenth and early nineteenth centuries, but the Italian craftsman's talents were shown less in the creation of such intimate little objects than in furnishing the sumptuous saloons of great palaces in Rome, Naples, Florence, Genoa and Turin. Richly carved, lavishly gilded and upholstered in the most opulent Lucchese silks and Genoese cut velvets, the furniture which stands beneath the vast frescoed ceilings of Italian *palazzi* is outstanding for its air of grandiose magnificence and princely splendour.

It must be admitted that Italian furniture does not show the consistently high finish of French or English work. In fact, its construction is sometimes distinctly shoddy. Yet this is not to deny it high quality in other respects. Generally speaking, the Italian cabinet maker seems to have been more interested in the design and decoration than the finish of his work, and he seldom bestowed much attention on those parts which were not intended to be seen – the backs of cupboards or the insides of drawers, for example. But such slip-shod methods did not always, or everywhere, prevail. In the Renaissance period painters gave as much care to the decoration of a *cassone* as to a great fresco, and in the seventeenth and eighteenth centuries several sculptors carved chairs, console tables and frames with the same accomplished freedom of hand as they lavished on independent statues. Fantastic armchairs by Brustolon (Plate 83A), inlaid tables and cabinets by Piffetti (Plate 84B) and lacquer furniture exquisitely painted by a host of anonymous Venetian artists, reveal impeccable standards of craftsmanship in their design and decoration even if they occasionally appear somewhat rough and ready in their carpentry.

To speak of Italian furniture as we speak of English or French furniture is, however, somewhat rash. The regional differences which are familiar to every student of Italian painting and sculpture are no less marked in the minor arts and crafts. Although Venice is but 90 miles from Bologna and Bologna no more than 60 miles from Florence, radical differences of style distinguish the furniture produced in these three centres until well into the eighteenth century. The Renaissance which was born in Florence did not affect the Venetian painter, let alone the cabinetmaker, for some fifty years. Similarly, the neo-classical style appeared in Venice long after it had been accepted in Rome and Turin. Moreover, different types of wood requiring different treatment were available in the various districts and helped to produce regional styles. In the South, olive wood was often used. In Lombardy and Tuscany where a rich variety of nut and fruit tree woods were available much inlaid furniture was made while at Venice, where the finer types of wood seem to have been difficult to obtain, a considerable proportion of the furniture was lacquered. We also find that much of the furniture made at Lucca and Genoa was designed mainly to show off the magnificent textiles those cities produced. In general, however, walnut was the wood most widely used in all districts from the middle of the sixteenth century until the late eighteenth century. Mahogany never achieved the same popularity in Italy as in England or France, probably for economic reasons.

The foreign influences which played an important part in Italian furniture designed after the middle of the seventeenth century were felt more forcibly in some regions than in others. French influence was, of course, exerted throughout the peninsula as in the rest of Europe but was at its strongest in Liguria and Piedmont. Venice was subject to a limited German and Austrian influence, while the Kingdom of the Two Sicilies produced furniture which owes a certain debt to Spain. After the middle of the eighteenth century the English pattern books of Thomas Chippendale and later of Sheraton and Hepplewhite circulated in Italy and seem to have been copied by cabinet-makers in many districts. With the Napoleonic conquests the Empire style became generally accepted and, for the first time in history, a general pattern was imposed on the furniture production of the whole country.

In view of the considerable local differences in style, it is hardly surprising that no wholly satisfactory comprehensive account of Italian furniture has ever been written. Books have appeared on the furniture of various districts and periods, but Italian furniture as a whole awaits a historian. Bearing local variations of style in mind, it is, however, possible to sketch the broad outlines of this fascinating and neglected subject.

Renaissance Furniture: very few examples of Italian furniture can securely be dated before the beginning of the fifteenth century, the most important exceptions being two thirteenth-century X stools in the Cathedral at Perugia and the Austrian Museum at Vienna. Similar X chairs and some three-legged stools of a type used in the fourteenth century are also known, but as these objects retained their popularity until well into the sixteenth century it is seldom possible to date them with any precision. A few *cassoni* and *armadi* decorated with somewhat primitive paintings or flamboyant Gothic carving have been preserved but most of them derive from northern districts where the Gothic style lingered on after it had given way to the Renaissance in Tuscany. The history of Italian furniture therefore begins with the Renaissance. Yet to study the furniture even of this period we must supplement our knowledge of existing pieces by reference to paintings. The *prie-Dieu* at which the Virgin kneels or the desk at which St Jerome studies in *quattrocento* paintings give us a better idea of the furniture of the period than any surviving examples. And it should be pointed out that the furniture which appears in these pictures acquired a sentimental charm which appealed very strongly to late nineteenth-century collectors for whom unscrupulous craftsmen produced a large number of similar works.

To judge from paintings, the majority of *quattrocento* furniture was very unpretentious and much of it was usually covered with linen or glowing Turkish carpets. It is, perhaps, significant that the most notable pieces of furniture to survive from this period are *cassoni* and *armadi* which were seldom muffled in drapery and were thus more richly decorated than the simple tables and *credenze*. *Cassoni* were often painted by the leading artists of the time, while *armadi* were treated in an architecturally monumental fashion. Indeed, these magnificent cupboards often have the same harmonious proportions and noble simplicity of decoration as the façades and interiors of early Renaissance palaces and churches. As the early Renaissance developed into the high Renaissance and, finally, the mannerist style, so furniture makers enriched their designs, making greater use of figurative carving. Mid-sixteenth-century refectory tables have their legs carved with mythological and human figures, and the *armadio* is often provided with a broken pediment and low relief panels on its doors. At about the same time Bolognese craftsmen began to apply brass handles in the form of cherub or satyr heads to their furniture and maintained this style of decoration throughout the first half of the seventeenth century.

Baroque and Rococo Furniture: early in the seventeenth century, the nervous angular mannerist line broke into the easy baroque flame in painting, sculpture and architecture. The baroque style also affected the cabinet-maker who now developed a greater feeling for three dimensional form. The top line of the *armadio* swells into a ponderous curve and the front occasionally bellies out in the centre. Richness is supplied by the free use of bulging balusters, by inlays of rare woods or, on the most sumptuously palatial furniture, by panels of semi-precious stones. At the same time, chairs began to take on a more grandiose appearance with carved and gilded backs which sometimes erupted into a profusion of scrolls at the sides; they were often upholstered in rich velvets or damasks and were made more comfortable. As the century advanced the use of gilding on all articles of furniture increased and further tones of opulence were added to the palace interior by the introduction of objects of mainly decorative value such as console tables and *reggivasi*. The consoles were particularly magnificent, with vast slabs of rare and brilliantly coloured marble supported by human figures, mythological creatures or gigantic seashells. Furniture made in England to the designs of William Kent in the early eighteenth century reveals the influence of these works.

Whereas Italian furniture had influenced the rest of Europe in the sixteenth and, to a less marked degree, the seventeenth century, it began to succumb to French influence before the beginning of the eighteenth century. Indeed, French models were so widely copied in Italy that one is tempted to classify Italian furniture in French periods from *Régence* to *Empire*. Eighteenth-century Italian furniture was also affected by a change in the manner of living; for now the daily life of the palace moved from the great saloons on the *piano nobile* to the smaller rooms on the mezzanine floor which demanded more delicate furnishings, usually derived from French models.

As the rococo style won general acceptance in the second quarter of the eighteenth century, broken *rocaille* decorations took the place of the great sweeping baroque scrolls, and figures vanished from all furniture except the *giridoni* and *reggivasi*. The new patterns which came from France were not slavishly copied, however. Venetian craftsmen, who were surely the most accomplished furniture makers in early eighteenth-century Italy, indulged their flair for fantasy by exaggerating the French designs, giving *bombé* commodes more absurdly bellying fronts, extending the sofa to an inordinate length and applying a greater profusion of rococo twists and turns to the woodwork. Elsewhere, especially in Rome and Naples, French patterns seem to have been toned down and made more rigid.

Neo-classical and Empire Furniture: the neo-classical style which began to influence painters and sculptors in Rome soon after the middle of the eighteenth century hardly affected the cabinet-maker until the 1770s; though some furniture made in the 'sixties reveals a greater simplicity of line and severity of decoration. In Rome classical term figures and winged lions began to reappear as the supports of console tables, but the force of the new style was most strongly felt in Piedmont where it was employed by G. M. Bonzanigo. Only the Venetians remained obstinately rococo, treating the new patterns from France in a distinctly frivolous fashion. But France was not the only country to influence the Italian cabinet-maker, for in the second half of the eighteenth century English designs were also copied and the *salone* might include examples of Italian Chippendale and Sheraton furniture jostling Italian Louis XV and Louis XVI pieces.

The greater rigidity of Louis XVI designs paved the way for the acceptance of the Empire style which spread over Italy almost as fast and inexorably as the advance of Napoleon's armies. In the early 1800s the slender columns, the Egyptian heads and the elegant ormolu mounts which had over-run the salons of Paris began to appear also in the great Italian *palazzi*. Much of this furniture was imported from France, but many pieces of high quality were made in Florence and Lucca under the guidance of French *ébénistes*. Moreover, the Empire style

ITALIAN FURNITURE

(A) Bedroom, formerly in the Palazzo Davanzati at Florence. All the furniture is Florentine. The bed, chairs and stools date from the fifteenth century, and the *cassapanca* on the left wall from the sixteenth century.

(B) Veronese *cassone* with painted panels attributed to Bartolomeo Montagna, late fifteenth century. *Museo Poldi Pezzoli, Milan.*

PLATE 81

ITALIAN FURNITURE

(A) Tuscan table, late sixteenth century. Formerly in the Palazzo Davanzati, Florence.

(B) Florentine *cassone*, late sixteenth century. *Museo Nazionale, Florence.*

(C) Florentine *cassapanca*, mid-sixteenth century. *Museo Nazionale, Florence.*

(D) *Armadio* with *tarsia* decorations, late sixteenth century. Monte Oliveto, Siena.

(E) Sixteenth-century chairs, probably Florentine. *Museo Nazionale, Florence.*

ITALIAN FURNITURE

(A) Venetian chair by Andrea Brustolon, late seventeenth century. *Palazzo Rezzonico, Venice.*

(B) Venetian throne, late seventeenth century. *Palazzo Rezzonico, Venice.*

(C) Marchigan bureau decorated with gilt chinoiseries on a grained wood ground, early eighteenth century. *Private Collection, Milan.*

(D) Genoese looking-glass frame, carved by Domenico Parodi, early eighteenth century. *Palazzo Reale, Genoa.*

(E) Console table, in gilt wood, probably Roman, late seventeenth century. *Palazzo Reale, Turin.*

PLATE 83

(A) Lucchese bed, early eighteenth century. *Palazzo Mansi a S. Pellegrino, Lucca.*

(B) Bureau, inlaid with ivory and rare woods, by Pietro Piffetti of Turin, *c.* 1730. *Palazzo Quirinale, Rome.*

(C) Gilt wood console table probably executed after a design by Filippo Juvarra at Turin, *c.* 1730. *Palazzo Reale, Turin.*

ITALIAN FURNITURE

(A) Carved console table probably by Andrea Brustolon, one of a pair, early eighteenth century. *Stoneleigh Abbey, Warwickshire.*

(B) Late eighteenth-century console table made at Turin. *Castello di Stupinigi, Turin.*

(C) Chest of drawers, Roman or Neapolitan, mid-eighteenth century. *Palazzo Quirinale, Rome.*

(D) Genoese arm-chair upholstered in *petit point* embroidery, late eighteenth century. *Palazzo Reale, Genoa.*

(E) Piedmontese firescreen by Giuseppe Maria Bonzanigo, *c.* 1770. *Castello di Stupinigi, Turin.*

(F) Sicilian chair decorated with glass over wood painted in imitation of marble, formerly in the Villa Palagonia at Bagheria, late eighteenth century. *Ringling Museum, Sarasota.*

PLATE 85

ITALIAN FURNITURE

(A) Gilt bronze table designed by Pelagio Palagi, 1836–40. *Palazzo Reale, Turin.*

(B) Two chairs, probably Florentine, *c.* 1820. *Palazzo Pitti, Florence.*

(C) Writing-table, probably by Giovanni Socchi of Florence, *c.* 1810. *Palazzo Pitti, Florence.*

VIENNESE FURNITURE IN THE EIGHTEENTH CENTURY

(A) Writing-table with two vase stands (guéridons) in the Boulle manner. First quarter of the eighteenth century. *Hofburg, Vienna.*

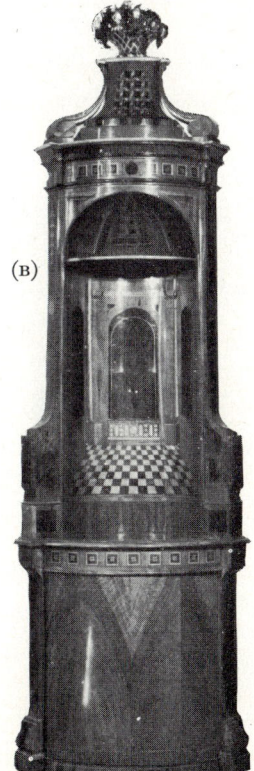

(B) Corner cupboard of the Baroque period, walnut and cherry inlay, c. 1735–40. *Palais Harrach, Vienna.*

(C) Small bombé commode, 'Palisander' ormolu mounts, c. 1750. *Palais Czernin, Vienna.*

PLATE 87

(A) Library table with four chairs, from the old University Library in Vienna, c. 1735. *Oesterreichisches Museum für angewandte Kunst, Vienna.*

(B) Armchair and small table, carved, white-gold mounts, c. 1770. *Oesterreichisches Museum für angewandte Kunst, Vienna.*

VIENNESE FURNITURE IN THE EIGHTEENTH CENTURY

(A) Dressing-table in cherry, c. 1760. *Palais Schwarzenberg, Vienna.*

(B) Commode of the period of Josef II, with Italian style inlay. 'Palisander', c. 1780–90. *Palais Schwarzenberg, Vienna.*

PLATE 89

VIENNESE FURNITURE IN THE EIGHTEENTH CENTURY

(A) Upholstered walnut settee, after 1740. *Palais Schönborn, Vienna.*

(B) Rococo settee in beech, walnut stained, *c.* 1755. *Palais Czernin, Vienna.*

(A) Low armchairs, beech, carved and gilded (re-covered), c. 1750. *Palais Harrach, Vienna.*

(B) Two side-chairs and one armchair of the period of Josef II, 1765–80. *Palais Schwarzenberg, Vienna.*

VIENNESE FURNITURE IN THE EIGHTEENTH CENTURY

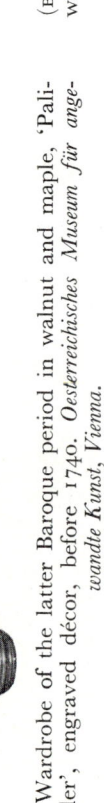

(B) Secretaire commode with pediment ('tabernacle-cabinet'), walnut inlay, c. 1735. Oesterreichisches Museum für angewandte Kunst, Vienna.

(A) Wardrobe of the latter Baroque period in walnut and maple, 'Palisander', engraved décor, before 1740. Oesterreichisches Museum für angewandte Kunst, Vienna.

VIENNESE FURNITURE IN THE EIGHTEENTH CENTURY

(B) Wardrobe of the period of Josef II in oak and cherry, 1770–80. *Palais Schwarzenberg, Vienna.*

(A) Rococo tall secretaire in alder, with inlay of different kinds of wood, c. 1760. *Palais Schwarzenberg, Vienna.*

PLATE 93

VIENNESE FURNITURE IN THE EIGHTEENTH CENTURY

(A) Armchair with high back. The property of Prince Eugene of Savoy (from his hunting lodge, the Schlosshof near Vienna), c. 1730. Now in the *Oesterreichisches Museum für angewandte Kunst, Vienna*.

(B) Four-post bed. Walnut and maple with engraved decoration, before 1750. *Palais Harrach, Vienna.*

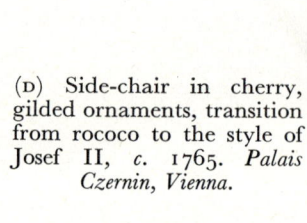

(C) Side-chair and stool, as above (Fig. A).

(D) Side-chair in cherry, gilded ornaments, transition from rococo to the style of Josef II, c. 1765. *Palais Czernin, Vienna.*

PLATE 94

FRENCH FURNITURE

(B) Walnut cabinet, second half of the sixteenth century. *Victoria and Albert Museum, London.*

(A) Carved walnut dresser, second half of the sixteenth century. *Victoria and Albert Museum, London.*

PLATE 95

FRENCH FURNITURE

(A) Chest of drawers (*commode*), made by A. Gaudreau and J. Caffiéri in 1739, for the bedroom of King Louis XV at Versailles. A perfect example of the Louis XV style on a monumental scale. *Wallace Collection, London.*

(B) Chest of drawers (*commode*), by Charles Cressent. It seems probable that Cressent himself also executed the mounts. *Wallace Collection, London.*

long outlived the Napoleonic regime in Italy. It was very successfully used by Pelagio Pelagi to decorate the throne room of the Palazzo Reale in Turin in the late 1830s: and, even in the 1840s, one Peters, an English cabinet-maker, was producing somewhat ponderous Empire furniture at Genoa. In Naples, palatial furniture of a late Empire character, in what may be termed the Bourbon style, was made to fill the vast apartments of Capodimonte and Caserta in the late 'thirties and early 'forties. The revival of old patterns had, however, begun and soon cabinet-makers were everywhere busy producing solid *credenze*, *armadi* and *cassoni* to furnish houses in the 'Dantesque' fashion. Italy still rejoices in numerous craftsmen of great ability who work in a tradition which has been handed on from master to *garzone* for generations. The collector should, perhaps, be warned that many of them devote themselves to making furniture on old designs and with old materials.

Italian Cabinet-Makers: relatively few pieces of Italian furniture can be attributed to named cabinet-makers or designers. Household accounts of many great palaces record payments to the *intagliatori*, or wood carvers, and the same palaces are filled with furniture. But the task of associating the names of the craftsmen with the works they produced still remains to be done. Indeed, it is not until we reach the last years of the seventeenth century that it becomes possible to ascribe any individual pieces of Italian furniture to known craftsmen. Of these the most notable was probably the Venetian **Andrea Brustolon** (1662–1732), a highly accomplished sculptor in wood who executed the superbly fantastic chairs, *reggivasi* and *giridoni* supported by blackamoors, carved out of ebony and box wood, now in the Palazzo Rezzonico at Venice (Plate 83A). Chairs decorated with *putti*, and a grandiose looking-glass frame in the Palazzo Rezzonico have been attributed to **Antonio Corradini** (1668–1752), a Venetian sculptor who otherwise worked in marble. The notable Genoese wood sculptor **Anton Maria Maragliano** (1664–1739) may well have been responsible for some of the finely carved console tables supported by mythological creations in the palaces of his native city. Another Genoese sculptor, **Domenico Parodi** (1668–1740), carved a magnificent looking-glass frame for the Palazzo Balbi, now Reale (Plate 83D), at Genoa and may also have produced console tables. All these artists were, however, *intagliatori* rather than cabinet-makers and their works are distinguished primarily for the quality of the carving. Moreover, they are all, with the exception of Brustolon, better known for their statues than for their furniture.

Early in the eighteenth century the architects to the court of Savoy, **Filippo Juvarra** (1676–1736), designed furniture (Plate 84C,

Fig. 1. Design by Filippo Juvarra for a console table for the King of Savoy

Fig. 1) for the great palaces he built in and near Turin (see *The Connoisseur*, November, 1957). A little later the same court was served by **Pietro Piffetti** (c. 1700–77), the first Italian to merit the title of *ébéniste*. He was a brilliant craftsman, but his furniture looks fussy and over-elaborate, as he tended to sacrifice the general design to the details, concentrating on the exquisite panels of inlaid ebony, ivory and mother-of-pearl with which they were embellished (Plate 84B). **Francesco Ladatte** (1706–87), a notable sculptor in bronze, supplied the fine mounts for some of Piffetti's furniture. In Lombardy **Giuseppe Maggiolini** (1738–1814) produced furniture in the Louis XVI style, decorated with *intarsia* panels representing portraits, bunches of flowers and ruins. At about the same time, in Turin, **Giuseppe Maria Bonzanigo** (1744–1820) was producing a few exceptionally fine works in the same style, notably a secretaire and a firescreen (Plate 85E), which are carved with a delicacy and precision seldom equalled even in France. In 1782 the Lombard architect, **Giocondo Albertolli** (1742–1839), published the only important Italian pattern book of furniture designs which shows, perhaps, too strict a regard for archæological accuracy. During the Empire period fine furniture was produced at Lucca under the French *maître ébéniste*, **Youf,** and at Florence by the Italian **Giovanni Socchi** many of whose works are still in the Palazzo Pitti. (Plate 86c.)

BOOKS FOR FURTHER READING

MORAZZONI, GIUSEPPE, *Il Mobile Veneziane* (Milan, 1958); *Il Mobilio Italiano* (Florence, 1940); *Il Mobile Genovese* (Milan, 1949).

PIGNATTI, TERISIO, *Lo Stile dei Mobile* (Verona, 1951).

VIENNESE FURNITURE IN THE EIGHTEENTH CENTURY

By Dr FRANZ WINDISCH-GRAETZ

THE photographs accompanying this study show examples of furniture from the reigns of the Emperor Charles VI (1711–40), of the Empress Maria Theresa (1740–80) and of the Emperor Josef II (1780–90).[1]

The cultural life of Vienna in the eighteenth century reached a high degree of brilliance, and its traces still determine the character of the city today. The Court, the Church and the nobility contributed to her restoration and embellishment by their extensive rebuilding activities, in which the gentry joined in increasing numbers during the latter half of the century. Celebrated architects, especially Johann Bernhard Fischer v. Erlach (1656–1723), Johann Lucas v. Hildebrandt (1668–1745) and the former's son, Josef Emanuel Fischer v. Erlach (1693–1742), were destined to carry out the typical work of the period.

Vienna was the Emperor's official residence, and as such was the capital of the Holy Roman Empire as well as the capital of the Habsburg territories, which made her one of the most important political centres of Europe at that time. In addition to these political ties, which bound her to all countries, Vienna was also the focal-point of all-round artistic influences. Among them those of the Italian states and their leading art centres should be particularly mentioned, together with those of France.

As the great architects produced their imperial buildings and palaces for the nobility from a synthesis of ideas on secular monumental architecture, so the cabinet-makers evolved their furniture from a similar synthesis of ideas. Generally speaking, research has failed so far to trace the names of well-known Viennese craftsmen, as is the case in other countries.[2] With the help of illustrations we can now follow up the development of Viennese furniture.

Plate 87A: Writing-table with two Vase Stands (guéridons); Hofburg in Vienna. Height (of back), 116 cm.; width, 110 cm.; depth, 68 cm. Tin, brass, tortoise-shell and ebony; first quarter of the eighteenth century.

The ornamentation of rich foliage, scrollwork and palmettes corresponds to the French style propagated by Jean Bérain (1640–1711). The technique of using tortoise-shell inlay in connexion with metal is a form of decoration developed to perfection by André Charles Boulle (1642–1732), and was therefore named after him.

The style of Bérain also spread to Austria, so much so that his decorative treatment became the characteristic feature of the first four decades of the eighteenth century. This period was ruled entirely by his influence. His ideas were universally adopted for every kind of ornamentation and material, whether stucco or furniture intarsia. But the Boulle technique was restricted to the Court and to the highest circles of the nobility and the Church.

In fact, when it concerned an important order, Vienna so far recognized the artistic superiority and leadership of France as to submit to her influence in that respect. She thus showed her unbiased attitude to art even though the political relationship between the two countries was anything but cordial. The Imperial Court, and above all the Emperor himself, was on bad terms with France, particularly during the reign of Leopold I (1658–1705). The reason for this was the perpetual difficulties which Imperial policy had to meet from that quarter.

Though the décor is French, there is something fundamentally Viennese about the simplicity of construction, wherein all the usual sumptuousness of Paris is eliminated. This will be noticeable again in other examples.

Plate 94A and 94C: Furniture from the Schlosshof. These well-known pieces, of which the majority have remained intact in the Museum für angewandte Kunst and in the government furniture depository in Vienna, form part of the original contents of the hunting-lodge – the Schlosshof – near Vienna. This magnificent castle was designed by the celebrated architect Johann Lucas v. Hildebrandt, who had it built by order of Prince Eugene of Savoy during the years 1725–29. Its contents are probably of the same date or a little later; possibly *c.* 1730.

Armchair with high back (Plate 94A): overall height, 126 cm.; height of seat, 43 cm.; front width, 66 cm.; depth, 56 cm. Walnut. Side-chair (Plate 94C): overall height, 100 cm.; height of seat, 50 cm.; front width, 50 cm.; depth, 47 cm. Walnut. Stool (Plate 94C): height, 47 cm.; width and depth, 44 cm. Walnut, recovered; *c.* 1730.

These pieces reveal the extensive artistic horizon and extravagant taste of the princely owner of the Schlosshof. His foreign origin, his knowledge of the world and his patronages are reflected in the French (Plate 94A) and Italian (Plate 94C) influence in the form and in the exquisite manner of execution. The ideas are derived from the leading art centres which propagated the style of the period. The richly ornamented armchair (Plate 94A) is somewhat conservative and essentially of the beginning of the century. There are innumerable closely related examples in France. The other two (Plate 94C) have a more modern look about them, and their imaginative construction resembles Italian workmanship. It must be remembered that the contemporary furniture of Italy and France (of the 'Regence') is, on the whole, more pompous, more richly carved and more elaborately adorned with figure motifs, than the native Austrian.

Vienna, as the capital city of the Empire, could afford to allow those foreign ideas expression because her native talent and influence were strong enough to turn them to her own uses as and when she wished. She came to develop her great baroque architecture by the same process.

Plate 88A: Library Table with four Chairs. These are at the Oesterreichisches Museum für angewandte Kunst, Vienna. The four chairs, with their collapsible backs, can be drawn out of the hollow body of the table side. The corresponding parts of the table are attached to the back of each chair. Height, 82 cm.; length, 159 cm.; width, 112 cm. of the table top. Length, 137 cm.; width, 92 cm. of the lower plinth. Predominantly walnut. The lighter inlay of the table top is of maple, showing a checkered pattern and the inscription 'charitas'; date *c.* 1735.

This is part of a particularly beautiful suite of the Baroque period. The table belonged to the library set of the old University in Vienna.[3] The ceiling of the great apartment still shows the old fresco displaying the various branches of science in allegorical representations. It is signed and dated 'Anton Herzog, 1734'. The side walls were covered with bookcases from the ceiling to the floor, and the upper rows were accessible from a richly ornamented gallery.

But the interior architectural composition would not have been complete had only the ceiling and the walls been considered in the scheme. The furniture was to be so constructed as to correspond. It was made massive to match the solemn architecture. The great library table is made to look like an altar and resembles a sarcophagus, as was often the case with Baroque altars.

The idea of constructing such a table is in keeping with the typical Baroque conception of associating the real world with the world of ideas. The mythological imagery is so consistently related to real life by the allegorical interpretations in the painted ceiling that the solemn, altar-like shape of the table is inevitably made to blend with their illusionism and theatrical effect. The work which the scholarly artist carries out here under the eyes of his patrons becomes a ritual. It was to heighten the massive effect of the table that the chairs were constructed in such an original fashion. Thus there is nothing at all to disturb the architectural unity of the composition.

In Baroque composition, the nature and peculiarity of the material is of little importance compared to the ingenuity employed to arrive at the desired effect. Everything is entirely subordinated to the artistic and intellectual components of form. Here the wood is cleverly carved to look like the work of a sculptor, an illusion which demands great skill on the part of the cabinet-maker. But when the most ingenious technique is employed at the same time to embellish the surface of the wood in order to show its quality to the best advantage, the idea becomes a contradiction, which is one of the fascinating features of Baroque furniture.

The master craftsman of this table is not known. But since the library belonged to members of a religious order, it is probable that it, like the rest of the furniture in this apartment, was made by lay brothers of the community, as in the majority of similar cases in Austria. Its date of origin probably corresponds to that of the fresco (1734). The structure is in keeping with the architecture of that period, and has all the boldness of form characteristic of the Imperial style of Viennese Baroque introduced by Fischer v. Erlach.

Plate 87B: Corner Cupboard. At the Palais Harrach, Vienna. Height, 275 cm.; overall width, 78 cm.; overall depth, 41 cm. Predominantly walnut, combined with lighter shades of cherry. The lighter inlay, particularly the architectural motifs and the narrow banding on the door of the base section, is of maple; c. 1735-40.

This is a particularly original example of the classical style of Viennese Baroque. The composition is based entirely on architectural principles. The components are clearly grouped into sections, which become less heavy towards the top. The plinth is massive and more uniform, the middle section is more broken up by the shape of the recess and the decorative detail of inlaid motifs, which is brought to a head by the mobile design and plasticity of the crowning members.

Observe the varied use of scrolls. In the lowest section they merely serve as a pilaster base, in the main section they become important architectural and decorative components. Yet they are 'edged' and sharp. Only the top section shows the true moulding of a scroll breaking away with a smooth, elegant curve from the massiveness of the rest of the structure. The treatment of the wood is similar to the technique employed in the library table (Plate 88A), especially with regard to the pinnacle. Imaginative ingenuity is of primary importance: the material has to yield to skilful craftsmanship.

The inlay ornaments correspond to essential features of the first third of the century, the fine, clear lines on the door being derived from the banding commonly used. The architectural inlay is also taken from contemporary ideas, and includes the fretted panels of the dome and frieze, lattice-work in the pediment, a silhouetted string of bell-flowers (on the side of the pilasters) and the balustrade design.

Plate 92B: Secretaire Commode with Pediment (tabernacle). In the Oesterreichisches Museum für angewandte Kunst, Vienna. Overall height, 212 cm.; height of commode, 88 cm.; depth of commode (at sides), 59 cm.; depth of pediment (side), 30·5 cm. Walnut; c. 1735.

This is in the typical Viennese style of the latter period of Charles VI. The native craftsman uses his discretion when conforming to the general Baroque tendencies of vigorous movement, rich grouping and general usefulness. The last point is particularly well thought out and successfully achieved. This is confirmed by the great popularity of such pieces up to the present day. The bulbous and hollow surface curves are modified, the structure is complete and clearly defined, the inlay motifs are sporadic and full of movement, but not excessively so. This piece of furniture therefore represents a happy medium which distinguishes it as a product of the Imperial capital, where many potentialities and incentives meet and harmonize. With one swing of the pendulum we find influences from the north-east – the Netherlands – showing sometimes greater severity or a heavy, somewhat bombastic unwieldiness. With the other, the more elaborate forms, more costly materials, a profusion of ornaments and a lack of tectonics, often found in Italian and German furniture construction, tend to produce an ostentatious and unbalanced effect. French sumptuousness is also reduced to a happy medium with a certain savour of preciosity.

Plate 92A: Wardrobe of the latter Baroque period. In the Oesterreichisches Museum für angewandte Kunst, Vienna. Height, 226 cm.; width, 182 cm.; depth (side), 63 cm. Walnut and maple with rosewood veneering, graphic decoration; before 1740.

The door-panels are adorned with canopies, foliated scrolls, urns and lambrequins which are typical of the 'Regence'. On closer inspection, however, one notices a curious transformation about them. The foliage is less like a real plant, but more like graphic renderings of carvings. They have lost the realistic style of the beginning of the century. Moreover, there is a new form of moulded bracket (on the pilasters and bottom drawer) that tends to asymmetry. It is one of the first elements of *rocaille* ornamentation that seems to suggest a revival of seventeenth-century ornamentation, but which in fact corresponds to a new sense of movement and spaciousness, with a certain preference for the bizarre. This tendency also becomes apparent in the bulbous and hollow pilasters frequently recurring on very mannered early Baroque wardrobes. The acceptance of these particular decorative effects is a sure sign of a return to Mannerism. And what else, indeed, is the early approach of Rococo, if it is not a mannered, late form of Baroque? There is little change in the general structure of the wardrobe. It still retains all the massiveness, vigorous movement and bold grouping of the Baroque style.

Plate 90A: Upholstered Settee. Palais Schönborn, Vienna. Overall height, 96 cm.; height of seat, 45 cm.; height of arm-support, 79 cm.; length, 203 cm.; depth, 66 cm. Walnut, light gold relief on carvings; after 1740.

Plate 94A and 94C have already shown the extravagant elaboration of the majority of chairs. Their massiveness in particular gave ample scope to the skilled cabinet-maker in exploiting his fancy for a carved, plastic, decorative effect.

In place of earlier forms used by Bérain – palmettes, shells, masks, foliage and bandings – there appears a new motif, resembling shells and breakers, of a whimsical form which is in no way bound to conventions, and can therefore be used in every conceivable combination of ideas. This is the *rocaille* ornament, original and lavish. We now formally approach the Rococo. But the presumptuous appearance of this settee and its dimensions have nothing yet in common with the intimate character of Rococo and still look formal and solemn. In the Palais Harrach there is a wardrobe which is architecturally almost identical with the one shown in Plate 92A. One could well assume that they were both done in the same workshop. The ornaments, too, are engraved in both cases.

Nevertheless, there is the distinct difference that the décor consists of fully developed *rocaille*. At the same time the 'Regence' ornaments in the panels are replaced by figurative details and graceful little scenes adapted from the School of Watteau and his successors. The tester is crowned (Plate 94B) with imaginatively flourished, delicate carvings. All this is typical of Rococo.

There is probably a decade between the two wardrobes. In studying the development of the style of Viennese furniture, it should be observed that the embellishment is in accordance with the principles of the new fashion, whereas the basic structure remains essentially true to Baroque tradition.

Plate 94B: Four-post Bed. Palais Harrach, Vienna. Height of headboards, 202 cm.; width, 157 cm.; height of footboard, 115 cm.; width, 157 cm.; length, 210 cm.; height of

VIENNESE FURNITURE IN THE EIGHTEENTH CENTURY

canopy (including the 'vase' motif), 263 cm. Predominantly walnut, centre and side panels of maple, bandings of rosewood and maple. All carvings are of lime, walnut stained; posts of walnut, engravings on panels of maple. On the footboard and sides are pastoral scenes of the four seasons – flowers, corn-harvest, fruit and grape gathering, sledging scene. On the headboard is a shepherd and shepherdess representing the Madonna and Child. Its date is *c.* 1750.

This bed is decorated in the same style as the wardrobe in Plate 93B. The two belong together. The engraved ornaments are far more rich, intricate and imaginative than on the older wardrobe (Plate 92A), but not as precise and the figures are more primitive.

Apart from a strong element of rococo in the décor, the whole construction of the bed speaks quite a different language than would have been the fashion during the first four decades of the century. The decisive factor is that the contours have become soft and flowing. It is significant that the shape of the headboard follows the curvilinear movement of the floral design. From now on and during the Rococo period, severe construction gives way to an easy flowing outline which links up the *rocaille* ornamentation with a realistic treatment of floral motifs, and this is the most distinctive feature of the style of Rococo furniture. The turned members of the posts are characteristic of Viennese conservatism, a seventeenth-century motif.

Austrian furniture is rarely found to be so true to the French style of Rococo as to correspond to it both in construction and decorative treatment. As a rule, the French influence is restricted to the ornamentation, but is found there in great measure and a variety of ways. The Rococo period produced some of the finest and most successfully constructed examples of Viennese eighteenth-century furniture, and they still remain popular. The structure has not changed much, but the general appearance is softer and more graceful than it used to be. There is a strong international element about those period pieces that have more in common with the French style. This is only to be expected, as they belonged to a cosmopolitan and cultured section of the society. All the same, they are not excluded from this study.

Plate 91A: Open Armchairs. Palais Harrach, Vienna. (Left to right): Overall height, 87 cm.; height of seat, 42 cm.; front width, 62 cm.; depth, 53 cm. Overall height, 93 cm.; height of seat, 42 cm.; front width, 66 cm.; depth, 54 cm. Overall height, 85 cm.; height of seat, 42 cm.; front width, 60 cm.; depth, 53 cm. Beech, carved and gilded, recovered; date *c.* 1750. Observe the straight back of the centre chair and the curved hollowed one of the two others made to fit the figure of the occupant. The one in the centre therefore looks stiffer and more old fashioned. Another interesting point is the elegant continuity of the design, the *rocaille* ornament and realistic floral décor being in keeping with the whole construction. The latter is more typically Austrian than French in its ponderous and solid style.

Plate 87C: Small Bombé Commode. Palais Czernin, Vienna. Height, 95 cm.; overall width, 67 cm. diminishing to 40 cm. Rosewood of various kinds and colouring. Very fine ormolu mounts; *c.* 1750. Here the French influence is decidedly marked in the quality of the wood, the construction and finish of the mounts and the graceful contours of the body of the furniture. The swelling curve of the outline gives it a realistic, lively and unusual appearance.

Plate 90B: Rococo Settee. Palais Czernin, Vienna. Overall height, 94 cm.; height of seat, 40 cm.; overall width, 144 cm.; depth, 48 cm. Beech, walnut stained, caned seat and back; *c.* 1755. Compared with earlier examples, this piece of furniture is very typically Viennese in its simplicity and unpretentiousness. It is well balanced and elegant. The parallel spacing that runs all along between the edge of the seat and the back, from one arm-support to the other, accentuates the neatness. The moulded arm-support is made to resemble a small cushion and shows great originality.

Lacquer was a painting medium of great popularity in other countries – particularly in Italy where it produced some of the most enchanting results so typical of Venetian Rococo – but apparently found little support in Austria and Vienna. Neither are there many pieces extant which were decorated with lacquered work. There is one example where two table tops of the second quarter of the eighteenth century are decorated with flowers and chinoiserie of painted lacquer. They belong to a set of furniture from the porcelain room in the Palais Dubsky, Brünn.[4, 5] Not only are they carved and gilded, but small porcelain plaques are inserted into the wood. This was another very favourite decorative fancy for furniture at that time. In this case there are floral miniatures made by the Du Paquier porcelain factory in Vienna. The rare and costly material of these delicately coloured insertions raised the price of the furniture much above the usual. (In Venice, the town renowned for the finest glass, cut plate-glass was used to decorate furniture by the same method.) Although the set belonged to Brünn (it is now the property of the Museum für angewandte Kunst, Vienna), it can be assumed with certainty that most of the workmanship is Viennese.

There is another lacquered piece of a later date, in the same museum, which must originally have come from Austria, perhaps Vienna – a secretaire with a small cabinet on top, signed and dated *P. Georgius Henner e S.I. Anno* 1788. It shows very fine paintings of flowers, animals and allegorical figures in gold-framed fields, representing the four continents. The great beauty and originality of this piece makes up for the rare use of this technique in Vienna.[6]

Plate 93A: Rococo Tall Secretaire. Palais Schwarzenberg, Vienna. Overall height, 225 cm.; height of commode, 88 cm.; front width, 135 cm.; depth, 66 cm. Larger areas of alder, dark inlay of 'Palisander', light inlay of rosewood, cornice bordered with olivewood, mounts of a later date; *c.* 1760.

Here is a curious example, but typically Viennese, where the characteristic style of Rococo and the traditions of Baroque are combined. The first is noticeable in the carvings on the upper section and on the curved apron below. But it is above all marked in the shape and contours of the furniture itself, the kettle-shape of the sides, the serpentine front.

The endeavour to render the piece as generally useful as possible is traditional, in contrast to France where furniture is usually made for a specific purpose. The cabinet is furnished with drawers and compartments of many different sizes. To allow enough room for them, this section was made more massive. This gives it a slightly unbalanced appearance, but it is just that utility of the upper section which renders it so typically Viennese. The pilaster bases of the cabinet are again bulbous and hollow, like those of the Baroque wardrobe (Plate 92A), and this time even pierced. The interlaced rings and quatrefoil design are interesting features. The latter was a favourite French ornament of the style of Louis XVI. Should this and the strictly geometrical circles suggest perhaps the approaching change of style and diversion from the bizarrerie of Rococo? The use of native, less costly woods is another pointer in that direction. The mounts are already typically Josef II

Plate 89A: Dressing-table. Palais Schwarzenberg, Vienna. Height, 77 cm.; length, 94 cm.; depth, 53 cm. Cherry, cross-banded in plum wood. The centre of the top opens to display a mirror, the side members folding over to the left and right, uncovering two partitions of which one is deeper than the other. Its date is *c.* 1760.

The reigns of Maria Theresa and Josef II are marked by the reforms of both rulers. Josef II could never have become the reformer except for the first and probably decisive impulse given him by his Imperial mother. Both the liberal education he received from her and the example of her initial reforms in particular had a bearing on his later course of action. In fact, just as the reforms of Maria Theresa served to prepare for those of Josef II, so in the sphere of art the one reign led on to the other. The new style, named after the young Emperor, had already been initiated long before his reign, during the lifetime of his mother.

The reforms had a far-reaching effect on class distinction and social developments, including the standard of living and social customs. They are, therefore, found to have left as strong a mark on furniture and domestic arrangements. The appreciation of practical usefulness, simplicity and excellence, together with the tendency to give first consideration and prominence to everything native, is very much in evidence. The example (Plate 89A) shows this so clearly that comment is almost superfluous. The preference given to native products is found in the choice of woods employed. But this dressing-table is still essentially Rococo, and therefore of the period of Maria Theresa. A notable point is that the table edges and the legs appear to be inseparable, in each case one merges into the other. The usual rules of furniture construction normally applicable to these two component parts are here concealed in order to fulfil the aesthetic purpose of an easy flowing outline.

Another similar example is in the government furniture depository, a writing-desk which is said to have been used by the Emperor Josef II. The simplicity of design in combination with the principles of tradition and the use of cherry wood, all confirm what has already been said.[7]

Plate 94D: Side-chair. Palais Czernin, Vienna. Overall height, 98 cm.; height of seat, 50 cm.; width, 47 cm.; depth, 45 cm. Cherry, the carvings gilded; c. 1765. The curious thing about this is the combination of two styles in the construction and décor. The shape of the back is Rococo (Venetian influence?), so is the modest *rocaille* ornamentation. Yet the front legs and the decoration generally are typically Josef II.

Plate 88B: Open Armchair and Small Table. Oesterreichisches Museum für angewandte Kunst, Vienna. Overall height, 106 cm.; height of seat, 44 cm.; width, 68 cm.; depth, 58 cm. Height of table, 81 cm.; length, 89 cm.; width, 55 cm.; c. 1770. This set belonged to the Schlosshof, which, as has been said, was owned by Prince Eugene of Savoy. In 1775 it was bought by Maria Theresa, and in 1760 was rebuilt, enlarged and partly refurnished for the requirements of the Court.

The century-old differences between the two Courts and governments of Vienna and Paris were brought to an end at the treaty of alliance between Austria and France in 1756. Doubtless this also paved the way for a closer relationship between their culture and art, so that Vienna was much more ready to accept the artistic attitude of Paris from then onwards. This is evident in this set of furniture. The ornamentation is typically Louis XVI. But it must be remembered that Austria's classical tendencies were also to a great extent influenced by Italy, since Italy's ties with Vienna were as strong then as they had been before.

Now and again the habitual over-elaboration of the Baroque and Rococo ornamentation of the Imperial style continues to prevail as it is applied to the new decoration. The varied use of small detail and accumulation of motifs have little in common with the decorative treatment of French furniture. There the ornamentation is more discreet and delicate. These examples therefore mark a stage of transition to the more simple style of Josef II.

Plate 91B: Two Side-chairs and One Armchair. Palais Schwarzenberg, Vienna. (Left to right): Overall height, 91 cm.; height of seat, 46 cm.; front width, 43 cm.; depth, 42 cm. Mainly walnut, the turned members framing the back of lime. Writing armchair: overall height, 88 cm.; height of seat, 41·5 cm.; front width, 60 cm.; depth, 51 cm. Beech, walnut stained. Side-chair: Overall height, 91 cm.; height of seat, 45 cm.; front width, 45 cm.; depth, 41 cm. Cherry. Small carvings in a dark, painted softwood; c. 1765–80.

With these chairs we have reached the period of Josef II. The back of the centre chair may still show some form peculiar to Rococo, but the general design has no longer anything in common with the past. One of the most important features of the new style, and one that already determined the form of the two previous examples (Plate 94D and Plate 88B), is the manner in which the seat and legs are conjoined. There is no more of that easy flowing continuation and concealment shown in Plate 89A. The useful purpose of the seat, to carry weight, and its support are well defined in the structural design. The individual components of the piece of furniture are clearly differentiated.

The writing arm-chair in particular shows

211

that they were no longer interested in a coherent, continuing outline, though all the past had led in that direction. The joint of the arms and seat is obvious enough in the hard effect of the two supports. How different it would have been had it been Rococo!

The chair shown on the right of Plate 91B has a particularly interesting back. Its form shows a strong tendency to imitate the English style of Hepplewhite. But the result is coarser and heavier, in accordance with Viennese-Austrian preference for massiveness, plasticity and volume, though these attributes are by no means to be associated with stockiness or clumsiness, which is important. On the contrary, there is something graceful about it. In those days, English influence won more and more support in every sphere, and is, moreover, also expressed here in the desire to preserve the particular quality and beauty of the wood.

Plate 93B: Wardrobe. Palais Schwarzenberg, Vienna. Height, 208 cm.; width, 163 cm.; depth, 64 cm. Highly polished, solid oak with inlays of cherry and 'Palisander' (instead of ebony) and walnut. Carvings of solid oak; c. 1770–80.

There is here still much of the Baroque wardrobe: the pilasters on the corner edges and the centre piece, the solid base and cornice. But details are altered in accordance with the new style. This is particularly obvious in the cornice. The easy flowing composition of the top mouldings of Baroque and Rococo wardrobes is here converted into a straight crown of dentil moulding, which is far removed from the variety of shells and carvings. The panels also are no longer filled with interlaced designs. The main idea is to display the beauty of different kinds of wood in a framed décor. Veneering is so applied as to accentuate the grain of the wood at its best. Light-coloured, native wood is again in evidence.

Plate 89B: Commode. Palais Schwarzenberg, Vienna. Height, 87 cm.; width, 122 cm.; depth, 58 cm. Larger areas in 'Palisander', cross-banded with rose-wood, maple and dark-stained wood inlay; c. 1780–90.

The structural element and decorative treatment of this commode display features rarely found in Vienna. It is a pretentious piece of furniture, and the décor is distinctly Italian. There, and particularly in Lombardy, it was a common thing to find such a delicate, extravagant and somewhat sensuous form of classicism. It should be remembered that Lombardy was then a part of Austria and Vienna was always in close contact with her Italian provinces. Therefore the commode is another apt example of the liberal and unbiased attitude of the Habsburg capital in its relationship to all its peoples. Indeed, it was only to be expected that all the different trends which the cultural life of the monarchy had to offer should be reflected in one of the noblest estates of the land.

This survey of Viennese furniture, which concludes with the description of this period piece, was intended to cover the particular era of the eighteenth century which began when the spirit of Baroque and its influence on intellectual and social values was at its highest, and which ended when these were gradually giving way to the new trends of the emancipation and Classical period. The fundamental principles which led to the intellectual and social changes have been traced, and their tendency to move away from the rule of an hierarchical authority in order to make room for a natural, individual common-sense expression.

Just as the simplicity of Viennese furniture strikes us in comparison with the contemporary workmanship of other countries, so the very refusal to submit to an exaggerated pomp and refinement, together with the desire to reproduce the natural beauty of a well-balanced design, contributes most to its particular charm. Surely it is no mere coincidence to find this tendency most marked during the reign of so maternal a ruler as Maria Theresa, when furniture was constructed in a happy, gracious manner to suit the home and family in their intimate surroundings. This has remained a salient feature of Viennese furniture ever since.

NOTES

[1] Since 1765, German Emperor and co-ruler with his mother, Maria Theresa, his influence affected all the

activities of his subjects, and was as strongly felt in the sphere of culture.

[2] The two most important publications on Viennese furniture, though limited to time and subject-matter, are: Eduard Leisching (Vienna), *Theresianischer und Josephinischer Stil, Kunst und Kunsthandwerk*, XV, 1912, pp. 493-563 (Verlag von Artaria, Vienna). Also published in a separate issue (Staatsdruckerei, Vienna, 1912). Marianne Zweig, *Wiener Bürgermöbel aus Theresianischer und Josephinischer Zeit* (1740-90), Kunstverlag Anton Schroll, Vienna, 1921.

[3] Before its new erection on the Ring (1873-83), the University was housed in the extensive buildings of the Jesuit College, and the Jesuits were in charge of it until their religious order was dissolved in 1773. The library of this University was, therefore, also one of the most important of this order in Austria, and in its artistic excellence was clearly meant to compete with other beautiful monastic libraries in the country.

[4] The entire room, including the windows, doors, wainscoting, chimney (of porcelain) and the complete set of furniture were removed and re-installed in the Oesterreichische Museum für angewandte Kunst in Vienna.

[5] Julius Leisching (Brünn), *Das Brünner Porzellanzimmer aus Dubsky'schem Besitze*, Kunst und Kunsthandwerk, XVI, 1913, pp. 281-99 (Verlag von Artaria, Vienna).

[6] Eduard Leisching (Vienna), *Neuerwerbungen des K.K. Oesterreichischen Museums Seit Kriegsbeginn*, Kunst und Kunsthandwerk, XIX, 1916, pp. 185, 210, 215 (Verlag von Artaria, Vienna).

[7] Marianne Zweig, *Wiener Bürgermöbel, op. cit.* (note 2) Plate 49, p. 26.

The author wishes to acknowledge the help and assistance of his sister Princess Mathilde Windisch-Graetz in the translation of this article.

FRENCH FURNITURE

FROM 1500 TO THE REVOLUTION

By R. A. CECIL

To collectors and connoisseurs in England French furniture, and particularly that of the late seventeenth and eighteenth centuries, presents certain problems. Firstly, the range of materials employed on the embellishment of certain pieces extends far beyond wood; secondly, the wealth and admixture of motifs, veneers, inlays, and the profusion of metal ornament are often alien to English taste; and thirdly, the number of craftsmen to be found in Great Britain who are competent to appreciate and repair French furniture is still so small that valuable pieces are in constant danger of being badly treated with the wrong substances.

From the historical point of view, the various periods and styles have become so bound up with the reigns of the three Kings of France, Louis XIV, XV and XVI, that it is frequently difficult to realize that these styles and fashions in designing and decorating furniture often began long before, and ended long after, the rather arbitrary dates connected with them.

Nevertheless, the regnal divisions into which the subject has been conventionally split up have their uses in indicating the approximate style and period in which a piece of furniture may have been produced, and they have therefore been retained for the purposes of this study.

THE RENAISSANCE AND SEVENTEENTH CENTURY

In spite of the large amount of furniture which was made in France in the sixteenth century, not very much has come down to us, and what has is almost completely undocumented. We are thus very seldom in a position to say when a given piece of furniture was made, for whom it was made, or by whom. A great deal of research has at one time or another been devoted to distinguishing between the various provincial centres where furniture was produced in the sixteenth century – whether, for instance, at Lyons or in the *Ile de France* – but the theories put forward are not very convincing, and it is safer to assume that most of the best furniture was made in Paris and probably for the Court, and that such known provincial pieces are variations on a style existing at the central point.

By far the largest number of such pieces to have survived are made of walnut, usually elaborately carved. The most common piece is the dresser (q.v.), but tables, chairs, beds, cabinets and cupboards are also found. These take various forms and are often covered with carving, the dressers particularly receiving the most elaborate treatment in this respect.

The carving is usually in the Italian style, imported into France by the wars of Francis I, and the engravings of Du Cerceau and others were important in distributing knowledge of the motifs which were employed at Court. The absence of any local inspiration for design meant that the Court style became predominantly Italian in character, as did the architecture of the period also. Often a decorative motif on a piece of French Renaissance furniture is taken direct from a known Italian engraving or plaquette. It is also important to remember that furniture at this date was intended easily to be taken to pieces and moved about (hence the word *mobilier*), and this can almost always be done with the pieces which we are considering.

With the more secure ways of life which came in with the seventeenth century, furniture began to become more stable, and thus the opportunities for decoration more appropriate. But France sadly lacked the craftsmen to carry out the elaborate inlays which were the fashion in Italy and which were favoured at Court after the arrival of Marie de Médicis as Queen of Henri IV. Up to the foundation of the Gobelins factory in 1663, therefore, the period is one of constant infiltration of foreign craftsmen, from whom, of course, Frenchmen in the next generation were to learn much.

The engravings of Adam Bosse, however, show how sparsely furnished the rooms of the prosperous members of society were, and do not show the elaborate cabinets and *bureaux* which have come down to us, and which must have been not only rare luxury products but almost entirely made by foreign craftsmen. These often incorporate elaborate carving, marquetry, and also intricate mirror arrangements in the interiors. They are usually designated as French in the absence of knowledge as to who actually made them, but it seems likely that Italian and Flemish craftsmen must have been largely involved. The taste for the Italian style was further extended by the rise to power of Cardinal Mazarin, himself an Italian, whose personality dominated the French scene through the minority of Louis XIV.

THE LOUIS XIV PERIOD

Le Roi Soleil came to the throne in 1643 at the age of five. It can be well imagined therefore that the artistic characteristics which have become associated with his name did not come into existence at once. Indeed, the changes of style in furniture did not begin to appear until the King's majority and the establishment under Colbert of that great organization for the production of objects of art, the *Manufacture Royale des Meubles de la Couronne* at Gobelins in 1662. This foundation, as much an act of policy as everything else, was intended to co-ordinate control of all the applied arts in France to the glorification of the Crown and the State, and under its brilliant first director, Charles Le Brun, achieved its aim at least for a generation. The establishment of the *Manufacture* is, in fact, the cardinal event in the history of French decoration and furnishing, for it was under its aegis that all the foreign and native talent and experience which had been employed for two generations previously was incorporated and made to serve as a foundation for the establishment of new standards of taste and craftsmanship, this time wholly French in style and intended to serve a national aim.

As is well known, the first great task awaiting the *Manufacture* soon after its foundation was the decoration and furnishing of the new palace at Versailles, which was to become the cradle of French decorative taste for the centuries to come, and to demand an output of lavish expenditure unparalleled in history. It is only the more unfortunate that almost all the furniture produced during the first years of the *Manufacture*'s existence has disappeared, and even the celebrated silver furnishings of Versailles were later all melted down to provide bullion to support the various wars of the later years of the reign.

What remains, then, must be regarded as only a fraction of what once existed, and by far the most important series of furnishings which have come down to us are the productions of the workshop of André Charles Boulle (1642–1732), the most celebrated cabinet-maker of the whole period, and the great exponent of the marquetry which bears his name. Boulle was trained under foreign influences, and his achievement lies in his adaptation of foreign techniques to his own original ideas, and to the combination of a new monumentality and elegance of design with a perfection of craftsmanship in a very complicated and elaborate technique.

In his early years he almost certainly worked in wood marquetry, following designs similar to those produced in Italy and Flanders, and to this was sometimes added the use of small amounts of metal for decorative purposes; but the intricate marquetry of tortoiseshell and brass with which we associate his name is, to all intents and purposes, an individual creation.

The principal innovations in furniture design during the period were first of all the chest of drawers, or *commode*. It can be said to date from about 1700, though it probably did not come into general use until rather later. The other main type to be evolved was that of the writing-table, or *bureau*. This first begins to appear before the turn of the century in the form of a table-top with two sets of drawers beneath, flanking a knee-hole, and later took on its more usual form of a flat table with shallow drawers under the top.

The demand for Boulle furniture diminished in the middle years of Louis XV's reign but returned in full force in the last quarter of the eighteenth century, when the neo-classical style came into its own. Often the same designs, motifs and techniques were used, and it is sometimes extremely difficult to be certain in which period a piece was made when the quality of marquetry and bronze are the same.

It must be remembered that all furniture at this time, and indeed later, was made in order to harmonize with the rich carving and painted decoration of the setting for which it was intended, and designs which may appear over-elaborate when isolated would often seem at home in their original positions.

THE LOUIS XV PERIOD

When considering the characteristics of anything connected with what has become known as the Louis XV or rococo styles in France, it is important to remember that their evolution was gradual, and indeed began some years before the date when the *Grande Monarque* actually died. The genesis of rococo design can, in fact, be traced back to the last years of the seventeenth century, and the engraved compositions of an artist such as Jean Berain provide ample evidence of the new feeling which finally usurped the classicism, formality and monumentality exemplified by the creation of Versailles.

It was, however, the removal in 1715 of the central personality in the formal and centralized Court and Government, and the succession of a small boy, with the consequent reign of a pleasure-loving Regent, which provided the circumstances for the change in taste which can be so readily observed in the years which immediately followed. It is, however, a mistake to isolate the style of the Regency with what followed and to try to identify objects as belonging to the *Style Régence* unless they can be proved to have been created within the years 1715 to 1725. It is much more sensible to regard the products of these years as the first-fruits of what was to become the *Style Louis Quinze* proper, and the absence of documentary evidence providing the necessary dating makes this course more prudent.

The new style inevitably, however, received its first impetus from the Court of the Regent Orléans at the Palais Royal, and almost at once there is a lightness to be observed in interior decoration and furniture. The relaxation of the rigid etiquette of the Louis XIV's court, caused apartments, and therefore furnishings, to be smaller and less formal, and gave opportunities for lightness, fantasy and colour impossible twenty years before. Gradually, therefore, the heavy monumental furnishings made for Versailles at the Gobelins gave place to smaller, more elegantly contrived pieces suited to the lighter and more informal atmosphere of the new type of interior decoration.

More and more, furniture was adapted and decorated to harmonize with wall decoration, which, being also almost exclusively of wood, created a harmony of design and craftsmanship never equalled outside France. The Boulle technique passed temporarily out of fashion, though the *atelier* continued to produce furniture throughout the eighteenth century and Boulle himself did not die until 1732. The new taste favoured elaborate wood marquetry overlaid with delicate gilt-bronze mounts, and during the period the combination of these types of decoration reached a perfection of design and execution only surpassed by the subsequent period. The opening up of trade routes with the Far East brought a large number of oriental goods on to the home market, with the result that a taste for lacquer was created, both applied in the original from China or Japan, or imitated in France and applied locally. A number of oriental woods useful for marquetry were also imported, notably kingwood and, later, purple-wood, which was used very widely. Other woods used for veneering and inlaying were tulip-wood, hazelwood, satin-wood, casuarina and sycamore, often mixed in elaborate floral, pictorial or geometrical designs, framed with fillets of box and holly. The range of design was very wide and soon began to be used with remarkable skill.

Apart from relaxation in formality, the earlier part of the reign did not witness any very startling change in the actual types of furniture used, and the forms prevalent under Louis XIV still lingered on, particularly the wardrobe, or *armoire*, and the chest of drawers. The former, however, while keeping its monumental proportions, was often constructed of plain wood undecorated except for carving; while the latter underwent a number of changes in design. The main tendency was for straight lines and flat surfaces to become curved and *bombé*, and for the functional purposes of the piece to be concealed beneath the general scheme of decoration. The two commodes on Plate 96 show these characteristics well, the divisions between the drawers being invisible beneath the designs of the marquetry and mounts. There is, however, not one straight line to be found on either piece. The extreme rococo tendency towards asymmetry did affect mounts and *bronzes d'ameublement*, though not for very long.

The latter part of the reign, with its increase of luxury expenditure, saw the creation of a large number of new types of furniture, mainly small, and nearly always intended for female use. The *secrétaire à abattant* began to appear in the fifties, also the *bonheur du jour*, the *bureau-toilette*, work-tables and other pieces, while commodes, chairs, sofas and *bronzes d'ameublement* of all kinds were produced in large quantities. This is the period also of the greatest *ébénistes*, including Oeben, Riesener, Leleu, Dubois and others, and it is in the sixties that foreign craftsmen, particularly Germans, began to arrive in Paris to seek their fortunes, usually finding them, in the profusion of demands for furniture.

Madame de Pompadour played a large part in forming the taste of her time by her constant purchases of objects of all kinds and the *Livre-Journal* of Lazare Duvaux, from whom she bought so much, gives a very clear picture of how much money was spent. She was not responsible for the introduction of the neo-classic Louis XVI style, however, as she died in 1764, and many of the portraits of her, even just before her death, show her surrounded by furniture, particularly in the advanced Louis XV style.

A word should be said here about the actual creation of a piece of eighteenth-century French furniture. First of all a designer, sometimes the *ébéniste* himself, though sometimes equally a decorator, produced a drawing of the piece. This was then made by an *ébéniste* in wood, veneered and inlayed if necessary. Mounts and fittings were then produced by a sculptor and a *fondeur*, and if required were gilded by a *doreur*, thus often involving members of three craft guilds and two artist designers. Occasionally painters were also involved, thus bringing in yet another guild. When one considers the number of different craftsmen employed on a single piece of furniture, the harmony and perfection so often achieved are the more remarkable.

THE LOUIS XVI PERIOD

As is well known, the main characteristic of the Louis XVI style is the return to classical forms and motifs after the exuberance and fantasy of the rococo. This tendency begins to make itself felt at least twenty years before Louis XV died, and it is indeed this particular regnal division which is so misleading. Between 1750 and 1774 a very large amount of furniture was made incorporating classical tendencies, and it is most important to realize this when attempting in any way to date a given piece of furniture from stylistic evidence. The change of taste was very gradual, as the artistic writings of the time show, and, as elsewhere in Europe, was motivated very largely by the discovery of the Roman remains in the old Kingdom at Naples, at Pompeii and Herculaneum. The subsequent interest in classical subjects aroused by such writers as de Caylus and the contempt poured on the rococo also played its part. From a purely stylistic point of view it can be said that the Louis XV style proper had worked itself out and the return to classicism came therefore as a necessary reaction, and antidote. In spite of the enormous expenditure on furniture in the seventies, both by the Court and private patrons, no very striking innovations took place in actual furniture design. The main feature of the reign was, however, the perfecting of processes used hitherto to an unprecedented degree. This is particularly the case with ormolu, which has never attained before or since such refinement as it did at the hands of Gouthière, Thomire, Forestier (q.v.), and others. Apart from the elaboration and refinement of marquetry, plain woods, and particularly mahogany, begin to be used as veneers, and the rather controversial embellishment of furniture with porcelain begins to make its appearance. The large number of German *ébénistes* increased, of which Weisweiler and Beneman (q.v.) were probably the most celebrated. The work of Jacob in making chairs also reached its highest peak, and Boulle furniture became fashionable again and was produced in large quantities.

The influence of Queen Marie Antoinette on the taste and craftsmanship of her time, with particular reference to furniture, has often been stressed. It is true that she employed extensively and lavishly the incomparable craftsmen whom she found in Paris on her arrival as Dauphine, but, apart from this expenditure and a liking for beautiful objects, it is doubtful if she possessed any real understanding of the visual arts, and she certainly was no rival of Madame de Pompadour in this respect. It has also been suggested that her nationality attracted many German-born craftsmen to Paris but, in fact, the influx of foreign workmen had started and become an established fact long before there was any question of her being Queen of France. She undoubtedly did employ Riesener, Weisweiler and Beneman very extensively, but chiefly because of their qualities as craftsmen, and only then on the advice of the *Garde Meuble*.

AUTHOR'S NOTE

I would like to acknowledge with gratitude the assistance I have received from the writings and advice of Mr F. J. B. Watson in compiling this article.

FRENCH CABINETMAKERS AND CRAFTSMEN

BENEMAN, Jean Guillaume
German by birth. Came to Paris *c.* 1784 but seems to have been trained prior to this date, when he is first mentioned as being employed by the *Garde Meuble de la Couronne*. In 1785 he became a *maître-ébéniste* but without going through the normal formalities. His employment by the Crown coincides with the disfavour into which Riesener fell owing to his high charges. Beneman made a large amount of furniture for Queen Marie Antoinette and the Court, and was employed also to repair earlier furniture in the possession of the Crown. He collaborated with all the leading craftsmen of the time, including Boizot and Thomire, but his furniture retains usually a rather heavy Teutonic appearance. He seems to have specialized in making commodes and *meubles d'entre deux*. He was officially employed under the Directoire and Consulate, but his name disappears about 1804. He used the stamp:

G·BENEMAN

BOULLE, André Charles
Born in Paris in 1642, the son of a carpenter, and died there in 1732. His training was very various, and he appears to have worked at different times as a painter, architect, engraver and bronze worker, as well as an *ébéniste* of importance. He worked as an *artisan libre* from 1664 onwards, but in 1672 he was appointed *ébéniste du Roi* through the intervention of Colbert. From this time he worked continually for the Crown and established a workshop in which he employed about twenty assistants, who were constantly at work providing furniture for the new palace at Versailles.

Boulle did not invent the marquetry which has become associated with his name, the combination of metal and tortoiseshell in the form of an inlay being used since the sixteenth century in Italy and Flanders; but he did evolve a particular type which he adapted to the taste and requirements of the time.

He possessed a large collection of old master drawings from which he may easily have drawn inspiration for his mounts. His ingenuity as a designer was very great, as can be seen from a series of engravings which he published, and from a number of his drawings which exist. But throughout his career his actual style changed very little. He never signed his work and his authenticated productions are very rare. The only pieces which can be said definitely to be by him are two commodes originally made for the Grand Trianon and now in the palace at Versailles.

CAFFIÉRI, Jacques
Born 1678, son of Philippe Caffiéri, and came from a large family of sculptors. Became one of the chief

FRENCH FURNITURE

(A) Writing-table (*bureau-plat*) of deal veneered with ebony and Boulle marquetry of a general type, showing the Louis XIV development of this type of furniture. *Wallace Collection, London.*

(B) Chest of drawers (*commode*), veneered on oak with mahogany, and stamped by J. H. Riesener. *Wallace Collection, London.*

PLATE 97

FRENCH FURNITURE

French toilet mirror of oak veneered with ebony and Boulle marquetry of brass on tortoiseshell. A good example showing marquetry of a design in the manner of Jean Bérain. *Wallace Collection, London.*

Wardrobe (*armoire*) veneered on oak with ebony and Boulle marquetry of brass and tortoiseshell. Attributed to André Charles Boulle and perhaps made for a member of the Royal Family. A perfect specimen of the monumental style of the Boulle *atelier*. *Wallace Collection, London.*

PLATE 99

FRENCH FURNITURE

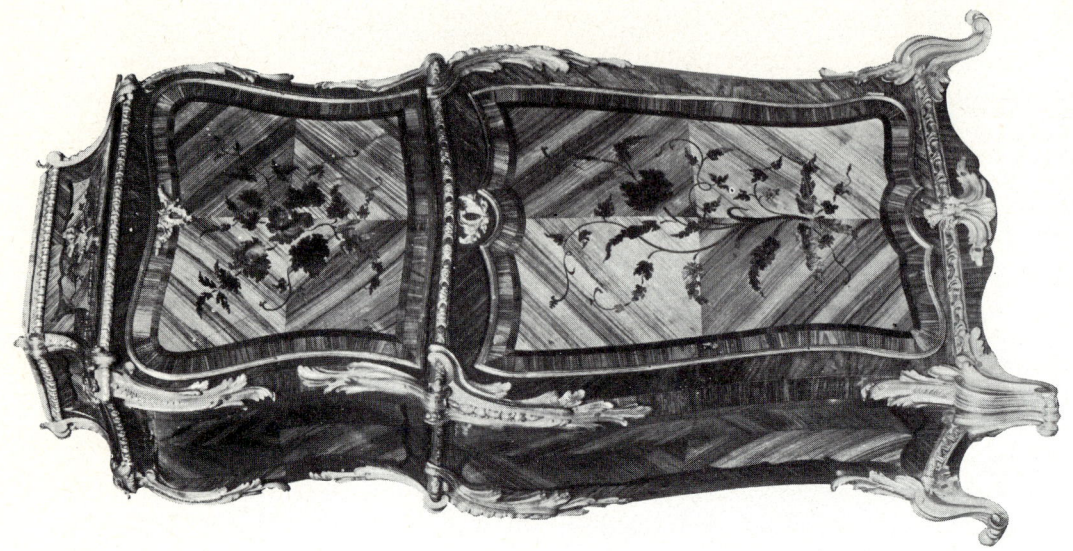

(B) *Secrétaire* veneered with tulip-wood and king-wood, and mounted with ormolu. A typical Louis XV design, *Victoria & Albert Museum (Jones Collection)*

(A) *Secrétaire à abattant* made by J. H. Riesener in 1780 for the use of Queen Marie Antoinette at Versailles. Repaired by G. Beneman in 1788 and moved to Saint Cloud. A particularly fine example of this type of piece. *Wallace Collection.*

PLATE 100

FRENCH FURNITURE

(A) Combined work-, writing- and reading-table veneered on oak with tulip-wood and mounted with plaques of Sèvres porcelain. By M. Carlin. *Wallace Collection, London.*

(B) Arm-chair of birch carved, gilt, and upholstered with Beauvais tapestry. Stamped by G. Jacob. A typical product of the Jacob *atelier. Wallace Collection, London.*

PLATE 101

FRENCH FURNITURE

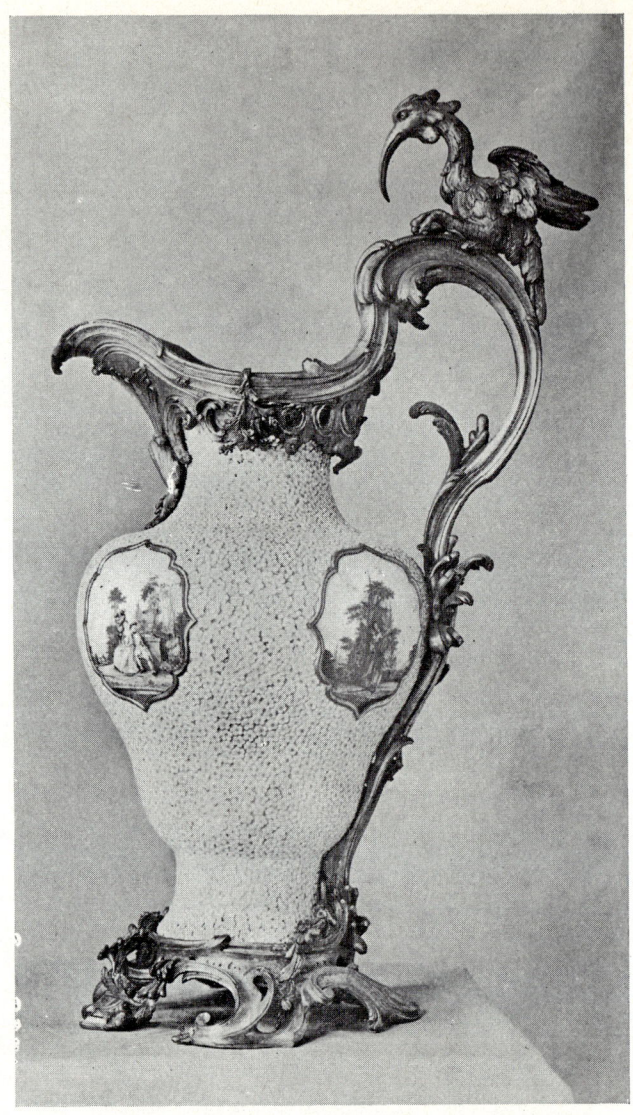

(B) Ewer of Meissen porcelain mounted with ormolu, and made between 1745 and 1749. *Wallace Collection.*

(A) Cartel Clock. The case made by C. Cressent, c. 1747. A particularly fine example of a Louis XV clock-case. *Wallace Collection.*

PLATE 102

FRENCH FURNITURE

French mantel clock of ormolu, perhaps by P. P. Thomire. *Wallace Collection, London.*

PLATE 103

FRENCH FURNITURE

(A) Wall-light (*applique*) of ormolu in the manner of J. Caffiéri. *Wallace Collection.*

(B) Candelabrum of ormolu in the manner of P. Gouthière. *Wallace Collection.*

(C) Fire-dogs (*chenets*) of ormolu. Attributed to J. Caffiéri. *Wallace Collection.*

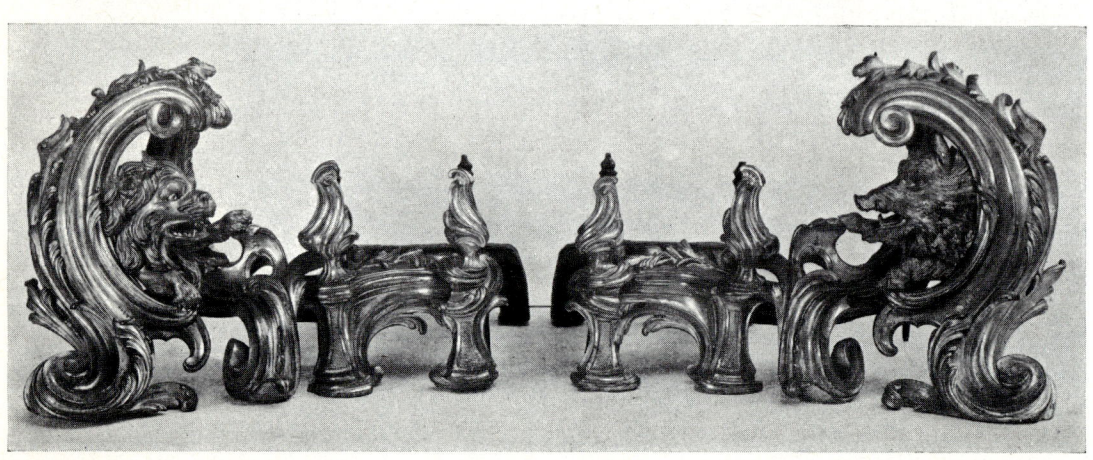

CHEST FURNITURE

Chest fitted with a tea equipage in Dresden porcelain. Eighteenth century.

PLATE 105

CHEST FURNITURE

Writing box or table desk covered with painted and gilt leather and bearing the heraldic badges of Henry VIII and Katherine of Aragon. 16 × 11½ × 9½ in., c. 1525. *Victoria & Albert Museum.*

PLATE 106

CHEST FURNITURE

(A) A fitted compendium, second quarter of the nineteenth century. Rosewood inlaid with pearl. Red leatherwork, stamped in gold, the fittings are of cut steel. *Presented to Bethnal Green Museum by Her Majesty Queen Mary.*

(B) Cabinet covered in raised needlework known as stump work. On the left Eliezer offers betrothal gifts to Rebecca, and on the front Abraham kneels to an angel. An unusual feature is the tray set out as a formal garden. Late seventeenth century. *Victoria & Albert Museum.*

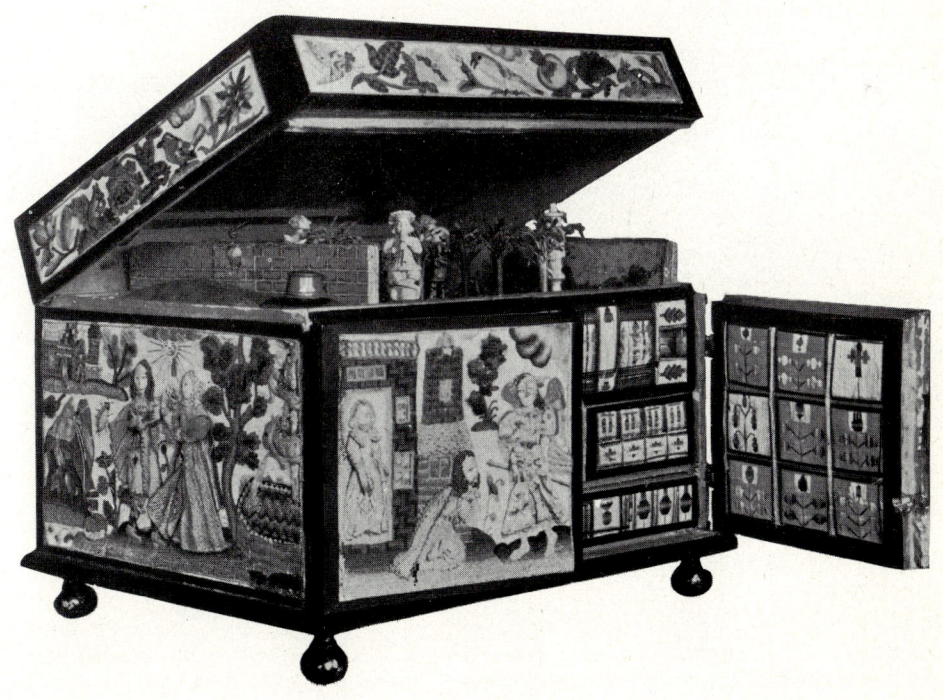

PLATE 107

(A) A superb casket equipped for various hobbies, covered with pearl and ormolu, made by Nicholas Rozet at Vienna in the first half of the nineteenth century. *By gracious permission of Her Majesty the Queen.*

(B) 'Lace box' covered with floral marquetry of a shape that would have proved equally convenient for writing equipment. Early eighteenth century. *Victoria & Albert Museum.*

CHEST FURNITURE

(A) Cabinet and boxes in Tunbridge ware marquetry showing the shaded-cube effect and vandykes, and, at the back, the marbled effect created by cutting the veneer from the glued-together shavings of the variously coloured natural woods. *Tunbridge Wells Museum.*

(B) Writing-box and associated woodwork decorated with elaborate Tunbridge ware, the mosaics of naturally coloured woods worked into popular souvenir views. The writing box shows Battle Abbey, the tray Hever Castle before restoration, the boxes, below, Eridge Castle and Penshurst Place. *Tunbridge Wells Museum.*

(D) Writing box of papier-mâché with a sloping hinged lid most delicately painted. *Victoria & Albert Museum.*

(C) Cabinet or casket ornamented with straw-work in dark and light tones of green, red and blue. Attributed to French prisoners of war, *c.* 1800. *Bethnal Green Museum.*

PLATE 109

CHEST FURNITURE

(A) Cabinet enriched with oyster veneers and the early naturalistic style of marquetry. Below the frieze drawer the front opens downwards, hinged at the bottom, to reveal eighteen short drawers and one long one for coins or similar curios. *Mallett & Son.*

(B) Cabinet enriched with oyster veneers and marquetry; another view, showing the front open. *Mallett & Son.*

CHEST FURNITURE

(A) Writing-box, of ash, decorated with glued pear-wood, bogwood, etc. Length 30½ in., depth 22 in., height 10 in. Early seventeenth century. *Victoria & Albert Museum.*

(B) Blanket chest in the mule chest tradition made of mahogany, on its own cabriole legs. Early Georgian. *John Bell Collection.*

(D) Papier-mâché cabinet of the early nineteenth century. Decorated with gold and slabs of shell tinted with transparent paints.

(C) Travel chest that expands into a writing desk. The lid may be opened to make two table flaps and the legs fold flat. *John Bell Collection.*

PLATE III

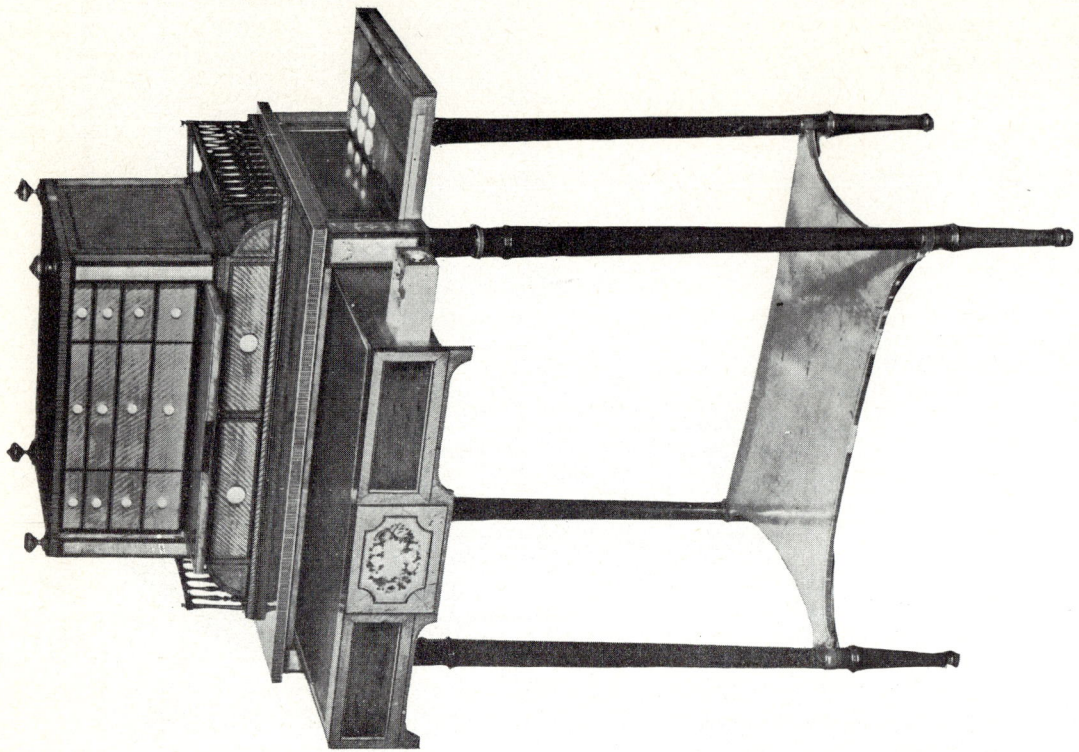

(B) Writing equipment at its most elaborate – a charming little *bonheur du jour*, the pull-out writing drawer fitted with a tiny ink-well drawer, painting equipment at the side and the table section topped by a fall-front cabinet. *Mallett & Son.*

(A) Cabinet in filigree paper work. Both cabinet and stand are covered in designs created with rolls of paper around pictorial medallions. Late eighteenth century. Height 58 in. *Lady Lever Art Gallery.*

exponents of the rococo style in France and was employed extensively by the Crown at Versailles, Fontainebleau and elsewhere. He also occasionally worked as a portrait sculptor. He often signed his bronzes with his surname only, and his chief works are to be found at Versailles, the Louvre, Paris, the Wallace Collection, and elsewhere. Died 1755.

His son, Philippe Caffiéri, was also a sculptor of note, and occasionally collaborated with his father in bronze work.

CARLIN, Martin
Very little is known about the life of Carlin. His place and date of birth are unknown. He died in Paris in 1785. He is first mentioned in 1763 and became a *maître-ébéniste* in 1766. He worked for Queen Marie Antoinette and the Royal Family, but it is uncertain whether he received an official appointment with the *Garde Meuble*. He supplied a large amount of furniture through the dealer Darnault.

Carlin was a most refined and delicate craftsman. He worked particularly in lacquer and with plaques of Sèvres porcelain.

CRESSENT, Charles
Born at Amiens in 1685, the son of François Cressent, a sculptor, and grandson of a cabinet-maker. He was apprenticed to his father, but probably learned cabinet-making from his grandfather. He became a member of the *Académie de Saint Luc* in Paris in 1714, and in 1719 married the daughter of Joseph Poitou, an *ébéniste* working for the Duc d'Orleans, and he also at this time was given commissions by the Regent. After this he seems officially to have abandoned sculpture for *ébénisterie*, but he was several times prosecuted by the *Corporations des Fondeurs* and *Doreurs* for casting and gilding his own mounts. In 1723 he was actually forbidden by law to produce mounts not made by a qualified *fondeur*. This type of litigation was repeated from time to time throughout his life.

The Regent died in 1723 but Cressent continued service with his son Louis, Duc d'Orleans, as late as 1743, on the Duc's retirement from public life. He also worked for important private patrons in France, and carried out important commissions for King John V of Portugal and the Elector Karl Albert of Bavaria. With the profits from the sale of his furniture Cressent formed an impressive collection of works of art, which he three times tried unsuccessfully to sell owing to financial difficulties. The first sale in 1748 was, in fact, withdrawn owing to fresh orders received for work. Cressent died in 1768.

His best work is never stamped. Towards the end of his life he did use the stamp: C. CRESSENT, but it never appears on pieces of very great quality and should always be treated with suspicion in view of his fame in his lifetime and later. The identification of his work therefore depends almost entirely on documents and tradition.

DUBOIS, Jacques and Réné
Jacques Dubois was born in Paris c. 1693. He became a *maître-ébéniste* in 1742, and was elected a *juré* of the guild in 1752. He specialized in the use of lacquer both Oriental and European, and died in 1763, the same year as Oeben, whose stock he helped to value. He used the stamp:

FRENCH FURNITURE

IDUBOIS

After his death his widow carried on the business with the help of her sons, the most celebrated of which was Réné (born 1757), who always used his father's stamp. He became a *maître* in 1754, was much patronized by Marie Antoinette, both before and after she became Queen, and also by the Court and nobility. He worked mainly in the Louis XVI style and eventually abandoned cabinet-making for selling furniture. He died in 1799.

FORESTIER, Étienne Jean and Pierre Auguste (1755–1838)
Two brothers, the sons of Étienne Forestier (c. 1712–68). All three were *fondeurs-ciseleurs*, and after the father's death his widow carried on the business with her two sons. Their names constantly occur in the Royal accounts, and they are known to have worked at Versailles and Compiègne, and for the Prince de Condé. After the Revolution, Pierre Auguste established a successful workshop, supplying furniture, *bronzes d'ameublement*, etc.

GAUDREAU, Antoine Robert
One of the most celebrated of the known *ébénistes* of the Louis XV period. He was born c. 1680, and was in the Royal service from 1726. He became a *syndic* of the *ébénistes* guild in 1744, and worked for the Crown and also later for Madame de Pompadour. Among his most important works are a medal cabinet and a commode, which were made for the King's private apartments at Versailles. On the latter he collaborated with J. Caffiéri, who signed the bronzes. It is now in the Wallace Collection (Plate 96A). He died in 1751.

GOUTHIÈRE, Pierre
The most celebrated of the late eighteenth-century *fondeurs-ciseleurs-doreurs*. Born at Bar-sur-Aube in 1732, the son of a saddler. He is known to have been in Paris by 1758, where he became a *maître-doreur*. He was employed by the Crown between 1769 and 1777, but after the latter date his name disappears from the Royal accounts. He had, however, a large number of private patrons, including the Duc d'Aumont and the Duchesse de Mazarin. He also worked for Madame du Barry at Louveciennes. He was constantly in difficulties financially, and his patrons were almost always behind with their payments. In 1788 he was declared bankrupt, and he never completely recovered, although he lived on until 1813 and died in poverty. Gouthière's signed works are exceedingly rare and can be supplemented by a few which are able to be identified by documents. Almost all bronzes of any quality of the Louis XVI period have been attributed to him, and it is only recently that the increased study of the Royal accounts have revealed the names of other *ciseleurs-doreurs*, who seem to have been his equals in many cases, even though we know little more than their names.

The attributions of bronzes to Gouthière on grounds of style alone should be made with great caution.

JACOB, Georges
Was born in Burgundy in 1739 and died in Paris in

1814. Little is known of his early life, but he was the founder of a long line of makers of furniture who specialized in the production of chairs. He is thus usually thought of as *menuisier*, although he did carry out some works in the *ébéniste*'s technique. He was made a *maître-ébéniste* in 1765 and carried on his business in his own name until 1796, when he sold it to his two sons, Georges II and François Honoré. On the former's death in 1803 the latter took the name of Jacob-Desmalter and joined with his father until the latter's death in 1814. He then carried on the business himself until 1824, and his son continued it up to 1847. The first Jacob was a craftsman with an extraordinary wealth of invention, and his designs for chairs are of the utmost elegance, but are also pleasantly varied so that they do not often repeat themselves. He also made a number of beds, which show the same qualities. He worked extensively for the Crown and in consequence was denounced at the Revolution, in spite of his friendship with the painter Jacques Louis David. His own work is usually stamped:

G ♦ I A C O B

LELEU, Jean François
Born in Paris in 1729, and died there in 1807. Trained under J. F. Oeben (q.v.), after whose death in 1763 he hoped to be chosen to take over the direction of the workshop. Oeben's widow's choice, however, fell on Riesener, whom she married, and Leleu never became reconciled to this. He became a *maître-ébéniste* in 1764, and worked both for the Court and for private patrons. He was also employed by Queen Marie Antoinette, Madame du Barry, and the Prince de Condé. He became successively *juré* and *député* of the *ébénistes*' guild, and in 1780 went into partnership with his son-in-law, C. A. Stadler, who succeeded to the business in 1792.

Leleu was a very versatile craftsman and worked in a number of styles; he seems to have been as equally at home in the advanced rococo as with the most severe neo-classic, and he also used Boulle marquetry and Sèvres porcelain to decorate his furniture. He used the stamp:

J·F·LELEU

OEBEN, Jean François
Born c. 1720, the son of a postmaster at Ebern in Franconia. He married in Paris in 1749, but we do not know the date of his arrival there from Germany. He entered the workshop of C. J. Boulle in 1751, and on the latter's death in 1754 Oeben succeeded him as *ébéniste du Roi* and was granted lodgings at the Gobelins, whence he moved in 1756 to the Arsenal. While working for Boulle, he was also employed by Madame de Pompadour and others, and after his move to the Gobelins he began in 1760 his most celebrated work – the monumental *Bureau du Roi Louis XV*, which, however, was not completed until after his death. Riesener, who was one of his assistants, succeeding him at the Arsenal, together with Leleu. Oeben also collaborated with Carlin and with P. Caffieri. He died bankrupt in Paris in 1763, when his widow carried on the business until 1767, when she married Riesener, who then carried on the business in his own name.

Oeben only became a *maître-ébéniste* in 1761 under special circumstances, having worked for the Crown for so long. His stamp on furniture is therefore rare, and when found it is more probable that the piece was made by Riesener before he took over the business, as Madame Oeben continued to use her husband's stamp while running the workshop herself.

After Cressent and Gaudreau, Oeben is the most celebrated *ébéniste* of Louis XV's reign. He specialized in elaborately-planned pieces, fitted with secret drawers and complicated locking devices, but, owing to the amount of furniture which must necessarily have left his workshop unstamped, his work cannot easily be identified.

RIESENER, Jean Henri
The most famous *ébéniste* of the eighteenth century in France. Born at Gladbeck, near Essen, in 1734, but it is not known when he came to Paris. He entered Oeben's workshop at the Gobelins about 1754, and moved with him to the Arsenal. At Oeben's death he was selected by the widow to take over the workshop, and he married her in 1768, the year when he became a *maître-ébéniste*. In 1769 Riesener completed the great *Bureau du Roi Louis XV*, which his predecessor had left unfinished (*see under* Oeben). In 1774 he succeeded Joubert as *ébéniste du Roi*, and for ten years enjoyed the patronage of the Crown to a hitherto unprecedented degree, as expenditure during that decade was higher than it had ever been. His wife died in 1776, and seven years later he remarried, but unhappily.

After 1784 his prosperity began to decline and he was made drastically to reduce his prices by the Treasury. It was at this time that Beneman to a certain extent succeeded him in the favour of the Court. Queen Marie Antoinette, however, seems to have remained faithful to Riesener throughout, for she continued to order furniture from him right up to the Revolution.

He continued in business during and after the Revolution but never actually reinstated himself. He seems to have retired in 1801 and died in Paris in 1806.

Riesener's stamp appears frequently on furniture of all kinds in the Louis XVI period, but it is probable that works bearing Oeben's stamp may also be by him, and made while he was working for Madame Oeben before their marriage (*see* Oeben).

J·H·RIESENER

He was the most versatile, and became the most accomplished *ébéniste* of the time, and certainly deserved the success he obtained. His work covers nearly all types of furniture in use, and he specialized in highly elaborate marquetry, mostly in geometrical designs.

THOMIRE, Pierre Philippe
Born 1751, the son of a *ciseleur*. Worked under the sculptors Pajou and Houdon. In 1783 entered the service of the Sèvres porcelain factory. From 1784 onwards he was frequently employed by the Crown to make mounts for furniture, and often collaborated with G. Beneman. In 1785 he was commissioned by the City of Paris to make a candelabra celebrating the American Declaration of Independance for presentation to General Lafayette (now in the Louvre).

He built up a large workshop, which is said to have employed as many as eight hundred workmen. He

FRENCH FURNITURE

worked extensively under the Empire and received a number of important commissions from the Emperor himself. The firm was known as *Thomire-Dutherne et cie*, and Thomire himself retired from business in 1823 but did not die until 1843. It by no means always follows that bronzes stamped with the name Thomire are by Pierre Philippe himself. More probably they are products of the workshop.

ROENTGEN, David
Born near Frankfurt in 1743, the son of the cabinet-maker Abraham Roentgen, whose workshop at Neuwied on the Rhine he took over in 1772 and developed considerably. He first came to Paris in 1774 and received patronage from Queen Marie Antoinette. This established his reputation which, by the time of his second visit in 1779, had increased considerably, and he established a depot in Paris for selling furniture, as he did also in Berlin and Vienna. He travelled widely and visited Italy, Flanders and Russia, where he sold a great deal of furniture to the Empress Catherine II.

In 1780 he was compelled to become a *maître-ébéniste* in Paris, using the stamp: DAVID, and in 1791 was made Court furnisher to King Frederick William II at Berlin. He was ruined by the Revolution and his depot in Paris was confiscated. His workshop at Neuwied was also overrun by Republican troops. He returned there in 1802, however, and died in 1807.

Roentgen specialized in furniture veneered with extremely elaborate pictorial marquetry and fitted with complicated mechanical devices, concealing secret drawers and multiple locks. His furniture was mostly made outside France and is seldom stamped.

WEISWEILER, Adam
Born *c.* 1750 at Neuwied and trained in the workshop of Roentgen (q.v.). Established in Paris before 1777. Became a *maître-ébéniste* in 1778. He worked for the dealer Daguerre and, through him, supplied a large amount of furniture for the Royal palaces, and particularly for Queen Marie Antoinette at Saint Cloud. He was a good business man, and in consequence survived the Revolution safely, and was employed under the Empire, during which time he executed commissions for Queen Hortense. He was still in business in 1810. He used the stamp:

A·WEISWEILER

BOOKS FOR FURTHER READING

G. H. BAILLIE, *Watchmakers and Clockmakers of the World*, 2nd ed., N.A.G. Press Ltd (London, 1947).
MARIE JULIETTE BALLOT, *Charles Cressent, Sculpteur, Ébéniste, Collectionneur*, published in 'Archives de l'Art Français', nouvelle période, tome X (Edouard Champion, Paris, 1919).
Le Décor Intérieur au XVIIIe siècle à Paris et dans la Région Parisienne. Boiseries sculptées et Panneaux peints. (G. Van Oest, Paris, 1930.)
ALFRED DE CHAMPEAUX, *Le Meuble.* Tome I: 'Antiquité, Moyen Age et Renaissance'. Tome II: 'XVIIe, XVIIIe et XIXe Siècles. 2 vols., 1885. (Paris, n.d.)
Dictionnaire des Fondeurs, Ciseleurs, Modeleurs en Bronze et Doreurs depuis le moyen-âge jusqu'à l'époque actuelle. 1st vol., A–C. (J. Rouam, Paris, 1886.)
HENRI CLOUZOT, *Le Style Louis-Phillipe-Napoléon III.* 'Arts, Styles et Techniques.' (Collection publiée sous la direction de Norbert Dufourcq.) (Larousse, Paris, 1939.)
PIERRE DU COLOMBIER, *Le Style Henri IV–Louis XIII.* (Arts, Styles et Techniques.) (Collection publiée sous la Direction de Norbert Dufourcq.) (Larousse, Paris, 1941.)
ÉMILE DACIER, *Le Style Louis XVI.* 'Arts, Styles et Techniques.' (Collection publiée sous la direction de Norbert Dufourcq.) (Larousse, Paris, 1939.)
DENIS DIDEROT AND J. LE R. D'ALEMBERT, *Encyclopédie, ou Dictionnaire raisonné des Sciences des Arts et des Métiers, par une Société de gens de lettres.* A–Z. 17 vols.; Supplément, 4 vols.; Planches, 11 vols.; Supplément aux planches, 1 vol. (Paris and Amsterdam, 1751–77.) Table, 2 vols.

LADY DILKE, *French Furniture and Decoration in the Eighteenth Century.* 4to. (George Bell & Sons, London, 1901.)
JULES GUIFFREY, *Les Caffiéri. Sculpteurs et fondeurs-ciseleurs. Étude sur la Statuaire et sur l'art de bronze en France au XVIIe et au XVIIIe siècles.* (Paris, 1877.)
Inventaire Général du Mobilier de la Couronne sous Louis XIV (1663–1715). 2 vols. (Paris, 1885.)
HENRY HAVARD, *Dictionnaire de l'Ameublement et de la Décoration depuis le XIIIe siècle jusqu'à nos jours.* 4 vols. (1887–90.) (Quanton, Paris, n.d.)
Les Boulle. 'Les Artistes Célèbres.' (L. Allison et Cie, Paris, 1892.)
GUILLAUME JANNEAU, PIERRE DEVINOY, and MADELEINE JARRY, *Le Siège en France du Moyen Age à nos jours.* (P. Hartmann, Paris, 1948.)
GUILLAUME JANNEAU and PIERRE DEVINOY, *Le Meuble Léger en France.* (P. Hartmann, Paris, 1952.)
ALBERT KEIM, *La Décoration et le Mobilier à l'Époque Romantique et sous le Second Empire.* (Nilsson, Paris, n.d.)
FISKE KIMBALL, *Le Style Louis XV. Origine et Évolution du Rococo.* Translated from English by Mlle. Jeanne Marie. (A. et J. Picard, Paris, 1949.)
DENISE LEDOUX-LEBARD, *Les Ébénistes Parisiens (1795–1830), leurs œuvres et leurs marques.* (Gründ, Paris, 1951.)
HECTOR LEFUEL, *Georges Jacob, Ébéniste du XVIIIe siècle.* Paris (Archives de l'Amateur, 1923).
ÉMILE MOLINIER, *Histoire Générale des Arts appliqués à l'Industrie.* Tome II: 'Les Meubles du Moyen Âge et de la Renaissance'. Tome III: 'Le Mobilier au XVIIe et au XVIIIe siècle'. (?1898.) (Paris, n.d.)

FRENCH FURNITURE

Le Mobilier Royal Français aux XVIIe et XVIIIe siècles. Histoire et description. 5 vols. (E. Lévy, Paris, 1902.)

JULIETTE NICLAUSSE, *Thomire, Fondeur-Ciseleur (1751–1843). Sa Vie-Son Œuvre.* Préface de Louis Réau. (Gründ, Paris, 1947.)

SEYMOUR DE RICCI, *Louis XIV and Regency Furniture and Decoration.* (Batsford, London, 1929.)

Louis XVI Furniture. (Heinemann, London, n.d.)

JACQUES ROBIQUET, *Gouthière, Sa Vie-Son Œuvre.* Essaie de Catalogue Raisonné. (Renouard, Paris, 1912.)

COMTE FRANÇOIS DE SALVERTE, *Les Ébénistes du XVIIIe siècle, leurs œuvres et leurs marques.* 4th edition. (G. Vanoest, Paris-Bruxelles, 1953.)

Le Meuble Français d'après les Ornemanistes de 1660 à 1789. (G. Van Oest, Paris, 1930.)

THOMAS ARTHUR STRANGE, *An Historical Guide to French Interiors, Furniture Decoration, Woodwork and Allied Arts during the last half of the Seventeenth Century, the whole of the Eighteenth Century, and the early part of the Nineteenth.* 3rd impression. (McCorquodale & Co. Ltd, London, 1950.)

ANDRÉ THEUNISSEN, *Meubles et sièges du XVIIIe siècle.* Menuisiers, Ébénistes, Marques, Plans et ornementation de leurs œuvres. (Éditions 'Le Document', Paris, n.d.)

PIERRE VERLET, *Le Style Louis XV.* 'Arts, Styles et Techniques.' (Collection publiée sous la direction de Norbert Dufourcq.) (Larousse, Paris, 1942.)

Le Mobilier Royal Français: Meubles de la Couronne conservés en France. I. (Éditions d'Art et d'Histoire, Paris, 1945.)

HENRI VIAL, ADRIEN MARCEL and ANDRÉ GIRODIE, *Les Artistes Décorateurs du Bois (Répertoire alphabétique des Ebénistes, Menuisiers, Sculpteurs, Doreurs sur bois, etc, ayant travaillé en France aux XVIIe et XVIIIe siècles).* 2 vols. 4to. (I: A–L; II: M–Z.) Paris. Vol. I: Bibliothèque d'Art et d'Archéologie, 1912. Vol. II: Libraire de la Bibliothèque d'Art de l'Université de. (J. Schemit, Paris, 1922.)

VICTORIA AND ALBERT MUSEUM, LONDON. *A Guide to the Salting Collection.* (Board of Education, London, 1926.)

The Panelled Rooms: III—The Boudoir of Madame de Sérilly. (H.M.S.O., London, 1915.)

Catalogue of the Jones Collection. Part I: Furniture, by Oliver Brackett. 4to. (H.M.S.O., London, 1922.) Part II: Ceramics, Ormolu, Goldsmiths' Work, Enamels, Sculpture, Tapestry, Books and Prints. (Board of Education, London, 1924.)

ROGER-ARMAND WEIGERT, *Jean I. Bérain, Dessinateur de la Chambre et du Cabinet du Roi (1640–1711).* 2 vols. Première Partie: Sa Vie-Sa Famille-Son Style. Deuxième Partie: L'Œuvre Gravé. (Editions d'Art et d'Histoire, Paris, 1937.)

Le Style Louis XIV. 'Arts, Styles et Techniques.' (Collection publiée sous la direction de Norbert Dufourcq.) (Larousse, Paris, 1941.)

E. WILLIAMSON, *Les Meubles d'Art du Mobilier National* (Choix des plus belles pièces conservées au Garde-Meuble et dans les Palais nationaux de l'Elysée, du Louvre, de Versailles, de Trianon, de Fontainebleau, de Compiègne et de Pau). 2 vol^s (1883–5.) (Baudry et Cie, Paris, n.d.)

CHEST FURNITURE

By THERLE HUGHES

TRAVELLING CHESTS

WHEN Charlotte, Princess of Savoy travelled in 1483 her personal luggage filled more than forty chests and coffers; Elizabeth I's retinue counted them by the hundred in her royal progresses. 'Our ancestors' taste for substantialness', that appalled Mrs. Lybbe Powis in 1757, was never more impressively demonstrated than in the chests and coffers, trunks and portmanteaux, standards and arks and fosselets, that delight and bewilder today's collectors. But one has only to read old English inventories – any household, any century – to appreciate the incalculable numbers of lesser specimens that these remaining treasures inadequately and untypically represent. In the 1585 inventory of William Shelley of Michelgrove, Sussex, for instance, the furniture included no fewer than twenty chests. In his wardrobe alone Sir William Ingilby of Ripley in 1617 kept 'one portmanteaux, 3 ould trunkes besides the trunke that keep Sir William's apparrell, an ould counter and 2 great chestes'.

Chest is a term that has been applied to a number of articles more or less box-shaped and opening with a rising lid. Records of the craftsmen who made chest furniture and of the guilds and companies, the churches and great houses, that used them, all contribute terms and definitions but constantly contradict each other. In this survey of chest furniture, this wide application of the word chest is accepted. Even as late as 1730 Bailey's dictionary made no attempt to be specific: a coffer was a chest or trunk, a chest was 'a sort of box, coffer or trunk'. Addison in 1700 used the term for a basket, 'a chest of twining osiers', such as one must assume Lady Grisell Baillie meant by her Dutch basket 'for my cloathes' in 1693. Moreover, chests in their hey-day served a multitude of purposes. Throughout the Middle Ages a man's possessions travelled with him, but when he settled down the chests in which they were packed or trussed became the furniture that displayed them. In later sections of this volume other types of chest furniture are reviewed, but it must be recognized that they, too, had a part-purpose in serving the traveller, whilst what may be regarded as specific travelling chests became accepted home furnishings.

The very word trunk indicates how early and primitive were men's first attempts to make stronger luggage than skin-covered osier baskets. A few ancient dug-outs remain, usually of oak, occasionally, as in Ackington Church, Worcestershire, of elm. The oldest dug-outs were succeeded first by the carpenter's hammered-up constructions, then gradually by the joiner's framed work until the cabinet, the chest at its most refined and most perfectly individualistic, became recognized as the most highly skilled creation in the whole craft of woodworking. But for the travel chest in particular the ancient rounded top of the dug-out was preserved. Since to truss was a familiar word meaning to pack or bundle goods, the traveller's chest was probably most frequently specified by the prefix 'trussing'. Numerous references may be found to trussing chests, such as in 1540, in an Act of Henry VIII. In the early seventeenth-century Howard Accounts, with their frequent references to freight, boat-hire and portage of luggage between London and the North, trunks and trunk chests appeared accepted terms.

The other term particularly associated with travelling chests is coffer. The cofferer was long recognized as the craftsman who covered chests and other furniture with leather. As early as 1483 the Guild of Cofferers protested against the competition of imported Flanders chests, and, until late in the eighteenth century, coffer-makers were listed among the officers of the royal household. But in common usage the term appears generally to have indicated a wide variety of strongly built chests, and will find further mention in later sections.

Boarded Chests: early, poor alternatives to the framed or jointed chest, the horizontal planks of wood forming the front and back being hammered to the vertical end-pieces or flush with heavy corner stiles, and frequently reinforced with corner-pieces of iron. As wood tends to shrink across the grain, the result was never satisfactory, and the horizontal planks usually show signs of splitting. Oak might be used, or planks of elm, large and comparatively little given to warping. The flush construction as contrasted with the loose panels of the mortise-and-tenon jointed chest offered a smooth surface for covering with leather or hair cloth.

Busse Chests: buscarles' or seamen's chests.

Close Nailing: brass convex-headed nails of a darkish tint of brass hammered with great exactitude by the cofferer, head beside head, were used all around the edges of the leather-covered chest and in sufficient numbers over the body of the piece to avoid any loose flapping of the inelastic cover. Similar treatment was given to hair cloth.

Coffers: a term that must be considered also in connexion with Plate Chests, but has always had particular association with the leather-covered travelling chest, the work of the cofferer. Randall Holme, in 1662, made the distinction that a coffer was called a chest if it had a straight and flat cover, a chest being like a coffer 'save the want of a circular lid or cover'.

Fitted Chests: coach travel became more popular and widespread in the seventeenth century, the experienced traveller taking his own fitted chest or case containing drinking glasses and square glass bottles, or a silver dining set consisting of a nest of tumblers, and knife, fork and spoons. Some eighteenth-century cases contained porcelain tea equipages (Plate 105). Doctors travelled with essential surgeons' chests, and craftsmen with tool chests that represented their livelihood.

Hair Cloth: cloth woven with horsehair was strong and rain-repellent, and was used like leather to cover wooden travelling chests and trunks. As it had no elasticity in the weft threads, it was close-nailed like leather. There is reference in the *Verney Memoirs*, 1653, to 'yelowe haire sumpter trunkes'. Some seventeenth-century writers specified fustian, others merely cloth to cover trunks, sometimes scarlet and even crest-embroidered, requiring an outer casing of leather. In the later eighteenth century hair cloth was available in a wide range of colours and stripes, and many a hair trunk studded with brass rosettes in a somewhat medieval manner was manufactured for the rough and tumble of coach travel in the early nineteenth century.

Hinges: *pin hinges* – the early medieval chest might have a rather clumsy pivot arrangement for opening the canted lid. A pair of horizontal pivots worked in slots cut in the back stiles of the chest. Often small iron plates were introduced, to protect the pivots. *Strap hinges* – these, of iron, were usual after the end of the thirteenth century.

Leather: cowhide close-nailed was the most usual covering for travelling chests, both standards and trussing coffers. Early leather might be enamelled and gilded, imported from Spain and Holland until an Englishman, Christopher, discovered their methods in 1638. Leather treated with oil and spirits was known as *cuir bouilli*, the applications rendering it supple enough to take incised ornament in addition to paint and gilding. The *Dictionary of Furniture* lists Richard Pegge, coffer-maker to Charles II, and Edward Smith, 1750–60, among suppliers of trunks to the royal household, covered in Russia leather (scented with oil of birch-bark). Pegge's were supplied with and without drawers, and included such details as one lined with sarcenet and quilted, and two covered with sealskin and bound with girdles of ox leather.

Linings: trunk lining became a specialized job, and in travelling chests particularly the work was important if the chest contents were to be protected from the drifts of dust that constituted roads and the rushes and rubbish scattered over flagstones or wooden flooring. Linen has always had terminological association with lining, and was the most suitable fabric until eighteenth-century cotton became strong and closely woven enough to be considered as a possible alternative. Paper, hand-made and soft textured, soon rubbed, but was widely used. It may be of particular interest to the collector; for sheets of unsaleable books were used when available, the plain backs printed in wood-block patterns.

Metal-work: travelling chests were frequently iron-bound, sometimes almost covered in iron; but these may be regarded as travelling safes and receive further consideration under the section on Plate Chests. The close nailing that protected the leather covering was reinforced with corner-straps, and often with a massive and handsome lockplate, early work being shaped cold by sawing like wood. Pepys mentioned in 1662 that 'we were forced to send for a smith, to break open her trunk'. Remaining specimens tend to have replacement locks, often with hinge pins too easily removed or damaged for any security.

Panelled Chests: typified joiners' as distinct from carpenters' furniture. The horizontal rails and vertical stiles and muntins that formed the framework to the loose panels of the chest were held together by mortise-and-tenon joints, allowing the wood to respond to atmospheric changes. Joiners' work in 1632 was defined to include dovetail joints, and the wide early style of dovetail may be noted down the corners of some chests in walnut, cypress and other woods that could be undercut in a manner impossible with oak. Plat in 1594 made reference to a 'foure square chest... close the sides well with dovetails or cement'. But corner dovetails in view on the outside of a chest are usually taken to indicate Continental work.

Pegged Chests: occasionally a chest is noted which can be dismantled for travelling or store by removing wooden pegs in the style of many early table trestles. Some are authenticated, but obviously the design was very much in the mood of the nineteenth-century's pseudo-medievalism.

Portmanteaux: a term introduced about the mid-sixteenth century, applied to cases specifically for horse travel yet large enough for bulky clothing. In the 1620s, for instance, the Howard Accounts refer to a leather portmanteau priced 10s. 1d., and in 1611 Cotgrave noted 'a portmantue with chaine and locke'. There are numerous references to portmanteau saddles, even to portmanteau horses, in the seventeenth and eighteenth centuries. Thus the *London Gazette* referred to 'a coloured leather Portmantle Saddle'. Such a saddle, according to Randall Holme, had 'a Cantle behind the seat to keep the Portmantle... off the Rider's back'.

Royal Crown on Travelling Chests: this may be found in close nailing or engraved on metal fittings, and is often assumed to indicate personal association with a monarch. It is thought more likely to indicate that the chest may have been used on Government service or by one of the palaces.

Standards: when a wealthy family travelled, their household goods might be conveyed in huge leather-covered, iron-bound, vividly painted standards. Here again is a term that must receive consideration also among other types of chest furniture.

Sumpter Trunks: a usual term for the pairs of travelling chests carried by sumpter- or baggage-horses or mules, or in the late eighteenth-century sumpter cars. Lady Grisell Baillie paid four pounds for a pair in 1715. Sumpter-horses were comparable with pack-horses. Bailey, in 1730, defined a pack as a horse-load of wool – about 240 pounds. Sumpter-cloths frequently bore the crest or cipher of their owner.

Tills: forerunners of the fitted tray in a modern trunk. Inside many a seventeenth-century chest a small tray was fitted on the right near the lid. Sometimes it was itself lidded, the lid hingeing into the framework of the chest; sometimes it was locked and occasionally had a false-bottomed hiding-place. Catharine of Aragon in 1534 had 'one cofar having four tilles therin, the forefronte of every one of them gilte'. The lidded box-like tills in a chest might be called drawing chests or drawers, although the chest-of-drawers, as a considerable piece of bedroom furniture and as distinct from a cabinet of tiny drawers, was evolved only in the seventeenth century. Thus, in 1599, Minshen referred to 'a great chest or standard with drawing chests or boxes in it'.

Trenails or Treenails: the old term for the cylindrical pins of hardwood used for fastening timber together, mentioned for instance in an inventory of 1571: 'iij houndrethe treenales viijd'. Square wooden pins might be used green, driven into round holes for greater firmness.

Trunks: probably the most common term for a travelling chest, leather-covered and with a rounded top to suffer as little as possible from wet weather. It was used in association with a number of terms regarding such chests. Thus the brass convex-headed nail used by the cofferer was a trunk nail, and there was a trunk saddle recorded as early as 1569. Moxon in 1677 distinguished between trunk locks, chest locks and padlocks.

Trussing Coffers: a frequent term for leather-covered travelling chests, usually implying smaller articles than standards; as, for instance, was indicated in a reference of 1622: 'Commodities packt up in Bundels, Trusses, Cases, Coffers or Packes.'

WRITING-BOXES

Early cabinets were mainly for the dilettanti. The majority of those who worked with their heads as well as their hands sought simpler means of keeping their office work within bounds, using what Cooper in 1584 (*Bibliotheca Eliotae*) defined as 'a littell holowe desk lyke a coffer whereypon men do write'. Old letters and inventories time and time again refer to the small portable desk that rested on a chest or table in the study or parlour, such as the 'wryghtyng box of syprese' in the *Paston Letters*, 1471. They were usually minor pieces; in 1586 Ralph Ewrie of Edgnolle, Co. Durham, had 'j wood deske 2d'. In 1587 William Jeneson, a Newcastle merchant, had two desks valued at 6s. 6d. in his hall to supplement a 'great counter' valued at 16s., three painted coffers and '2 bound coffers for writings, 10s'. The 1545 inventory of Marketon, Derbyshire, gives a vivid little picture of a well-equipped study:

'It' a red cofer bownd with yeron, with evidences, iiijs.
It' a payr balns and a pyle of troye weights vjs.
It' desk a sandbox and a payr golde ballanz xxd.
It' a Standyssh for pen ynk etc of fyrre xxd.
It' a wrytynn bord couered and ij forms j cusshyn ijs. iiijd.
It' a payr table of slate and a combe case ijs.'

In the sixteenth century only a very few specimens of English craftsmanship were ornate in the Continental manner, painted inside and fitted with compartments, like the 'desque with a Cabonett therein of crimson velvet laced xls', in the Earl of Northampton's inventory (1614). Not until late in the seventeenth century were larger units of furniture developed in any quantity comparable with modern desks, bookcases and filing cabinets. Thus, throughout the centuries dominated, though not monopolized, by oak furniture with its carving and panelling, inlays and glued embossments, its emphasis on massive effects in ornaments and mouldings and iron mounts, the writing-box was the one piece of furniture more specialized than a plain chest for a man of the standing of squire or farmer or lesser merchant. Here he kept his papers and his few, heavy books, and inscribed his records in the family Bible. It is this personal association with past owners that gives writing-boxes their peculiar appeal.

As they were placed on tables or chests, they were ornamented on all sides, but usually lacked legs, being based on wide convex mouldings. Such a box, perhaps as much as 2 feet 6 inches or 3 feet wide, frequently, though not always, had a sloping lid, the slope slight in early specimens, and the hinge at the top, desk fashion. In some instances a shallow box for quills or ink with a separate lid was included in the design, to the right of the main writing-box and mounted on the same reeded base moulding. By the later seventeenth century the style was changing, with a more steeply sloping front that might be hinged at the bottom to open down for writing with the interior fittings accessible. These at their most elaborate included small drawers with concave fronts shaped from the solid wood flanking pigeon-holes, and a central domed cupboard perhaps with secret compartments behind its tiny decorative pilasters. In the provinces it continued in popular use throughout the eighteenth century, and in Wales in particular its individuality has been demonstrated in an exceptionally handsome style of country furniture. But many more were sophisticated little pieces. *The Cabinet-Makers' London Book of Prices* (1788) put a price of 30s. for a traveller's specimen fitted for shaving as well as for writing.

By the beginning of the nineteenth century every kind of compendium, for the writer, artist, needlewoman was being made as dainty and elaborate as highly competitive ingenuity could devise. Thus by the mid-nineteenth century there were yew-tree writing-boxes with fittings of ebony and mounts of bronze, ebony boxes with 'medieval mounts', and every kind of lavish but finely made compendium under the general classification of 'elegancies for presentation'.

Bonheur du Jour: a dainty piece of furniture derived from the writing-box that enjoyed a short spell of popularity in France around 1760 and was copied in England. It suggested a shallow writing-box backed by a small cabinet and mounted on the period's slender, unencumbered legs. The top might be surrounded on back and side edges with a low ormolu gallery. When the cabinet portion rested on a slightly more extensive stand, there might be small wooden fences of spindles at its sides as letter racks (Plate 112B).

Bureaux: a term sometimes applied to writing-boxes before they became established as full-sized desks. It was derived from the colour of the rough woollen forerunner of baize commonly used for writing-tables – *burrus*, Latin for the colour of fire.

Coffor Bach: the Welsh Bible-box, peculiar to the Principality and an attractive little piece of furniture, suggesting a diminutive mule chest. The authors of *Welsh Furniture* state that it was usually made of oak or elm, occasionally inlaid with holly, and most commonly dated from the second half of the eighteenth century onwards, including many twentieth-century copies. The upper chest portion was intended for the Bible, and the two small drawers below for family papers.

Compendiums: *see* section on Cabinets.

Counters: frequent accompaniments to writing-boxes in homes of merchants and the like. In 1459 Margaret Paston wrote to her husband regarding 'your coffers and your cowntewery'. They were distinguished from other flat-topped storage chests by being scored for reckoning.

Crofts: Seddon, Sons and Shackleton in the late eighteenth century manufactured and sold an attractive little piece of desk furniture that they claimed would serve 'men of method' and particularly those who had to travel and wished not to disarrange their business papers. A small table top with D-shaped drop-flaps was fitted over a partitioned drawer with a sliding lid for writing on while the drawer was extended. Below were small drawers and partitions enclosed by a wide door. The makers claimed that corners, hinges and so on were finished so as to cause the minimum of inconvenience if the owner travelled with it in a post-chaise. Sir Ambrose Heal has traced the name to the Rev. Sir Herbert Croft, Bt., who at one time proposed to issue a revised version of Johnson's dictionary.

Cypress: hard, durable, coniferous wood almost imperishable and used for writing-boxes, coffers, etc, sometimes bearing incised ornament that suited its close grain. It was usually assembled by dovetailing.

Derbyshire Desks: term for oak writing-boxes, carved and sometimes dated.

Lace Boxes: many delightful boxes now go by this name, although their original purpose must have been less restricted. They became most conspicuous in the late seventeenth and early eighteenth centuries when bedroom furniture was being given the handsome treatment fitting the furnishings of what was often in practice an office, study and reception-room for the head of the household. These boxes frequently bore floral marquetry patterns that originally must have matched similar work on the chests of drawers they accompanied. Lace was, of course, vastly important at a period when William III could spend £290 on the lace for half a dozen razor-cloths, but obviously the shallow box had many possibilities, for the family Bible and often as a fully adequate writing-box (Plate 108B).

Ladies' Work-boxes: the implication that such boxes were solely or mainly associated with needlework is comparatively new. Even in the early nineteenth century they were usually equipped for writing, often also for drawing and painting as well as for needlework. Inkpots might be contained in a special drawer at the right side of the box that could be kept open during use. Such boxes were intended to meet their users' every imaginable need at a period when fierce competition made every manufacturer struggle for novelty and elaboration. The box might be covered in satinwood, more often pre-dating 1800, rosewood, tooled and gilt-stamped leather, tortoiseshell veneer. Fittings might be of gold and mother of pearl, the mounts brass or steel (Plate 108A).

Ornament: applied on all sides since the box might rest on a centrally placed table. It included simple repetitive carving, such as deep lobe mouldings, guilloche braids, etc; inlay in green and brown stained holly, box, sycamore and bogwoods; even intarsia work in the manner of large Nonsuch chests (p.133). The base moulding usually received careful treatment, whether in the plain wide thumb moulding of an early Stuart table or in more elaborate egg-and-tongue outline. Eighteenth-century work included the expected range of japanning and marquetry in the early years and satinwood in solid and veneer late in the century, ornamented with the marquetry ovals and fan shapes and the box and ebony stringing associated with this wood. By the early nineteenth century rosewood was supplemented by the wealth of ornament – japanning, Tunbridge ware and even glue-on varnished prints—that in early Victorian days so easily descended into tawdriness.

Papier Mâché: by the early nineteenth century writing-boxes were made in this amenable material, their highly decorative surface finish requiring only a simple design of box. The pulped paper, like the layered construction of earlier 'paper ware' made before the 1840s, was given its superb silken finish with numerous varnishings, long, slow stovings in a japanners' oven and hand rubbing with bare hands occasionally dipped in cold water. Ornament most usually took the form of flowers and butterflies, hand-painted in the crowded manner of the period (Plate 109D). Slabs of nautilus shell might be introduced by other firms, while the Birmingham japanners, Jennens and Bettridge, held the patent for grinding shell paper-thin and shaping it delicately with acid. Some boxes had a suggestion of Oriental lacquer work, part of the ornament being in raised composition covered with gilding – but never gold paint. Some were competently painted with souvenir views, such as the many Oxford scenes issued by Spiers and Son of that city.

Reed Top: whereas a large desk might open with a solid cylinder lid, a writing-box might have the space-saving opening associated with tambour tables. In this the rounded top could be pushed out of sight inside the box, being constructed of lengths of thin moulded beading glued side by side on to a back of strong canvas, pliable enough to move in curved runners.

Satinwood: some delightful writing-boxes appeared in this wood, either solid or in veneer, early imports before about 1795 being comparatively unfigured. While demand exceeded supply, sycamore and chestnut were substituted. The greenish wood known as harewood was sycamore suitably tinted. Often these little boxes were tall, the upper half rounded at the front, somewhat in the manner of contemporary knife-boxes. This uprising portion was often ornamented with a fan or shell motif, such as specialist marquetry men prepared and sold in quantity to furniture makers. Inside, the box was divided into compartments.

Screen Writing-tables: late eighteenth-century devices by Gillow and others with adjustable screens of pleated silk.

Sheverets or Chevrets: A late eighteenth-century term used by Gillow and others for small pieces of table furniture associated with writing. The back half of the top offered housing for books, while the front might open forwards to serve for writing.

Tunbridge Ware: early Tunbridge-ware writing-boxes were often in attractive parquetry patterns, such as shaded cubes and the deep vandykes suggested by the backgammon boards that were another Tunbridge-ware speciality. In the subsequent mosaic veneers a writing-box might carry a picture on its upper front or sloping lid, such as a view of Hever, Eridge or Tonbridge castle, or some similar local sight of souvenir value. Such mosaics were built up from the various local woods, only their natural colours being approved and the greenish shade caused by the local spring water. Strips of these woods in appropriate colours were assembled by hand like so many matchsticks, fastened together by their sides so that the tiny squares of their ends together formed the picture. These could then be thinly sliced across their length, so that every slice would bear the same mosaic picture ready for mounting on the box. Occasionally one sees a marble box, the veneer consisting of a haphazard assembly of the various coloured shavings glued and sliced in the same way as the mosaic pictures (Plates 109A and B).

Writing-box Stands: The post-Restoration writing-box might be placed on a stand instead of a table. This had gate-legs and the fall-down flap of the box opened on to them for writing. Even towards the end of the seventeenth century box and stand might be separate, although the box was acquiring the characteristic shape of the more elaborate desk, with the writing portion based on a chest of drawers. The simplest stands were without drawers, and resembled some of the first toilet looking-glass boxes. Early legs were turned and tapering, linked by flat, waved stretchers. By about 1705 simple cabriole legs were coming into use.

CABINETS

To this day the most expert furniture craftsman is the cabinet-maker, and cabinets are unquestionably the most fascinating as well as the most technically perfect pieces of furniture ever evolved. They represent the chest at its most refined and personal, the antithesis of the old clumsy chest with its casual disregard for orderliness. Their very perfection rules out any very ancient pedigree for English work. The Earl of Northampton was ahead of his times in his collection of lovely furniture, and the inventory taken in 1614 lists no fewer than eight – ebony inlaid with white bone, crimson velvet laced with silver and gold lace and similar exotic beauties. But only twenty years before the very term cabinet had been a rarity and the Dean of Durham's wife, for instance, referred in her will to 'one coffer with boxes in y[t] standinge onn a frame'. In 1620 Lord William Howard bought what had to be described as a 'cabbinnit with 21 drawboxeis' for 7s. 3d. As late as 1730 Bailey's dictionary defined a cabinet first as a closet in the king's palace, and only secondly as 'a sort of chest of drawers, also a kind of little trunk to put things of value in'.

In late Stuart and early Georgian days, however, for china, shells, coins, curios, cabinets achieved a remarkable maturity and range of design and material, and even in the nineteenth century new treatments were being evolved. In silver and papier-mâché, in lacquer, tortoiseshell and ivory, in needle-work, straw-work, paper filigree and every delicate and decorative treatment of wood-work – inlay, marquetry, carving and paint – the cabinet declared man's admiration for patient, exquisite craftsmanship. Basically it was the development of hardwoods that enabled craftsmen to accomplish the small-scale joinery of countless fitted drawers and compartments, this necessarily limiting its execution to the most skilled.

The idea of immensely valuable, ornate chests for storing one's treasure is almost as old as the valuables themselves, but early specimens might be classed as caskets. The costly brilliance of such work may be visualized from such contemporary sources as the summary of the 'chests' in the 1536 inventory of Salisbury Cathedral. These included: 'A fair chest, curiously and cleanly made, covered with cloth of gold, with shields of noblemen, set with pearls, with lock, gemmels and key silver and gilt. Item one fair chest, painted and gilded, with precious stones and knops of glass, broidered with coral, seven of them wanting, and painted within like silver. Item, three other chests, very fair, and ornate with precious stones, with gemmels of silver and gilt.... Also divers chests... some covered with cloth of blue and silver, and others ornate with ivory and gemmels and locks.'

Even by the date of this inventory cabinets with small compartments for jewellery had a considerable history in Italy, and they had become extremely ornate before English craftsmen began to give much attention to such work in response to seventeenth-century demand. Ivory inlay was associated with Milan, damascened iron with Milan and Florence, glass encrustations with Florence, mother of pearl with Venice. The *varguenos* of Spain were conspicuous for their characteristic horizontal shaping, long hinges and other gilded ironwork. But before the end of the seventeenth century men were looking beyond these lovely creations. Charles II's queen brought Bombay as her scintillating dowry, and the so-called Portuguese cabinets that the king presented to his favourites – ornate gold-mounted treasures incrusted with mother of pearl or ivory – came mainly from India, from the Portuguese colony at Goa. And even these could not compare with the wealth of magnificent colour and fantastic design displayed by some of the cabinets introduced in the seventeenth century from China.

By the late seventeenth century English cabinet-makers were devising a range of furniture variously termed cabinet bookcases, desks, scrutoires, bureaux and so on in which the cabinet-maker's skill was tested to the full on the small compartments, drawers, shelves and hiding-places that constituted the cabinets themselves. But in this brief survey such furniture can receive only passing mention. During the eighteenth century the tendency was to develop smaller pieces that possessed the dainty charm of early table cabinets yet which were complete in themselves.

Cabinets on Stands: large cabinets mounted on stands are especially associated with the late seventeenth and early eighteenth centuries. Early specimens retained the rectangular outline of the chest on stand, becoming less massive after about 1670, but with a heavy, straight cornice and often a drawer in the swelling frieze, and another in the tall table-like stand. Two vertical doors usually embraced the whole front of the cabinet, finely ornamented and with handsome lock-plates. Inside, the space was filled with drawers, cupboards, pigeon-holes.

Alternatively the cabinet was combined with a bureau, the doors replaced by a wide fall-front hinged at the bottom to provide writing space when open. Such a piece was most usually mounted on a chest of drawers. By the late seventeenth century there were numerous variants. There were even a few display cabinets with glazed fronts, plain rectangles of glass being framed in heavy glazing bars. From the 1680s a china or book cabinet might be mounted over a bureau with a slanting fall-down flap, charming interior fittings and deep drawers below. Some were narrow, to fit against the piers between the windows, and all lent themselves to the architectural furniture treatment of their day. A few were of oak, many more in veneer, such as walnut, burr elm banded with foreign wood, or mulberry, associated with stringing in pewter.

Mahogany appeared more widely once the import tax was removed in 1733, and was used in the early Georgian style associated with William Kent, followed by lighter mid-century work with rich naturalistic carving. Some had fret-cut, pierced cresting boards, several thicknesses of wood being glued together in different ways of the grain to avoid warping. There was more use of clear glazing in place of heavy mirror-plate fronts, the lighter glazing bars that could be cut from mahogany dating from about 1750 onwards. But shapes and styles in the mid-eighteenth century were numerous, followed by the more restrained, formal designs of the neo-classic mood. In the late eighteenth century a delightful style of little cabinet consisted of about six graduated drawers beneath a lifting top rebated on a plain stand with the entirely unencumbered legs, tapering only on their inner sides, associated with Hepplewhite's day. Such a cabinet was typically of satinwood, with simple but precise bandings of richer tulip-wood.

Caskets: a frequent term for small decorative chests that contained jewels, letters and similar highly valuable articles with some degree of security and with great decorative effect. Until the term cabinet became widely current, caskets and chests of draw-boxes were in common usage. References are endless. As early as 1467 a guild record was 'to be put in a boxe called a Casket'; in 1471 in the *Paston Letters* there is allusion to 'Syche othyr wryghtynges and stuff as was in my Kasket'. Some extremely finely made caskets date to the first quarter of the nineteenth century, when they might be known as compendiums, with lift-out fitments for a wide variety of purposes. Treatments varied endlessly, but a typical specimen might be of rosewood, perhaps pearl-mounted and with interior mountings of gilt-stamped leather and fittings of cut steel.

Compendiums: *see* Caskets.

Drawer Construction: by Tudor days the early wide dovetail was in widespread use in England, but by about 1695 the lap dovetail was preferred under veneers, as the old through dovetail exposed too much end-grain for satisfactory glue-work. Some Dutch work continued the earlier style. Oak was used for drawer linings to take the rub of wear. As early as 1655 the Marquess of Worcester patented 'a total locking of Cabinet-boxes'.

Ebony: this brittle, difficult wood was first employed to supplement the native woods used for decorative inlays, but it so fascinated the early cabinet-maker that it prompted the development of the veneer technique. Corfe Castle in 1643 was typical of wealthy establishments in containing a 'rich ebony cabbonett with gilded fixtures', and a very large ebony cabinet, in contrast to a more simply constructed casket covered with mother of pearl that was catalogued as a trunk.

Filigree Cabinets: throughout the 18th century filigree was a popular amateur ornament for small cabinets, calling for neat fingers and considerable patience. The ornament entirely covered the main panels of the cabinet, creating pictorial designs and arabesque patterns in an effect of metal filigree. This was achieved solely with tiny rolls of paper arranged so that they projected edgeways from their background. To complete the effect, they were gilded or coloured on their exposed edges (Plate 112A).

Forsets, Fossets, Fosselets: terms defined by Bailey in 1730 as small chests or cabinets. They were smaller versions of the forser or fosser, an early form of strong box such as the Cockesden 'waynscott fosser' (1610) and the 'grete joyned forser' with two keys owned by the Pewterers' Company in 1488–9.

Handles: the quality of the work depended more upon cost than period. Early cabinets might have turned ivory or wood handles, or solid, pendant 'knobs of tin' or iron. The brass handles of the later seventeenth century most often consisted of slender loops, rings, stirrup and ellipse shapes on circular plates and held by strips of metal folded outwards at the back in the manner of brass paper-clips. The wide, low, loop handles of Queen Anne cabinets might have their back-plates incised, but piercing for such work dates mainly from about the 1720s. They hung on the nutted bolts that held the back-plates. By the 1730s heavier drop loops had their bolt heads mounted on separate moulded circles. Showy, asymmetrically shaped 'French' mounts were popular around the mid-century, followed by the austere circles and ellipses of Adam's day, cast until about 1777 when stamping was used in Birmingham to make back-plates with patterns in relief. From about 1790 many heavy cast handles were used, including wreaths of flowers and the most familiar ring-holding lion heads.

Inlay: *see* the section on Blanket Chests.

Japanning: *see* Lacquer.

Lacquer: 'Right Indian' and 'Right Japan' were indiscriminate terms for Oriental lacquer to differentiate it from the poorer paint and varnish imitations executed in England. Many Oriental and Dutch cabinets were made in a distinctive plain rectangular silhouette notable for elaborate lock-plates and many fine hinges. Their crestings, like their stands, were English, carved and gilded or silvered; first in the florid Renaissance style, and then more restrainedly, with tapering trumpet legs. Stands ornamented with low-relief gilded gesso were followed by early Georgian stands like contemporary side-tables. Good-quality English japanned imitations of Oriental cabinets were frequently based on the gesso process of building up a ground of whiting and size that would be coloured, lac varnished and gilded. Sometimes the cabinet's softwood carcase was veneered – inside and out of the heavy doors – to provide a lastingly smooth surface to the lacquer substitute. Black was the most usual ground, red rarer, blue and white still rarer. Black and red were sometimes used for 'counterfeit tortoiseshell'.

Marquetry: *see* under Blanket Chests, p. 133 (Plate 110).

Needlework Cabinets: 'A coffer maid in broderie upon reid satine' was listed among Elizabeth I's movables in 1561. This was a forerunner of innumerable examples characteristic of English needlework around the mid-seventeenth century. Every well-to-do young lady, it would appear, then embroidered a set of satin pieces for mounting on a little wooden cabinet fitted either with doors or with a fall-front to allow access to jewellery drawers and toilet compartments. In some examples the interior above the drawers consisted of a little well surrounded by lidded boxes for toilet accessories, and ornamented with pieces of the still-novel looking-glass and perhaps carpeted with a hand-coloured print. But the major work went into the exterior mountings, usually embroidered on the narrow rich satin, then newly available, that allowed the embroidery to break away from the customary ground-covering tent stitch into speedier ornament that left some of the ground visible.

Most often the main embroidery was scenic, such as one of a few favourite scriptural scenes—the story of Rebecca, or Jephthah and his daughter, perhaps. Always the tendency was to crowd the scene with fascinating, disproportionate detail in the Elizabethan manner. Often some of the main figures were padded and stitched separately, their faces and hands of wood, silk covered, their clothes exquisitely wrought with minute lace stitches and decked out in all the trinket ornaments that age has rendered somewhat tawdry. Beads and coral, feathers and tinsel, were freely used in what was then termed raised work but has become known as stump work.

Those who condemn the extraneous ornament on the raised work must remember that its creators were usually girls barely into their teens, who had graduated to this fanciful exercise through the rigours of an elaborate sampler of flat coloured stitches and another of alphabets and cut-works in white. And even the most frivolous are usually in meticulous stitchery.

Such conspicuous trifles have tended to overshadow the many cabinets mounted with flat embroidery, either in a wide variety of stitches or in the fine unemphatic grace of tent stitch, known also as *petit point*, although this term has now been transferred by some collectors to the comparatively clumsy cross stitch (Plate 107B).

Ormolu: originally gold ground to powder for gilding metals, and hence the gilded bronze that decorated fine furniture, so that the term came to mean an alloy of copper, zinc and tin, gold coloured. Ure's *Dictionary of the Arts* (1875) defined it as 'a brass in which there is less zinc and more copper than in ordinary brass, the object being to obtain a nearer imitation of gold than ordinary brass affords'. English manufacture was launched by Matthew Boulton; in 1778 the *English Gazetteer* referred to Birmingham ormolu as highly esteemed all over Europe.

Painted Cabinets: some of the earliest English casket cabinets were painted inside and out, often with heraldic motifs. But it was about 1780 before this again became an important medium. Then the cabinet was often of satinwood, solid or in veneer, and slightly painted with ribbons and swags of flowers. Some cabinets were painted all over, either white in the Pergolesi manner or a pale straw colour to suggest a satinwood background to painted medallions of cupids and the like in the Cipriani-Kauffmann style. After about 1800 exotic wood veneers were generally preferred.

Parquetry: some attractive small cabinets were veneered in regular patterns created with squares, diamond shapes, triangles, etc, of matching and contrasting grain patterns.

Porcelain Cabinets: Mary II owned several for Chinese porcelain and Delftware, but they are associated especially with the mid-eighteenth century when English porcelain was a spectacular novelty. They offered wide scope for fantastic 'Chinese' designs, some in fine mahogany and many more in softwoods, japanned and painted or partly gilded. Then followed slighter, classic carving with much use of peardrop cornice mouldings, after 1770, on straight cornices, urn-crested.

Straw-work: professional as well as amateur ornament on small cabinets, achieved with delicate and precise arrangements in split and variously coloured straws. These might be red, green, blue, as well as buff and black and white. The colour has proved fleeting, but cabinet interiors are often bright. Crude little pictures in this straw parquetry, often of buildings, are usually ascribed to French prisoners of war around 1800 (Plate 109C).

Stump-work: late nineteenth-century term for seventeenth-century raised or embossed work.

Tills: term occasionally noted in connexion with cabinets as well as chests. In 1561 Elizabeth I was presented with a 'cobonett full of tylls'.

Tunbridge Ware: small fitted cabinets were largely made in the styles of parquetry and wood mosaic that formed a distinctive craft in the Tonbridge and Tunbridge Wells area. (*See* the section on Writing-boxes.)

Walnut Cabinets: in 1687 the *London Gazette* referred to 'a drawing Walnut Tree Box, with two Drawers in it ... to put Mathematical Instruments in'. This might have been in solid walnut with rich undercut and cross-grained carving. Or it might have been in walnut veneer, hand-sawn, one-sixth or one-seventh of an inch thick, to display the beautiful pattern of the grain without regard for strength, and glued to a deal framework. Burr walnut, most difficult to lay, came from the tree stump where the roots showed as minute veins. The plumed effect was obtained from crotches or branch junctions; the 'oyster' was sliced across a small branch, often of laburnum or olive wood instead of walnut. Some walnut veneers were further enriched with marquetry. Suggestions of panelling on the flat surface might be achieved with narrow lines in contrasting veneers, mitred at the corners in high-quality work; diagonal grain especially between 1680 and 1705; cross grain with the herringbone or feather grain especially 1695–1715; cross grained alone especially after 1710. English, then French, then the 'black' Virginia walnut was used for cabinet work.

BLANKET CHESTS

'In ivory coffers I have stuff'd my crowns,' declared Gremio in *The Taming of the Shrew*:

In cypress chests my arras, counterpoints,
Costly apparel, tents, and canopies,
Fine linen, Turkey cushions boss'd with pearl,
Valance of Venice gold in needle-work,
Pewter and brass, and all things that belong
To house or house-keeping.

Heavy and rich, laboriously woven or embroidered, sumptuously lined and trimmed, the fabrics of earlier centuries were made to last for generations – and presented the housekeeper with the monumental problem of their safe keeping from the ravage of moth and the tarnish of damp. Chests were evolved as a refuge centuries before wardrobes became pieces of furniture instead of rooms, or chests of drawers broke free of the lidded-box design, and they have never entirely disappeared from use.

Very many of the splendid chests in churches were required for robes and vestments, even to the inclusion of a few quarter-circle and half-circle designs for most highly treasured copes. In 1480 the Pewterers' Company had streamers made to decorate their barge in a water pageant, and at once the accounts recorded the consequence: 'Item, payed for a cofyn for the sayde strem^rs xijd.' In 1550 this typical guild owned a wainscot chest for napery, and their records even included occasional payments for 'bagges of Rose leaves and lavender ffor tje chest of lynnen xviijd.'

As late as Tudor and early Stuart days, every room in the old rambling self-sufficient house might have its bed pitched like a tent and with a tent's semi-privacy among the tools of the establishment's innumerable trades, and more often than not every bed had its own accompanying furnishings, a blanket chest at the foot and probably another alongside serving instead of chair or table, such as Robert Belassis of Morton recorded, 'the great Danske chest at the bedde feete and a littell Chest at the bedd syde'. Inventories give fascinating glimpses of this confusion. They also testify to the importance of chests as furniture. Robert Barker, for instance, mayor of Newcastle from 1577 to 1585, had two danske chests in the nursery in 1588, a danske chest and a danske coffer in the fore parlour, and two more danske chests, one of fir, a little counter and a banded chest in the back parlour. In the previous year an inventory of a Newcastle merchant, William Jeneson, furnished a servants' chamber solely with two beds, four cupboards and five danske chests.

The mid-seventeenth century introduced mule chests and the gradual evolution of the big chest of drawers, but even in the eighteenth century's more polished household blanket chests received the consideration of good design and excellent workmanship. Evelyn and his daughter, in *Mundus Muliebris*, described the bed-chamber of a late Stuart society lady, and among the expected cabinets, tea tables, and all the rest she was furnished with 'trunks on stand'. It must be remembered, of course, that household linen was stored in immense quantity by every lady of any substance, and handed down from generation to generation.

The contemporary names of many of these chests indicate that they were imported from abroad—Danske, Spruce, Flanders and so on. The Act of Tonnage and Poundage, 1689, indicates that they came in nests of three, fitting inside each other, and duty rates were calculated on this assumption; whereas chests of iron were dutiable singly, and small painted chests and gilt-leather covered coffers by the dozen. The duty on cypress-wood chests was more than five times as great as on spruce or danske chests or iron-bound coffers. While many were specifically for blankets, linen or napkins, this style of chest was widely used for household storage. Cedar-lined chests have never been ousted for protection against moth and damp.

Armour was stored in chests, as described in Chambers' *Cyclopaedia*, 1751, and in 1789 Dr Burney referred to the custom in music-loving families of possessing chests of viols – two trebles, two tenors and two basses. Various food chests were developed with local names: in the north-east, for instance, an ark was often a ventilated chest. 'The

CHEST FURNITURE

Mule chest covered with brown leather, finely close-nailed and with notable pierced mounts. This bears the monogram of William III and Mary. Late seventeenth century. Measurements 3 ft. 2 in. × 1 ft. 10 in. × 2 ft. 3 in. *Victoria & Albert Museum.*

PLATE 113

CHEST FURNITURE

(A) Chest for storage, early Stuart period. The chest ends slide in grooves and when drawn up show two drawers beneath a false bottom. Measurements 3 ft. 11 in. × 2 ft. × 2 ft. *Victoria & Albert Museum.*

(B) Beautifully carved walnut chest, late fifteenth century. *Victoria & Albert Museum.*

(C) Late fifteenth-century chest, carved oak banded with iron. Measurements 6 ft. 11½ in. × 2 ft. 3 in. × 1 ft. 11 in. *Victoria & Albert Museum.*

(D) Seventeenth-century oak mule chest. Low-relief carving mainly lacking surface modelling. Lower part contains only one small drawer, flanked by two cupboards. Measurements 5 ft. × 2 ft. × 3 ft. *Victoria & Albert Museum.*

(E) Chest of very simple nailed-up construction, the vertical ends continued and shaped to form legs. Elm, *c.* 1630. Measurements 3 ft. 3 in. × 1 ft. 3 in. × 1 ft. 8 in. *Victoria & Albert Museum.*

(F) Thirteenth-century chest, chip-carved in roundels. Measurements 3 ft. 7 in. × 1 ft. 7 in. × 1 ft. 8 in. *Victoria & Albert Museum.*

CHEST FURNITURE

(A) Leather-covered chest with brass lockplate and close-nailing. Dated 1666. Measurements 4 ft. 6 in. × 2 ft. 6 in. × 2 ft. 7¾ in. *Victoria & Albert Museum.*

(B) Mule chest, early eighteenth century, the front of burr walnut veneer with wide herringbone bandings. *Victoria & Albert Museum.*

(C) Nonsuch chest of oak ornamented with various woods. Late sixteenth century. Measurements 5 ft. 11½ in. × 2 ft. 3 in. × 2 ft. 2 in. *Victoria & Albert Museum.*

(D) Oak panelled chest painted with formal flower groups. Seventeenth century. Measurements 4 ft. 10 in. × 1 ft. 10 in. × 2 ft. 2 in. *Victoria & Albert Museum.*

(E) Chest of cypress wood, incised on front with grotesque birds and dragons among formal ornament. Early seventeenth century. Measurements 5 ft. 3 in. × 1 ft. 10 in. × 1 ft. 11 in. *Victoria & Albert Museum.*

(F) All-over strapwork in low relief around panels finely inlaid with flower-and-vase motifs on an early seventeenth-century chest. The feet are formed by the corner stiles, overlapped by the applied base moulding. *Hotspur Ltd.*

PLATE 115

CHEST FURNITURE

(A) Chest decorated with Japanese lacquer in relief. Gilded base and engraved brass mounts are English, c. 1750. *H. Blairman & Sons.*

(B) Chest of carved mahogany, design taken from Verrochio's tomb of the Medici in St Lorenzo, Florence, 5 ft. long × 2ft. 9 in. wide × 2 ft. 10 in. high, c. 1730. *Victoria & Albert Museum.*

(C) Plate chest of oak veneered with lignum vitae. Seventeenth century. Measurements 14¼ in. × 9⅜ in. × 8½ in. *Victoria & Albert Museum.*

(D) Chest of camphor wood from the Dutch East Indies, the brass mounts cut and chased. Late seventeenth century. Measurements 5 ft. × 2 ft. 4 in. × 2 ft. 6 in. *Victoria & Albert Museum.*

(E) Wrought-iron plate chest with painted ornament, dated 1597. Mounted on iron wheels. 4 ft. 5¼ in. long and 2 ft. 8¾ in. high. *Victoria & Albert Museum.*

(F) Casket, substantially made of wickerwork with ornamental brass mounts. Eighteenth century. 22 in. × 12 in. × 14¼ in. *Victoria & Albert Museum.*

Kedleston Hall, Derbyshire. The dining-room by Robert Adam, showing candle-stands, sconces, knife-cases, and fire-screen.

SMALLER FURNITURE OF ALL PERIODS

(B) Late eighteenth-century plate-pail with brass handle, and cellaret of octagonal form. *Mallet & Son.*

(A) Mahogany Canterbury music-stand, c. 1810. *Hotspur, Ltd.*

(C) Mahogany tripod pole screen with needlework panel, c. 1750. *Frank Partridge & Sons.*

(D) Late eighteenth-century mahogany tripod basin-stand with shelf and drawer and soap receptacle. *Hotspur, Ltd.*

SMALLER FURNITURE OF ALL PERIODS

(B) Mahogany kettle-stand, *c.* 1755, with aperture for kettle spout, and slide; enriched with rococo carving. *Formerly in the F. H. Reed Collection.*

(A) Mahogany tripod kettle-stand, *c.* 1755, with lattice-work gallery, kettle and heater. *Mallett & Son.*

(C) Hepplewhite period mahogany urn-stand with slide. *Frank Partridge & Sons.*

PLATE 119

SMALLER FURNITURE OF ALL PERIODS

(A) Library steps made to fold into a small table, *c.* 1790. *Hotspur, Ltd.*

(B) Chair and steps combined, *c.* 1810. *Hotspur, Ltd.*

PLATE 120

SMALLER FURNITURE OF ALL PERIODS

(A) Sconces: Early eighteenth-century, carved and gilt. *Frank Partridge & Sons.*

(B) *c.* 1760, in the Chinese taste, carved and gilt. *Frank Partridge & Sons.*

(C) Late eighteenth-century, in the classical style, with cut-glass ornament. *Frank Partridge & Sons.*

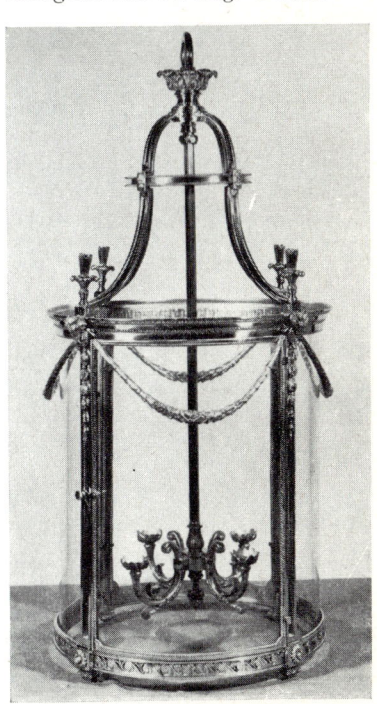

(D) Late eighteenth-century metal lantern with classical ornament. *Mallett & Son.*

PLATE 121

SMALLER FURNITURE OF ALL PERIODS

(A) Mahogany wine cooler inlaid with satinwood, c. 1775. *Mallett & Son.*

(B) Kingwood and satinwood 'French Work-table' with tray, and trestle feet, c. 1790. *Frank Partridge & Sons.*

PLATE 122

SMALLER FURNITURE OF ALL PERIODS

(A) Top of writing-table shown in 123C below.

(B) Gate-leg writing-table with folding top, c. 1690. *Private Collection.*

(C) Writing-table with drawer and folding top decorated with floral marquetry, c. 1690. *Private Collection.*

PLATE 123

SMALLER FURNITURE OF ALL PERIODS

(A) Late eighteenth-century mahogany night-table with tray top. *Hotspur.*

(B) Late seventeenth-century brass-bound casket on a George II period carved mahogany stand. *Private Collection.*

(C) Walnut bureau or secretaire on turned legs with curved stretchers and finial, *c.* 1690. *The Hart Collection.*

PLATE 124

EUROPEAN LACQUER FURNITURE

(A) English lacquer cabinet, c. 1620. *Victoria and Albert Museum, London.*

(B) Dutch lacquer doll's house cupboard, c. 1700. *Rijksmuseum, Amsterdam.*

(C) Dutch lacquer casket, early seventeenth century. *Rijksmuseum, Amsterdam.*

EUROPEAN LACQUER FURNITURE

(A) English lacquer cabinet on carved gilt stand, c. 1670. *H. Blairman and Sons Ltd.*

(B) English lacquer secretaire, early eighteenth century. *William Rockhill Nelson Gallery of Art, Kansas City.*

(C) English lacquer commode, first half of the eighteenth century. *Collection of Sir James and Lady Horlick.*

EUROPEAN LACQUER FURNITURE

(A) Commode decorated with a veneer of Oriental lacquer on the front and English japan on sides and borders, c. 1765. *The Shaftesbury Estates Co.*

(B) English lacquer display cabinet, probably by Thomas Chippendale, c. 1750. *Collection of Sir James and Lady Horlick.*

(C) English green lacquer bracket clock by Thomas Windmills, early eighteenth century. *Moniz Galvãos Collection, Lisbon.*

(D) English lacquer cabinet, c. 1830. *H. Blairman and Sons Ltd.*

PLATE 127

EUROPEAN LACQUER FURNITURE

(A) French console table decorated with a panel of Japanese lacquer by Bernard van Risen Burgh, c. 1750. *Collection of M. de Cailleux.*

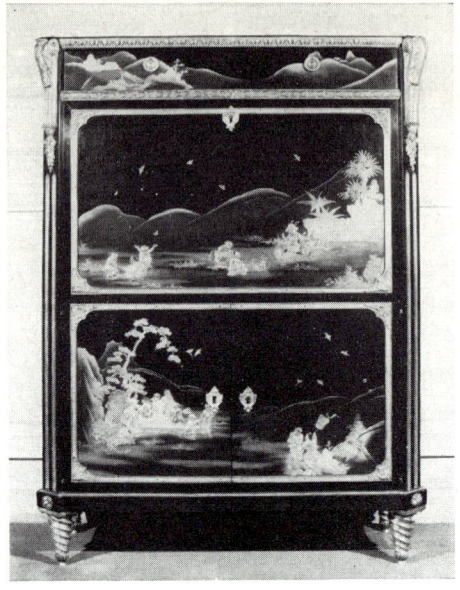

(B) French secretaire decorated with panels of Chinese lacquer by P. Garnier, c. 1770. *Louvre, Paris.*

(C) Chest of drawers veneered on oak with panels of Japanese and French lacquer, probably by René Dubois, c. 1770–80. *Wallace Collection, London.*

PLATE 128

cheese in arke, the meill in Kist' (Henryson, 1450) was reiterated in innumerable later inventories. But Warwick's St Mary's Church in 1464 listed 'i grete olde arke to put in vestments &c'. In East Anglia the term hutch was widely used for a kitchen chest. Spices, salt and candles all had their own chests. Some idea of the widespread demands may be gained from a wholly typical late sixteenth-century inventory: in 1580 John Lawson of Chester had a counter, a salt kytt and a danske chest in his hall; two old chests and a leather-covered chest in his chamber; a chest, a coffer and another little chest in his parlour – no chairs, no tables – and a 'great arke' in the kitchen.

Carved Chests: it is impossible to differentiate entirely between ecclesiastical and domestic chests. Surviving medieval specimens probably represent only the finest work. Some of the earliest ornament consisted of chip-carved roundels. Always the tendency has been for the ornament to suggest, superficially, the architectural construction of building in stone: thus an early panel would have chamfering on the top edge of the lower rail because this allowed water to drain off a stone sill. Until well into the sixteenth century foreign influence was mainly Flemish. Some of the richest remaining fourteenth- and fifteenth-century chests are 'Flanders chests' carved with representations of 'Gothic window' tracery, although attention has been drawn to the fact that in some instances a chest's frontal carving may originally have formed the reredos associated with a church's stone altar (Plate 114F and B).

Other low-relief carving more simply followed linenfold and similar fabric patterns. High-relief carving was used for naturalistic ornament. In medieval and early Tudor chests various real and mythological creatures were carved and occasionally there were even pictorial scenes, followed by more sophisticated pilaster figures, caryatides and the heavy round-headed Roman arch that has become symbolic of Renaissance decoration. Soon this Roman arch was surrounding panels of inlay instead of carving. In the seventeenth century there was a vast amount of dull repetitive work, much of it lacking even surface modelling. After the interruption of smooth-faced veneers and lacquers there came a return to some heavy architectural carving in early mahogany and by the mid-eighteenth century some good cut-card work was appearing on mahogany chests, but it became more usual to fret-cut and apply it, instead of carving from the solid and smoothing the background. Late-eighteenth- and nineteenth-century oak chests were often coarsely carved, being only faintly reminiscent of simple work of earlier centuries (Plate 114).

Cassoni: a pair of Italian dower chests constituted important furnishings in the sixteenth and seventeenth centuries. Some were elaborately painted, the wood covered first with glue-on canvas, then perhaps with gesso, then with paint. Others were richly carved or decorated with marquetry. The Earl of Leicester in 1588 had 'fower faier flatt [i.e. not rounded trunk-tops] Venetian chests of Walnut tree carved and gilte'. English work is occasionally noted in similar vein.

Cedar Chests: Cedar veneer made an excellent lining for a blanket chest. John Houghton stressed in 1727 that the wood 'is of so very dry a nature that it will not endure to be fastened with *nails*, from which it shrinks, therefore *pins* of the same are better . . .' Cedar chests were extensively imported from Holland in Queen Anne's reign.

Chest Stands: towards the end of the seventeenth century many blanket chests were fitted with stands. These resembled their period's side-tables, with trumpet-shaped legs, waved diagonal stretchers and heavy ball or bun feet. Soon after the turn of the century, low cabriole-legged stands might be used, or a chest might be mounted merely on plain bracket feet. Oriental lacquered chests were mounted on stands made in England, first with heavy naturalistic carving and then in more formal designs. Some were gilded but many more were silvered to accord with the late seventeenth century's craze for silver furniture, and only assumed a golden tone as the protective varnish lost its original clarity. Around the mid-eighteenth century some blanket chests were mounted on straight-legged, fret-cut stands in the English 'Chinese' manner.

Commodes: Sobry in *Architecture* (1718) stated that 'coffers and arks are commonly called commodes. Some have a lid, others have drawers'. But the term is more usually restricted to a cupboard design with doors and drawers. While bedrooms remained customary visiting and reception rooms, all bedroom furniture tended to be disguised and some bedroom commodes were constructed to resemble chests or trunks.

Construction: *see* section on Plate Chests.

Counters: *see* section on Plate Chests.

Cypress Chests: introduced early in the sixteenth century, but by the late seventeenth century were subject to heavy import tax. Some bore all-over ornament in low relief, incised or in cheap poker work. John Houghton reported in 1727 that such chests were made in Venice for the wood 'resists the *worm* and *moth*, and all putrefaction to *eternity* . . . nothing outlasts it, or can be more beautiful, especially than the roots of the wilder sort, incomparable for its *crisped undulations*'. Houghton also referred to the use of juniper wood for chests (Plate 115E).

Danske Chests: frequently appear in Elizabethan records and might be assumed to be imports from Denmark, but probably there was more or less generalized use of the terms spruce (Prussia), danske and danszig for chests of Baltic fir wood.

Dowry Chests: for centuries a chest of linen was a bride's usual contribution to her new home, but the term dowry chest appears of comparatively recent popularity.

Feet: early chests merely had their corner stiles prolonged to raise them from the floor, a frequent detail consisting of a semicircular shaping on the inner side of each front stile partly filled with a turned spindle or a vestige of such ornament. In heavily carved Elizabethan chests, the feet might continue the pillar motif. But during the seventeenth century separate feet were often applied, consisting of balls or bun shapes. In 1633 the turners complained that the joiners were wrongfully making their own. Low cabriole and simple bracket feet, sometimes on a separate stand, came with the eighteenth century (Compare Plates 114A, 114F, 115B and 115F).

Flanders Chests: more vaguely defined as overseas work in some inventories. They were in great demand by the sixteenth century; as early as 1483 the Cofferers' Guild was protesting at their importation. Inventoried specimens were generally priced at about five shillings in the late sixteenth century, and were in general use throughout the house. Some remaining specimens may have been preserved because of the exceptional richness of their traceried 'church window' carving, attached sometimes instead of carved from the solid. In the seventeenth century the ornament associated with Flanders included a range of unambitious glued-on decoration intended to simulate elaborate constructional work.

Gesso: among the richest, most ornate furnishings of many a flamboyant late Stuart and early Georgian household were chests covered with gilded gesso. These tended to follow the heavy baroque designs of other gesso furniture, contrasting with extremely delicate work in low relief on the lid where intertwining arabesques shaped by brush in the gesso composition were set off by the customary ground of subdued matting. The gesso was suitably coloured and then covered with gold or silver leaf, and this protected with varnish.

Inlay: pieces of contrasting wood about one-eighth of an inch thick sunk into the solid oak or walnut of the chest. It was associated especially with the seventeenth century, but introduced much earlier, at first with native wood, then with ebony, with ivory and mother-of-pearl fostered by the monarchs' associations with Spain in Mary's and James I's reigns, with silver, pewter and the ubiquitous tortoiseshell. John Houghton in 1727 referred to the practice of inlaying holly under ivory 'to render it more con-

CHEST FURNITURE

spicuous'. An alternative term was set-work. Thus Robert Atkynson, a former sheriff of Newcastle, owned a 'great Danske Chyste with sett wourke', valued at £5 in 1596 when a more usual valuation of a danske chest was five shillings (Plate 115F).

Joined Chests: *see* section on Plate Chests.

Jousting Chests: an attractive name given to chests carved in high relief with naturalistic scenes of secular subjects, such as jousting and hunting. These may have been created as early as the fourteenth or fifteenth century, but they have prompted many nineteenth- and twentieth-century copies.

Lacquer: first the Dutch and then the English East India Company imported great quantities of Oriental lacquer boards in the later seventeenth century, and these were often made into handsome blanket chests. Pepys in 1661 wrote of the Duke of York's 'many fine chests covered with gold and Indian varnish given him by the East Indy Company of Holland'. Lacquer trunks were listed in 1700 among the goods sold at East India House. But many more were made up in England. Some Oriental lacquer panels were framed up in English japanned work, usually an unattractive combination. Others were wholly of English japanning. 'Lackered Ware Truncks' were advertised in the *London Gazette* in 1687. (*See* section on Cabinets.) The liking for Chinese work never entirely disappeared, and around the mid-eighteenth century many Chinese rooms were created with lacquer or japanned chests among their handsome furnishings.

Leather: some blanket chests were covered with leather, closely studded with nails but lacking the metal angle-pieces and bandings that would fit them for travel. Some were mule chests.

Lids: for household use chests had flat table tops, the flat boards secured by cross battens fitting outside the chests themselves. Stuart chests had thinner lids from about 1600, and they might be framed up in loose panels after about 1625.

Mahogany: by George II's reign these chests ranged from extreme plainness to the most richly carved work. A mule chest, for instance, might be entirely plain save for the metal mounts and the cock's head beading around the drawers, and many depended upon the beauty of their rich Cuban veneers (Plates 111B and 116B).

Marquetry: achieved much the same effect as inlay (q.v.), but the contrasting pattern and its background were both created in wood veneer thinly covering the wood that formed the chest. Veneering proved the most successful method of using the hard, brittle ebony that came into fashion in the seventeenth century. Inlay usually appeared on panelled chests and in association with carving; marquetry required a flat, unbroken surface. Nothing elaborate was attempted on chests and much of the naturalistic flower-and-bird work that remains appears to be Dutch.

Metal Mounts: Wrought-iron, often gilded, largely ceased to ornament chests during the fourteenth century, apart from security bandings and heavy lock-plates, and the strap hinges that were replacing wooden pin hinges. Iron was costly and the wood was smooth enough for carving. Some Elizabethan hinges were decoratively shaped to form a pair of rounded Es, one in reverse. Handles were of iron until the mid-seventeenth century when brass might be used. Screws were cut and filed by hand, and were rough and less perfectly regular than modern machine work. Their heads varied perceptibly in size and their ends were blunt.

Mule Chests: here the usual box construction was combined with one or two drawers below. Some were of oak, many more of walnut; mid-eighteenth-century work might be in mahogany. For drawer construction, *see* the section on Cabinets (Plate 111).

Nonsuch Chests: decorated with a kind of wood mosaic known as intarsia, a geometrical inlay prepared in bulk and cut off into lengths as required to fill hollows sunk in the wood. This work possibly dated to about 1500 onwards. In the Nonsuch designs quaint buildings were portrayed, perhaps, as Fred Roe has suggested, intended to represent the Nonsuch House on old London Bridge, a timber construction brought over from Holland in prefabricated sections early in Elizabeth I's reign (Plate 115c).

Ornament: probably the earliest chests were brightly painted: the Carpenters' Company paid 13s. 4d. for a chest to be painted and gilded in 1484. Carving observed a sequence of modified Gothic and Renaissance Greco-Roman styles followed by much raised applied ornament. Inlay appeared in the sixteenth century and was developed in the seventeenth, and there was some intarsia work in the Continental manner. There was some simple marquetry, and a little sumptuous silvered or gilded gesso, as well as much English japanning. Early Georgian mahogany might bear such simple classic enrichment as dentil moulding, and there was some mid-eighteenth-century pseudo-Chinese cut-card work.

Settles: often merely chests with tall panelled backs and arm-rests, and sometimes placed at the bed-foot. Sir Thomas Ramsey in 1590 possessed several, their style indicated by an entry 'a wainskot settle wth two locks vs'.

Spruce Coffers: *see* Danske Chests.

Trunks: this term is so usually associated today with travelling that it is well to realize its wider implication, as in G. Greene's reference, 1591: 'At the bed's feete stood a hansome truncke, wherin was very good linnen.' Even the Carpenters' Company in 1648 used it as a term for linen chest, and the Company's writings, too, were 'locked up in a trunke'. (*See* the section on Travelling Chests.)

PLATE CHESTS

Chests were the forerunners of the modern safe throughout century after century of pillage and pilfering, of unbridled violence and the petty tricksters who, one suspects, must have been major pests in the big households that dominated Tudor and Stuart life. As early as the thirteenth century the majority of towns were acquiring self-rule and arranging that city dignitaries should be responsible for the keys that trebly locked each muniment chest and iron-bound coffer. A number of churches testify to the security of their thirteenth-century treasure chests. Liveried companies record many among their possessions, such as the Pewterers' in 1488–9: 'A grete joyned forser peintyd w^t the armys of the crafte and lockyd w^t ij keys pryc viijs.'

This Company's records at this time indicate the range of chests used for safe keeping; consecutive items in their books included 'boxis contayning dyverse evydences', 'a Casked lokt with the jury booke', and other documents (this had become 'an olde boxe or Casket' by 1549, and was supplemented then by a black, leather-covered chest bound with iron), 'a box with xxiiij byllys of paper' and other documents, 'a blak cofyr containing iij chapelets of Rede Saten, ij lelypottys' and other silver, and 'a grete Chest bounde with Iren called a standard'. Another chest with two locks was acquired seven years later. But it is not always remembered that this problem of safe-keeping continued far beyond the troubled days of medievalism. Henry VIII commanded that parish registers should be kept in coffers with two locks and keys, and valuables in chests of iron. Some early specimens found in old churches may date to the day when Edward VI commanded every parish to supply a strong chest, trebly locked and with a hole in the top for collecting money for the poor. But it was by no means unusual for a church to have custody of a family's plate chest.

By Elizabethan days a man of considerable wealth would have a jewel coffer such as was owned by the Earl of Leicester in 1588: 'A jewel coffer, with sundry boxes and partitions of redd leather, guilte, covered with fustian of Naples, nailed all over with yellow nails, barred with iron and w^t iij lockes and keies.' But for larger articles of plate he might use his 'great redd standard bound with iron, with lock and key'. The Earl at this time possessed nine other chests, covered with leather or Naples fustian, and also four Venetian chests, of carved and gilded walnut. The 1666 fire in London resulted in a great demand for new and stronger boxes for documents and valuables: the Pewterers, for instance, resorted to the purchase of two 'Sea Chests to secure ye Books, Deeds and Records.' Still later, the end of the seventeenth century witnessed an extreme intensity of hoarding, and Georgian furniture with its many hiding-places testifies to the continuance of the nagging anxieties of possessions. Some extraordinarily elaborate strong-boxes date to the seventeenth and eighteenth centuries.

The collector traces the development of the plate chest from the earliest dug-out through the medieval thick-planked trunk, the wood as much as 2, occasionally 3, inches thick, too heavy to move, doubly or trebly locked, banded with iron and perhaps guarded at the hinges with iron chains or perhaps chained to the wall. The chest, 11 feet long, in Chipping Sodbury (Gloucestershire) town hall, dating to about 1500, is so heavily banded with iron bolted to the thick oak that its weight has been calculated at one and a half tons. Ironwork ornament had been superseded by cheaper alternatives by the fourteenth century, but the idea of chests constructed wholly of metal is not so ancient. Even the Blacksmiths' Company themselves in 1496 kept their valuables in 'a gret Cheste of elme in length VII fote di w^t a box Thereynne w^t III lokks and III keies'. Some chests were banded with iron in both directions. When this developed into the chest wholly of iron this so recommended itself to the rich liveried companies that even such craftsmen in wood as the Carpenters bought an iron chest in Charles I's reign for keeping their stocks and bonds, worth over £4,000 (Plate 116E).

By the late seventeenth and throughout the eighteenth century many of the most elaborate strong-boxes were imported from Germany. These were long associated, erroneously, with the Spanish Armada, and are described under the usual popular name of Armada chests.

Adze-surfaced Wood: some late medieval and early Tudor chests of heavy, strong construction show a pleasing irregularity of surface under the metal bandings, due to being faced with an adze. This tool, resembling a hatchet but with the blade at right angles to the shaft, inevitably left the surface faintly patterned with ridges and saucer-shaped hollows.

Armada Chests: these iron strong-boxes were imported from Germany in the late seventeenth century and throughout the eighteenth, and have no association in fact with the Spanish Armada. They were copied by English craftsmen, but not usually in such elaboration. In the typical design the whole lid was a gigantic lock, with as many as a dozen bolts – occasionally twice that number – which when shot caught under the turned-in edges of the sides. A false keyhole was usually included in the front, although this must have been too well known to any potential cracksman to have any security value; the real keyhole was in the lid hidden by a small plate that sprang up when a knife was pushed under one of the metal straps. For further security there might be looped hasps or staples for fastening with padlocks. But the metal itself was thin and would not offer much resistance to a modern safe-breaker. The lock often had a highly decorative plate, engraved and pierced, and in some instances the whole chest was ornamented with wrought-iron scrolls. Further decoration was provided with painted pictorial work.

Coffers: term frequently applied in circumstances that indicate a strong-box, and in the plural bearing a direct association with money, as for instance Dryden's 'Money in our Coffers'. In the king's household, Bailey's dictionary (1730) points out, the cofferer was the name for the second officer under the comptroller, responsible for paying the other officers their wages. Early references are numerous. Beket in 1300 had 'a lute cofre' in which at least £800 was kept, and as late as 1732 Lediard referred to 'several coffers and cabinets filled with stuffs and gold'. But here again it is unwise to be over-precise; for one finds, for instance in a Bury will of 1463, a more general and typical application – 'a lityl grene coffre for kerchys'.

Compartment Chests: when safe keeping was the main preoccupation, a large chest or standard, and its lid, might both be divided into two or more parts, each fitted with its own lock.

Construction: it is important to recognize that primitive construction is no guarantee of age. The first advance from pegged or hammered-up plank construction towards a framed style may be dated to as early as around the mid-fifteenth century; the four big upright pieces, stiles, were grooved to receive one or more tongued horizontal side planks placed flush with the stiles and often cross-banded at the corners with iron. But village carpenters and other craftsmen continued to meet local needs long after the joiner became established in England making his joined chests (q.v.). It is interesting to note that in 1500 the Carpenters' Company went to a joiner to make them a chest. In the early seventeenth century many of the elaborate effects of panelling were achieved merely with glued-on ornament, and decorative panelling gave place to veneering. By the eighteenth century all constructional methods were in use. As an additional security, a plate chest might have its ends drilled with vertical holes so that it could be screwed to the floor.

Counters: usually large, strong chests, found especially in merchants' houses, with their flat lids scored for reckoning. They are often noted in inventories of the main halls in Elizabethan houses.

Ironwork: some of the most interesting early work was fashioned by hammering the hot iron into chilled iron dies. Some extremely attractive flower-and-leaf patterns were achieved in this way, which may be compared with the grille on the tomb of Queen Eleanor in Westminster Abbey dating to 1292. Otherwise the bands were wrought by the blacksmith in a manner so traditional that it is virtually impossible to date it. The metal itself, of course, may be distinguished from modern iron, but not easily from Tudor or early Stuart work. Charcoal-smelted iron has a black tone, and never the fresh bright rust of modern work. Some bands were let into the wood of the chest to their full thickness, but more usually projected to take the rub of wear, especially on their massive nail heads. The majority were plain or had simply ornamented terminals. Iron ornament returned only with the pseudo-medieval castings of the nineteenth century. Even apart from any question of security, the everyday usage of earlier, rougher centuries demanded strong construction. Catherine Parr complained that the royal children Mary and Elizabeth smashed all the furniture in their Hatfield apartments except what was made of cast-iron or massive oak (Plate 116c).

Jewel Chests: in some instances a chest of the so-called Armada type would hold a rich family's jewels, although these are more particularly associated with companies and official holders of securities. Ralph, first Earl Verney, in his will in 1752 referred to his wife's little iron jewel chest, but indicated that more jewels and money were concealed in a cabinet in the trunk-room. Obviously one of the major requirements of the small many-compartmented cabinet was as a container for jewellery, handsome enough to be worthy of its contents. These are considered under the section on Cabinets.

Between these extremes, very many small chests were made of other sturdy materials for jewellery. Often they were trunk-shaped with rounded lids, substantial lock-plates and heavy metal corner-pieces. The earlier iron-work was replaced by brass in the course of the seventeenth century, this often being engraved in the eighteenth century and sometimes including four small brass feet. The trunk itself, perhaps 18 inches wide by 12 inches high, might be veneered in decorative burr or oyster walnut, or covered in leather or japanning, or even made of wickerwork (Plate 116c and F).

Joined Chests: few survivors may be dated earlier than the sixteenth century. In these the horizontal rails and vertical stiles and intervening muntins were secured with mortise-and-tenon joints, often by the drawbore process, and grooved on their inner sides to hold loose panels allowing for the wood's reactions to changing atmospheric conditions, especially important in the tough, widely used oak of standard and coffer. Panels tended to be small to minimise joining and yet avoid cutting into the centre of the tree's heartwood, most liable to warp. In 1632, when some sort of agreement was attempted between carpenters and joiners, the joiner's work was defined to include 'all Sorts of Chests being framed duftalled pynned or Glued' (Plate 115D).

Locks: these followed the styles used on other contemporary woodwork, early specimens depending on quantity rather than intricacy, although the provision of a number of locks on a parish or company chest was mainly a safeguard against a dishonest or careless key-holder, different officials each being responsible for one key. In some instances a plate or muniments chest with three locks had iron staples so arranged that a bar run through them would make it even more difficult to prise open the lid until all were unlocked.

Locksmithing was a well-established craft in London by the twelfth century, the principle of the warded construction remaining unchanged until late in the eighteenth century. Plate locks were the rule until the late fifteenth century, and continued in most general use until mid-Victorian days. The exposed working parts, perhaps slightly ornamented, were riveted to a heavy hatchet-shaped plate of wrought-iron fixed flat against the wood. While iron and steel were very costly, the comparative cheapness of plate-locks was a strong recommendation. It must be stressed, however, that there was an Early Victorian craze for reproducing early plate-locks, distinguishable by the fact that they were riveted to rolled or cast-iron plates instead of hammered iron. Improvements in the locks' appearance were made in the sixteenth and early seventeenth centuries, but the metal itself wore badly. The most decorative might bear hand-sawn Gothic pierced ornament or coats-of-arms, and were bright with paint and gold leaf. Damascening on steel lock cases was introduced in the late sixteenth century and by the 1620s lock-cases were being engraved as a specialist trade, and afterwards fire-gilded to prevent rust.

Meanwhile lock-cases of latten had come into use, mostly Dutch metal until the 1730s, except for a period of monopolistic action when flawed English metal had to be used; such locks usually dated between 1660 and 1675. Early decoration on brass locks was punched. By the end of the seventeenth century locks were sometimes sold with matching accessories, such as hinges and key escutcheons. Greatly improved English brass replaced the latten in the mid-eighteenth century. In considering late locks, the collector may note that cases and parts for cheap locks were first cut from sheet iron by fly press, punched and bolstered, in 1796. Keys were hand-forged until 1812, and thereafter might be of stamped wrought-iron or, after 1816, might be cast.

Riven Wood: this was much used in early strong chests, saving labour although wasting wood, and ensuring enduring work, little subject to warping and splitting that would render a plate chest useless. The tree trunk was split or riven along the natural growth lines of dense, non-cellular tissue radiating from the tree centre. These rays show a relief on old, weathered, riven timber, and probably suggested the early linenfold patterns.

Silver: at periods when silver was lavishly used as a fashionable medium, silver caskets for jewels were devised. As early as 1494 Fabyan in his *Chronicles* wrote, 'he ordeyned a cheste or Trunke of clene sylver, to thentent yt all such juells and rych gyftes should be kept'. More date to the late seventeenth century, or to the 1820s onwards, when they suited the vogue for loading silver vessels with impressively heavy ornamental castings.

Standards: the most frequent term for large plate chests, described, for instance, in an inventory quoted by T. H. Turner: 'A square standard & covered with black letheir, & bowden with yrne, with 2 lokys.... A great red standard, full of stuff... a gret standard bound with ierne, with 2 lokks.' Many references might be noted, usually concerning wealthy households with considerable possessions. For instance, Henry VIII's privy purse expenses in 1530 included: 'for ij standards for to carry plate from yorke to hampton courte'. Wolsey in 1526, according to a quotation by Cavendish (1893), was sent three or four cartloads of stuff by the king 'and most parte thereof was lokked in great standerds'. (*See* also the section on Travelling Chests.)

SMALLER FURNITURE OF ALL PERIODS

By E. T. JOY, M.A.

A FAIRLY wide interpretation has been given here to the term 'small furniture'. It includes, in general, those smaller pieces which were not dealt with in the chapters on furniture in the previous volumes of this series, or which were there given only a passing mention. It has also been assumed that readers will be familiar with the main developments of English furniture styles, to which smaller furniture, as well as the larger, conformed; with the warning that 'country' furniture might continue to be made in a style which had passed out of fashion, perhaps some considerable time previously, in London and the chief provincial towns.

The collection of small pieces of furniture can be a most fascinating pastime, not only for obvious financial reasons but also because they are a constant delight to the eye, and – a point of special weight in these days when living room is not so spacious as in times gone by – because they can be frequently used as their original makers and owners intended.

The study of the evolution of smaller articles of furniture can also be a study of social history; for they portray, as Horace Walpole wrote of the furniture in Hogarth's pictures, 'the history of the manners of the age'. One can see how they came into use as the rooms of houses began to take on their separate character and as new conventions established themselves in society. Note, for example, how, at the end of the seventeenth century, the two new fashions of tea-drinking and displaying china produced a whole range of small pieces among which can be included, on the one hand, tea-boards, kettle-stands and caddies, and, on the other, china-stands, brackets and shelves. With the coming of home manufacture of mirror glass, the development of special processes of decoration such as Tunbridge ware and straw-work and the introduction of new materials like Clay's papier-mâché, many new articles came into production or new forms and modes of decoration were given to older ones. The great diversity of small pieces in Georgian dining-rooms tells its own story of the importance placed by the upper classes in those days on eating and drinking.

With regard to the furniture which is described hereunder, one might be tempted to write, as did Sheraton in his *Cabinet Dictionary*, that 'the reader will find some terms which he will probably judge too simple in their nature to justify their insertion'. One feels, however, that this apology is unnecessary; the simplest articles are often the most useful, and their names, though no doubt very familiar, do not give what is, after all, the intention of this section, viz. their history and development. It might be added, in conclusion, that Sheraton's own period delighted in small furniture which combined, to a greater degree than at any other time, usefulness with extreme delicacy of appearance.

BOOKS FOR FURTHER READING

RALPH FASTNEDGE: *English Furniture Styles* (1955).
MARGARET JOURDAIN: *Regency Furniture* (1948).
PERCY MACQUOID AND RALPH EDWARDS: *The Dictionary of English Furniture* (rev. 1954).
F. GORDON ROE: *English Cottage Furniture* (1950).

The design books by Chippendale, Hepplewhite and Sheraton make many references to the smaller furniture of their periods, while SHERATON's *Cabinet Dictionary* (1803), provides a great deal of information.

EUROPEAN LACQUER FURNITURE

By HUGH HONOUR

GREAT cabinets, bureaux, console tables, day-beds and chairs of green, vermilion or jet black lacquer, added the final touch of opulent magnificence to many a late seventeenth- or early eighteenth-century salon. 'What can be more surprising than to have our chambers overlaid with varnish more glossy and reflecting than polisht marble?' asked Stalker and Parker, the authors of the first English *Treatise of Japanning and Varnishing*, in 1688. 'No amorous nymph need entertain a dialogue with her Glass, or Narcissus retire to a fountain to survey his charming countenance when the whole house is one entire speculum.' They even went so far as to declare that 'the glory of one country, Japan alone, has exceeded in beauty all the pride of the Vatican at this time and the Pantheon heretofore'. Lacquer had already been introduced into Europe and soon there was hardly a great house in England, France, Germany or Italy that could not boast a few pieces of lacquered furniture, if not whole rooms 'overlaid with varnish more glossy and reflecting than polisht marble'. Many such works in lacquer have survived to our own day, mellowed but hardly decayed by time, and in their shining surfaces, between the exotic birds and wispy trees, we may still catch a reflection of the brilliant world for which they were created.

Before proceeding to an account of how and when lacquer was used for the embellishment of European furniture a few words must be said about the substance of this brilliant paint or varnish. Although intended to imitate Oriental lacquer, European lacquer was, perforce, made in a different way. Chinese and Japanese craftsmen derived the lac, the basic constituent of the varnish, from the resin of a tree, the *Rhus vernicifera*, and applied it to the wood they wished to decorate in many layers, each of which was allowed to dry before the next was applied. The surface was then highly polished and decorated with designs in gold leaf. As the resin from which true lac was obtained was unavailable in Europe and could not satisfactorily be imported from the East, craftsmen had to resort to other means to achieve the same effect, and they propounded a wide variety of different receipts. Filippo Bonanni, an Italian who wrote a treatise on lacquering in 1720, listed some ten different methods employed by English, French, German, Italian and Polish craftsmen. Usually the wood was prepared with a mixture of whitening and size and then treated with numerous coats of a varnish composed of gum-lac, seed-lac or shell-lac, different preparations of the resin broken off the twigs of the tree on which it is deposited by an insect, the *coccus lacca*, and dissolved in spirits of wine. The decorations were outlined in gold size, built up with a composition made of gum arabic and sawdust, coloured, polished and gilt with metal dust. The surface was burnished with a dog's tooth or an agate pebble. Such methods could not, of course, produce a substance as hard and glittering as Oriental lacquer, but as experiment succeeded experiment, European craftsmen gradually improved their technique and were eventually able to produce a varnish of great beauty. Some, indeed, thought they had improved upon their models and Voltaire rhapsodized over

    . . . les cabinets où Martin
    A surpassé l'art de la Chine.

By the irony of chance, time has dealt more kindly with these European imitations than with Oriental lacquer of the same period, much of which has now faded to a drab and unappetizing hue.

Importations of Oriental Lacquer: although considerable quantities of Oriental porcelain had been brought to Europe before the end of the sixteenth century, importations of Chinese and Japanese lacquer had been on a much more modest scale. Two varnished boxes which were in the collection of the Queen of France in 1524 and a 'purple box of Chine' which the Emperor sent from Aachen to Queen Elizabeth in 1602, may have been lacquered, but we cannot be sure. There is no doubt, however, of the attention which Oriental lacquer held for sixteenth-century travellers to the East. 'The fayrest workemanshippe thereof cometh from China,' wrote Van Linschoten in 1598, in the account of his voyage. And he went on to praise the 'desks, Targets, Tables, Cubbordes, Boxes, and a thousand such like things, that are all covered and wrought with Lac of all colours and fashions'. By 1610, indeed, one Jacques l'Hermite had sharpened his taste for lacquer to such a degree that he was able to despise a consignment sent to Holland from Bantam, declaring that it was far inferior to that which came from Japan.

Lacquer was imported into Europe in ever-increasing quantities during the first half of the seventeenth century. An inventory of 'goodes and household stuffe' belonging to the Earl of Northampton in 1614 refers to a 'China guilt cabinette upon a frame' and in the same year the East India Company's ship *Clove* returned to London, after the first English voyage to Japan, loaded with a cargo of Japanese wares which included 'Scritoires, Trunkes, Beoubes (screens), Cupps and Dishes of all sorts and of a most excellent varnish'. Lest the market should be flooded, these objects – the first of their kind to reach England in quantity – were sold off slowly to inflate their commercial value. This device had such good effect that 'small trunkes or chests of Japan guilded and inlaid with mother of pearle having sundry drawers and boxes' which fetched £4–5–0 and £5 in 1614 commanded as much as £17 apiece four years later. Lacquer was also popular in France during this period. By 1649 Mazarin had three Chinese cabinets in his collection of orientalia, besides many pieces of Eastern porcelain and embroidery, and he acquired more lacquer furniture in the next few years.

Mid-seventeenth-century travellers to China, whose *Voyages* were translated into many languages and read throughout Europe, were full of admiration for the lacquer they had seen in Peking and elsewhere. John Nieuhoff, the steward to the abortive Dutch embassy to the Emperor of China in 1655, described the process by which it was made, enlarging on the beauty and utility of lacquer: 'There is also in divers places throughout the whole Empire, a certain sort of Lime which they press from the Bark of a Tree, being tough and sticking like Pitch; of this, which I suppose I may call a Gum, they make a certain sort of Paint wherewith they colour all their Ships, Houses, and Household-stuff, which makes them shine like Glass; and this is the reason that the houses in China, and in the Isle of *Japon*, glister and shine so bright, that they dazzle the eyes of such as behold them. For this paint lays a shining colour upon Wood, which is so beautiful and lasting, that they use no Table-cloaths at their Meals; for if they spill any grease, or other liquor upon the Table, it is easily rubbed off with a little fair water, without loss or damage of colour.'

In addition to the painted lacquer – of the type described by Nieuhoff – incised Coromandel lacquer was extensively imported into Europe in the seventeenth century, mainly from the Dutch trading station at Bantam in the Malay peninsula, whence it derived the name 'Bantam work'. Cabinets and vast six-fold Coromandel screens were brought to Europe but enjoyed a somewhat wavering fashion, perhaps on account of their gaudy, if not garish, colour schemes which have only now faded to an attractively subdued tone (fragments of Coromandel lacquer preserved inside cabinets give one an idea of its startling pristine colours). In 1688 Stalker and Parker, who were certainly prejudiced in favour of painted lacquer, declared that Bantam ware was 'almost obsolete and out of fashion' in England. 'No person is fond of it, or gives it house-room,' they scornfully remarked, 'except some who have made new Cabinets out of old Skreens. And from that large old piece, by the help of a Joyner, made little ones ... torn and hacked to joint a new fancie ... the finest hodgpodg and medly of Men and Trees turned topsie turvie.' Without any regard for the figures of the design, strips of Coromandel were used in this way to face the drawers of cabinets or to frame looking-glasses, like that which is still to be seen at Ham House. Nevertheless, Coromandel screens retained their popularity in some circles, and the Duke of Marlborough included one among the furniture he took with him on his campaigns. In Germany and Holland the vogue for Coromandel seems to have been steadier and of longer duration than in England.

The Earliest European Lacquer: the first attempts to imitate Oriental lacquer in Europe were made in the early seventeenth century. Marie des Médicis is known to have employed a skilful cabinet maker named Etienne Sager to make 'with lacquer gum and gold decoration in the manner of the same country (China), cabinets, chests, boxes, panelling, ornaments for churches, chaplets, and other small articles of Chinese goods'. She also established a vendor of Oriental wares in the Louvre and his shop would, no doubt, have contained articles of European lacquer as well. At about the same time imitations of lacquer were produced in Italy and when William Smith wrote to Lord Arundell from Rome in 1616 he was able to list among his many accomplishments that he had 'been emploied for the Cardinalles and other Princes of these parts, in workes after the China fashion wch. is much affected heere'. Imitations were also made in England, as is shown by the inventory of furniture belonging to the 1st Earl of Northampton on his death in 1614. In addition to a few genuine Oriental articles, Lord Northampton owned several examples of 'china worke' (i.e. European lacquer). He had, for instance, a 'large square China worke table and frame black varnish and gold,' a 'small table of China worke in gold and colours with flies and wormes upon a table suteable,' and a 'Field bedstead of China worke blacke and silver branches with silver with the Armes of the Earl of Northampton upon the head piece'. These must have been European and were perhaps of English lacquer. Next year, in 1615, Lady Arundell was matching curtains to her 'bedde of Japan' which may also have been of English make. Unfortunately, none of these objects has survived, but a small group of English lacquer pieces dating from the second decade of the seventeenth century may give us some indication of what they were like. These consist of a ballot box dated 1619, in the possession of the Saddler's Company at London, a cabinet (Plate 125A) and a box of twelve roundels in the Victoria and Albert Museum. All are of oak painted in gold and silver with a curious *mélange* of European and Eastern motifs on a thickly varnished black ground. Similar lacquer work, though of somewhat higher quality, was also produced in Holland (Plate 125C). The fashion for imitation lacquer appeared in Denmark in the 1620s when a remarkable room in Rosenborg Castle at Copenhagen

FIG. 1. Panel of lacquer painted by Simon Clause, in the Rosenborg Castle, Copenhagen

was decorated with panels of dark green and gold lacquer, set in imitation tortoise-shell frames and painted by Simon Clause with views of fantastic buildings and fragile little junks. (Fig. 1.)

Although European craftsmen had greatly improved the technique of lacquering by the middle of the seventeenth century, they had not yet succeeded in producing wares which could vie with the genuine Oriental articles. Importations of chests and screens from China and Japan continued unabated. But Eastern cabinet makers did not produce all the objects of furniture deemed necessary for a European house, and merchants therefore sent out designs of various objects to be copied in the East. Here again there was a difficulty; for although Eastern craftsmen excelled in lacquer decoration their cabinet-making was found to be of surprisingly poor quality. As Captain William Dampier remarked in 1688, 'The Joyners of this country (China) may not compare their work with that which the Europeans make; and in laying on the Lack upon good or fine joyned work, they frequently spoil the joynts, edges, or corners of Drawers and Cabinets: Besides, our fashion of Utensils differ mightily from theirs, and for that reason Captain Pool, in his second voyage to the Country, brought an ingenious Joyner with him to make fashionable Commodities to be lackered here, as also Deal boards....' Very few such European carpenters seem to have been taken out to China, but unpainted furniture was occasionally shipped from Europe to the East to be lacquered and returned home for sale. This costly procedure was not practised for long, however, as European lacquerers had attained sufficient skill in their medium to satisfy all but the most fastidious connoisseurs before the end of the seventeenth century.

The great age of European lacquer begins in the late seventeenth century. French, English, Dutch, German and Italian craftsmen had discovered a means of imitating the fine hard polish of the Oriental substance; they had, moreover, learned to decorate it in a freer style with designs which expressed the European's strange vision of the infinitely remote and exotic lands of the East. At Versailles and in some of the greater English country mansions, whole rooms were lined with lacquer panels, of European or Oriental origin, and great Chinese, or Chinese style, cabinets mounted on ponderous gilt baroque stands became an essential feature in the furnishing of any truly grand house. Towards the end of the century the art of lacquering was also practised by amateurs in France and England where many a young lady spent her leisure hours 'japanning' any piece of furniture – large or small – on which she could lay her hands. Changing in style with the times, lacquer furniture maintained a fluctuating popularity until after the end of the eighteenth century. During this period lacquer was produced in England, France, Germany, Holland and Italy, and the furniture made in each of these countries must be considered separately.

English Lacquer: great square cabinets were probably the most popular objects of Oriental lacquer to be imported into England in the late seventeenth century and seem to have been the most widely imitated. Such cabinets have two doors, with elaborate metal hinges and lock guards, which open to reveal numerous small drawers and sometimes a central cupboard. Oriental examples can be recognized not only by the style of their gilt decorations but also by their metal work. In China such cabinets stood on the floor or on simple hard wood tables, but in England they were mounted on grandiose frames intended to set off their importance and make them harmonize with the other furniture of the rooms in which they were kept (Plate 126A). The cabinets themselves usually had black or imitation tortoiseshell backgrounds, but red ones were also made, especially for export to Spain and Portugal where this colour was preferred. England was indeed famous for its red lacquer which Bonanni, in 1720, declared to be of a colour more beautiful than coral – 'si bello che vince il colore di corallo'.

The stands for these cabinets were either gilt or, more usually, silvered and varnished so that they appeared to be gilt (it seems probable that most of the surviving silver stands were originally varnished in this manner). In the 1660s and 1670s the stands normally had four legs, sometimes crowned with *putti* or blackamoors, joined by aprons which were richly carved with figures, and swags of fruit and flowers, amid a profusion of swirling baroque scrolls. Towards the end of the century the design changed and stands were often made with three or four legs along the front connected by aprons carved in a lighter style. These stands usually had stretchers which were provided with round plates on which vases of Oriental porcelain might be placed. The top of the cabinet was sometimes enriched with a cresting carved in the same style as the stand, but was more often left free to serve as a table for more Oriental vases. In the second decade of the eighteenth century the heavy baroque stand went out of fashion and was replaced by a lighter and more elegant frame with cabriole legs, but these, alas, were seldom able to support the weight of the cabinets and relatively few have survived. At about the same time a few craftsmen departed from the traditional shape of the cabinet itself, giving it a shallow domed top.

When John Evelyn visited Mr Bohun in 1682, he noted that his 'whole house is a cabinet of all ellegancies, especially Indian; in the hall are contrivances of Japan skreens instead of wainscot.... The landskips of these skreens represent the manner of living and Country of the Chinese'. Many other such rooms, including those at Burghley House, Hampton Court Palace and Chatsworth, are mentioned in diaries of the period but none has survived and it is seldom possible to determine whether their panels were of Oriental or European origin.

Lacquer was at this date used for decorating nearly all articles of household furniture. In 1697 a company of 'The Patentees for Lacquering after the manner of Japan' (founded in 1694) was offering for sale 'Cabinets, secretaires, tables, stands, looking-glasses, tea-tables and chimney pieces'. Other lacquer objects made at the same time included chests of drawers, corner cupboards, clock-cases, day-beds, chairs and small articles for the dressing- or writing-table. These pieces were usually made of deal, oak or pear-tree wood on patterns which were identical with those of contemporary walnut furniture. The lacquer grounds were of various colours: black, vermilion, tortoise-shell, dark green (particularly popular for clock-cases), yellow or blue, and the gilt decorations represented a wide variety of fanciful scenes copied from genuine oriental objects, taken from Stalker and Parker's treatise or invented by the craftsman. Stalker and Parker claimed to have derived their designs from Oriental cabinets, somewhat ingenuously confessing that they had, perhaps 'helped them a little in their proportions where they were lame or defective, and made them more pleasant, yet altogether as Antick'. In the late 1720s chinoiserie decorations suffered a temporary eclipse and were replaced by flowers painted in naturalistic colours on a light ground.

In the late seventeenth century much lacquering, or 'japanning' as it was called, was executed by amateurs who applied themselves to the difficult art with a will, and the principal book on the subject, Stalker and Parker's *Treatise of Japanning and Varnishing* (Fig. 2), seems to have been designed mainly for a public of amateurs. By the 1680s the art of lacquering had taken its place among the genteel occupations suitable for young ladies, and in 1689 Edmund Verney permitted his daughter to take this extra subject at school, telling her: 'I find you have a desire to learn to Japan, as you call it, and I approve of it; and so I shall of anything that is good and virtuous, therefore learn in God's name all Good Things, and I will willingly be at the charge so far as I am able – though they come from Jappan and from never so farr and Looke of an Indian Hue and colour, for I admire all accomplishments that will render you considerable and Lovely in the sight of God and man....' That the art of lacquering – like watercolour painting in a later age – rendered young ladies lovely in the sight of man is, perhaps, confirmed by Dryden's lines to Clarinda (1687) in which he remarks that:

Sometimes you curious *Landskips* represent
And arch 'em o'er with gilded *Firmament*:
Then in *Japan* some *rural Cottage* paint.

Fig. 2. A design for a comb-box, from Stalker and Parker's *Treatise of Japanning and Varnishing*, 1688

Nothing was sacred to these eager japanners who seized on any object that could be decorated with Chinese figures. Sometimes they may have applied themselves to specially prepared furniture, but often they were content to lacquer ordinary walnut pieces. Nor was this pastime reserved for the young. Mrs Pendarves (later Mrs Delany) declared in 1729: 'Lady Sun(derland) is very busy about japanning: I will perfect myself in the art against I make you (Mrs Anne Granville) a visit, and bring materials with me'. 'Everyone is mad about Japan work,' she later remarked, 'I hope to be a dab at it. . . .' Even the Prime Minister's wife, Lady Walpole, applied herself to the art and it was to her that John Taylor dedicated his book: *The Method of Learning to draw in perspective. . . . Likewise a new and Curious Method of Japanning . . . so as to imitate China and to make black or gilt Japan-ware as Beautiful and Light as any brought from the East Indies* (1732). Horace Walpole preserved an example of his mother's handiwork – a cabinet – at Strawberry Hill.

Amateur japanners, it may be guessed, kept alive the vogue for lacquer furniture which, after a temporary eclipse, returned to fashion in the late 1740s. In 1749 Mrs Montagu – the Queen of the Blues – remarked that 'sick of Grecian elegance and symmetry, or Gothic grandeur and magnificence, we must all seek the barbarous gaudy *gout* of the Chinese. . . . You will wonder I should condemn a taste I have complied with, but in trifles I shall always conform to the fashion'. Accordingly, three years later she ordered a suite of japanned furniture, in full conformity with the chinoiserie taste of the moment, from Mr (presumably William) Linnell; some of it is now at Came House, Dorset. This revived fashion for chinoiserie did not, however, escape the attention of critics who poked merciless fun at the Mandarins and Mandarinesses of England. One of them, an anonymous writer in *The Connoisseur* (1755), gave a graphic description of a fop's dressing-table: 'But the toilet most excited my admiration; where I found everything was intended to be agreeable to the Chinese taste. A looking-glass, inclosed in a whimsical frame of Chinese paling, stood upon a Japan table, over which was spread a coverlid of the finest Chints. I could not but observe a number of boxes of different sizes, which were all of them Japan, and lay regularly disposed on the table. I had the curiosity to examine the contents of several: in one I found lip-salve, in another a roll of pig-tail, and in another the ladies black sticking plaister. . . .'

Many of the mid-eighteenth-century examples of English lacquer furniture were wholly designed in the Chinese taste, with fret-work doors and square legs carved with a similar fretted pattern. The cabinet and table made by Linnell for Mrs Montagu were in this style. Thomas Chippendale intended many of his designs for chinoiserie furniture (Plate 127B), especially the standing shelves designed for the display of Chinese porcelain, to be embellished with japanned decorations, but furniture in the current 'French' style, notably commodes and bureaux, were also decorated with panels of European or Oriental lacquer. A commode in the possession of the Shaftesbury Estates Company (Plate 127A) has a veneer of Chinese lacquer on the front and is painted with English japan on the top and sides. Many smaller articles, like those on the fop's dressing-table, were prettily lacquered with gay Oriental figures. Snuff-boxes and other trifles in lacquer were produced by John Taylor at Birmingham who seems to have made a fortune out of this trade.

After about 1765 the fashion for lacquer furniture began to decline in England, though the art of japanning remained a popular amusement among amateurs for whom such books were written as *The Ladies Amusement or the Whole art of Japanning made easy*. This valuable manual, illustrated with numerous plates after Pillement and others, advised its readers of the liberties which might be taken with Indian or Chinese designs, 'for in these is often seen a Butterfly supporting an Elephant, or things equally absurd'. Among amateur japanners of the late eighteenth century, the King's third daughter, Princess Elizabeth, was surely one of the most passionate and decorated two whole rooms at Frogmore, one with scarlet and gold and the other with black and gold lacquer. Perhaps it was from her that George IV acquired his fondness for chinoiserie which was largely responsible for the third revival in lacquer furniture towards the end of the century.

Although lacquer does not seem to have been used to furnish the famous Chinese drawing-room at Carlton House, it was freely applied to furniture in the Sheraton and Hepplewhite styles during the last decades of the eighteenth century. In 1804 the Prince Regent sent Dr James Grant to collect lacquer and other orientalia in the Far East, and the panels with which he returned were probably among those used to adorn the furniture of the Royal Pavilion at Brighton. Other pieces of furniture at Brighton were painted with English lacquer which also enjoyed a popular vogue, especially for the decoration of cabinets and book-cases. The design of such furniture conformed with the usual Regency patterns. Amateurs continued their labours for some time, and even as late as 1828 Mrs Arbuthnot, the Duke of Wellington's friend, could be found 'making up a japan cabinet I painted last year. . . . The cabinet is really excessively pretty'. Lacquer seems finally to have gone out of fashion in the late 1830s but at the Great Exhibition of 1851 Messrs W. W. Eloure were showing various *papier mâché* 'imitations of japan work. Cabinet doors, and folding fire screens in imitation of India-Japan, ornamented with gold and inlaid with mother of pearl'.

Dutch and Flemish Lacquer: of all European countries, Holland was perhaps the most closely connected with the trade in Oriental lacquer during the seventeenth century. Before the middle of the century Dutch merchants had, indeed, established a virtual monopoly in the export of lacquer from Japan. Nevertheless, a need seems to have been felt for a greater supply of lacquer than the trading ships could provide, and early in the century craftsmen set themselves to the imitation of lacquer in Holland. The style of their work, which was of much higher quality than contemporary English work, may be judged from a casket decorated with birds

EUROPEAN LACQUER FURNITURE

(A) Lacquer harpsichord case made at Paris by Pascal Taskin in 1786. *Victoria and Albert Museum, London.*

(B) Lacquer harpsichord case made at Hamburg in 1732. *Kunstindustrimuseet, Oslo.*

PLATE 129

Lacquer clock case and stand made at Augsburg, c. 1730. *Bayerisches Nationalmuseum, Munich.*

EUROPEAN LACQUER FURNITURE

(A) Venetian lacquer harpsichord case, *c.* 1750. *Museo Civico, Treviso.*

(B) Venetian lacquer commode, *c.* 1750. *Palazzo Rezzonico, Venice.*

PLATE 131

EUROPEAN LACQUER FURNITURE

Detail of Venetian lacquer door, *c.* 1760. *Palazzo Rezzonico, Venice*.

PLATE 132

(A) Mahogany arm-chair similar to one designed by Robert Adam for Alnwick Castle, *c.* 1760. *Messrs H. Blairman and Sons, London.*

Photo: *A. F. Kersting*

(B) Mahogany chair, English, *c.* 1760. *Arbury Park, Warwickshire.*

(C) Writing table, probably made by Thomas Chippendale, *c.* 1760. *Temple Newsam House, Leeds.*

GOTHIC REVIVAL FURNISHINGS

The salon at Arbury Park, Warwickshire, designed for Sir Roger Newdigate, 1761.

GOTHIC REVIVAL FURNISHINGS

A   *Photo: A. F. Kersting*   B
(A) Mahogany bookcase, English, *c.* 1760. *Victoria & Albert Museum, London.*
(B) Lectern made for the chapel at Alnwick Castle to the design of Robert Adam, *c.* 1760.
His Grace the Duke of Northumberland Collection, Alnwick.

C   D
(C) Mahogany cabinet, English, *c.* 1760–70, *Victoria & Albert Museum, London.*
(D) Arm-chair of Cuban mahogany, English, *c.* 1795. *Simon Sainsbury Collection, London.*

PLATE 135

GOTHIC REVIVAL FURNISHINGS

(A) Cathedral style book-binding, French, *c.* 1820. *Musée des Arts Décoratifs, Paris.*

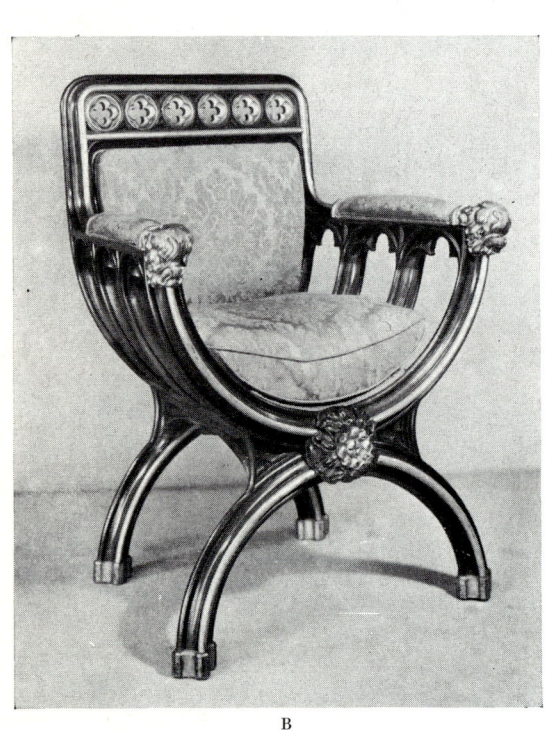

(B) Chair, one of a set of twelve, made for Eaton Hall, Cheshire, *c.* 1815. *Messrs Stanley J. Pratt Ltd, London.*
(C) Brass hall lantern, English, *c.* 1815. *Messrs Stanley J. Pratt Ltd, London.*

GOTHIC REVIVAL FURNISHINGS

Design in gouache for a room in the Gothic taste, French, *c.* 1825. *Musée des Arts Décoratifs, Paris.*

PLATE 137

GOTHIC REVIVAL FURNISHINGS

(A) Tapestry with the arms of the Solar de Belerril branch of the Castilian family of Campo, Aubusson, *c.* 1820. *Messrs William Young, Aberdeen.*

(B) Bronze clock in the troubadour style, French, *c.* 1825. *Musée des Arts Décoratifs, Paris.*

(C) Looking glass or 'Psyche' in the Gothic taste, French, *c.* 1815. *Musée des Arts Décoratifs, Paris.*

GOTHIC REVIVAL FURNISHINGS

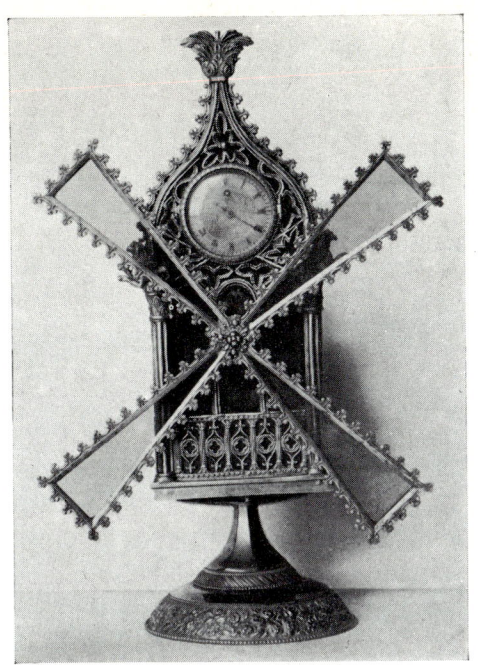 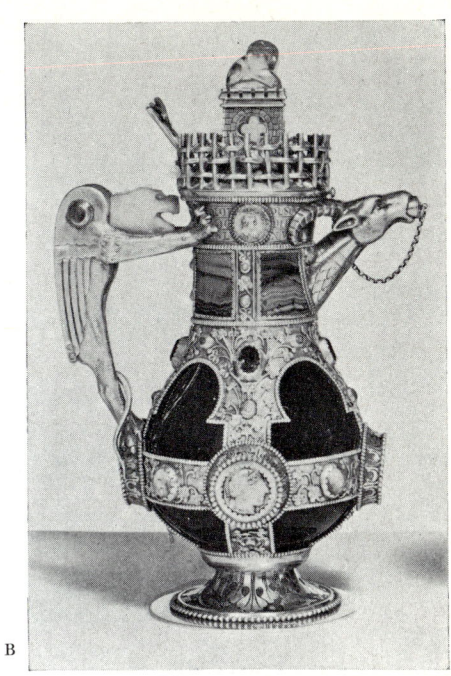

(A) Gilt bronze and amethyst-glass clock in the form of a Gothic windmill, French, c. 1825. *Musée des Arts Décoratifs, Paris*
(B) Glass and silver-gilt decanter designed by William Burges, c. 1860. *Victoria & Albert Museum, London.*

(C) Bronze oil and vinegar bottle stand, French, c. 1825. *Musée des Arts Décoratifs, Paris.*
(D) Design by Augustus Pugin the elder for a Gothic bed, published by R. A. Ackerman, 1820. *Private Collection, Asolo.*

PLATE 139

(A) Cabinet designed by A. W. N. Pugin, c. 1850. *Victoria & Albert Museum, London.*

(B) 'The Failure of Sir Gawaine', one of a set of tapestries representing the legend of the Holy Grail woven to the design of Edward Burne Jones, 1894. *City Museum & Art Gallery, Birmingham.*

FURNISHINGS IN THE EGYPTIAN TASTE

(A) Pair of carved pine sphinxes, English, c. 1790. *Messrs Stanley J. Pratt Ltd, London.*

(B) Silver tureen made at Turin, probably c. 1790. *Private Collection, Turin.*

PLATE 141

FURNISHINGS IN THE EGYPTIAN TASTE

(A) Arm-chair of wood painted black and gold, made to the design of Thomas Hope for the Egyptian room at his house in Duchess Street, London, 1804. *Messrs H. Blairman & Sons, London.*

(B) Porcelain sugar-bowl modelled on a type of vase represented in Egyptian hieroglyphics, made for Napoleon at the Sèvres factory, 1811–13. *His Grace the Duke of Wellington Collection, Stratfield, Saye.*

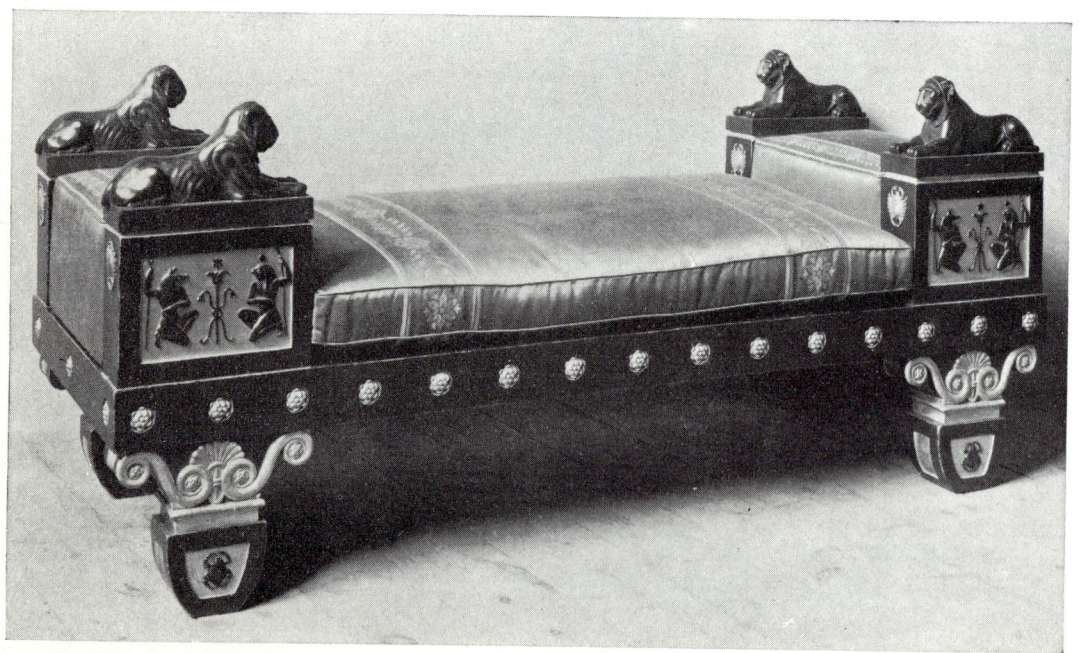

(C) Sofa from the Egyptian room in Thomas Hope's house. *Messrs H. Blairman and Sons, London.*

FURNISHINGS IN THE EGYPTIAN TASTE

(B) Red and black Wedgwood style bowl and lid, c. 1810. *Museum of Art, Hove.*

(A) Coin cabinet in ebony with silver decorations, made for Napoleon by Martin Guillaume Biennais, c. 1806 and modelled on the pylon at Ghoos. *Metropolitan Museum of Art, New York.*

(C) Mahogany commode in the Egyptian taste, French, c. 1810. *Musée des Arts Décoratifs, Paris.*

PLATE 143

FURNISHINGS IN THE EGYPTIAN TASTE

(A) Chest of drawers in the Egyptian taste, English, c. 1820. *Leonard Knight Collection, London.*

(B) Table designed by Agostino Fantastici at Siena, c. 1820. *Professor R. Bianchi-Bandinelli Collection, Siena.*

(C) Design for a 'hieroglyphic border' chintz by R. Ovey from a Bannister Hall pattern book, 1804. *Messrs Stead, McAlpin and Co. Ltd, London.*

perching among flowering plants, in the Rijksmuseum (Plate 125C). Dutch *Japanish Verlaker* – japanners – attained great skill in the second half of the century and produced some of the closest imitations of Oriental lacquer made in Europe. It has even been suggested, with some probability if no evidence, that Japanese lacquer workers were brought to Europe to school the Dutch craftsmen. Late seventeenth- and early eighteenth-century Dutch lacquer was usually somewhat sparsely decorated with chinoiserie designs in gold on a lustrous black ground. A good though miniature example, is provided by the doll's house cupboard in the Rijksmuseum (Plate 125B). Lacquer furniture decorated in

FIG. 3. Cabinet and stand by Gerard Dagly, *c.* 1700

colours on a cream or white ground was also popular in Holland. In style, Dutch lacquer furniture was similar to the walnut and marquetry pieces produced at the same time. Cabinets – whether Dutch or Oriental – which were as fashionable here as in England seem usually to have been mounted on scroll-shaped legs which were also lacquered (Fig. 3) rather than on gilt baroque stands. In the early eighteenth century lacquer with chinoiserie decorations was most notably applied to large chests of drawers and wardrobes. Good examples are in the collection of Graf van Aldenburg-Bentinck at Schloss Amerongen.

Spa, the watering place near Aix-la-Chapelle which was for centuries the Mecca of European hypochrondriacs, was the principal centre for the production of lacquer in Flanders. A lacquer industry grew up here in the late seventeenth century and its products, known as *bois de Spa*, soon became famous throughout Europe. All manner of large and small objects from snuff-boxes to corner cupboards were produced at Spa in the eighteenth century and purchased by those who came from far and wide to drink the famous medicinal waters or gamble in the scarcely less celebrated gaming-rooms. *Bois de Spa* was usually decorated with gilt chinoiserie motifs on a black ground. Spa was, moreover, the birthplace of one of the foremost masters of European lacquer, Gerard Dagly (*fl.* 1665–1714) who, though he executed most of his work in Germany, may fitly find mention here.

Gerard Dagly was born at Spa some time before 1665 and went at a fairly early age to seek his fortune in Germany. In 1687 he was appointed *Kammerkünstler* to the Kurfürst of Brandenburg and in this capacity was principally employed in producing lacquer work in the Chinese manner. In 1696 he lacquered four black and gold coin cabinets one of which is at Berlin—a fine piece of work mounted on a stand with twist-turned legs on which small floral motifs are picked out in gold. Another cabinet, formerly in the Hohenzollernmuseum at Berlin, was painted with a lovely prospect of mountains on the outside of the doors and dancing Chinese figures on the inside. He also produced very elegant lacquer furniture decorated in gold on a white ground; a good example of this type of his work is, or was, in the Schloss Monbijou. Other works by Gerard Dagly are to be found in the Royal Palace at Stockholm and the Museum at Brunswick. He attained wide renown in Germany and when the Kurfürstin of Hanover sent her Prussian son-in-law a clock-case she felt bound to remark that 'it comes from England but Dagly makes much better ones'. On the accession of Frederick William I to the Prussian throne in 1713 Dagly was among the many court employees who were promptly dismissed. He seems to have returned to Spa. For a full account of Gerard Dagly see *The Connoisseur*, 1934, vol. XCV, pp. 14 ff.

French Lacquer: in the earlier seventeenth century Oriental lacquer was imported in to France from Portugal and it was to the Portuguese stalls at the Foire de Saint Germain that Scarron directed the connoisseur's attention for 'beaux ouvrages de vernis'. After the foundation of the French *Compagnie des Indes* in 1664 importations were considerably increased and the vogue for lacquer furniture reached a new height. The French attitude to lacquer at this date and during much of the eighteenth century, was, however, somewhat unusual. Lacquer seems to have been prized more for its rarity and commercial value than for its style of decoration. Louis XIV evidently thought it in no way incongruous to have silver plaques engraved with the Labours of Hercules applied to a Chinese cabinet.

As we have already mentioned, lacquer was made in France early in the seventeenth century though no examples of it are known to have survived. Nor is much known of the productions of 'Les Sieurs Langlois, père et fils' who, in 1691, were making 'cabinets et paravents façon de la Chine, d'une beauté singulière' with ormolu mounts which were expressly intended to make them harmonize with other pieces of furniture in the great salons. Like the English, the French occasionally sent furniture out to the East to be lacquered, and it seems probable that Mme de Sévigné's writing-desk in the Musée Carnavalet at Paris, which is of a normal French pattern embellished with oriental lacquer, is one such piece.

In 1713, or shortly after, the Flemish craftsman Jacques Dagly (1655–1728), brother of Gerard **Dagly** (see p. 299) settled in France and obtained a licence to 'establish . . . a factory to make varnish', but this paint seems to have been primarily intended for application to textiles. Not until some years later did French craftsmen succeed in producing lacquer of conspicuously high quality. Between 1733 and 1740 the Duc de Bourbon was maintaining at Chantilly an atelier where, according to a contemporary, lacquer furniture was produced in such close imitation of Chinese models that even the greatest connoisseurs had been deceived by it. Meanwhile, the brothers Martin – Guillaume (d. 1749), Etienne Simon (d. 1770), Julien (d. 1782) and Robert (*fl.* 1706–65) – had perfected the lacquer to which they gave their name, *vernis Martin*. Letters patent, issued in 1730 and renewed in 1744, granted them the exclusive monopoly of 'toutes sortes d'ouvrages en relief et dans le goût du japon ou de la Chine' for twenty years. They did not, however, confine themselves to decorations in the Chinese style and many of the best examples of *vernis Martin* are either without any ornament or simply stippled with gold specks – like the sedan chair made for the Montmorency children and now in the Musée de Cluny at Paris. *Vernis Martin* was produced in several colours of which the green was the most celebrated. Among the larger works undertaken by the Martins were the decorative paintings in several of the *petits appartements* at Versailles. They were also much patronized by Mme de Pompadour.

Lacquer was extensively used for the decoration of furniture in the Louis XV period but, whether of French or Oriental make, was usually treated in a cavalier fashion. The curling tendrils of rococo mounts were allowed to clamber over it and obscure much of the pattern, whilst handles were screwed on without any regard for the figures on the design. On a chest of drawers in the Wallace Collection – the so-called Marriage coffer of Marie Antoinette (Plate 128c) – the exquisite panels of Japanese lacquer on the front and those of French lacquer at the sides are half hidden behind bronze fret-work grilles. Here the lacquer seems to have been considered purely as a precious substance which could add the final touch of opulence to a magnificent piece of furniture. The famous *ébéniste B.V.R.B.* (recently identified as Bernard van Risen Burgh) treated lacquer, which he very frequently used, in a much more respectful manner. But he, too, chose to emphasize the beauty of its glossy substance rather than the charm of its gilt decorations. (Plate 128A.)

With the development of the Louis XVI style this attitude seems to have changed. The greater rigidity of the furniture produced in this period enabled *ébénistes* to show off panels of fine Japanese lacquer much more effectively. Indeed, objects like the secretaire by P. Garnier in the Louvre (Plate 128B) seem to have been conceived mainly as frames for exquisite panels of lacquer. Much of the furniture bought in Paris for George IV and now at Windsor Castle is of this type. French lacquer was applied to various types of furniture but perhaps most notably to these pieces which could not easily have been veneered with oriental lacquer. In the Victoria and Albert Museum there is an exceptionally fine harpsichord made by Pascal Taskin in Paris in 1786 and painted on the lid and sides with engaging little gilt Chinamen dancing on a puce ground. (Plate 129A.)

The taste for lacquer does not seem to have survived the French Revolution. Lacquer furniture clearly had no place amid the Greek and Egyptian style objects of an Empire salon. It may perhaps have been used after the Restoration by those cabinet makers who reverted to the production of furniture in the Louis XVI style.

German Lacquer: as miniature versions of Versailles sprang up outside the capitals of nearly every German principality in the late seventeenth and early eighteenth centuries, so the taste of the French court spread throughout Germany. Lacquer consequently became an accepted, indeed, an all but essential feature of palatial decoration. Rooms panelled from floor to ceiling in lacquer and provided with whole suites of furniture to match were installed in many a stately *Schloss* and *Residenz*. Small lacquer objects were also produced in Germany before the end of the seventeenth century, and a pattern book of the period gives designs for tobacco boxes and trays to be painted with Chinese scenes from the plates in John Nieuhoff's *Embassy*.

In the last two decades of the seventeenth century the Flemish craftsman Gerard Dagly (see p. 299) was producing exceptionally fine lacquer at Berlin. He attracted several imitators who were probably responsible for some of the pieces of lacquer furniture which are, or were until the war, in the Charlottenburg Palace. These included a table, a writing-table and a harpsichord decorated with little chinoiserie figures on a white ground – the harpsichord is mounted on a base painted with purely European floral motifs. Among Dagly's named followers was Martin Schnell who worked with him from 1703 to 1709 and then returned to his native town of Dresden where he produced some splendid examples of lacquer work besides providing designs for porcelain during the subsequent three decades. Schnell is best known for his small lacquered trays – the finest of their kind – of which there are good specimens in the Residenzschloss at Dresden. He was also responsible for furniture and decorations in Schloss Pillnitz – the *Japanische Palais* – which contains one of his most notable works, an English style fall-front secretaire.

Lacquer furniture was also made at Augsburg in the first half of the eighteenth century, and a notable example of it is provided by a clock in the Bayerisches Nationalmuseum at Munich (Plate 130). The clock itself is of a baroque architectural pattern with columns at the corners, and stands on a low table. All the woodwork, including the columns, is decorated with chinoiserie motifs in colours on a white ground, and a painted mandarin squats on the stretcher of the stand. Another centre for the production of lacquer was Hamburg where a very fine harpsichord was made in 1732. (Plate 129B.)

One of the earliest of the several surviving German lacquer rooms was that built for the Kurfürst Lothar Franz von Schönborn in the Neue Residenz at Bamberg in about 1700. It is decorated with a series of panels of black and gold lacquer set amidst a profusion of carved swags, and contains a handsome lacquer cabinet, similar to those popular in England but without doors, set on very short legs to serve as a chest of drawers. Between 1714 and 1722 one Johann Jakob Saenger painted the magnificent lacquer-room in Schloss Ludwigsburg, at Württemburg, with chinoiserie birds and dragons sporting in a garden which is decorated with baroque urns. In the Pagodenburg Pavilion in the Nymphenburg gardens there is a room decorated with red and black lacquer panels of 1718. The Residenz at Munich had a bedroom of about the same date which was adorned with large panels of lacquer each painted with three or four chinoiserie scenes placed inconsequentially one above another. At Schloss Brühl, near Cologne, there is an exceptionally attractive *Indianische Lackkabinet* painted for the Kurfürst Clemens August between 1720 and 1730 with gay, brightly coloured chinoiserie scenes· on a cream ground. A later example of a lacquer-room is that in Schloss Nymphenburg, decorated by J. Hörringer in 1764.

Frederick the Great, an admirer of Oriental lacquer (he gave his sister Amelia the Coromandel panels for a room which is still in the Neue Residenz at Bayreuth) also patronized European lacquer workers, acquiring them in much the same way as he gathered literary lions to adorn his court at Potsdam. In 1747 he commissioned Jean Alexandre Martin, the son of Robert Martin, to decorate the *Blumenkammer* – otherwise known as the *Voltaire Zimmer* – at Sanssouci: and some twenty years later he again lured him away from Paris, appointing him *vernisseur du Roy*. In 1765 Frederick commissioned another French lacquer worker, Sebastian Chevalier, to decorate an oval room in the Neuen Palais at Potsdam. He then encouraged Jean Guérin the son-in-law of Johann Heinrich Stobwasser, who had for long been providing lacquered canes for Prussian army officers, to set up a lacquer industry at Berlin. Stobwasser himself remained at Brunswick where he produced the many exquisite snuff-boxes, canes, etc., which won him European renown. He also developed the art of lacquering on *papier mâché* in the English manner. As late as the 1790s the Stobwasser workshop at Brunswick was producing little lacquered objects and small pieces of furniture painted in lacquer with classical figures and motifs.

Italian Lacquer: Venice was already famous for its lacquer in 1668 when Maximilien Misson remarked that 'La Lacque de Venise est comme on sçait en réputation: il y en a àtoute sorte de prix'. Unfortunately no examples dating from this early period can be identified, but a few later seventeenth-century pieces show that the Venetian craftsmen produced both black and vermilion lacquer decorated with gold chinoiserie subjects. A notable example of this style of work is the writing-table formerly in the collection of the late Mr Arthur Spender of Venice and exhibited in the 1938 exhibition of Venetian lacquer. As in other parts of Europe, lacquer was applied to furniture of normal design, but the Venetian attempts to imitate the substance of Oriental lacquer were rather more perfunctory. The base of white wood or *cirmolo* (a type of pine from Cadore) was treated with successive layers of *gesso* each of which was polished, gold paint was then applied to the raised decorations, which were generally reserved for the main surfaces, and other portions were painted in tempera, the whole piece was then given a coat of transparent varnish. In the early decades of the eighteenth century the Venetians excelled in the production of dark green lacquer with gold decorations, of which the finest examples are probably those now in the Palazzo Rezzonico at Venice. (Plate 131B.)

Venetian eighteenth-century lacquer was the work of the guild of *depentori* which had, in earlier centuries, included all painters but from which the painters of pictures (*pittori*) had split away in 1691. Iseppo Tosello who is mentioned in a document of 1729 as a *depentor alla chinese* was one of many who produced lacquer, but his name has survived only by chance and we know of none of his productions. It is also possible that some of the great *settecento* painters occasionally worked in lacquer and a pair of doors in the Palazzo Rezzonico (Plate 132) has tentatively been ascribed to G. B. Tiepolo, though not, it must be admitted, with much confidence. Whether the work of modest *depentori* or of *pittori*, Venetian lacquer of the eighteenth century is distinguished for its gay colours no less than for the accomplishment and frivolity of its decorations. Early in the century chinoiserie figures in gold or colours on a ground of black, green, red or yellow, seem to have been the invariable rule but a preference was later shown for floral motifs or little landscapes painted in the style of Zais or Zuccarelli. All manner of objects were thus decorated – from great *armadi* and secretaires (known as *bureaux trumeaux*) to little boxes, fans, trays, brushes and small ornaments in the form of animals. Perhaps the most satisfying of all non-chinoiserie examples of Venetian lacquer is the harpsichord in the Museo Civico at Treviso (Plate 131A), sprinkled with exquisitely painted little bunches of midsummer flowers on a brown ground. Similar floral decorations were very happily applied to the undulating surfaces of chests of drawers. These pieces, like so many examples of later Italian furniture, show how the craftsmen concentrated their attention on the decoration rather than the structure and their joinery is often of poor quality.

Venetian lacquer of the type already described seems to have been reserved for the grander palaces and villas. But a cheaper substitute was also made in the eighteenth century and enjoyed a very wide popularity in Venetia. Works of this type were painted all over in a uniform colour, then decorated with cut-out prints produced for this purpose by the Remondini of Bassano and others. The prints were painted or gilded and the whole surface covered with a coat of transparent varnish. Furniture decorated in this manner looks from a distance as if it were lacquered but can easily be distinguished on close inspection. Despite their somewhat rustic character the decorations themselves are often attractive. Most of the surviving examples of furniture decorated with this *lacca contrafatta* are *armadi*, chests of drawers or secretaires.

Although Venetian lacquer was the most famous, lacquer furniture was made in several other Italian towns in the eighteenth century. At Florence lacquer was made for Cosimo III with ingredients brought back from the Far East, and good examples of Genoese and Lucchese lacquer, little inferior to Venetian, are also recorded. During the second quarter of the eighteenth century there was a vogue for rooms wholly panelled with lacquer in Piedmont. The most notable is that designed by the great architect, Filippo Juvarra, in the Palazzo Reale at Turin. Records show that sixty of the panels in this room were bought at Rome in 1732, but the decorative scheme was not completed until 1736 when one Pietro Massia provided further panels in the same style. Painted with birds and flowers in red and gold, the panels are set within elegant gilded rococo scrolls on a vermilion wall and produce a remarkable impression of sumptuous grandeur. A somewhat simpler room executed at about the same time or a little later was in the Villa Vachetti at Gerbido, near Turin, and is now at the Rockhill Nelson Gallery of Art at Kansas City, Missouri. Here the panels are red and gold set against walls of celadon green. The designs used for the panels of both rooms reveal an Italian interpretation of chinoiserie.

The use of lacquer declined in Italy towards the end of the eighteenth century. Much fake eighteenth-century lacquer was, however, produced after the revival of interest in later Italian furniture in the 1920s.

Lacquer made in other Countries: lacquer furniture was produced in several other European countries during the eighteenth century. The Portuguese produced a certain amount, the most notable pieces being secretaire cabinets, usually with gold chinoiserie decorations on a red ground, containing shrines in their upper parts. But both Portugal and Spain imported English lacquer during the first half of the eighteenth century. Giles Grendy, the maker of a red and gold day bed now in the Victoria and Albert Museum, seems to have specialized in catering for this export trade.

Surprisingly little lacquer seems to have been produced in Austria. A few examples of Viennese lacquer are in the Museum für angewandte Kunst at Vienna. (See p. 210.) Lacquer was also produced to a limited extent in Denmark and Sweden.

BOOKS FOR FURTHER READING

EDWARDS, R. AND MACQUOID, P., *A Dictionary of English Furniture* (London, 1954), Vol. II.
HUTH, HANS, *Europäische Lackarbeiten* (Darmstadt).
LORENZETTI, G., *Lacche Veneziane del Settecento* (Venice, 1938).

GOTHIC REVIVAL FURNISHINGS

By HUGH HONOUR

THE buildings and furnishings produced under the impetus of the Gothic Revival have been returning to favour during the last thirty years. Pinnacled and crocketted chairs, writing desks and cabinets adorned with delicately carved tracery derived from fourteenth-century windows, clocks shaped like Gothic churches and book-cases like Gothic quire-stalls, are no longer subject to sneers from the artistically 'knowing'. After having been despised and derided for more than a century, Strawberry Hill has become a Mecca for all admirers of eighteenth-century taste. The heavier and bulkier products of the nineteenth-century Gothic Revival have also won their admirers. Created to satisfy a romantic longing for the medieval past, these eighteenth- and nineteenth-century objects and buildings have now acquired a period charm. An eighteenth-century arm-chair in the Gothic taste calls to mind the elegant world of antiquaries and men of taste described in the letters of Horace Walpole rather than the Norfolk of feudal squires revealed in those of the Paston family; a richly decorated washstand by Burges reminds us of the piety and ardour of the artists of the nineteenth rather than the thirteenth century.

Students of English architecture have traced the origin of the Gothic Revival back to the early seventeenth century when many country masons and carpenters were still working in a tradition handed down from the Middle Ages. The question therefore arises of the distinction to be drawn between Gothic Survival and Gothic Revival. Generally speaking the term 'Gothic survival' can be applied to those buildings – tithe barns and additions to (or restorations of) churches – which were created in a debased Gothic style because their craftsmen knew no other. Gothic Revival works, on the other hand, reveal a conscious desire to evoke the past. It was, for instance, with a wistful look backwards to the ritualistic splendours of the unreformed Church that high churchmen built in the Gothic Revival style. One of the most prominent, Lancelot Andrewes, revived the use of the chalice (as opposed to the Elizabethan Communion cup). The chalices made either for him or under his influence were based on a late fifteenth-century prototype with a knopped stem and sexagonal base with ornamental terminals to the points. To the horror of Puritans, such vessels were often engraved with the figure of the Good Shepherd or a Crucifix. During the Commonwealth, chalices of this type were made for private chapels and they returned to general favour after the Restoration (for a full examination of this aspect of Gothic Revival silver see: C. Oman: *English Church Plate*, London, 1957). Other fittings of the Laudian Church may also have harked back to the Middle Ages (an altar frontal worked for Hollingbourne church in the 1650s incorporates winged cherubs of a vaguely medieval type) but very few have survived.

After the Restoration, churches and university college buildings were occasionally erected or enlarged in a Gothic style similar to that employed for Laudian churches and chapels. But early in the eighteenth century a new note was struck by Sir John Vanbrugh who evolved a medieval castellated manner. Of his work at Kimbolton he wrote in 1707:

'As to the outside, I thought it absolutely best, to give it something of the castle air, tho' at the same time to make it regular ... I'm sure this will make a very noble and masculine show; and is of as Warrantable a kind of building as any.' For himself, Vanbrugh built at Blackheath a castle with round crenellated towers which stressed the picturesque qualities of medieval architecture. But he was clearly attracted to Gothic architecture on account of its forms rather than its associations. Vanbrugh's associate, Nicholas Hawkesmore, worked in a very different Gothic style when he built the north quadrangle and elegant, if somewhat thin, towers at All Souls, Oxford, where he was attempting to work in harmony with the existing medieval buildings. The Gothic of Vanbrugh and Hawkesmore has no counterpart in the minor arts.

With the growth of the sensibility cult in eighteenth-century England, Gothic buildings, preferably ruined, acquired a new attraction.

Come let me range the gloomy Iles alone
(Sad luxury! to vulgar minds unknown),

wrote Thomas Tickell in 1721. This movement coincided, and partly accounted for, the development of the landscape garden where a mouldering pile of medieval masonry thickly overgrown with ivy, the haunt of moping owls, was a coveted incident among the newly planted clumps of trees and the newly excavated lakes. Those so unfortunate as to possess no such monument were forced to create one if they were to indulge to the full that pleasing melancholy which medieval buildings stimulated. They might, Batty Langley suggested in 1728, 'be either painted upon canvas or actually built in that manner with bricks and covered with plaster'. The sham ruin consequently came into being and with it the Gothic summer house – a more elegant and lighthearted affair suitable for gay picnicking parties. Before long, Gothic motifs were being applied to the exterior of the house itself.

By 1742 the Gothic Revival had won sufficient popularity for Batty Langley to publish his notorious set of designs, *Gothic Architecture Improved*, which provided Gothic versions of the five classical orders. In 1750 W. and J. Halfpenny began to bring out their little builder's pattern books which included designs in the Gothic taste, the Chinese taste and a mixture of the two. Four years later a critic in the *World* sarcastically remarked 'how much of late we are improved in architecture; not merely by the adoption of what we call Chinese, nor by the restoration of what we call Gothic, but by a happy mixture of both'. These Gothic buildings and pieces of furniture did not, of course, have any of that solemnity which marked sham ruins. They gave, as Horace Walpole remarked in his unregenerate days, 'a whimsical air of novelty that is very pleasing'. Indeed, they are, together with chinoiseries of the same period, expressions of that reaction from classical solemnity which marked the rococo style.

A writer of 1753 declared that 'a few years ago everything was Gothic; our houses, our beds, our book-cases, and our couches', and spoke of the Gothic taste as a thing of the past. But, in fact, the Gothic Revival had only just begun to exert its influence on the design of furniture. Indeed, most surviving examples of eighteenth-century Gothic Revival furniture date from the later 1750s and 60s. They are, with few exceptions, in an elegant and delightfully 'incorrect' style, richly and whimsically crocketted and carved. The most notable examples are those which are similar to the many Gothic designs included by Thomas Chippendale in the various editions of the *Gentleman and Cabinet-Maker's Director* (1754–62). Most prominent among the exceptions are the furnishings made for Horace Walpole and his friends in a more 'correct' if only slightly less elegant style.

Horace Walpole acquired in 1750 a small house – Strawberry Hill – which he gradually converted into the most famous neo-Gothic building in England, if not in all Europe. At first he regarded the style as a mere whimsicality but as he investigated medieval buildings his respect for Gothic developed into a passion. Soon dissatisfied with the mongrel enrichments of Batty Langley and the Halfpennys, he and his friends who formed the 'Strawberry committee of taste', rummaged the old folios on the English cathedrals for details which might be adapted to domestic use. An archbishop's tomb at Canterbury was found to provide a suitable design for a chimney piece, a rose window served as the model for a plaster ceiling, an octagonal chapter house was reduced to the scale of a parlour. Fragments of Gothic tracery were copied on the furniture and the wall papers. It was Horace Walpole's intention that the detail should be no less correct than the classical ornamentation used at the same time, and he employed it with a similar lack of respect for its original purpose. For Strawberry Hill was neo-Gothic in the same way that Robert Adam's Kedleston was neo-classic: a similar archaeological attitude marks the design of both houses.

By the 1760s the Gothic Revival had ceased to be a laughing matter. No longer was it, like chinoiserie, a frivolous alternative to the correct antique manner. More eagerly than ever before, men of letters were investigating Britain's medieval past, and as a wave of nationalist zeal swept across the land, Gothic was declared to be the true national style. As a result Gothic detail was used with greater respect, though no-one seems to have thought, as yet, of imitating medieval furniture. The grandeur and mysterious solemnity of Gothic architecture was also better appreciated than hitherto, as is strongly evident in *The Castle of Otranto* and many later novels in the same vein. The picturesque qualities of the style were exploited by William Beckford and his architect James Wyatt when Fonthill Abbey was, with such disastrous rapidity, run up in the last years of the century. Both the nationalistic and picturesque qualities are notably expressed in Windsor Castle which owes its present monumental aspect almost entirely to Sir Jeffry Wyatville's remodelling in 1824. The Gothic Revival furniture made for early nineteenth-century houses was much solider, harder and heavier than any that had appeared in Strawberry Hill. Some tables at Fonthill, for instance, were based on a sixteenth-century design, and a set of chairs made for Eaton Hall is adapted from the medieval pattern (Plate 136B). Nevertheless, clocks were still made to look like miniature churches and looking glasses were placed in frames of Gothic arcading. Prominent among the artists who designed such wares was the elder Augustus Pugin (a French émigré) (Plate 139D), many of whose delicate aquatints for Gothic furniture – including elegant sofas, fire-tongs and keys enriched with cusped tracery – were published in Ackerman's *Repository of Arts* in the 1820s.

England was not the only country to indulge in a Gothic Revival. In Germany a ruined Gothic chapel was built in the park at Nymphenburg in the late 1720s. In Italy one masterpiece of Gothic Revival decoration was painted in the *foresteria* of the Villa Valmarana at Vicenza by G. D. Tiepolo in about 1757. Several manifestations of romantic gothicism also appeared in France. As early as 1675 a set of tapestries depicting scenes from medieval romances accurately dressed, was woven at Beauvais. Silk embroidered arabesque panels in the style of Bérain, dating from the first quarter of the eighteenth century, sometimes include ladies in fifteenth-century dress among their classical motifs. But these isolated objects are merely evidence of a false start. French visitors to Strawberry Hill in the 1760s were not impressed. Indeed, Horace Walpole declared that a sight of his house had cured Mme de Boufflers of her Anglomania. And Mme du Deffand told him that her compatriots thought such buildings were 'natural enough in a country which had not yet arrived at true taste'. Under the influence of the cult for troubadour poetry, however, France was soon to succumb to the Gothic craze, and to produce a strongly Gallic version of the style which was called 'le style troubadour'. In the 1770s Gothic architecture began to appear in the backgrounds to hunting scenes on Lyonnaise brocades. A medieval fête and tournament with fifty knights in armour, was staged by Monsieur in honour of the Queen in 1780. During the subsequent decade Gothic ruins and buildings were added to the caprices of many a *jardin Anglo-Chinois*, at Armainvilliers there was a 'salle de bains gothique', at Bagatelle a 'tour des paladins', at Ourscamp a Gothic chapel and observatory, and in 1787 Kléber diversified the park of the Prince de Montbéliard with numerous Gothic buildings including an Anabaptist chapel, a concert hall, and a shooting gallery.

Even during the Revolution the neo-gothic style continued to grow in popularity while, ironically enough, genuine medieval buildings were being destroyed and disfigured. In 1791, for instance, the Théatre du Marais was rebuilt in the Gothic manner 'absolument l'architecture de nos anciennes chapelles'. Two years later a writer commented: 'nous avons tant épluché les modes, tant raffiné sur les goûts, tant retourné les meubles et les ajustements, que rassasiés, épuisés de jolies choses, nous redemandons le Gothique comme quelque chose neuf, nous l'adopterons; et nous voilà revenus tout naturellement au XIVe siècle'. Further impetus was given to the style by Napoleon for whose coronation in 1804 those arbiters of Empire taste, Percier and Fontaine, built a false neo-gothic front to Notre Dame, liberally decorated with the Emperor's cypher in medieval style frames. Next year Jacob Desmalter made for the chapel of the Petit Trianon four *prie-Dieu* – 'la planchette du dossier découpée en forme gothique'. Pictures of troubadours won ever-increasing popularity, and J.-A. Laurent executed several for Queen Hortense and for Josephine who, in 1805, had a Gothic gallery built at Malmaison (destroyed). Furniture and ornaments in the troubadour style also became very fashionable.

In Restoration Paris the Gothic style won further ground and became as poular as in England where, indeed, many of the leaders of fashion had spent their exile. The Duchesse de Berry, an enthusiastic reader of troubadour poetry, played an important part in the movement and appeared at fancy dress balls dressed as a *reine du moyen âge*. The furniture, clocks and ornaments produced in the troubadour style to satisfy the Gothic rage were similar to English objects of the time, delicately adorned with tracery and little statues. Greater accuracy was soon demanded by patrons who wished not merely for correct Gothic detail but for accurate imitations of medieval furniture. Looking back after several years Théophile Gautier remarked: 'Rien ne ressemblait moins au moyen âge que pendules et troubadours qui fleurissaient vers 1825. C'est un des grands mérites de l'école romantique d'en avoir radicalement débarrassé l'art.' But the Gothic chairs, tables, armoires, silver cups and jewels made in Gautier's time seem to modern eyes to bear a resemblance to medieval objects little closer than the works in the outmoded troubadour style. To judge from engravings, and such an example as the reliquary designed by Viollet le Duc for Notre Dame, they were slightly heavier and, if possible, more elaborate than those made in contemporary England. But in France Gothic Revival furnishings seem to have been going out of fashion in the 1860s in favour of more recent historical styles and *japonaiserie*. The Italian Gothic Revival passed through phases similar to those of the French. In the 1820s such elegant buildings as the conservatory at Racconigi were built and furniture was decorated with Gothic tracery. Later, imitations of medieval buildings (in the Lombard Gothic style) and thirteenth-century furniture (usually called Dantesque) were in demand. The cassone, solid credenza and uncomfortable chair once again took their places in the Italian villa and palazzo. But Italians generally favoured their own early Renaissance style rather than true Gothic.

There can be little doubt that the best Gothic Revival furniture made in nineteenth-century Europe was that produced in England, by A. W. N. Pugin (Plate 140A) in the 'thirties and 'forties, by William Burges (Plate 139B) in the 'sixties and 'seventies and by William Morris and his associates in the last forty years of the century. Such furniture, which is well worth the attention of collectors, is fully described on p. 109.

BOOKS FOR FURTHER READING

CLARK, SIR KENNETH, *The Gothic Revival* (rev. ed. London, 1950).
EVANS, JOAN, *Pattern* (Oxford, 1931, vol. II, pp. 160–187).

FURNISHINGS IN THE EGYPTIAN TASTE

By HUGH HONOUR

Of all exotic fashions surely the most extraordinary was the vogue for Egyptiana which swept across Europe in the eighteenth and nineteenth centuries, leaving in its wake a charming array of pyramids, obelisks, sphinxes and a few rooms and entire buildings decorated with pseudo-hieroglyphics. Among its more familiar manifestations are such pieces of household furniture and ornaments as couches with Egyptian lions sitting impassively on their arms, cabinets and tables decorated with lotus bud columns and winged solar discs, chimney pieces supported by sturdy Egyptian caryatids, and lamps and candlesticks in the form of Egyptian slaves. All such objects passed until recently under the name of the 'retour de l'Egypte' style, and were supposed to have been derived from the drawings made during Napoleon's Egyptian campaign of 1798. But, in fact, the vogue for the Egyptian style in architecture, interior decoration and furniture was already well established in Europe long before Napoleon was born. Indeed, imitations and adaptations of Egyptian objects have been produced from time to time since the dawn of the Renaissance.

The revival of interest in classical art led inevitably to a study of certain Egyptian antiquities which the Romans had introduced into Italy. Some of these objects – the obelisk now in the Piazza di S. Pietro, and the Egyptian capitals re-used in the church of S. Maria in Trastevere at Rome – had been visible throughout the Middle Ages. Before the end of the thirteenth century the Egyptian sphinx had begun to exert its fascination on Italian sculptors. At least four were carved, one of which (Museo Civico, Viterbo) is signed: *Fra Pasquale*, 1279. In the excavation of building sites more Egyptian objects, usually connected with the cult of Isis, were unearthed. The bizarre characters with which they were decorated naturally excited the curiosity of Renaissance scholars one of whom discovered a transcript of a fifth-century text on hieroglyphics which was published in 1463 and widely read. Egyptian motifs therefore began to make their appearance in Italian art: Ghiberti included a pyramid in the background to one of his scenes on the Baptistry doors at Florence (c. 1435), Mantegna painted hieroglyphics in his *Triumph of Caesar* (1486), as did Pinturicchio in the Borgia apartments of the Vatican (1493–95), while the anonymous illustrator of the *Hypnerotamachia Polifili* included numerous hieroglyphics and obelisks in his woodcuts. Early in the fifteenth century Raphael incorporated two painted caryatids, clearly derived from those found in Hadrian's Villa and now in the Vatican Museum, in his *stanza dell'Incendio* (1514–17). Carved figures derived from the same pair of caryatids were used in about 1540 to decorate a gateway at Fontainebleau. Later in the century sphinxes began to appear as the supports for the sarcophagus on sepulchral monuments in both Italy and France, probably derived from an antique prototype in the Vatican gardens.

There can be little doubt that Egyptian motifs appealed to the Renaissance patron and artist (as they were to appeal also in the early eighteenth century) mainly on account of their classical, rather than their pharaonic, associations. But they also exerted a special fascination on the mystagogue for whom Egypt was revealed as the most intriguing land of arcane mystery. This aspect of Egyptian art and religion was further developed in the seventeenth century, notably by Athanasius Kircher who published numerous folios of wholly fantastic Egyptology. At the same time, however, travellers were visiting Egypt in greater numbers than hitherto, examining her monuments and bringing back drawings of them. On such drawings Bernard de Montfaucon relied for the illustrations of Egyptian architecture in his *Antiquité Expliquée* (1719–24) and Bernard Fischer von Erlach for those in his *Historiche Architektur* (1721) both of which reveal the baroque capabilities of Egyptian motifs.

In the early eighteenth century Egyptian monuments seem for the first time to have won popularity for their ornamental, as well as their associative, value. Sir John Vanbrugh had a passion for obelisks with which he decorated both houses and gardens, and in the park at Stowe he planned to build a pyramid which a contemporary described as 'a copy in miniature of the most famous one in Egypt and the only thing of this kind I think in England'. Within a short time such pyramids were liberally scattered through English parks; though it should be remembered that they probably reminded the erstwhile grand-tourist of the monument of Caius Cæstius at Rome rather than Egyptian pyramids. The sphinx also came into fashion as a garden ornament, especially useful for decorating lodge gates and balustrades. These creatures, usually female and coyly smiling, were treated with such rococo elegance that it is sometimes difficult to remember that they derive ultimately from solemn Egyptian ancestors. Egyptian motifs were handled in a still more exuberantly rococo manner by Johann Melchior Dinglinger, the court jeweller at Dresden, who made in 1731 a remarkable *Apis Altar* (Grünes Gewölbe, Dresden) of precious and semi-precious stones, incorporating such motifs as bird-headed men and topped by an obelisk decorated with hieroglyphics.

A change in the attitude to Egyptian art became apparent soon after the middle of the century and found expression in the Comte de Caylus's *Recueil d'Antiquités, égyptiennes, étrusques, grecques et romaines* (1752–62). De Caylus was deeply impressed by the massive solidity and simplicity of Egyptian temples which, he said, made later buildings appear like 'châteaux de carte chargés de colisfichets'. Significantly enough he was also among the pioneers in the appreciation of the Grecian Doric architecture. From this time onwards, small schemes of interior decoration and even whole buildings in the Egyptian style were created in far greater quantities. The Egyptian taste made a strong appeal to neo-classical artists and patrons for it provided a style which could be treated in perfect conformity with Grecian rules of nobility and simplicity while answering the perennial demand for exoticism which had hitherto been satisfied by chinoiserie and turquerie. Indeed, the Egyptian style was often confused with the Grecian in the neo-classical period even as Gothic and Chinoiserie had been intermixed a generation earlier.

The most important and probably the earliest manifestation of neo-classical *égyptiennerie* was the interior of the English coffee house in Rome, designed by G. B. Piranesi and painted with decorations in the Egyptian taste which covered the entire wall surface. The room was in the form of a fantastic hypæthral Egyptian temple liberally adorned with sphinxes, caryatids and hieroglyphics and pierced by windows and tapering doors commanding views of a sandy desert sprinkled with pyramids and obelisks. This decorative scheme, which nearly every English visitor to Rome must have seen in the latter years of the century (and on which several commented unfavourably), was given further publicity when Piranesi included a series of engravings of it, together with several designs for fantastic fire-places in the Egyptian taste, in his *Diversi Manieri d'Adornare i Cammini* of 1769. A few years later A. R. Mengs, aided by C. Unterberger, painted an appropriately Egyptian style ceiling to the Camera dei Papiri in the Vatican library, with sphinxes, caryatids and hieroglyphics. At the Villa Borghese a *Sala Egizia* was created in 1781 with a ceiling depicting *Cybele Pouring her Gifts upon Egypt*, by Tomaso Conca, supported by Egyptian figures in stucco by G. B. Marchetti and a tessellated floor inlaid with kneeling figures of Egyptians and pseudo-hieroglyphics. Mention should also be made of a room in Palazzo Braschi, painted in about 1805 probably by L. Coccetti, which conforms in style with those other pre-Napoleonic manifestations of the Egyptian taste. It might well be supposed that this minor craze for the Egyptian style at Rome influenced the minor arts, but as yet only one small object has been recorded: a soup tureen made at Turin (Plate 141B). Others in a similar style may well be found.

From Rome the fashion for Egyptian style decorations seems to have spread to both England and France, for in the late eighteenth century most architects of promise completed their studies by visiting the Eternal City. John Dance the younger, who had been in Rome in the 1760s, made a design for a fireplace in the Egyptian taste for Shelbourne House in about 1779. Sir John Soane, who had also been to Rome, published an 'Egyptian temple' in his *Designs in Architecture* of 1778. In 1792 James Playfair, the year after his visit to Rome, designed a Billiard Room (which still survives) in the Egyptian taste at Cairness House, Aberdeenshire. This was a distant and somewhat faint echo of Piranesi's English coffee house. And it was from Rome in 1796 that C. H. Tatham sent designs for Egyptian candlesticks for Carlton House to Henry Holland. These candlesticks, now at Buckingham Palace, are in the form of Egyptian slaves with lotus flowers to hold the lights (a somewhat similar candelabrum and pair of candlesticks had been made for the Earl of Yarborough in 1791). Among other examples of late eighteenth-century English Egyptiana is a fireplace carried by black marble Egyptian caryatids designed by Nathaniel Dance, in about 1794, for the library at Lansdowne House where the wall decorations between the book-cases and the bird capitals also owe their inspiration to Egypt. Dance later used Egyptian motifs at Stratton Park. The Egyptian taste clearly enjoyed considerable popularity in England in the 1780s and 1790s. It therefore seems probable that many of the objects usually assigned to the early years of the nineteenth century were in fact made in the eighteenth.

In France *égyptiennerie* was hardly less fashionable than in England. Avant garde architects like Boulée and Ledoux made frequent use of pyramids in their vast and optimistic projects, and J.-L. Desprez produced some striking aquatints of Egyptian sepulchres. Other manifestations of this style are less forceful. Sphinxes were more than ever popular as garden ornaments. As early as 1775 Clodion carved figures of a male and female Egyptian for the church of Orsay (unfortunately they have vanished) and somewhat later the statuette of an Egyptian girl now in the Louvre. In 1786 the salon of the financier Bouret's house in the Place Vendôme was decorated in the Egyptian taste, and in the following year an Egyptian temple front was erected as a folly by J.-B. Kléber in the park at Étupes. Furniture was also made in the Egyptian taste. Gouthière made two porphyry-topped tables supported by Egyptian figures for Louis XVI, and in 1783 Marie Antoinette is recorded as owning a tripod table which stood on Egyptian caryatid legs.

The prevalence of Egyptiana in Europe before the French Revolution in no way lessens the importance of Napoleon's famous North African campaign of 1798. He took with him several draughtsmen, notably the Baron Vivant Denon, who published in 1802 his handsome folio work *Voyage dans la Basse et la Haute Egypte* which provided the first accurate drawings of Egyptian buildings and furniture. But even before this book appeared a swarm of Egyptian figures, sphinxes and winged solar discs had begun to settle on the salons and bedrooms of Paris. Denon himself commissioned Jacob to furnish his bedroom with a bed mounted on sphinxes, decorated with silver reliefs of Egyptian suppliants and guarded at the head by a statue of Isis, and surrounded by stools supported on sphinx-headed terms. The Egyptian devices used at this period were much more 'correct' than those of pre-revolutionary days, answering an increased demand for archæological accuracy. The revived Egyptian style won great popularity and since it appeared at the very moment when Napoleon was about to crown himself Emperor, it was naturally associated with him. And as a manifestation of the official Empire style it spread in the wake of the French armies throughout Europe.

Denon's book appeared during a brief lull in the war between England and France, and it could therefore be translated into English without delay. The plates exerted a strong influence on George Smith and Thomas Hope who both derived details from it for the design of furniture. Thomas Hope's *Household Furniture* of 1807 is chiefly remembered for its Grecian designs but it also included a plate of the Egyptian room which this wealthy dilettante created at his house in Duchess Street, London. This room was decorated with an Egyptian frieze, some genuine Egyptian antiquities, and furniture made specially in the Egyptian taste: sofas, chairs and tables of black and gold painted wood embellished with hieroglyphics and such archæological devices as miniatures of the canopic vases in which ancient Egyptians preserved the entrails of their mummified dead. Two chairs and a sofa from this room have recently been identified (Plate 142A). Hope's aim in publishing his book was, he said, to 'induce several professional men, upholders, cabinet makers, and others, to abandon in some degree the old beaten track' and to produce 'correct' imitations of the stone furniture recently discovered in Egyptian tombs or depicted in ancient carvings. But in this ambition he was unsuccessful, for cabinet-makers and their patrons seem to have preferred more comfortable and less correct pieces of furniture which were only faintly tinged with an exotic Egyptian aroma: sideboards, writing tables and cabinets of a slightly tapering outline, beds, cupboards, chairs and tables with Egyptian caryatids or sphinxes decorating the corners (Plate 143C). In 1812, however, the Egyptian Hall, with a façade which combined elements from several ancient Egyptian temples, was built in Piccadilly by P. F. Robinson; a versatile architect who had worked in the Hindoo taste at Brighton and was later to win fame for his essays in the Swiss Cottage style. During the next thirty years several Egyptian buildings were erected in England, some based on Robinson's hall (the house in Chapel Street at Penzance, for instance), others based directly on Egyptian temples (a warehouse about 1840 at Leeds, inspired by the temple of Dendera). Strangely enough the vogue for Egyptian furniture and ornaments did not last as long as that for buildings, and none seems to have been produced after the early 1830s.

The Empire style lived on in Italy long after Napoleon's armies retreated and dispersed. With it the Egyptian taste also survived. In the late 1820s or 1830s Luigi Canina built the very handsome Egyptian gateway to the gardens of the Villa Borghese at Rome. At about the same time a Sienese architect, Agostino Fantastici, was making designs for furniture several of which included Egyptian motifs (Plate 144B). Specimens of Egyptian architecture were also produced in several other European countries, including Russia where a very imposing gateway was built at Peterhof by Merelaws in 1829. The taste for Egyptian architecture also appeared in the United States at this period.

The foregoing summary account of the principal monuments to the taste for Egyptiana reveals that this strange fashion persisted in Europe from the late 1760s until the 1830s. Yet nearly all the surviving examples of furniture and ornaments in the Egyptian taste have usually been ascribed to the ten years after the publication of Denon's book in 1802. Unfortunately it is very seldom possible to date specimens of the minor arts with the same precision as buildings and schemes of painted decoration and the question must be left open as to whether many of the surviving examples of Egyptiana belong to the last decades of the eighteenth century, the Empire period, or the two decades after the end of the Napoleonic wars.

BOOKS FOR FURTHER READING

HONOUR, H., *The Connoisseur*, May, 1955, p. 242 ff.
PEVSNER, N. and LANG, S., *The Architectural Review*, May, 1956, p. 242 ff.

GLOSSARY

Acanthus. The leaf used in classical and Renaissance architectural design, particu-

Fig 1.

larly on Corinthian capitals. Adapted later as a motif in furniture design. Most important in Chippendale furniture as decorative motif on the knees of cabriole legs.

Acorn clock. American shelf or mantel clock, generally about 2 feet high, with the upper portion shaped somewhat like an acorn. Popular in New England about 1825.

Ambry (aumbry, almery; *Fr.* **armoire).** Enclosed compartment or recess in a wall or in a piece of furniture, the original sense of the term having been usurped by cupboard, which originally had a different connotation. "Cuppbordes wyth ambries" are mentioned

Fig. 2

in inventories of Henry VIII's furniture. To-day aumbry, etc., is principally used architecturally and ecclesiastically, as of the doored compartments or recesses for the Reservation of the Blessed Sacrament, this usage perpetuating the original sense. The French form *armoire* is often applied to large presses or press-cupboards.

Apple. A fruitwood much used in America for turnings, also often in case pieces, such as slant-front desks, etc., to show off the rich-coloured pink-brown wood.

Appliques. *See under* Wall-lights.

Apron-work. Prolongation downwards, beyond what is essential to construction, of the lower edge of a member, such as the shaped lower edge of the front of certain boarded chests, or the lower frontal framework, below

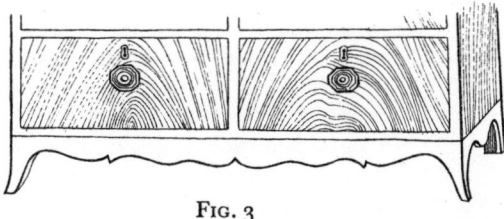

Fig. 3

the drawers, of certain dressers. In such cases an apron is purely ornamental; in others, e.g. the seating of close-chairs, its purpose is that of concealment.

Ark. Term frequently encountered in medieval inventories, seemingly meaning: (*a*) a chest with a coped or gabled lid; (*b*) perhaps a structure resembling a reliquary (*Fr. chasse*), as exemplified by the sixteenth-century almery in Coity Church, Glamorganshire. That ark was a distinct term is shown by such entries as the following from an inventory of the contents of St Mary's, Warwick, 1464:

"It: in the Vestrye i gret olde arke to put in vestyments etc.

"It: in the Sextry above the Vestrye, i olde arke at the auters ende, i olde coofre irebonde having a long lok of the olde facion, and i lasse new coofre having iii loks called the tresory cofre and certeyn almaries." (Quoted by Philip Mainwaring Johnston, F.R.I.B.A.: *Church Chests of the Twelfth and Thirteenth Centuries in England*; 1908, p. 60.)

Armadio. The French *armoire*, a large cupboard, usually of a somewhat monumental character, which seems first to have been used to supplement the *cassoni* in the furnishing of Italian houses in the late fourteenth century. Early examples are usually about 4 feet in height, and some are decorated with flamboyant Gothic carving in low relief. An early fifteenth-century example (in the Museo Bardini at Florence) is in the form of a long, low cupboard with several very simply decorated doors and a panelled backboard of the same height as the cupboard. In the sixteenth century two-story *armadi* became popular. They were often decorated with two orders of pilasters or pilasters above elongated consoles (there is a good Tuscan example of this type in the museum at Berlin). Sometimes the two stories were separated by a projecting drawer. This pattern was superseded in the seventeenth century by a still more massive type, with pilasters some 6 feet tall at either end, and sometimes with a pair of drawers in the plinth. When a less ponderous effect was desired the cupboard was mounted on turned legs. The tops of seventeenth-century *armadi* are often shaped in baroque curves. In the eighteenth century the *armadio* was usually made on a lighter and more elegant pattern and was often designed to stand in a corner. But with the introduction of the chest of drawers the *armadio* lost much of its former popularity in the house.

Many of the early surviving *armadi* were intended originally for the sacristies of churches, where they were used for the storage of vestments, and it is often difficult to distinguish these from domestic examples except when they have specifically religious motifs in their decoration. After the sixteenth century such *armadi* were usually built-in furnishings of the sacristy. Sometimes they were richly carved or decorated with *intarsia* panels.

Arming chest. Chest for the housing of armours and weapons. Arming chests might be fitted with compartments of varying size to accommodate breast-plate, etc. (*see* Chest). (In navigation an arming box contains tallow for the "lead".)

Armoires. *See under* Wardrobes.

Artisans libres. The name given to French craftsmen who chose to work outside the guild jurisdiction and who sought refuge in what were known as *lieux privilégiés* in Paris. Being exempt from guild charges and regulations, they were a continual source of irritation to the guilds, particularly as they included a large number of foreign *ébénistes* who came to Paris in the mid-eighteenth century. These included some of the finest craftsmen of the time, a number of whom later became *maître-ébénistes*.

Ash. The American ash, a cream-coloured hardwood with oak-like graining; much used for furniture parts, such as upholstery frames, where strong, but not heavy, wood was desired. In England it was used in eighteenth-century furniture, particularly for the hooped backs of Windsor chairs.

Athénienne. A form of candelabrum consisting of an urn supported on a classical tripod, invented in 1773 by J. H. Eberts, editor of the famous *Monument de Costume*. The name derives from a painting by J. B. Vien entitled "*La Vertueuse Athénienne*", which shows a priestess burning incense at a tripod of this type. They were made of patinated bronze with ormolu mounts or in carved giltwood, but not many survive. They are, however, typical of the classicizing tendencies of the last quarter of the eighteenth century.

Bail. Half-loop metal pull, usually brass, hanging from metal bolts. First used in America about 1700; slowly grew into use for drawers of William and Mary pieces. The reigning fashion from 1720 to 1780 for drawers of Queen Anne and Chippendale pieces.

Ball-and-claw foot. *See* Claw-and-ball foot.

Ball foot. U.S. term for Bun foot

Banister-back chair. Probably simplified from the cane chair (*q.v.*) but with vertical split-banisters in the back. Generally maple, often ebonized. Widely used in rural America,

1700–25 until the end of the century (Fig. 4).

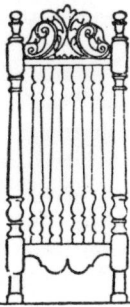

FIG. 4

Banjo. Modern name for the American wall clock with a longish pendulum, the whole housed in a case shaped somewhat like a banjo. Invented in the 1790s by Simon Willard, and patented by him about 1800. Decoratively attractive, its popularity spread from 1800 through the next half-century.

Bargueño (or **Vargueño**). Spanish cabinet with fall-front enclosing drawers and often mounted on a stand. Mixed materials are found.

Barley-sugar. *See* Twist-turning.

Baroque. The late Renaissance style of vigorously elaborate furniture with sweeping curves and resplendent ornament. It originated in sixteenth-century Italy, spread through Europe, but was little practised in England, and known in American only in *bombé* case-pieces and in greatly simplified forms of some William and Mary and Queen Anne furniture (*see* Rococo).

Basin-stand. *See* Washing-stand.

Bedstead. So far as practical collecting is concerned, main basic types are the box- (or enclosed) bedstead, wainscot- (including bedsteads panelled at head and foot), post- (with two or four posts supporting the tester), stump- (or low type), and the truckle- or trundle- (with wooden wheels at base of uprights). These are not hard-and-fast definitions; one type may well overlap another (e.g. box and wainscot). Parts of bedsteads have been re-used for other purposes of a decorative nature, such as overmantels. We know little of the shape of Italian beds before the sixteenth century, save from those which appear in such paintings as Carpaccio's *St Ursula* or Ghirlandaio's *Birth of the Virgin*. One of the earliest is that formerly in the Palazzo Davanzati at Florence (Plate 81A), a handsome piece of furniture mounted on a wide plinth. Sixteenth-century examples often have rich carving on head and foot and are without the plinth. In Sicily iron bedsteads with four posts supporting a canopy were popular from the late sixteenth century. The use of four posts was, however, unusual on later Italian beds, which sometimes have stumps at the corners and are covered by canopies supported from the wall. Lucchese examples (Plate 84A) are often richly covered with fabric which is matched on the bedspread.

Beech. A smooth, close-grained wood of light colour less frequently used in America than England. Found in the underframes of New York Chippendale pieces and occasionally in New England Chippendale as well as early turned pieces.

Beer-wagon. *See* Coaster.

Bell flower. Conventionalized hanging ("belle") flower-bud of three, occasionally five, petals carved or, more often, inlaid one below the other in strings dropping down the legs of a table or chair or, sometimes, a chair splat. Seen in American Hepplewhite and Sheraton, notably Maryland furniture (Fig. 5). It is practically the same as the English "husk" motif.

FIG. 5

Bell seat. The rounded, somewhat bell-shaped, seat often found in late Philadelphia Queen Anne side chairs. Nowadays often called balloon seat. Mostly about 1740–55.

Bench. A long seat, backed or backless, fitted or movable (*see* Form, Settle, Table-bench).

Bible-box. Popular term for a variety of box, generally of small size. That some such boxes were used to hold the family Bible, or average meagre domestic library, is probable,

Fig. 6A

though they doubtless served other purposes. Lace-boxes enter this category.

Bibliothèque-basse. A low cupboard fitted with shelves for books, and doors often of glass but sometimes fitted with grilles.

Bilbao or **"Bilboa"**. U.S. wall mirror framed in coloured marbles or marble and wood with a scrollwork headpiece and gilded mouldings. Adam or Hepplewhite followers might have designed them, yet they are believed to have originated in the Spanish seaport Bilbao. Stylish in New England seaport towns 1780–1800.

Bilsted. Word used in colonial New York for sweet-gum wood.

Birch. Hard, close-grained wood. Stained to substitute for mahogany in country furniture. Resembles satinwood in certain cuts. The American variety, *betual lenta*, was exported to England in the second half of the eighteenth century.

Bird's-eye. A marking of small spots, supposed to resemble bird's eyes, often found in the wood of the sugar maple. Used and much prized from the earliest to present times.

Blister. A marking, thought to resemble a blister, found in various woods – cedar, mahogany, poplar, pine, and, especially, maple.

Block front. A whole range of forms – chests of drawers, chests-on-chests, knee-hole dressing-tables, slant-front desks, secretaries, etc. – in which thick boards, usually mahogany, for the fronts of the drawers and cabinets are cut so that the centres recede in a flattened curve while the ends curve outwards in a flattened bulge. At the top of the three curves, one concave and two convex, a shell is often carved or glued on. Should the piece be in two sections, often only the lower section is block-fronted. The origin of block-fronting is unknown; the development is believed to be American, evolved about 1760–80, by John Goddard of Newport, Rhode Island, perhaps with the aid of his associate, John Townsend. They may have arrived at it by straightening the curves of the Dutch cabinet. The late American authority Wallace Nutting called block fronts "the aristocrats of furniture". The English antique furniture authority, Cescinsky, described them, especially the secretaries, as "the finest examples of American furniture". They are much sought after.

Boat bed. American Empire style bed shaped somewhat like a gondola. A variant of the sleigh bed.

Bombé. Lit. "inflated, blown out", i.e. of convex form generally on more than one axis.

Bonheur-du-jour. A small writing-table usually on tall legs, and sometimes fitted to hold toilet accessories and *bibelots*. It first appeared in France *c.* 1760, but remained in fashion for a comparatively short time.

Bonnet top. When the broken-arch pediment of tall case-furniture covers the entire top from front to back, this hood is called a bonnet top (Fig. 6B). It is usually cut in the

Fig. 6B

same curves as the arch, but is sometimes left uncut, a solid block of wood behind the arched fronting. 1730–85. Same as "Hood".

Bookcase. In England bookcases, either fitted or, in some cases, contained in other furniture, were known medievally, but the domestic bookcase mainly derives from the period of Charles II (1660–85). In Italy bookcases were less frequently made individually than as part of the built-in decorations of a library. In Venice there is an excellent example of a late seventeenth-century library with cases carved by German craftsmen in the monastry of S. Giorgio Maggiore (now *Fondazione Cini*) and an exquisite small, early eighteenth-century library, with painted cases, in the Ca' Sagredo. Both of these have two tiers of bookcases which fill the walls. In houses that could not afford to give up a whole room to the library the books were probably kept in an ordinary *armadio*. Eighteenth-century bookcases resemble either a section of a complete library or, more usually, an *armadio* with wire grilles in place of panels in the doors. Although a few enormous early bookcases exist, bookcases were seldom made in America as an article of furniture before 1785-90, the average family before then keeping their books in locked chests, cupboards, and the tops of secretaries. Bookcases are generally large and heavy until about 1800, when the smaller type came in (*see* China cabinet).

Book-rest. A stand used in Georgian libraries to support large books, consisting of a square or rectangular framework with cross bars, the upper bar being supported by a strut which was adjusted on a grooved base. This kind of stand was sometimes fitted into the top of a table.

Book-shelf. *See* Shelves.

Boston rocker. In America the most popular of all rocking chairs. Apparently evolved from the Windsor rocker (*q.v.*). Usually painted, it has curved arms, a tall spindle back, broad top rail generally showing stencilled designs – a kind of ornamental panel – and a "rolling" seat, curved up at the back and down at the front. When standardized and mass produced (after 1840) it is not a true antique.

Boulle marquetry. The name given to the type of inlay evolved for use on furniture in the late seventeenth century by André Charles Boulle (1642–1732) (*see* under French furniture).

The process involves the glueing of one or more thin layers of tortoiseshell to a similar number of brass. The design of the marquetry is set out on paper, and this is pasted on to the surface. The pattern is then cut out by means of a saw. After this, the layers of brass and tortoiseshell are separated and can be made to form two distinct marquetries by combining the materials in opposite ways: either with the design formed by the brass on a ground of shell, known as *première partie* or first part, or the exact opposite, known as *contre-partie*, or counter-part, with the design in shell on a ground of brass. These two types of inlay can then be glued on to a carcase in the form of a veneer. Often the two types are found side by side as part of the same design, in order to give contrast. Again, when pieces are made in pairs one is often veneered with *première partie* and the other with *contre-partie* marquetry.

The brass in the *première partie* marquetry was often engraved naturalistically, frequently very finely, and was sometimes combined with other substances, such as pewter, copper, mother-of-pearl, and stained horn, again usually to give contrasts and naturalistic effects to the design. Additional colour was also given occasionally by veneering the shell over coloured foil, usually red or green.

The carcases on to which Boulle marquetry is veneered are usually found to be of oak or deal, and the parts which are not covered by the inlay are veneered with ebony, coromandel-wood, or purple-wood, in order to tone with the shell of the inlay.

Finally, Boulle furniture is usually lavishly mounted with ormolu, so as to protect the corners and the more vulnerable parts of the inlay, but the mounts are frequently also adapted in a decorative manner to form hinges, lock-plates, and handles. It will be noticed that the ormolu is sometimes fully gilt, which provides a strong decorative contrast with the inlaid brass; equally, the bronze is sometimes left ungilt, and therefore harmonizes with the metal inlay to a greater extent.

Boulle furniture, so much in demand in the reign of Louis XIV, went out of fashion during most of that of his successor, but it did not cease to be made, and the Boulle *atelier* continued to turn out pieces from time to time. They were therefore ready when, under Louis XVI and the classical revival, the taste for this type of furniture returned, and at this period a very large number of pieces were made, often using the original designs, mounts, and processes as in the former period. It is thus often extremely difficult to tell whether a piece was made in one period or another, and it is better not to be too dogmatic about this, as there are very few distinguishing characteristics. Two may perhaps be mentioned: the engraving of the brass inlay is less common in the Louis XVI period and, when it does appear, of inferior quality;

GLOSSARY

secondly, the use of other metals than brass and freer designs are slightly more common.

In the earlier period a large number of designs for Boulle marquetry are derived from the engravings of Jean Berain, who was, like Boulle, also employed by the Crown.

Boulle marquetry is sometimes erroneously referred to as Buhl. This is a Teutonic adaptation of Boulle's name for which there is no justification.

Bow back. *See* Windsor chair.

Bow-front. A curving front used on case pieces in New England during the Chippendale period.

Box and casket. Boxes were among the most attractive of the smaller pieces of furniture, and were used from medieval times for a multitude of purposes – personal effects, toilet and writing materials, valuables, documents, etc. Tudor and early Stuart boxes were usually square in shape and made of oak, carved, inlaid, or painted, and occasionally stood upon stands, few of which have survived. In the later seventeenth century walnut was commonly used (sometimes decorated with marquetry or parquetry), but other materials included parchment, tortoise-shell, and stumpwork, the latter particularly on the boxes kept by ladies for their cosmetics, etc. The interiors were often ingeniously fitted with compartments and drawers. In the eighteenth century some beautiful mahogany and satinwood boxes were made, until they were gradually replaced by small work-tables, though boxes on stands, conforming to the prevailing decorative fashions, were to be found. Among other examples were Tunbridge ware (*q.v.*) boxes, and travelling boxes fitted with spaces for writing, working, and toilet requisites. About 1800 work and toilet boxes covered with tooled leather were in vogue (Plate 124B).

Boxwood (*buis*). A very closely grained wood of a yellow colour found frequently in Europe and elsewhere. Extensively used in France for fillets to frame panels of marquetry.

Boys and crowns. Old term for a type of carved ornament on the cresting of late seventeenth- and quite early eighteenth-century chairs, day-beds, etc. (*see* under Restoration). The motif, a crown, usually, though not necessarily, arched, supported by two flying or sprawling naked boys, derives ultimately from the flying *putti* frequently found in renaissance design. In England, the idea was familiar long before it achieved (*temp*. Charles II) a vogue on chair-backs.

Bracket. The detachable wall-bracket, as distinct from the fixed architectural feature, appeared towards the end of the seventeenth century, and seems to have been used at first for displaying china. Its prominent position in the room singled it out for special decorative treatment in carving or gilding. In the early Georgian period the bracket was often used to support a bust or vase, and as a result it tended to become larger in size and more heavily ornamented; but with the return of the fashion for displaying china about 1750 and the growing use of the bracket for supporting lights, it became altogether more delicate in appearance, and was adapted to the various styles of the Chippendale and Adam periods. The wall-bracket supporting a clock was a popular form of decoration in the later eighteenth century.

Bracket foot. A foot supporting a case piece and attached directly to the underframing. It consists of two pieces of wood, joined at the corner. The open side is generally cut out in a simple pattern. The corner end is sometimes straight, at other times curved in an ogee pattern.

Bras de lumière. *See under* Wall-lights.

Brazier. A portable metal container used from Tudor times for burning coal or charcoal; with handle and feet, or sometimes mounted on a stand.

Breakfast table. A small table with hinged side leaves that can be used by one or two people. After the Chippendale period the name Pembroke is often applied to the type.

Brewster chair. A seventeenth-century American arm-chair of turned spindles and posts with rush seat (Plate 46B). The back has two tiers of spindles. There is a tier under the arms and one under the seat. The chair is usually of ash or maple. Named after William Brewster, elder of Plymouth Plantation, whose chair is preserved at Pilgrim Hall, Plymouth, Massachusetts. Similar to the Carver chair.

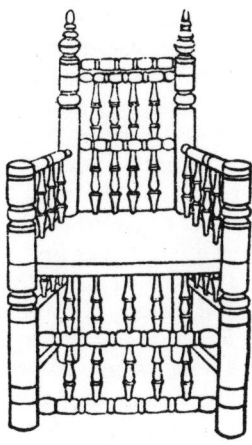

FIG. 7

Broken arch. *See* Scroll top.

Bronzes d'ameublement. A term with no exact English equivalent covering all furniture, practical or decorative, made of bronze, patinated or gilt. It embraces such items as candelabra, candlesticks, wall-lights, chandeliers, fire-dogs, clock-cases, mounts for furniture and porcelain, etc. Their manufacture was the particular province of the *fondeurs*, *ciseleurs*, and *doreurs*.

Buffet. Term variously applied to open, doorless structures, of more than one tier (*see also* Court cupboard, Livery cupboard).

Bull's eye. A popular term for the small round mirror with convex or concave glass and an ornate gilt frame. The type was fashionable 1800–20, and often of English or French manufacture. An alternate meaning is the reference to clear glass with a large centre drop or gather employed as window glass and in cabinets.

Bureau. In America, ever since the eighteenth century, the word bureau means a chest of drawers, with or without a mirror, and regularly used in the bedroom (Fig. 8). Originally, and still in England, a desk. Examples were made in the William and Mary style, dating 1700–10, but the form dropped completely out of use until revived about 1750. They are found in the Chippendale and every style thereafter, the revival probably springing not from the earlier form but from Chippendale's designs. Many authorities describe bureaux according to the shape of the front – serpentine, reverse serpentine, bow or swell, and straight front – but that is mere grouping, not classification proper. In England the word denotes a writing-desk with a fall, a cylinder, or a tambour front.

FIG. 8

Bureau-plat. A writing-table supported on tall legs with a flat top with drawers beneath. Began to appear in France towards the end of the seventeenth century.

Bureau table. A dressing-table with drawers on short legs and a knee-hole recess.

Bureau-toilette. A piece of furniture for female use combining the functions of a toilet- and writing-table.

Burl. A tree knot or protruding growth which shows beautifully patterned grainings when sliced. Used for inlay or veneer. Found in some late seventeenth- and much eighteenth-century American furniture, and chiefly in walnut and maple burls.

Butler's tray. A tray mounted on legs or on a folding stand, in use throughout the eighteenth century. The X-shaped folding stand was in general use from about 1750, the tray normally being rectangular and fitted with a gallery. Oval trays were sometimes made in the later part of the century.

Butterfly table. A William and Mary style drop-leaf table with solid swinging supports shaped a little like butterfly wings. The

FIG. 9

GLOSSARY

supports are pivoted on the stretchers joining the legs. Assumption that the type is of American origin is probably incorrect.

Cabinet. The glass fronted cabinet intended for the display of a collection of porcelain or other *objets d'art* is an eighteenth-century invention. Such cabinets were made in Italy in conformity with the rococo and neo-classical styles.

Cabriole leg. The curving tall furniture leg used in American Queen Anne and Chippendale furniture, and almost universally used in the eighteenth century. The adjective is from the French noun, which is a dancing term meaning a goat leap, and is used in the idiom *faire le cabriole* to refer to the agility and grace of a person. The leg is inspired by an animal form, unlike the earlier scroll and turned shapes and is terminated in the claw-and-ball foot, the hairy paw, or the scroll in the Chippendale period and earlier the claw-and-ball, the pad, trifid, or slipper foot.

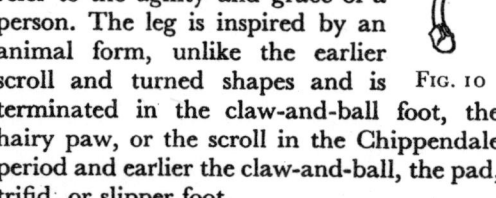

Fig. 10

Camel back. Colloquial term for a chair or sofa, such as Hepplewhite, with the top curved somewhat like the hump of a dromedary (Fig. 11).

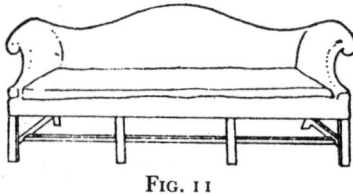

Fig. 11

Canapé. The ordinary French word for a sofa. Evolved in many forms during the Louis XV period.

Candelabrum. A lighting appliance with branches supporting sockets for more than one light. They took many forms, but are usually made of ormolu, sometimes with figures in patinated bronze. They were often made in pairs or sets of four.

Candle-box. A cylindrical or square box, of metal or wood, widely used in the Georgian period for storing candles.

Candle-stand. A portable stand (known also as a lamp-stand, *guéridon*, and *torchère*) for a candlestick, candelabrum, or lamp. After 1660 the fashion arose of having two candle-stands flanking a side table with a mirror on the wall above; the stands usually took the form of a baluster or twist-turned shaft, with a circular or octagonal top and a tripod base. At the end of the century more elaborate kinds, copying French stands, became fashionable, with vase-shaped tops and scrolled feet, all carved and gilded. Other examples were of simpler design, but had rich decoration in gesso or marquetry. In the early Georgian period, when gilt stands followed architectural forms, the vase-shaped tops and baluster shafts were larger, and the feet curved outwards, replacing the scrolled French style. About 1750 stands became lighter and more delicate, many of them being enriched with rococo decoration. There was a distinct change in design in the later eighteenth century: the traditional tripod continued, often in mahogany, with turned shaft and a bowl or vase top in the classical taste; but a new type, which was originated by Adam, consisted of three uprights, mounted on feet or a plinth, supporting usually a candelabrum, or with a flat top. Smaller examples of the latter type were made to stand on tables (Plate 117). A much smaller version of candle-stand was also popular after 1750 – with a circular base and top, and sometimes an adjustable shaft.

Candlesticks (*flambeaux*). A portable lighting appliance with one socket for a single light or candle. Large numbers were made almost exclusively of ormolu in the late seventeenth and eighteenth centuries, usually in pairs or sets of four, but sometimes in larger quantities.

Cane chair. First produced in England in Charles II's reign, it was very popular in London because it was cheap, light, and durable. It was used in America first in about 1690, in William and Mary tall-backed chairs (Plate 51A). The type occasionally occurred in Queen Anne, but was revived in the classical style. Duncan Phyfe used it. Caning was introduced from the Orient through the Netherlands.

Canted. Sloping, at an angle.

Canterbury. (1) A small music-stand with partitions for music-books, usually mounted on castors, and sometimes with small drawers,

GLOSSARY

much used in the early nineteenth century (Plate 118A); and (2) a plate and cutlery stand particularly designed for supper parties in the later eighteenth century, with divisions for cutlery and a semicircular end, on four turned legs. "The name 'Canterbury' arose", wrote Sheraton, "because the bishop of that See first gave orders for these pieces."

Carolean. Term of convenience strictly applicable to pieces made in the reign of Charles I (1625–49), those made under Charles II (1660–85) usually being dissociated. Actually the Carolean style is as much an extension of the Jacobean as the latter was of the later Elizabethan.

Cartonnier. A piece of furniture which took various forms. Usually it stood at one end of a writing-table (*bureau-plât*) and was intended to hold papers. It was sometimes surmounted by a clock. Also sometimes called a *serre-papier*.

Cartouche. A fanciful scroll; used in America mostly as a central finial for the tops of Philadelphia Chippendale highboys, clocks, and, occasionally, mirrors.

Carver chair. Modern term for an early seventeenth-century "Dutch" type arm-chair made of turned posts and spindles. It has three rails and three spindles in the back (Fig. 12). Such chairs may be seen in seventeenth-

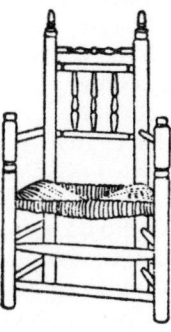

FIG. 12

century paintings of humbler Dutch interiors, though the source of the American ones was probably an English model. Usually of ash or maple, with rush seats. Named after John Carver, first governor of the Plymouth colony, who is said to have brought one to America with him in the *Mayflower*. Made until the end of the century. Many examples survive, the earliest dating perhaps about 1650. (*See* its variant, Brewster chair.)

Caryatid. Upright carved in semblance of a human figure or, more frequently, a demi-figure on a terminal base. Strictly, Caryatid implies a female, Atlanta or Atlas figure a male figure, though Caryatid is used for either. The term derives from the legend of the women of Carya, enslaved and immured for their betrayal of the Greeks to the Persians. Atlanta refers to the myth of Atlas upholding the heavens (Plate 3B).

Cassapanca. A wooden bench with a built-in chest under the seat. Early *cassapanche*, like that of the fifteenth century in the Ca' D'Oro at Venice or the magnificent sixteenth-century example in the Bargello at Florence, are in the form of a *cassone* with back and arms. After the *cassone* went out of fashion in the early seventeenth century the *cassapanca* survived as a useful piece of entrance-hall furniture. Seventeenth- and eighteenth-century examples often have immensely high backs of thin wood painted with mythological beings or a coat-of-arms amid a profusion of scrolls.

Cassone. The *cassone*, or chest, was clearly one of the most popular pieces of furniture in fifteenth- and sixteenth-century Italy. It was also the most richly decorated, and, for this reason, perhaps, numerous examples have survived. It was used to hold linen or clothes and might also serve as a seat (with or without the upright back which made it into a *cassapanca*). *Cassoni* are frequently referred to as dower chests, and although they were often made to hold the supply of linen which a bride took to her new home, there is no reason to suppose that the majority were intended for this purpose. The *cassone nuziale*, or dower chest, can be recognized as such only if it bears the coats-of-arms of two families between whom a marriage took place.

The earliest *cassoni* were probably very unpretentious affairs, but a few of the early fifteenth-century examples which have survived are decorated with Gothic curvilinear carving or rough paintings of heraldic achievements. In the Renaissance period great ingenuity was expended on their design and adornment. Some were decorated with gesso friezes of *putti* sporting on the front and sides and others were fashioned like antique sarcophagi, but most seem to have been painted on the front (some were also painted inside the lid). Several highly able Florentine *quattrocento* painters, like the famous Master of the Jarves *Cassoni*, seem to have specialized almost exclusively in the decoration of furniture of this type: and some more important artists, like Bartolomeo Montagna (Plate 81B), occasionally turned their hands to this decorative work In Florence paintings of battles and the triumphs of Roman generals were in particular demand, elsewhere religious and mythological scenes seem to have enjoyed great popularity, but in Venice patterns of ornamental motifs were generally preferred. *Intarsia* views of real or imaginary architecture were also employed to decorate *cassoni*. In the sixteenth century the painted *cassone* seems to have gone out of fashion, and most surviving examples from this period are simply carved with abstract decorations. A few later sixteenth-century *cassoni* are adorned with mannerist term figures at the corners and low reliefs in the same style on the front. The *cassone* survived the sixteenth century only in the form of the *cassapanca* (*q.v.*) or of a simple unembellished utilitarian travelling chest.

Cat. A stand used after about 1750 to warm plates in front of the fire; it had three arms and three feet of turned wood (or three legs of cabriole form). The turning was well ringed to provide sockets for plates of various sizes.

Causeuse. A large chair or small sofa to accommodate two persons. Roughly corresponds to the small English settee. Sometimes referred to colloquially as a love-seat.

Cedar. Handsome pieces of furniture were occasionally made of colourful red cedar wood, though cedar – both the red and the white – was usually set aside for drawers, chests, linings, etc.

Cellaret. The name given generally after 1750 to a case on legs or stand for wine bottles; prior to that date, from the end of the seventeenth century, the same kind of case was called a cellar. In the early eighteenth century cellarets, lined with lead and containing compartments for bottles, stood under side-tables, and they were still made later in the century (Plate 118B) when sideboards, which had drawers fitted up to hold bottles, came into general use. Sheraton classified the cellaret with the wine cistern (*q.v.*) and sarcophagus, and distinguished them from the bottle-case, which was for square bottles only.

Chair. In its old sense chair meant, as like as not, an arm-chair, what is now called a single- or side-chair being a back-stool (stool with a back).[1] To what extent the chair originated from such box-forms as the chest is suggested by early surviving examples of box-like structure. Development from the wainscot chair to the open-framed variety with panelled back belongs in general to the late sixteenth century. Folding or rack-chairs and X-chairs (so called from their shape) have also a long history. Certain sixteenth-century chairs with narrow backs and widely splayed arms are so-called caqueteuse or caquetoire. The so-called farthingale chair (a term freely applied to many pieces, mostly of the earlier seventeenth century) has its back-support raised clear of the seat. Upholstery (not unknown earlier) had arrived, seats and back-pads being covered in velvet or in "Turkey-work". Leather was used, especially on Cromwellian chairs, some of which date from the Interregnum, though the type endured until relatively late in the seventeenth century. Leather or Russia chair are old terms for such items. About the middle of the seventeenth century are found what are often termed "mortuary" chairs, a term of doubtful origin for chairs with a small moustachioed and bearded head (supposedly allusive to King Charles I) in the centre of the shaped and scrolled back-rails. Similar chairs occur without the masks, and the type is a variation of Yorkshire or Derbyshire chair, the geographical distribution of which is undefined.

Cane chairs (*q.v.*) achieved main popularity in the second half of the seventeenth century, their backs and seats being caned. Scrolling, curlicues, boys and crowns, etc., were favoured as carved ornament. Backs lengthen, assuming the form of a narrow panel or centre (often caned or stuffed) flanked by

[1] 'Back chaier' occurs (e.g. Unton Inventory, 1620).

GLOSSARY

uprights. Already had been reached the period of barley-sugar turning (*see* Twist).

Corner-chairs, some of triangular formation, and sundry related types, were already in being. A later variety has the seat disposed diagonally to the low, rounded back. Elbow-chair and roundabout-chair are synonyms in use. An allied type is the circular chair (with circular seat), often Dutch, and known as burgomaster or (again) roundabout-chair, such terms being jargon. Thrown-chairs of various shapes, with much turnery, have been often assigned to the sixteenth century, though many are certainly later. Though scarcely belonging to the Age of Oak, the Windsor chair (*q.v.*) may have owed something to older types. The basic characteristic of Windsors is not the bow- or hoop-back, but the detail that back and under-framing are all mortised into the wooden seat, itself frequently saddle-shaped and "dished", but sometimes circular, etc. The bow-back type (late eighteenth century and later), preceded by the comb- or fan-back (early eighteenth century and later), was itself followed by other formations on more or less "Regency" lines. Types are many with much overlapping; woods are mixed. Scole or Mendlesham chairs are East Anglian types on Windsor lines. Yorkshire and Lancashire Windsors usually show "frilly" splats and developed turnery, but the type was not confined to the North of England. In America Windsors were made from the early eighteenth century, and include some fine types. Lancashire chair is also applied to an extensively made type of bobbin back, much favoured in the eighteenth and early nineteenth centuries, but, here again, as with Yorkshire and Derbyshire chairs in general, the geographical location has been overstressed (*see* Close-chair and -stool; *also* Restoration).

In the Renaissance period those made in France were on the whole very simple, constructed of plain wood, usually walnut, and carved with conventional motifs in the Italian style. Often they are of the ecclesiastical type with high backs carved in relief. Others have carved arms and stretchers. These types continued into the early seventeenth century, usually accompanied by some upholstery.

Such chairs of the Louis XIV period as have come down to us are also almost always of plain wood, carved in the classical manner. The backs are high, often with elaborately carved cornices. The legs are also elaborately carved and are often joined with stretchers. The chairs are upholstered on seats and back, either with embroidery, velvet, or with cane. Tapestry does not appear until later in the eighteenth century.

In the Louis XV period the design of chairs became less formal and the carving soon began to be carried out in the rococo manner. The outlines of the upholstered backs and seats, and the legs, gradually became curved and bowed until there is not a straight line in the whole design. Often chairs of the Louis XV period are of considerable size and of rather a heavy appearance. They are upholstered usually with silk, velvet, or brocade, but sometimes with tapestry, which begins to make its appearance at this time.

In the Louis XVI period chairs, in particular, take up the prevailing neo-classical style, the change being noticeable soon after 1755. Legs gradually become straighter, as do the outlines of backs, seats, and arms, and the motifs employed in the carving derive from classical sources, the most commonly found being the acanthus leaf in various forms, the wave-like band and the Ionic capital, as well as symmetrical garlands of flowers. It was at this time that the carving of chairs, particularly those produced by G. Jacob, reached the very greatest refinement, both of design and detail.

The frames of chairs of the Louis XV and Louis XVI periods are usually made of beech, birch, or walnut, and they are often gilt. It is important to remember, however, that they may not originally have been so. Sometimes the wood forming the frames was left plain and unadorned, more often they were painted white, or white and partly gilt. Equally, a chair may have been originally plain or painted, and then gilt before the end of the eighteenth century. More often gilding or regilding was carried out in the nineteenth century, and often very coarsely. Collectors should bear this in mind when judging both the style and condition of French chairs.

The earliest Italian chairs were probably no more than square stools to which a back and arms had been added, but they do not seem to have been in general use until the fifteenth century. Folding chairs (*sedie pieghevole*) were made before the beginning of the fourteenth century, however, and one or two fourteenth-century examples have survived. The most popular form of chair in the fifteenth century seems to have been the so called "Dantesque" or X-chair which might also, if necessary, be folded for travelling. Two thirteenth-century wooden X-chairs are known, but most chairs of this type seem to have been made of metal rods. At first the X-chair was without any form of back but this was added in the sixteenth century, and many examples survive from this period. The so-called Savonarola chair was a development of the simple X-chair with a number of struts following the curve of the design. Chairs of both these types were made throughout Italy in both the fifteenth and sixteenth centuries. Wooden tub chairs seem to have enjoyed a limited popularity in the fourteenth and fifteenth centuries (a good example is in the Horne Museum at Florence). The "Andrea

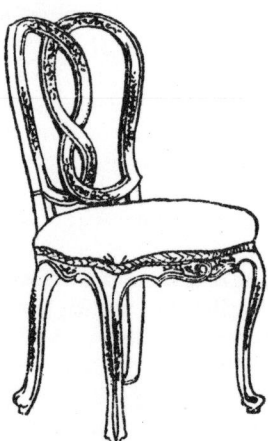

Fig. 13. Chair with figure of eight back; Venetian; mid-eighteenth-century

del Sarto" chair, which has a semicircular seat above which a thin strip of wood supported on balusters serves as both back and arms, was introduced into Tuscany in the early sixteenth century.

In the course of the sixteenth century the upright chair with straight back and arms was developed and ornamented, eventually becoming the standard pattern. Seventeenth-century craftsmen used it as the basis for their richly carved and gilded thrones, such as the one in the Palazzo Rezzonico at Venice (Plate 83B). The easy-chair (*poltrona*) does not appear in Italy until the late seventeenth century. During the eighteenth century Italian chairs differed little from those made elsewhere in Europe (Plate 85D). In Venice, however, chairs with backs in the form of a figure of eight (Fig. 13) enjoyed great popularity.

Chamfer. Bevelled edge, as when the sharp edges of a beam are bevelled off. A dust chamfer (i.e. to throw off dust) is a smooth bevel at the lower edge of framework of a panel, the other edges being moulded, or part moulded and part of rectangular cut. Of stop chamfer there is no better simple definition than Walter Rose's in *The Village Carpenter*: "where slope finishes and square begins" [to arise].

Chandeliers. A branched lighting appliance consisting usually of several lights which can be suspended from a ceiling. Large quantities were made in France in the seventeenth and eighteenth centuries, but not many have survived. They were made of various materials: ormolu, wood, crystal, glass, and occasionally porcelain.

Cherry. A hard, close-grained, reddish or pinkish brown wood, it was used in England for chairs and panels in the seventeenth and eighteenth centuries, though few examples remain. It was often used in America for furniture of the finest design and workmanship. In use as early as 1680. Joseph Downs says cherry was a favourite wood among New York cabinet-makers; was more often used than mahogany in Connecticut, and quite often used in Pennsylvania, Virginia, and Kentucky furniture.

Chest (*see also* Coffer). One primitive form of chest is the dug-out or trunk, its interior gouged in the solid. Some dug-outs are of considerable antiquity; others may be of more recent date than their appearance suggests. In name and rounded lid the travelling trunk, as it is still known, recalls the ancient use of a tree-trunk. Framed chests are also ancient, the earliest surviving medieval examples being formed of great planks so disposed as to present an almost or wholly flush surface at front and back (Fig. 14A). Panelled chests were being made in the fifteenth century, later becoming very popular. The earlier "flush" con-

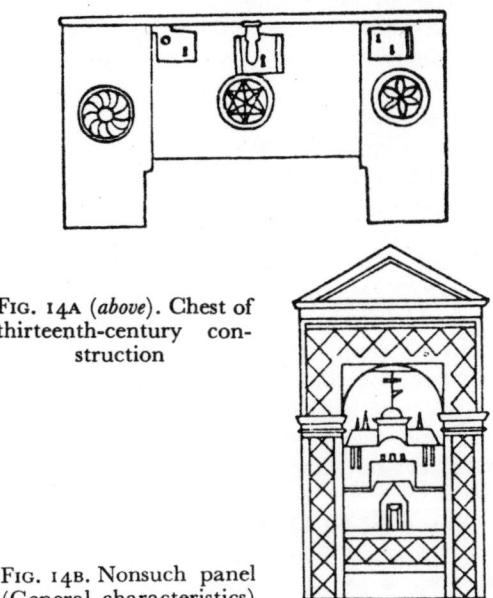

Fig. 14A (*above*). Chest of thirteenth-century construction

Fig. 14B. Nonsuch panel (General characteristics)

struction was, however, to some extent perpetuated until a very late period in the boarded chest, made entirely of boards, including the ends, which also form the uprights (*cf.* Wainscot). Unusually long examples are sometimes, but not necessarily correctly, called rapier chests. The validity of the term is uncertain. Popularly called "non(e)such" chests (Fig. 14B), mainly of the latter part of the sixteenth century, are inlaid with formalized architectural designs, thought possibly to represent the Palace of Nonsuch, or Nonesuch, at Ewell, Surrey. Such architectural motifs are, however, exploitations of a Renaissance design favoured on the Continent, though a possible affinity exists between them and the crowded towns in Gothic art. Mule-chest (implying a hybrid) is collectors' jargon of no validity for a chest-*with*-drawers.

Chest of drawers. This derives in name, and to a considerable extent in principle, from the chest, a link being the chest-with-drawers, with a single range of drawers beneath the box. Such pieces were in being by the latter part of the sixteenth century, a gradual tendency to increase the drawer-space at the expense of the box resulting in the chest-of-drawers. At the same time various structures enclosing a quantity of drawers were also in being, on the Continent and in England, as with the "new cubborde of boxes" made by Lawrence Abelle in 1595 for Stratford-upon-Avon or the "cubborde with drawing boxes" of the Unton Inventory, 1596. "Nests of boxes" is another old term (*see also* Bargueño, Writing-cabinet). The chest of drawers was introduced into Italy, probably from France, in the late seventeenth century. An early example in the Palazzo dei Conservatori at Rome is of a square pattern adorned with pilasters at the corners, but the French *bombé* shape was generally preferred (Plate 85c). In some mid-eighteenth-century Venetian examples the curve of the belly has been ridiculously exaggerated and the top made considerably larger than the base (Fig. 15). In

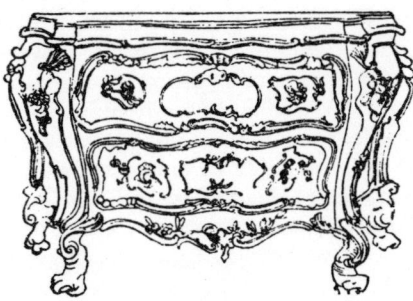

Fig. 15. Chest of drawers; Venetian; eighteenth century

Rome and Naples rather more reticent designs were adopted. In Venice and Genoa chests of drawers were frequently lacquered or painted, while Lombard examples were often decorated with *intarsia*. Elaborate bronze mounts in the French style are rare on *cassettoni* made outside Piedmont. In the United States it was not common in the Queen Anne period, but was revived, especially in New England, during the Chippendale period. Serpentine, oxbow, and block-front shapes are found on New England Chippendale chests.

Cheval-glass. A larger type of toilet mirror in a frame with four legs; also known as a horse dressing-glass; dating from the end of the eighteenth century. The rectangular mirror either pivoted on screws set in the uprights or moved up and down by means of a weight within the frame ("the same as a sash-window" – Sheraton). Turned uprights and stretchers were often found on these pieces about 1800.

Cheveret. *See* Secretaire.

Chiffonier. A piece of furniture which has given rise to a certain amount of confusion. The French chiffonier was a tall chest of drawers, but the *chiffonière*, a quite different piece, was a small set of drawers on legs. It was the latter which seems to have been copied in England in the later eighteenth century. Another form of chiffonier was popular in the Regency period – a low cupboard with shelves for books. As this was similar to contemporary commodes, it can be taken that the English version of the *chiffonière* was the only true small piece of furniture.

Child's furniture. Mostly small-scale furniture for children's usage, distinct from toy furniture. Some confusion exists between tables and the square joined stool (with unsplayed legs) which certainly existed as such. Chairs follow full-scale design, or are high-chair pattern, some of enclosed or wainscot fashion, others elevated on tall legs. A framework on wheels to support a toddler has been given various names, e.g. baby-cage or go-cart.

China cabinet. Seldom, if ever, found in America as a separate piece of furniture before 1790–1800. Even then it is perhaps a "bookcase" (*q.v.*) used for displaying china. In early examples the lower portion is often a shallow cupboard on legs. Most American china cabinets date after 1800 and are in the Sheraton or a later style.

China-stand. An ornamental stand for displaying china or flowers, introduced at the end of the seventeenth century and at first taking the form of a low pedestal on carved and scrolled feet, or of a vase on a plinth. In the early eighteenth century the form was sometimes that of a stool with cabriole legs, in mahogany. More fanciful designs, in the rococo taste, were evident after 1750, as in the "Stands for China Jarrs" presented in Chippendale's *Director*. In the Adam period some attractive stands for flower-bowls resembled the contemporary candle-stands with three uprights. Little four-legged stands with shelves were also made at this time for flower-pots.

Chip-carving. Lightly cut ("chipped") surface ornament, mostly of formal character and including whorls, roundels (*qq.v.*), etc. Such work, known medievally, persisted on items of much later date.

Classical style. Basically any humanistic style emphasizing ancient Greek ideals, and in the arts a style inspired by Greek and Roman art and architecture. In American furniture the style reflected the innovations of Robert Adam, the British architect who was inspired by ancient Roman design. The design books of Hepplewhite and Sheraton helped communicate the style to America, where it has been called after them by dividing the style into two tendencies, the Hepplewhite and Sheraton. This is a difficult distinction to make.

Claw-and-ball foot. An adaptation, probably from the Chinese, of a dragon's claw grasping a pearl. Perhaps first adapted in Europe by the Dutch, it spread to England, from whence it was introduced into America about 1735. Enormously popular as the foot of American cabriole leg furniture in the Queen Anne and Chippendale styles. It remained much in fashion as late as the 1790s. In America a bird's claw was generally used, mostly the eagle's.

Clock-cases. Elaborate clock-cases made their appearance in France in the Louis XIV period and were often treated in the most monumental manner. They became a special product of the Boulle *atelier*, as they did of the workshop of Cressent later. In the Louis XV and Louis XVI periods they took almost any form which appealed to their creators, and a great deal of ingenuity, both of design and craftsmanship, went into their production. Roughly, they divided themselves into five main types: wall or cartel clocks, mantel clocks, pedestal clocks, *régulateurs*, and bracket clocks, the names of which are self-explanatory.

GLOSSARY

If the movement or make of a clock is known and the date is established the collector should remember that it may have originally been placed in another case. This is not uncommon.

Close-chairs and **close-** or **night-stools.** Were sometimes chair-shaped, sometimes rectangular or drum-shaped boxes (possibly covered and padded), and sometimes rectangular boxes on legs. A type of joined stool with a box-top was so usable, though it does not follow that all stools with this feature were for sanitary usage.

Coaster. A receptacle which came into use before 1750 for moving wine, beer, and food on the dining-table; also variously known as a slider, decanter stand, and beer-wagon. For ease of movement, the coaster was normally fitted either with small wheels or with a baize-covered base, and the materials used in good examples included mahogany, papier mâché, and silver. Beer-wagons were sometimes made with special places for the jug and drinking vessels.

Cock's head. Twin-plate hinge of curvilinear shape, the finials formed (more or less) as a cock's head. Frequently found on woodwork of the late sixteenth and first half of the seventeenth centuries.

Coffer. Term freely confused with chest. In strict definition a coffer was a chest or box covered in leather or some other material and banded with metalwork, but it seems likely that the term was not always precisely used. It may not be wrong to class as coffers various stoutly built and/or heavily ironed strong-chests and -boxes, even though they do not fulfil all the above requirements. Trussing coffers were furnished with lifting rings and shackles or other devices for transportation; but chests and coffers not intended for transport might be chained to the wall for security.

Comb-back. *See* Windsor.

Commode. The normal French word for a chest of drawers, which seems to date from the early eighteenth century.

Concertina action. A device on card and gaming tables for extending the frame to support the table top when it is opened. The back half of the frame is made up of two hinged sections that fold in to reduce the frame size when the top is closed.

Connecticut chest. So named because chiefly made in seventeenth- and eighteenth-century Connecticut. Decorative chest with or without a bottom drawer or two. Ornamented with applied bosses and split spindles

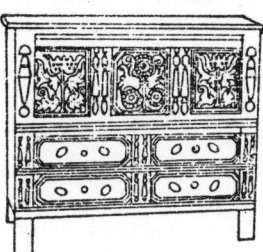

Fig. 16

which set off three front panels carved, low relief, in conventionalized flowers—centre panel, sunflowers; other panels, tulips (Fig. 16).

Constitution mirror. A term of obscure origin, perhaps a misnomer, widely used in America when referring to a Chippendale-style wall mirror with strings of leaves or flow-

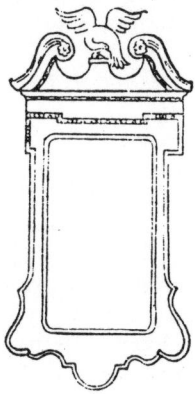

Fig. 17

ers at the sides, a scrolled-arch top, and a fanciful finial, generally a bird. The frame is usually in walnut or mahogany and partly gilded (Fig. 17).

Corner chair. A square or squarish seat supported by two side posts and a back post, the three extending above the seat to a low, strong, semicircular top rail. The fourth support, a leg, is added centre front. Made in America from about 1700 to 1775, it is found

GLOSSARY

in three styles – Dutch–Queen Anne transitional, Queen Anne, and Chippendale. Also called roundabout and writing chair. Some authorities say the American Windsor chair (*q.v.*) may have been evolved from it.

Corner-cupboard. This type of furniture consists of a triangular cupboard containing shelves and closed by a door, which is sometimes curved. It is made to fit into the right-angled corner of a room. *Encoignures* begin to appear in France during the Louis XV period, and are usually made in pairs, often *en suite* with a secretaire or chest of drawers. They continued to be made right up to the Revolution.

Coromandel or **zebra-wood.** A form of ebony with light-coloured striped markings found on the Coromandel coast (*see also under* Ebony).

Couch. A seventeenth- and eighteenth-century term for day-bed; not used as synonym for sofa or settee until recent times.

Counter. Hutch-like structure, sometimes approximating to a table with an under-compartment. The name (surviving in shop-counter, etc.) derives from the top being employed for reckoning accounts with counters or jettons disposed on a marked scale. When not so used the counter was available for a variety of other purposes.

Court cupboard. The earliest fine cupboard in America. A kind of Jacobean buffet (and called a buffet in England), with the upper portion enclosed, the lower open. Sometimes, however, the upper portion is partly open – that is, contains a closed central cupboard with splayed sides. When the bottom portion is also closed, whether with doors or as a chest of drawers, it is in America called a press cupboard (*q.v.*). Early ones are generally of oak, with much sturdy Jacobean ornament, and seldom, if ever, ornamented alike (*c.* 1650–70).

Courting mirror. Small mirror framed with mouldings and a cresting, the crested area often containing a painted picture or design. They were traditionally a courting gift in eighteenth-century New England. Lockwood says their source was a similar mirror made in China for the export trade.

Cradle. The cradle, which had hitherto been a fairly simple piece of furniture occasionally carved but otherwise of a type that might be found in any other European country, was developed into an object of extravagant fantasy in mid-eighteenth-century Venice. Here cradles were made with rippling rococo rims and lacquered with floral motifs or heavily carved with *putti* and gilded. The most fantastic of all is that formerly in the *Donà dalle Rose* Collection at Venice, in which the cradle itself is swung between two branches of a naturalistically carved tree, with a stork gazing at the occupant from the foot and a chinoiserie parasol suspended over its head.

Credence. Side-table as used ecclesiastically for the Elements prior to Consecration, and for the Cruets, etc., therewith associated. Such tables were sometimes of hutch-like formation, and the term credence has been loosely extended to cover other furniture of more or less similar construction.

Credenza. An Italian sideboard of buffet used as a serving-table on which silver might also be displayed. Fifteenth- and sixteenth-century *credenze* were either simple tables designed to stand by a wall or else long cupboards, sometimes with canted corners, the height of an ordinary dining-table (Fig. 18).

Fig. 18. *Credenza*; Tuscan; sixteenth century

As they were normally covered with linen, they were very simple in design and decoration. A recessed top story containing a cupboard was added to many *credenze* in the sixteenth century, and this was usual in subsequent periods.

Cresting. Shaped and sometimes perforated ornament on the top of a structure, as in the cresting of a chair.

Croft. A small filing cabinet of the late

GLOSSARY

eighteenth century (named after its inventor), specially designed to be moved about easily in the library; it had many small drawers and a writing-top.

Cromwellian. Term of convenience applied to English furniture of austere character, actually or supposedly made about the time of the Commonwealth or Interregnum (1649-60), but also used loosely of related types.

Cromwellian chair. Spanish-type chair with strips of leather for the seat and back; turned legs and stretchers, occasionally spiral turned. Generally ornamented with brass-headed tacks. A mid-seventeenth-century "Puritan" chair. Very few have been found.

Cross stretcher. X-shaped stretcher in straight or curved lines. Sometimes found on occasional tables, a few chairs, and in America as highboys and lowboys.

Cupboard. Originally cup-board, a species of sideboard for the display and service of plate, etc., and having no essential connection with enclosed and doored structures. When equipped with such features, these might be noted (*see* Ambry). The modern sense of cupboard, as an enclosed structure, is a long-standing usurpation, such items being mostly descended from the press, press-cupboard, etc. Livery cupboard (a much-abused term from Fr. *livrer*, to deliver) was a *doorless* structure, as is clearly stated in the Hengrave Hall contracts, 1537-8. That it was distinguished from the court cupboard is shown by such an entry as "ij court cubbordes, and one liverye cubborde", in Unton Inventory, 1596 ("Liverie table" is also listed). Court cupboard was likewise an open structure, or with a small enclosed compartment in the upper part (*see* R. W. Symonds, "The Evolution of the Cupboard", in *The Connoisseur*, December 1943, and "The Dynyng Parlor and its Furniture", op. cit., January 1944). The tendency to compartment such furniture eventually resulted in enclosed pieces of similar outline being called court cupboard, though press cupboard is preferable. Welsh varieties of the press cupboard are the cwpwrdd deuddarn (two-tiered) and the cwpwrdd tridarn (three-tiered, the top stage often more or less open) (Plate 6B). Dole-cupboard strictly applies to hanging or other structures open-shelved, or doored and railed, used in the charitable dispensation of bread, etc., in churches and other institutions. The term is often wrongly applied to food-cupboard, or, better, food-hutch. Spice-cupboard is a hanging "cupboard", usually of small dimensions, internally fitted with shelves or compartments and drawers, and fronted with a door. Doubtless many were used to hold spices, herbs, and medicaments, though they could have served various purposes. Corner cupboard is a triangular structure, doored or open, independent or fitted, and normally furnished with shelving.

Cupid's bow. A term used to describe the typical top rail of a Chippendale chair back which curves up at the ends and dips slightly in the centre.

Curly. The grainings of some woods – maple, walnut, birch, etc. – sometimes show feather-like, curly or tiger-stripe markings, which are much prized. Not to be confused with other markings, such as bird's-eye, wavy, blister, and quilted.

Cutlery Stand. *See* Canterbury (2).

Cylinder-top desk. A writing-table, incorporating drawers and writing accessories, the functional part of which is closed by means of a curved panel fastened with a lock. It is usually supported on tall legs and differs from a roll-top desk (*q.v.*) in that the curved panel is in one piece and not slatted.

Cypress. Fine furniture was sometimes made of the pale to dark brown (swamp) cypress, especially in South Carolina, Georgia, and other southern American states. More often used for drawers and linings, and for utility-type furniture. It is noted for its resistance to decay.

Daventry. A small chest of drawers with a sloping top for writing; said to be named after a client of the firm of Gillow who claimed to have invented it.

Day-bed. Known in England from the sixteenth century, though authentic examples are mostly of much later date. The original form approximated to a stump-bed with a sloped back at one end. In the period of Charles II, and later, day-beds were caned, their frames often being elaborately carved, quite likely *en suite* with cane chairs.

329

GLOSSARY

Decanter stand. *See* Coaster.

Desk. A term of varied meaning, but taken here to refer to two portable pieces. (1) The commonest meaning was that of a box (originating in medieval times) with a sloping top for reading and writing. Early examples in oak in the Tudor and Stuart periods had carving and inlay, and sometimes the owner's initials and date. When bureaux came into use at the end of the seventeenth century these small desks were too useful to discard, and were fitted with drawers and pigeon-holes; many were veneered with walnut, or japanned, and some were mounted on stands. In the Georgian period they became less decorative, and were usually of plain mahogany; few were made after 1800. (2) In the later eighteenth century "desk" was the current term for what would now be called a music-stand (which was also used for reading); it generally took the form of a tripod base supporting a shaft and a sloping, adjustable top.

Desk box. A rectangular box with sloping lid for the storage of books and writing materials; more popularly known in America as a Bible box.

Deuddarn. *See* Cupboard.

Document drawer. A thin narrow drawer in a desk for important papers.

Doreurs, Corporation des. The craft guild responsible for gilding in all its forms in France. The organization was similar to that of the *menuisiers-ébénistes*, except that the apprenticeship lasted five instead of six years. There were three hundred and seventy *maîtres-doreurs* at the end of the eighteenth century (*see also* Ormolu).

Dowel. Headless pin used in construction. Though, architecturally, dowels may be of other materials, wood is understood when speaking of furniture. Trenail (i.e. tree-nail) is another term for a wooden dowel (*see* Nails).

Dowry chest or **dower chest.** Is one made to store the trousseau of a prospective bride. Outstanding among American examples are the Hadley chest (Fig. 61), the Connecticut chest (Plate 46c), and the painted Pennsylvania-German chest.

Drake foot. *See* Duck foot.

Drawer. Box in a framework from which it can be drawn. In some simple or traditional constructions drawers merely rest on the framework, but a typical feature of the late sixteenth to seventeenth century was a groove on each side of a drawer, accommodating projecting runners on the framework. This gave way, in later furniture, to runner-strips at the base of the drawer itself, and the encasing of the interior framing with dustboards.

Dresser. On which food was dressed; a species of sideboard with or without a superimposed "back"; also for service of food, and/or storage of plates, dishes, etc. Some backless dressers are closely allied to the side-table. Dressers are wontedly furnished with storage accommodation (such as ambries, shelving, drawers, etc., or combinations of such). Welsh-dresser is used of local varieties of the tall-back dresser found virtually everywhere (Plate 6A). North Wales and South Wales types are differentiated.

Drop or **tear-drop handle.** The characteristic pull used on furniture with drawers, 1690–1720. Of brass, solid or hollow, this pendant hangs from a brass plate and is attached to the drawer by wire pins. Also called tear drop and pear drop, which picturesquely suggest its shape.

Drop leaf. A table with one or two hinged leaves which can be raised or dropped by bringing swinging legs or supports into use. Many kinds of drop-leaf tables have special names – butterfly, corner, gate-leg, library, Pembroke, sofa, etc.

Drum table. A circular top table on a tripod base with a deep skirt that may contain drawers. The type exists only in the classical style, and American examples appear late.

Duck foot. Colloquial American term for the three-toed club or Dutch foot, mostly found in Delaware River Valley furniture. Also called drake foot and web foot. For some reason the pad foot is often mistakenly called a duck foot.

Dumb-waiter. A dining-room stand, an English invention of the early eighteenth century, with normally three circular trays, increasing in size towards the bottom, on a

GLOSSARY

shaft with tripod base. This established design gave way to more elaborate versions at the end of the century; four-legged supports and rectangular trays were found; and quite different kinds were square or circular tables with special compartments for bottles, plates, etc.

Eagle, American. The Seal of the United States, adopted 1786, emblematizes the American bald eagle with wings outspread (Fig. 19). This emblem promptly became popular as furniture ornament in America – carved (free or engaged), inlaid or painted – replacing the fanciful phoenix which had been used since the mid-eighteenth century.

FIG. 19

Ébéniste. The ordinary French term for a cabinet-maker concerned in making veneered furniture as distinct from a *menuisier* (*q.v.*). The word derived from the ebony (*ébène*) to be found on the earliest veneered furniture in France. It is not found, nor are *ébénistes* associated by name with the *menuisiers*' guild, until 1743, by which time the use of ebony was more or less confined to pieces in the Boulle technique. Although permitted by guild regulations to work in plain wood like the *menuisiers*, an *ébéniste* usually confined his activities to techniques requiring veneer or inlay (*see also under* Menuisiers-Ébénistes).

Ebonize. To stain wood to look like ebony. This was often done in the seventeenth century for the applied ornaments on oak furniture. Also used in William and Mary period when contrasting colours in wood were sought.

Ebony. A hard wood, black and finely grained, sometimes found with brown or purple streaks. Found commonly in tropical climates in Asia, Africa, and America. Extensively used in France for veneering furniture, particularly in combination with Boulle marquetry (*see also under* Coromandel or Zebra-wood and Boulle marquetry). Grandfather and other clock cases were veneered with ebony in England in the seventeenth century.

Egg-and-tongue (egg-and-dart). Repeat ornament of alternated ovolo and dart-like motifs (Fig. 20); as much other ornament of

FIG. 20

classical origin, transmitted through Renaissance channels.

Elizabethan. Term of convenience, strictly applicable to furniture, etc., made in the reign of Elizabeth I (1558–1603), though loosely used of pieces of later date displaying Elizabethan characteristics. The reign was long; just as early Elizabethan furniture shows influences from previous reigns, so late Elizabethan merges easily into Jacobean.

En arbelette. An expression used for shapes and forms which have a double curve similar to that of a cross-bow.

Encoignures. *See under* Corner-cupboards.

Espagnolette. A decorative motif popularized by the engravings of Gillot and Watteau and consisting of a female head surrounded by a large stiff collar of a type worn in Spain in the seventeenth century. It was used frequently in the early eighteenth century as a mounted decoration for furniture.

Etagère. A small work-table consisting usually of shelves or trays sets one above the other. The word is of nineteenth-century origin, the ordinary term used earlier being *table à ouvrage*.

Fake or forgery. Furniture (or other objects) made or assembled in simulation of authentic antiquities, with deceptive intent. Fakes are of several kinds, of which a few may be listed: (*a*) the wholly modern fake, though quite possibly made of old wood; (*b*) the fake incorporating old and in themselves authentic parts; (*c*) the "carved-up" fake, as, for instance, a plain chest (itself antique) with modern carving added; (*d*) the "married" piece, of which all, or considerable portions, may be authentic, but which has been "made-up" from more than one source. Difficult of classification are certain items which have been liberally restored (*see* Restoration), each case demanding judgement on its own merits. Though over-restoration is reprehensible, cases occur of pieces reconditioned with innocent intent. An ordinary repair to a genuine antique need not disqualify it. At the same time a watchful eye should be kept for

GLOSSARY

an old faking trick of inserting an obvious "repair" for the sole purpose of making the rest of a spurious piece look older by contrast.

Fan-back. *See* Windsor chair.

Fan pattern. Description of the back of a chair when filled with ribs somewhat resembling the stalks of a half-open fan. Also said of any fan-shaped carving, inlay, or painted decoration. (*See* Rising sun.)

Fancy chair. Almost any variety of decorative occasional chair, generally light in weight, painted, and with a cane seat. The source was probably the late Sheraton occasional chair. Popular in all styles from 1800 to 1850.

Federal style. A term often used in America to describe furniture made in the United States between 1785 and 1830, the early days of the Republic. It includes works showing Hepplewhite, Sheraton, Directoire, and early Empire influence. An inexact, therefore unsatisfactory, term – though at times highly convenient.

Fire-dogs. An appliance, popular in France for use in a fireplace to support the logs of a fire. These were usually made in pairs of iron with bronze ends or finals, sometimes patinated and sometimes gilt. They took various forms during the Louis XV and XVI periods, when the ornamental parts are usually made of ormolu and are often of the finest quality.

Fire-screen. An adjustable screen made from the end of the seventeenth century to give protection from the intense heat of large open fires. Two main kinds were used. (1) Pole screen: with the screen on an upright supported on a tripod base; known as a "screen-stick" in the late seventeenth century; and in very general use in the eighteenth. The screen, often of needlework, was at first rectangular (Plate 118c), but oval and shield shapes were fashionable in the late eighteenth century. In the Regency period the tripod was replaced by a solid base, and the screen was a banner hung from a bar on the upright. (2) Horse or cheval screen – two uprights, each on two legs, enclosing a panel (Plate 117). Elaborate carving and gilding of the crests was often found until the end of the eighteenth century, when lighter and simpler screens were in vogue. Needlework was the popular material for the panel.

Fish-tail. The carving, somewhat resembling a fish tail, on the top rail of a banister-back chair.

Flag seat. Colloquial term sometimes used for a seat woven of rush-like material.

Flambeaux. *See under* Candlesticks.

Flame carving. A cone-like finial carved to represent flames, either straight or spiralling. Used on highboys, secretaries, grandfather clocks, etc.

Flemish scroll. A curving double scroll used on William and Mary style legs; also on the wide stretcher connecting the front legs.

Flower-stand. *See* China-stand.

Fluting. Narrow vertical groovings used in classical architecture on columns and pilasters. In furniture fluting is employed where pilasters or columns are suggested and on straight legs. It is of particular importance in the classical style, but is encountered in earlier work as well.

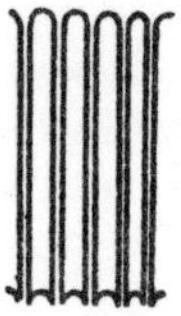

Fig. 21

Folding table. *See* Gate-leg table.

Fondeurs, Corporation des. The craft guild responsible for casting and chasing metal, either for sculpture, furniture, or *bronzes d'ameublement* in France. It was organized similarly to those of the *menuisiers-ébénistes* and *doreurs*.

Form. Long, backless seat, with any number of supports from two upwards. Of ancient lineage, the form is simply a long stool. "Longe stoole" occurs in old inventories.

Four-poster. Colloquial term widely used for a bedstead with four posts.

Frame. The style of picture frames altered with the style of painting. The earliest to be found in private houses were very simple, of painted or gilt wood. Late sixteenth-century artists seem sometimes to have designed and painted allegorical frames for their own works. Not until the seventeenth century did the richly carved and gilded frame come into its own. Some late seventeenth- and early eighteenth-century frames are, indeed, better and more elaborate works of art than the pictures they enshrine. Later, eighteenth-century frames are usually more discreet and simple.

332

GLOSSARY

Gadrooning. A carved ornamental edging of a repeated pattern which, on Chippendale furniture, is often no more than curving, alternating convex and concave sections. Particularly popular in New York and Philadelphia in the Chippendale period.

Garde Meuble de la Couronne. The department which dealt with all matters connected with the furnishing of the royal palaces in France. It was established by Louis XIV in 1663, and survived until the end of the monarchy. Very fortunately, its records survive more or less intact.

The first inventory of furniture belonging to the Crown was completed in 1673 and has been published in full by M. Emile Molinier in 1902 (*see* p. 117), but the most important item among the records is the *Journal*, instituted in 1685 and continuing until 1784. In it every piece acquired for the Crown was scrupulously entered and given a number, with dates of delivery, the name of the maker, costs and measurements, its eventual destination in the Royal palaces, and a full description. The numbers often correspond with those painted in the backs of existing pieces (*see* Inventory numbers), and these can be thus identified fairly closely from the descriptions and measurements.

The *Journal* consists in all of eighteen volumes and 3,600 pages, of which only a small proportion are missing, and is preserved in the *Archives Nationales* in Paris. After 1784 a new system of recording was introduced, but the same numbers were preserved, and these, in fact, continued to be used until well into the nineteenth century.

Gate-leg. A form of drop-leaf table with

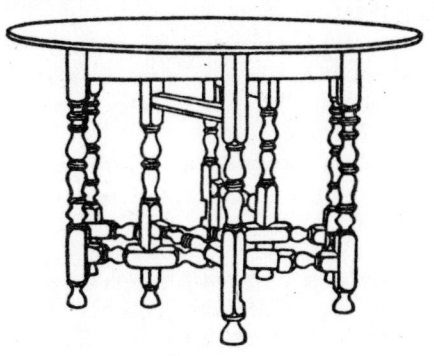

Fig. 22

swinging supports that are legs joined to the main frame of the table by upper and lower stretchers which make a gate. First used in the late seventeenth and early eighteenth centuries.

Gesso. Composition of plaster of Paris or whiting and size for making bas-reliefs and other ornaments. It came into fashion in England just before 1700 and was a popular form of decoration until about 1740.

Giridon. *See* Guéridon.

Glastonbury chair. Is collectors' jargon for a type of chair with X-supports and elbowed arms linking seat and top of back. The name derives from an example at Wells, supposedly associated with the last Abbot of Glastonbury. Examples of like construction have been made or embellished at various, including modern, periods.

Gobelins, Manufacture Royale des. The State-supported organization founded by Letters Patent at Gobelins in 1667 through the inspiration of Colbert, Louis XIV's finance minister. It was designed to provide, apart from tapestry, all products of the luxury arts, including furniture, and its first great task was the equipment of the interior of the Palaces of Versailles. It owed its success and great reputation to the energies of its first director, Charles Le Brun, who made it into the foundation stone of the organized applied arts in France.

Goose neck. *See* Scroll top.

Gothic. A twelfth- to fifteenth-century style revived superficially in the eighteenth century. Chippendale offered designs in the "Gothick Taste", occasionally followed by American craftsmen. These consisted of arcades of pointed arches and quatrefoils on chair backs. In the classical period there are also occasional designs employing Gothic motifs.

Grandfather clock. Long-case floor clock which appeared in England at the time of the Restoration. In America it was in standard use by 1750, though many earlier examples exist. Lockwood mentions one in a Boston inventory of 1652. American grandfather clocks generally follow English models, except when the decorative motives are American – e.g. block-front-and-shell.

Grandmother clock. Modern name for a

GLOSSARY

smaller floor clock, about half to two-thirds as tall as a grandfather clock.

Guéridon or **guéridon table.** A small piece of furniture, usually circular, intended to support some form of light. In the seventeenth century it sometimes took the form of a Negro figure holding a tray, and the name derives from that of a well-known Moorish galley-slave called Guéridon. Subsequently the term was extended to cover almost any form of small table on which candelabra, etc., might be placed.

Guilloche. Band of curvilinear ornament suggesting entwined ribbons (Fig. 24).

Hadley chest. So called because mostly found in and around Hadley, Massachusetts. A characteristic New England dower chest of 1690–1710. Its distinctive feature is the incised carving of tulips, vines, and leaves which cover the entire front (Fig. 23).

FIG. 23

Handkerchief table. A single-leaf table with leaf and top triangular in shape. Closed, the table fits in a corner, opened, it is a small square.

Hickory. Oak-like American wood often used for furniture parts needing strength without heaviness; also for bent parts; and almost always for spindles of Windsor chairs.

Highboy. Uniquely American tall chest of drawers mounted on a commode or lowboy (*q.v.*) and topped with a broken-arch pediment usually heightened with finials. Characteristically plain in New England; richly carved and ornamented in Philadelphia. It was made in three styles – William and Mary, Queen Anne, and Chippendale. The Philadelphia Chippendale highboy is sometimes thought to be the most remarkable creative achievement in American antique furniture design. The late authority on English antique furniture, Herbert Cescincky, wrote: "... there is little or no kinship between a Philadelphia highboy and anything ever made in England". Much sought today, they bring high prices – up to $43,000 for one; $44,000 for another.

Hitchcock chair. American adaptation of the late Sheraton-style painted and stencilled chair. It has round-turned legs, raked, and an oval-turned "pillow-back" top rail. Almost always painted black with stencillings of fruits and flowers in gold or colours. Named for Lambert Hitchcock, of Hitchcockville, Connecticut, who made them in quantity from 1820 to 1850.

Holly. A hard wood with a fine close grain. White or greenish white in colour. Found commonly in Europe and western Asia. Used extensively for fillets to frame marquetry (*see also* Boxwood).

Hoop-back. *See* Windsor chair.

Hope chest. Colloquial American term, widely used for dowry chest, which itself is a misnomer, since a chest normally serves more purposes across the years than holding a trousseau (*see* Dowry chest).

Horse-glass and horse-screen. *See* Cheval-glass and Fire-screen.

Horseshoe back. *See* Windsor chair.

Hutch. Enclosed structure, often raised on uprights, or an enclosed structure of more than one tier. The name derives from Fr. *huche*, a kneading-trough or meal-tub, but the significance of hutch was much wider. Food-hutch, often confused with dole-cupboard, is a name given to a hutch with perforated panels (Plate 1).

Inlay. Surface ornament formed by in-setting separate pieces of differently coloured woods, or bone, ivory, shell, etc., in a recessed ground (Fig. 25).

Inventory numbers. These are often found usually painted or branded on furniture made for the Crown or Royal Family of France. They often refer to the *Journal du Garde Meuble de la Couronne*, which has survived intact for some periods between the late seventeenth century and the Revolution. When accompanied by a palace letter (*q.v.*),

GLOSSARY

the numbers may refer to the inventories made of that particular royal residence which may or may not be still extant. Considering everything, the documents of furniture made for the French Crown have survived in an extraordinary number of cases.

The discovery of an inventory number of any kind on a piece of French furniture of whatever date is always worth the closest investigation, as it may be possible to identify it.

Jacobean. Term of convenience usually applicable to furniture made in the reign of James I (1603–25), and perhaps, though unusually, to that of James II (1685–8). In general, loosely applied to furniture styles in direct descent from the Elizabethan tradition. It is thus employed of certain types of furniture covering virtually the whole of the seventeenth century and even later, though from the time of Charles II it is generally restricted to pieces of unmodish or traditional character. Jacobean is not now favoured as a descriptive label by scholarly writers, except in cases of uncertain dating, preference being given to a more precise system involving such approximations as "c. 1620" or "first quarter of the seventeenth century", etc.

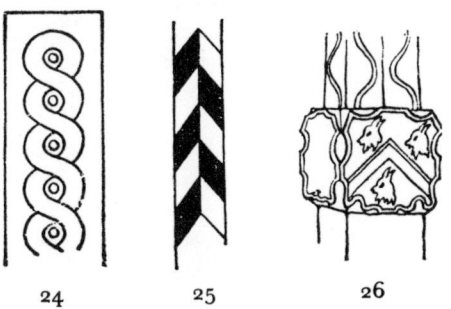

FIG. 24. Guilloche (seventeenth century)
FIG. 25. Herring-bone Inlay
FIG. 26. Knop on bedpost (sixteenth century)

Japanning. European and American version of Oriental lacquering often substituting paint for the layers of varnish on lacquered wares. Raised chinoiserie in plaster is generally the added decoration. The technique became popular in England late in the seventeenth century; a book of instructions, *Treatise of Japaning and Varnishing*, by Stalker and Parker, was published in 1688 in London. In America the technique was practised before 1715 and continued to be used throughout the century.

Jewel. Ornament with raised devices distantly suggestive of gem-stones, often combined with systems of reeding (*q.v.*) (Fig. 45).

Joined. Term used in describing furniture made by a joiner.

Kas. The Dutch word, *kast*, for wardrobe incorrectly spelled. Used to refer to the wardrobes made by Dutch settlers in America. They are generally large, with wide mouldings, heavy cornice, and on ball feet. Their style is of the seventeenth century, but they were made for a great part of the eighteenth.

Kettle-stand (also **urn-** and **teapot-stand**). A special stand which was introduced with tea-drinking in the later seventeenth century, of two main kinds. (1) A small table, tripod or four-legged, with a gallery or raised edge round the top. Slender four-legged tables were common in the later part of the eighteenth century, nearly always with a slide for the teapot. (2) A box-like arrangement set on four legs; the box was usually lined with metal, and had an opening in one side for the kettle spout, as well as a slide for the teapot. Another version of the box type had a three-sided enclosure with a metal-lined drawer. The two main types of kettle-stand persisted until the end of the eighteenth century, when they were superseded by occasional tables.

Kingwood. *See under* Rosewood.

Knife-case. A container for knives (and other cutlery) introduced in the seventeenth century for use in dining-rooms. Two distinct varieties appeared. (1) Until the later eighteenth century the usual shape was a box with a sloping top and convex front (Plate 117); the interior had divisions for the cutlery. Walnut, shagreen (untanned leather with a roughened surface), also made from shark skin, and later mahogany, sometimes inlaid, were the main materials. (2) This was succeeded by the graceful vase-shaped case, the top of which was raised and lowered on a central stem, around which the knife partitions were arranged; this type was designed to stand on a pedestal or at each end of the sideboard. Straight-sided cases were favoured in the early nineteenth century.

GLOSSARY

Knop. Swelling member on an upright, etc., a knob. Thus a knopped post (Fig. 64).

Knotted pine. Originally a second-best plank of pine with the rough knot showing in the wood and therefore used only when covered with paint. Today the paint is removed, the knot design being liked by enough collectors to make old knotty pine sought after.

Labelled furniture. Mid-eighteenth-century American and British chair- and cabinet-makers often pasted small paper labels, advertising their wares, on furniture leaving their shops. A number of these labels remain to this day on the furniture and, when genuine, help establish characteristics of a particular shop.

Lacche. The word *lacche* is used in Italian to cover all painted decoration applied to furniture, whether or not it has the hard gloss of Oriental lacquer (*see* p. 302). Painted furniture (*mobilia laccata*) was produced in most districts of Italy in the eighteenth century, but the most celebrated centre for it was Venice. Earlier examples were normally decorated with chinoiseries, but in the middle of the eighteenth century floral motifs were more popular and some *armadi* were painted with landscapes in their panels. Desks were occasionally painted with *trompe l'œil* prints and papers which appear to be pinned to them.

Lacquer. A form of resinous varnish capable of taking a high polish. Its chief application to furniture in France dates from the early eighteenth century, when it was imported for this purpose from China and Japan. The Oriental lacquer was also often imitated in France and then applied to furniture locally (*see also under* Vernis Martin).

Ladder back. A chair back with the vertical centre splat replaced by a series of horizontal bars cut in curving lines. Usually this type of chair has straight legs. It originated in the Chippendale period, but persisted until the end of the eighteenth century.

Lambrequin. A short piece of hanging drapery, often imitated in metal or wood for decorative purposes.

Lantern. A container for a candle or candles; portable, fixed to the wall or hung from the ceiling; especially useful for lighting the draughty parts of the house. Early lanterns (*c.* 1500–1700) were made of wood, iron, latten (a yellow alloy of copper and zinc), and brass, the most common filling being horn (whence the Shakespearean "lanthorn"). After 1700, when glass become more plentiful, lanterns were increasingly fashionable, particularly as they prevented candle-grease from falling about, and their frames, of metal, walnut, and mahogany, followed the main decorative modes of the times. In addition to these more elaborate kinds, simpler lanterns of glass shades, in a variety of forms, were in wide use in the eighteenth century.

Lazy Susan. *See* Dumb waiter.

Library steps. Found in libraries of large houses after about the middle of the eighteenth century, and of two main kinds: (1) the fixed pair of steps, some with hand-rails, and (2) the folding steps, sometimes ingeniously fitted into other pieces of furniture, such as chairs, stools, and tables.

Lighthouse clock. American shelf or mantel clock designed by Simon Willard about 1800 (Fig. 27). The case is judged to have been modelled after the lighthouse on Eddystone Rock in the English Channel. Miller declares that "because of mechanical difficulties . . . very few were made".

FIG. 27

Linenfold. Carved ornament suggested by folded linen, first found late in the fifteenth century, very popular in the first half of the sixteenth, and continuing in diminishing quantity for many years (Fig. 28).

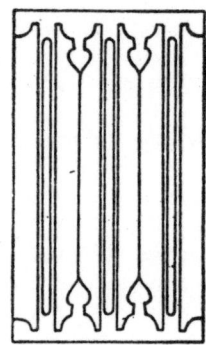

FIG. 28

Attempts to distinguish "true" (realistic) from "mock" (formalized) linenfold need not be taken too seriously. Some of the single-fold types (often cusped and foliated) have been differentiated as parchemin (Fr.), from a supposed resemblance to cut parchment. Apart from its obvious decorativeness, no satisfactory explanation of the origin of linenfold has been adduced. An attractive suggestion is that it was inspired by the Veil of the Chalice, though it could have arisen in other ways.

Linen-press. A frame with a wooden spiral screw for pressing linen between two boards, dating from the seventeenth century.

Lobby chest. Defined by Sheraton as "a kind of half chest of drawers, adapted for the use of a small study, lobby, etc."

Lock-plate (or **scutcheon**). Front-plate of a lock, or the plate protecting a key-hole.

Looking glass. In the sixteenth and seventeenth centuries looking-glass frames were similar to picture frames, though seldom as ornate as the richest examples. During the eighteenth century they were made with delicate mouldings in the wide diversity of shapes which the rococo taste approved and the mirror – unlike the painting – permitted. Large mirrors, or pier glasses, in elaborately carved frames were used in palatial decoration in the early eighteenth century. Small wall mirrors, framed in wood or pottery, and with designs engraved on the glass were popular in the mid-eighteenth century, especially in Venice. They were sometimes designed to serve as *girandoles*. Toilet mirrors with lacquered, gilt, or simple polished wood frames, similar to French and English examples, were made throughout Italy in the eighteenth century.

Loop-back. *See* Windsor chair.

Lowboy. Modern name for an American creation inspired by the English flat-top dressing-table with drawers, yet in its final development closer to the French commode. Attractively plain in New England, much carved and ornamented in Philadelphia. It occurs in three styles – William and Mary, Queen Anne, and Chippendale. Often made as a companion piece to the highboy (*q.v.*). Dressing-table, chamber-table, low chest of drawers were eighteenth-century names for it.

Lunette ornament. Formal carving composed of a horizontal system of semicircles,

FIG. 29

variously filled and embellished, frequently disposed in a repeat-band (Fig. 29).

Lyre. The lyre form as a furniture ornament was introduced to England from France by Adam in the second half of the eighteenth century and reached America after the Revolution and was increasingly used until about 1830 for chair backs and table supports in Hepplewhite, Sheraton, and, notably, Duncan Phyfe furniture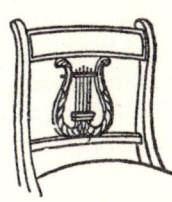

FIG. 30

(Fig. 30). American lyre-form clocks, late Empire style, were popular about 1825–40.

Mahogany. A dense, dark, heavy wood which in the eighteenth century was known in two varieties, the Spanish and the Honduras. The Spanish from Cuba, San Domingo, and Puerto Rico was darker and harder than the variety from Honduras. By 1750 it had supplanted walnut for the highest quality work in England, and at about the same time it became important in America.

Maple. A handsome, pale, satiny hardwood of close grain, plentiful in the northern part of America. Much used for furniture, especially in New England, ever since earliest times. Often it was the inexpensive substitute for walnut or mahogany, also for satinwood inlay, etc. Old maple takes on a rich honey colour. Its regular or plain graining is subject to several very attractive markings – curly (a tiger striping), bird's-eye, blister, and quilted Many pieces of furniture have been established as American because the underframing or secondary wood is maple.

Marlborough leg. Of obscure origin, perhaps originating in England as the trade term for a bed with square or square tapering (pillar) legs and block (plinth) feet. In America, by extension, a whole range of elegant furniture, mostly mid-eighteenth-century Philadelphian, with legs as described, generally with the inside edge chamfered to lighten the appearance. The authority, Horner, says: "A refinement and rival of the cabriole. . . . There were but few pieces of the Chinese-Chippendale ever made in Philadelphia, so that nearly all Pembroke tables and similar articles should be classified as Marlborough. . . ."

Marquetry. The ordinary word for a design formed of substances inlaid on a carcase in the form of a veneer. It can consist of various types of wood, combined with such materials as tortoiseshell, brass, pewter, copper, mother-of-pearl, etc. It first came into prominence in English furniture in about 1675. It is found in Italy, in the sixteenth century and in Flanders in the seventeenth century. It was from these sources that it came to be imported into France mainly by the foreign craftsmen working at the courts of Henri IV and Louis XIII. After the majority of Louis XIV, Boulle marquetry (*q.v.*) came to be used extensively. In the eighteenth century the possibilities of wood marquetry were developed until they reached their ultimate perfection in the works of J. H. Riesener (*q.v.*).

Martha Washington chair. Slender Chippendale – Hepplewhite arm-chair with tapered outlines; a "lady's chair", with upholstered, low, shallow seat and high back, which usually ends in a serpentine curve (Fig. 31). So named because Martha Washington is supposed to have used one at Mount Vernon.

FIG. 31

Martha Washington mirror. Walnut or mahogany wall mirror, Georgian style, with handsome gilded mouldings, strings of leaves, fruits, or flowers down the sides, a scroll top, and a bird finial. The base is cut in a series of bold curves. Made in America from about 1760 to 1800. So named because Martha Washington is supposed to have used one at Mount Vernon. (Same as Constitution mirror.)

Martha Washington sewing-table. Oval box-form sewing-table with rounded ends and hinged top. Fitted with drawers and sewing material compartments. The general style is Sheraton, but the particular type seems to be an American variant. It was so named because Martha Washington is supposed to have used one at Mount Vernon.

Melon-bulb. Jargon and comparatively modern term for the swollen member on legs or posts of furniture (Fig. 32). An exaggeration of the knop, it attained full development in the Elizabethan period, thereafter dwindling away.

FIG. 32

Menuisier. The term corresponds roughly to the English "carpenter" or "joiner". In France, as far as furniture was concerned, the menuisiers were responsible for making chairs, beds, and other furniture made from plain or carved woods, as distinct from veneered pieces, which were the province of the *ébénistes* (*q.v.*). Although permitted by guild regulations to work in both techniques, they seldom did so (*see also* Corporation des Menuisiers-Ébénistes).

Menuisiers-Ébénistes, Corporation des. The craft guild which embraced all craftsmen engaged in making wood furniture in France.

An apprentice began his training with a *maître-ébéniste* or *maître-menuisier* at the age of fourteen, and it lasted for six years, after which he entered on his next stage, known as *compagnonage*. This lasted for three to six years, according to whether the craftsman had served his apprenticeship in Paris or elsewhere. During this time the *compagnon* was paid for the work he did. After his *compagnonage* the craftsman was ready to become a *maître* of the guild, but often the period was extended because of lack of vacancies or because of his inability to pay the fees required. These were fairly large and were devoted to the running expenses of the guild. The number of *maîtres* was limited. In 1723 there were 985, and in 1790 this figure had not increased. The King, moreover, had the right to create *maîtres* on his own authority.

A *compagnon* had to submit a specimen of his work before receiving the *maîtrise*, but once a *maître*, he was permitted to open a shop in his own name, in which he could employ some *compagnons*, and was required to take in one apprentice at least. At his death his widow could continue to direct his business, provided that she had qualified *compagnons* to assist her.

After 1751 a *maître* was also required to stamp the furniture he put on sale (*see* Stamps).

In addition to the apprentices, *compagnons*, and *maîtres*, there were two other types of craftsmen involved in the guild organization. Firstly, the maintenance of standards was in the hands of a *syndic* and six *jurés*, elected once a year from among the *maîtres*, whose duty it was to examine the specimens submitted by aspiring *maîtres* and also to inspect all workshops in Paris four times a year and examine work in hand. All pieces of furniture approved by the *jurés* were stamped with the monogram J.M.E. (*juré*, or *jurande des menuisiers-ébénistes*) (*see also* Stamps).

Meuble à hauteur d'appui. A term used extensively in France at all periods for any low bookcase or cupboard, usually between 3 and 4 feet high.

Meuble d'entre deux. A term used in France in the eighteenth century for a type of furniture which usually consists of a cupboard or chest of drawers flanked at each side by a set of shelves. Often these are open, but sometimes are enclosed by a curved door forming a small cupboard with shelves.

Mirror-stand. An adjustable mirror mounted on a shaft and tripod base, resembling a pole-screen; popular at the end of the eighteenth century.

Misericord. In ecclesiastical woodwork, bracket on underside of hinged seat of a stall, to support an occupant when nominally standing during certain offices. From a "monastic" usage of L. *misericordia* (pity, compassion), in sense of "an indulgence or relaxation of the rule" (O.E.D.). Miserere is an incorrect alternative.

Mortise and tenon. For joining two pieces of wood. The mortise is a cavity, usually rectangular; the tenon, an end shaped to fill the cavity exactly; characteristic of Philadelphia chairs, where seat rail joins the stiles.

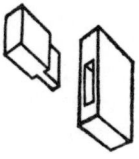

FIG. 33. Mortise and tenon

Mother-of-pearl. Inlay of nacreous shell slices, often used on early nineteenth-century American fancy chairs, tables, etc.

Moulding. Shaped member, such as used to enclose panels; or the shaped edge of a lid, cornice, etc.

Muntin. Upright (other than an outermost upright) connecting the upper and lower stretchers of a framework (Fig. 34). An instance is the bearer between the doors of the lower stage of a press-cupboard; but the number of muntins depends on the nature of the structure. (*See also* Stile.)

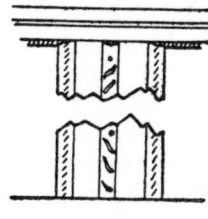

FIG. 34

Music-stand. See Canterbury (1) and Desk (2).

Nails. A popular notion that iron nails are never found in antique furniture construction is fallacious. In fact, metal nails have been known for centuries, though the use of the wooden dowel (*q.v.*) must not be minimized by implication. Old hand-made nails are very different from the modern, mass-produced variety; but the manufacture of hand-made nails (and screws) has been revived.

Name chests. Colloquial term for chests that bear the decoratively carved or painted name of the original owner.

Neo-Greek. Alternative term for furniture of the brief classical revival in early nineteenth-century America. Mostly said of the late Empire style, 1815–40.

Night-table. A pot cupboard which replaced the close-stool after 1750; sometimes also fitted as a washing-stand (*q.v.*). Among the features commonly found on these pieces may be noted a drawer under the cupboard, a tambour front, and a tray top (Plate 124A).

GLOSSARY

Some night-tables were given a triangular shape to fit into a corner.

Oak. A hard wood with coarse grain used almost exclusively up to the seventeenth century and as a secondary wood later. Its hardness made it difficult to carve but quite durable.

Occasional table. Any light table easily moved here or there to meet the occasion. Much used in America ever since early eighteenth-century times.

Ormolu. An English word in use from about the middle of the eighteenth century, derived from the French term "*bronze dorée d'or moulu*". Its most accurate equivalents are "*bronze dorée*" or gilt bronze. It was a French speciality, and when found on English furniture it is likely that it was done by French craftsmen. Ormolu is the substance from which all objects covered by the term *bronzes d'ameublement* are made, e.g. lighting fixtures, including candelabra and candlesticks, clock-cases, appliances for doors and fireplaces, as well as mounts for furniture. Its manufacture was the function of two craft guilds; the *fondeurs* (*q.v.*) and the *doreurs* (*q.v.*). Its preparation consisted of a model in wood or wax being produced by a sculptor, often of some note; this was then cast in bronze by a *fondeur*, usually by the *cire perdue* method, but sometimes from a mould of clay or sand (*see* article on Bronzes). The casting was then tooled and chased until the required degree of finish had been achieved. This last process (known as *ciselure*) was carried to an extraordinary degree of refinement in France in the eighteenth century, and the tools which the *ciseleurs* used are illustrated in the *Encyclopédie*, showing the precision which could be obtained. The bronzes when finished were often merely dipped in acid and then lacquered, and this often needed to be done more than once, when the surface became dirty.

If they were required to be gilt, this was usually done by the mercury process, of which detailed particulars are also given in the *Encyclopédie*. It consisted of coating the bronze with a paste formed by dissolving gold in heated mercury. The bronze thus coated was then itself heated, and the mercury driven off, when the gold was left adhering to the surface of the metal. The fumes of the mercury vapour produced at this stage were very dangerous and the heating had to be carried out in a furnace with a strong draught. Finally, when the process was completed the gold was either burnished or given a matt finish, according to requirements, but sometimes both types of finish were used on the same piece for purposes of contrast.

During the Louis XIV period the leaf-gilding of bronzes was sometimes employed, and occasionally bronzes were silvered, although this is rare at any time.

It is important to remember that only the finest bronzes were gilt in the manners described, the remainder being merely dipped and lacquered. The owners of furniture and *bronzes d'ameublement* in the eighteenth century were also not averse from having their ormolu regilt by the mercury process in order to keep it in a bright condition. So far as one can judge from contemporary accounts, ormolu was never allowed to become as dull or dirty as it often is today, and there seems to have been no taste for patina for its own sake.

The craft of making ormolu reached its height towards the middle of Louis XVI's reign, the chief exponents being Pierre Philippe Thomire, E. Forestier, and others. During the Napoleonic period the quality of ormolu declined, mainly owing to the cost of gilding by the mercury process. Later in the nineteenth century, however, with the advent of machinery and mass-production methods, fine ormolu was produced, and although it often lacks the personal perfection which the earlier craftsmen gave it, it is sometimes very difficult to distinguish between a piece produced in 1770 and another made in the same style in 1860. Connoisseurs and collectors should always keep an open mind about this.

Oxbow, oxbow front. The reverse serpentine curve, somewhat resembling the curve of an oxbow. Often employed in the finest eighteenth-century New England, especially Boston case furniture such as chests of drawers, secretaries, etc.

Palace letters. These, with inventory numbers (*q.v.*), are often painted or branded on furniture and occasionally stamped on *bronzes d'ameublement*, made for the French

GLOSSARY

Crown. On veneered furniture they are usually to be found on the carcase at the back or under marble slabs, but in the case of chairs and *menuiserie* generally, they are often in the under parts and sometimes on the bottom of the upholstered seats. They almost always take the form of the initial letter or letters of the palace concerned beneath a crown. Thus F = Fontainebleau; C.T. = Château de Trianon; W (two Vs) = Versailles; S.C. = Saint Cloud, etc. Like inventory numbers, their existence on furniture of any date is worth careful investigation.

Panel. Compartment usually rectangular, and sunk or raised from the surface of its framework. Panel is the filling of such framework, whereas panelling refers to the framework and its filling (*see* Wainscot).

Papier mâché. Moulded paper pulp used for many small articles and particularly suitable for japanning and polishing; the original process came to England via France from the East as early as the seventeenth century. Considerable stimulus was given to this kind of work in 1772, when Henry Clay of Birmingham, and later London, patented a similar material and began manufacturing various pieces, among which trays, boxes, tea-caddies, and coasters were prominent.

Parquetry. A word connected, as its French equivalent implies, with the laying of floors. It is sometimes used in connexion with furniture inlaid with geometrical cube designs in the manner of a parquet floor. It should be used with caution and is not really applicable to furniture at all.

Patina (and **colour**). Of furniture and woodwork, patina is the undisturbed surface, heightened by centuries of polishing and usage. Contrary to popular belief, some old oak furniture shows clear signs of having been originally varnished; some was also polychromed. Patination and colour pose problems to a faker. To some extent they can be simulated, but, when artificially produced, deteriorate (*see* Fake and Stripping).

Pear drop. *See* Drop handle.

Pedestal table. A table on a round centre support.

Pembroke table. A small table with short drop leaves supported on swinging wooden brackets. The term Pembroke is used in England first in the 1760s. Although Chippendale lists tables of this description as "breakfast tables" in the *Director*, he used the term on bills. Sheraton said this type of table was named after the lady who first ordered it. It was particularly popular in the classical period, and both Hepplewhite and Sheraton suggested designs for it.

Pennsylvania Dutch. The name applied to German settlers in Pennsylvania. Their furniture has many distinctive qualities, since it assimilates English and German peasant styles. Their cabinet-makers worked in soft woods, which they painted and often decorated with floral patterns and other motifs from the vocabulary of peasant design.

Pie-crust table. A round tilt-top tea-table on a tripod base. The top has a scalloped edge finished with a carved moulding which is suggestive of the notched rim of a pie crust; tables in the Chippendale style have pedestals elaborately carved. The tripod consists of three cabriole legs terminating generally in claw-and-ball feet (Plate 56B).

Pier table. A table designed to stand against the pier, the part of the wall between the windows. In America the term is used loosely to refer to a table designed for use against a wall, a side table.

Pilgrim furniture. Term used to describe American seventeenth-century furniture.

Pillar and scroll clock. American shelf or mantel clock by Eli Terry. Its wooden works are housed in a vertical rectangular case with a scrolled-arch top, small, round pillars at the sides, and delicately small feet. Same as the so-called "Terry" clock.

Pine. Often used for panelling rooms in eighteenth-century England. It was also used for the carcases of veneered furniture. From the time of the Pilgrims down to the present, much of the everyday utility furniture in America has been made of pine, especially the soft white pine of New England. Antique examples of it are much prized today for countrified settings. White pine was also much used for the unseen parts of furniture and other secondary purposes, as well as for overlaying with veneer. Its presence often identifies the furniture as American. Short-leaf,

341

yellow, hard pine is often used as the secondary wood in New Jersey, Pennsylvania, and Virginia furniture. The long-leaf, yellow, hard pine, so plentiful in the south, does not made good furniture.

Pin-hinge. Method of hinging, as found on thirteenth-century chests, the lid being pinned through the rear stiles and pendent side-rails of the lid.

Pipe-rack. A stand for clay pipes. Of the various wooden kinds in use in the eighteenth century one can distinguish: (1) the stand of candlestick form with a tiny circular tray on the stem, pierced with holes for holding the pipes, and (2) the wall rack, either an open frame with notched sides so that the pipes could lie across or a board with shelves from which the pipes hung down (cf. spoon-rack). In addition to these, metal pipe-kilns were widely used from the seventeenth century – iron fromes on which the pipes rested, deriving their name from the fact that they could be baked in an oven to clean the pipes.

Pipe-tray. A long and narrow wooden tray with partitions for churchwardens, in use throughout the Georgian period.

Plate-pail. A mahogany container with handle for carrying plates from kitchen to dining-room (often a long journey) in large houses in the eighteenth century; of various shapes, generally circular with one section left open for ease of access (Plate 118B).

Pole-screen. *See* Fire-screen (1).

Poplar. *See* Tulipwood.

Poppy- (popey-) head. Decorative finial of a bench- or desk-end, as in ecclesiastical woodwork. Plant and floral forms are numerous; human heads, figures, birds, beasts, and other devices are found. Derivation of term is uncertain, one suggestion (rejected by some writers) being from Fr. *poupée* (baby doll), or from poppet, puppet.

Porcelain. In the Louis XV and Louis XVI periods there were two important uses of porcelain in connexion with furniture. Firstly, for purely decorative purposes, actual pieces of porcelain were mounted with ormolu, often of very high quality. This is what became known as "mounted porcelain", and the pieces so embellished came not only from the French factories of Vincennes and Sèvres but also from Meissen, and particularly from the Far East, *celadon* and *famille rose* being specially favoured. The ormolu decoration is usually confined to ornamental bases and bands for the necks of vases, but is sometimes extended to form handles, knobs for lids, etc. It is screwed on to the porcelain by means of a hole bored in the latter. The types of porcelain chosen are usually vases of various shapes, shallow bowls, ewers, and particularly the famous bunches of flowers from the Meissen factory, which were imitated at Vincennes. Sometimes groups of *biscuit de Sèvres* were similarly mounted. The demand for all these types was very high and extended right up to the Revolution, the usual changes in style being noticeable.

The other principal use to which porcelain was put did not come into fashion until the latter part of Louis XVI's reign. This consisted of the inlaying of plaques of porcelain into the veneered surfaces of pieces of furniture. This method of decoration, although it sometimes produces an extremely sumptuous effect, is often criticized on the grounds that it lies outside the scope of practical cabinet-making, and it has always been foreign to English taste. The covering of parts of furniture with porcelain does certainly make the pieces much more fragile, and there is evidence to show that a number of the plaques adorning extant pieces are not in fact the originals.

The porcelain so used almost always came from the Sèvres manufactory and often, therefore, has the royal monogram with or without date letters or painters' marks. If a date letter is found and is genuine it may help to date the piece of furniture fairly exactly, but it is always possible that the plaque is not the original, and may have replaced another, in which case the date letter may bear no relation to the year in which the furniture was made.

The porcelain is let into cavities in the carcase and kept in position originally by means of ormolu fillets. Martin Carlin and Adam Weisweiler were two *ébénistes* who appear to have specialized to some extent in making furniture of this kind, and the custom of mounting porcelain of any date on furniture was particularly prevalent in the nineteenth century, during the Restoration and reign of

Louis Philippe. Collectors should always bear in mind that the porcelain on furniture may be a later addition or replacement, and this is particularly to be suspected if there is any lack of harmony between the furniture and the plaques, or any confusion of dating.

Press. Broadly, a tall, enclosed, and doored structure comparable to the modern wardrobe or hanging cupboard. Not to be confused with linen-press, in the sense of a framework with a screw-down smoother. (For press-cupboard *see under* Cupboard.)

Prie-dieu. The earliest surviving examples of the *prie-dieu* in Italy date from the sixteenth century and are simple contrivances with a step for the knees, an upright panel or shallow cupboard, and a shelf on top. Two or three drawers occasionally replaced the cupboard in the seventeenth century and the whole object was treated more decoratively. A magnificent early eighteenth-century example in the Palazzo Pitti at Florence is enriched with swags of fruit in *pietre dure*. Later in the eighteenth century the *prie-dieu* was made in conformity with rococo taste, usually with a single curving column supporting the shelf. Other more substantial examples were made to fold up into chairs.

Puritan. A term applied to simpler seventeenth-century American furniture.

Purple-wood. A wood with an open grain which is fairly hard. It is brown in its natural state, but turns purple on exposure to the air. Found chiefly in Brazil and French Guinea. Very extensively used for marquetry in France in the eighteenth century.

Rail. The horizontal piece in framing or panelling. In a chair back the top member supported on the stiles.

Reeding. Similar to fluting but with the ornament in relief (Fig. 35).

Fig. 35. Combined reeding and fluting

Reggivaso. A vase stand, a purely decorative piece of furniture which enjoyed widespread popularity in Italy in the eighteenth century. *Reggivasi* were made in the form of *putti*, satyrs, chained Negro slaves, or blackamoor page-boys and are often minor works of sculpture of great charm. A superb example by Andrea Brustolon in the Palazzo Rezzonico at Venice is made in the form of a group of river gods holding trays for the porcelain vases.

Renaissance (Fr. for rebirth). Applied to the effects of the revival of learning and embracing the use (often very freely interpreted) of classical as opposed to Gothic motifs. Originating in Italy in the fifteenth century, Renaissance design spread throughout Europe, beginning to make itself felt in England in the early sixteenth century.

Restoration. (1) A proper renewal of a piece by a candid replacement of hopelessly damaged or missing parts; (2) restored is sometimes used to indicate either that a piece has been over-restored or that the extent of its restoration is dubious.

Restoration Furniture. Term applied to certain elaborately carved and scrolled chairs, etc., their backs surmounted by crowns or boys and crowns. It was said that such pieces recorded the restoration of King Charles II (1660), but many so-called Restoration chairs are now known to date from late in his reign when not from a subsequent period. Such chairs may be of mixed woods, and other than oak.

Rising sun. When a fan-shaped ornament is carved half-circle, and the resulting spray of stalks suggests sun rays it is picturesquely called a rising sun (Fig. 36). "Setting sun" is sometimes used. It was so often the only decoration on New England highboys that its presence generally indicates the New England origin of the piece. James (later President) Madison recalled that when the Constitution of the United States was finally adopted after much contention, Benjamin Franklin pointed to a decoration of this type painted on the back of the chairman's chair and said he had looked at it many times

Fig. 36

GLOSSARY

during the sessions "without being able to tell whether it was rising or setting, but now I . . . know that it is a rising . . . sun".

Rocking chair. A chair of almost any simple type mounted on bends, rockers. An American institution, the rocking chair may also be an American invention. Authentic "slat-back" examples are said to date as early as 1650–1700, though 1800 would seem to be safer. Special types were developed (*see* Boston rocker, Salem rocker, Windsor).

Rococo. An ornate style developed in France from the Chinese forms. It came to England in the Chippendale period. It appeared in its most characteristic forms on sconces, mirror-frames, and console tables, all elaborately carved and gilded by special craftsmen. The American version only barely suggests the exuberance of the Continental rococo style. Ornament rococo in spirit is used on American Chippendale furniture, particularly in Philadelphia, but the lines of the furniture are more conservative.

Roll-top desk. Similar to a cylinder-top desk (*q.v.*), but the writing-table and fittings are enclosed by a curved slatted panel.

Romayne work. Old term for Renaissance carving with heads in roundels, scroll-work, vases, etc., some few heads being portraits, but most purely formal (Fig. 37). The taste was widespread in Europe, and traditional traces survived in Brittany until quite a late period. The vogue for romayne work in England was under Henry VIII (1509–47), thereafter dwindling.

Rosette. A round ornament in a floral design.

Rosewood or **kingwood.** A coarse-grained wood, dark purplish brown or black in colour, varying considerably in hardness. Found in India, Brazil, and the West Indies.

Roundabout. *See* Corner chair.

Rounded ends. The top rail of early Chippendale chairs is sometimes made with rounded ends, somewhat in the style of a Queen Anne chair (*see* Cupid's bow).

Roundel. Circular ornament enclosing sundry formal devices on medieval and later woodwork (Fig. 91); also human heads as in romayne work (*see also* Whorl).

Runner. Alternative term for the rocker of a rocking chair.

Rush seat. A seat woven of rushes. Used in America from the earliest times, generally with simple furniture. Still popular for country chairs (*see* Splint seat).

Sabre leg. A term used to describe a sharply curving leg in the classical style which has also been called scroll-shaped and even likened to the shape of a cornucopia. It is generally reeded. This leg is found on small sofas attributed to Duncan Phyfe.

Saddle seat. When the seat of a Windsor chair is cut away from the centre in a downward slope to the sides the shape somewhat resembles the seat of a saddle, and is picturesquely so named.

Salem rocker. Salem, Massachusetts, variant of the Windsor rocker (*q.v.*) and with a lower back than the Boston rocker (*q.v.*), early nineteenth century.

Salem secretary. Salem, Massachusetts, variant of Sheraton's secretary with a china cabinet top; also, by extension, a Salem sideboard with a china cabinet top (*c.* 1800–20).

Salem snowflake. A six-pointed punched decoration resembling a star or a snowflake found as a background in the carved areas of Salem, Massachusetts, furniture.

Fig. 37. Romayne work with head in roundel

GLOSSARY

Sample chairs. A group of six chairs thought to have been made by Benjamin Randolph, a Philadelphia cabinet-maker, as samples of his skill. The group of chairs (one wing and five side chairs) is in the most elegant Philadelphia Chippendale style.

Satinwood. A fairly hard wood, with a very close grain. It is yellow or light brown in colour and has a lustrous surface somewhat like that of satin. It is found in central and southern India, Coromandel, Ceylon, and in the West Indies.

Sawbuck table. A table with an X-shaped frame either plain or scrolled. Frequently found in rural New England and in Pennsylvania German examples.

Sconce. A general name for a wall-light consisting of a back-plate and either a tray or branched candle-holders. Metal seems to have been the chief material from later medieval times until the end of the seventeenth century when looking glass became fashionable for back-plates (and when "girandole" was another name for these pieces). The use of looking glass meant that sconces tended to follow the same decorative trends as contemporary mirrors, but metal back-plates continued to be made, and for a period after 1725 there was a preference for carved and gilt wood and gesso-work, often without looking glass. About 1750 sconces provided some of the freest interpretation of the asymmetrical rococo mode, either with looking glass in a scrolled frame or in carved and gilt wood only; Chinese features were often blended with the rococo. In contrast, the sconces of the Adam period had delicate classical ornament in gilt wood or in composition built up round a wire frame. Cut-glass sconces were in vogue at the end of the century.

Scoop pattern. Popular term for a band or other disposition of fluted ornament, gouged in the wood, the flute having a rounded top and, sometimes, base (Fig. 38). A motif of Renaissance origin, its use was widespread (*see* Fluting).

Screen. Although frequently used in the church, screens do not seem to have been introduced into the house until the late seventeenth century. In Italy, as in England, Coromandel screens imported from the East were very popular, but screens, either hung with silk or painted with floral motifs, standing figures, etc., enjoyed a considerable vogue. The fire-screen was more widely used. An excellent example carved by G. M. Bonzanigo, is in the Castello di Stupinigi at Turin. (Plate 85E.)

Scroll top. A curved broken-arch pediment used on case pieces. Also called gooseneck, swan-neck, etc.

Scutcheon. Shield on which are armorial bearings or other devices, and, by extension, sundry shield-shaped ornaments and fitments (*see* Lock-plate).

'Scrutoire, escritoire. Eighteenth-century American term for an enclosed writing-desk, often with a cabinet top. Lockwood differentiates three varieties: fall front, slant top with ball feet, and slant top with turned legs. In England called a bureau or bureau-bookcase.

Secretaire (or **secretary**). The name somewhat loosely applied to different kinds of writing furniture, of which two small varieties call for mention here. (1) At the end of the seventeenth century appeared the small bureau mounted on legs or stand, very similar to the contemporary desk on stand (*q.v.*) (Plate 124C). This kind seems to have been designed for ladies' use, and sometimes had a looking glass at the top. (2) In the late eighteenth century large numbers of light and graceful secretaires were made, one popular kind taking the form of a small table with tapering legs enclosing a drawer and supporting a little stand with drawers and shelf. The stand, which was used as a small bookshelf, was often provided with a handle so that it could be lifted off. This type of table was also known as a cheveret.

Serre-papier. *See under* Cartonnier.

Settee. A low, long seat with upholstered

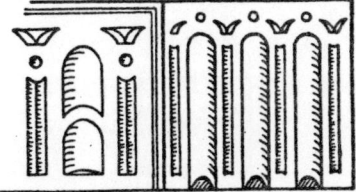

Fig. 38. Double Scoop and Fluting (*left*); Reeding and Fluting (*right*). Seventeenth century

GLOSSARY

back and arms, which developed along the same lines as the arm-chair.

Settle. Long, backed seat with boxed base, or on legs, and at each end side-pieces or arms (Plate 5). Fixed or movable, the settle represents a stage preceding the settee, a derivative of the chair. Some quite late settles have one end scrolled like a sofa-head. Some, mostly country-made, settles have a storage press in the back, such being loosely known as bacon-cupboard.

Sewing-tables. *See* Work-table.

Shaker furniture. A whole range of furniture – chairs, tables, chests of drawers – made by early nineteenth-century Shakers, a celibate American sect. This furniture, while provincial, is of such sheer simplicity, so pure in line, so lean and functional in form, so well proportioned and soundly constructed, that it is much prized today. Usually in pine, maple, walnut, or fruit woods (Plates 79, 80).

Shearer, George. English furniture designer, contemporary of Hepplewhite and Sheraton, whose work first appeared in the 1788 *Cabinet-Maker's London Book of Prices*. The sideboard, as usually made in the classical style, appeared first in his book of designs.

Shearer, Thomas. English furniture designer whose drawings, first published in the *Cabinet-Maker's London Book of Prices*, 1788, influenced many American cabinet-makers from 1790 to 1810, though the credit has to this day gone to his contemporaries, Hepplewhite and Sheraton, both of whom took many a leaf from Shearer's book (*see* Sideboard).

Shelves. Taken here to refer to hanging or standing shelves without doors, for books, plate, and china. Small oak shelves of the Tudor period were square in shape; while arcaded tops appeared in the early seventeenth century. Carving was the chief decoration, and this became more ornate after 1660. It is probable that many walnut shelves were made, but few of these seem to have survived. It was at this time that shelves were used for displaying china; a fashion which continued into the early eighteenth century, but was then replaced by that of keeping china in cabinets and cupboards. Open shelves, however, returned to favour in the Chippendale period, when they were often decorated in the Chinese taste, and had fretted sides and galleries. Simple, light shelves were generally in vogue in the later eighteenth century (Fig. 39), for books or china;

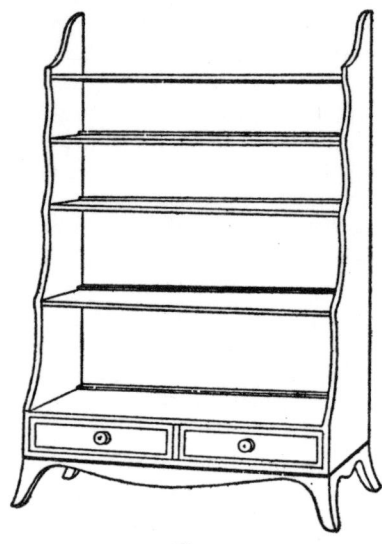

FIG. 39

Sheraton emphasized that shelves should be light enough for ladies to move about and to contain their "books under present reading".

Sideboard. Literally a side-board (as a cupboard was a cup-board); a side-table or other structure convenient for the display and service of plate, foodstuffs, etc., and possibly including storage facilities such as ambries, drawers, etc. A near relative of the dresser, and in some cases indistinguishable from such.

Slant-front desk. A frame or chest of

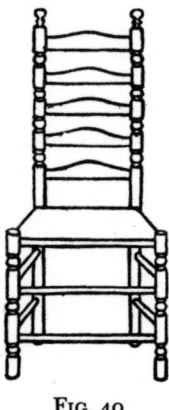

FIG. 40

346

drawers with a top section as an enclosed desk for writing, the hinged lid sloping at a 45 degrees angle when closed. Called in England a bureau.

Slat back. A seventeenth-century style chair made of turned posts connected by horizontal slats across the back. Persisted in rural areas to the twentieth century (Fig. 40).

Sleigh bed. American French Empire bed somewhat resembling a sleigh.

Slider. *See* Coaster.

Sofa. The sofa as we know it developed in the Louis XIV period out of the day-bed (or *lit de repos*). It became established more or less in its present form in the Louis XV period as a regular part of a *mobilier de salon*, and was often made to match a set of chairs and *causeuses*, in which case it was upholstered similarly. The sofa was first introduced into Italy in the late seventeenth century. Its stylistic history follows that of the chair: indeed, many Italian sofas resemble a row of chairs joined together. Extraordinarily long sofas with carved wooden backs and, usually, rush seats, were much favoured for the furnishing of eighteenth-century ballrooms (Fig. 41). Padded sofas with outcurving arms were

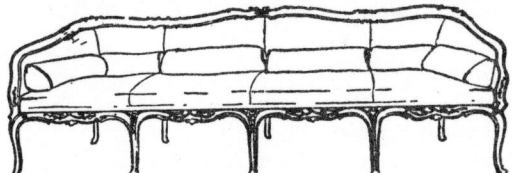

FIG. 41. Venetian sofa; mid-eighteenth century

popular in Venice in the eighteenth century, and some were made in the form of folding beds.

Sofa table. Small, narrow, rectangular table with two front drawers in the apron and hinged leaves at each end; the underframe of two legs at each end, or graceful bracket supports connected by a stretcher. First made in America about 1800 from Sheraton's designs. Duncan Phyfe developed several fine variants. Popular until the passing of the Empire fashion about 1840. Rare today in America but common in England.

Spanish foot. William and Mary, also early Queen Anne, chair or table foot, with

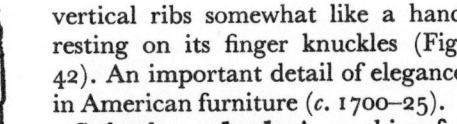

FIG. 42

vertical ribs somewhat like a hand resting on its finger knuckles (Fig. 42). An important detail of elegance in American furniture (*c.* 1700–25).

Spinning wheel. A machine for making yarn or thread, employing foot or hand power. As a piece for the home, it was generally made of turned parts. Used through the nineteenth century in rural areas.

Splint seat. A seat made of oak or hickory strips interlaced. Used in country furniture through the eighteenth century.

Spool. A turning in the shape of a row of spools which was employed for long, thin members such as legs. Introduced after 1820 and continued through the Victorian period in rural work.

Spoon-back. Colloquially used of a Queen Anne chair with a back, curved like a spoon, conforming to the human back.

Spoon-rack. A stand for hanging spoons, dating from late Tudor times when metal spoons came into general use. The usual form, until the end of the eighteenth century, resembled a miniature dresser – a wooden board with small slotted shelves for spoons, and, attached to it at the bottom, a box for knives and forks.

Stamps. Various names and letters are often found stamped on French furniture made in the eighteenth century or later. The principal and most important of these is the stamp (*estampille*), giving the name and often the initials of the *ébéniste* who made the piece of furniture concerned, which, after 1751, he was compelled by guild regulations to strike on all his work, unless he happened to be a privileged craftsman working for the Crown. Before 1751 *estampilles* are very rarely found.

These stamps are a most important means of identifying the makers of individual pieces of furniture, but it must be borne in mind that sometimes they refer only to the repairer of a piece as distinct from its original maker. Thus some pieces bear more than one *estampille*, and it is often doubtful which *ébéniste* was the actual maker. The importance of the stamps, however, was only rediscovered in 1882, as a result of an exhibition held in Paris under the

GLOSSARY

auspices of the *Union Centrale de Arts Décoratifs*, and as an unfortunate consequence, a number of false signatures have been applied to furniture since that date by unscrupulous dealers. Connoisseurs and collectors should be on their guard against this and also against the attribution of unstamped pieces to individual *ébénistes* on grounds of style alone.

The *estampille* is of roughly uniform size and format, usually incorporating the *ébéniste*'s name and initials, but sometimes the surname only (*see* pp. 116-18. They are usually found in an inconspicuous place on the carcase of the piece, often on the bottom or top rails, front or back, under marble tops, etc. Very occasionally they appear on the surface of the veneer itself, and sometimes panels of marquetry are signed in full by their makers.

Another important stamp to be found on furniture after 1751 is that of the *jurés*. It consists of a monogram incorporating the letters JME (*juré* or *jurande des menuisiers-ébénistes*), and its presence implies that the piece concerned has passed the standard required by the *jurés* of the guild (*see* Menuisiers-Ébénistes, Corporation des).

In addition to the *estampille* and the *juré*'s stamp, furniture made for the Crown sometimes, though by no means always, bears the stamp of the *Garde Meuble de la Couronne* (*q.v.*). Inventory numbers and palace letters (*q.v.*) are usually painted or branded, but seldom stamped, on furniture.

In the eighteenth century *bronzes d'ameublement* are very rarely stamped, but sometimes they do bear signatures. Jacques Caffiéri frequently signed his work with his surname. Inventory numbers and palace letters are even rarer, but they do occasionally occur on bronzes, and where they can be checked with existing documents they are found to be of eighteenth-century origin.

Stars. American ornaments often inlaid or painted on clocks, mirrors, tables, desk tops, etc., usually celebrating the number of states in the Union. The date of the article is sometimes traceable to the number of stars thus employed: the thirteenth state, Rhode Island, being admitted in 1790; the fourteenth, Vermont, in 1791, etc.

Stile. In construction an outermost upright, as a muntin is an inner one.

Stool. Small, backless seat. Apart from rack- or folding stools, the main basic types are trestle and legged. Trestle, with two uprights out from the solid, on the same principle as the ends of a boarded chest, may be included among stools of wainscot. Stools with legs may have three or four supports, and some quite common, and indeed modern, stools of traditional form are of very ancient lineage.

Joined stool (joint is a corruption): is proper to stools made by joinery. The term coffin stool invariably used by beginners is only correct when the use of joined stools as a coffin-bier (as in some old churches) is known. It is incorrect for the domestic article. For close-stool see that section. An old term for a box-top stool was "stool with a lock" (*see English Cottage Furniture*, p. 28).

Folding X stools, with the seat placed on top of the X – and not just above the crossing as in X chairs – were very popular in the fifteenth and sixteenth centuries in Italy. Elegant but very uncomfortable three-legged stools with small octagonal seats and tall, narrow backs, called Strozzi stools (Fig. 43) were made in Tuscany in the fifteenth century. In the sixteenth and seventeenth centuries stools with legs formed out of two carved and shaped planks were usual, but in the eighteenth century the stool was regarded principally as the appendage of a chair or suite of chairs and designed in conformity.

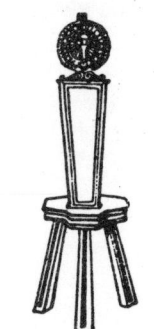

FIG. 43. Strozzi stool; Tuscan fifteenth century

Strapwork. Of carving, band of ornament more or less suggestive of plaited straps, often

FIG. 44

GLOSSARY

highly formalized; distinct from guilloche (Figs. 44 and 45).

FIG. 45. Strap and jewel carving. First half of the seventeenth century

Straw-work. A method of decorating furniture, particularly smaller pieces, with tiny strips of bleached and coloured straws to form landscapes, geometrical patterns, etc. This craft came to England from the Continent towards the end of the seventeenth century and

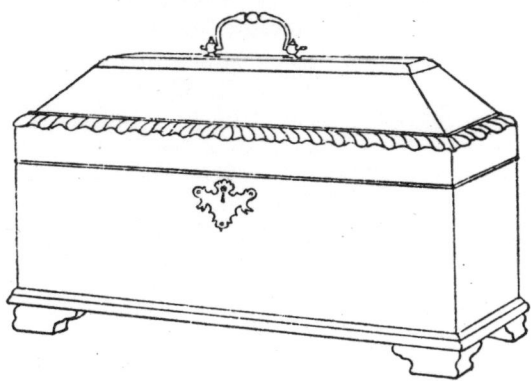

FIG. 46. Rectangular Tea-caddy

was centred at Dunstable. There was a big increase in output during the Napoleonic Wars, when French prisoners, many of whom were craftsmen who had been conscripted into the French Navy, decorated articles in this way during their captivity in England. Among the chief pieces thus decorated were tea-caddies, desks, and boxes.

Stretcher. A horizontal member connecting uprights.

Stripping. Furniture, the old surface of which has been removed and reduced to the wood, is said to have been stripped. Though stripping can be properly used, it should never be lightly indulged, as for a supposedly aesthetic advantage (*see* Patina).

Stump leg. A simple, thick rear leg curved at the corners; used on Queen Anne and Chippendale chairs.

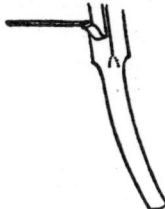

FIG. 47

Stump feet. A plain turned foot – the "stump" of the leg – much used on the back legs of American Queen Anne and Chippendale chairs, etc., with cabriole front supports, particularly in Philadelphia.

Sunburst. English source of the American rising sun ornament (*q.v.*).

Sunflower. From earliest American times the conventionalized sunflower was a popular carved ornament on Connecticut desks and chests (*q.v.*).

Swan-neck. *See* Scroll top.

Sweet gum. Close-grained, silky, red-brown American wood easily stained to look like mahogany and sometimes used as a substitute for it in less-expensive furniture. Miller says that during the Revolution, when mahogany was not obtainable, American sweet gum wood, then called "Bilsted", was often used.

Swing-leg table. A hinged leaf table with a swinging rather than a gate-leg. Handsome examples, some of them cabriole, survive.

Table. Primarily, board forming the top only of such furniture, and by later extension the whole structure. "Table tretteau" (table trestles) in the famous *Epitaphe* of François Villon is thus a precise, as well as a poetic, statement. The trestle table is a very old form (Plate 12), an advantage being in its ease of clearance and storage, but trestle-supports are often ponderous. The other main basic type of table is that supported by a developed framework with a leg at each corner and possibly others along the sides. Of about the early sixteenth century frame-tables constructionally ancestral to later types are in evidence, though authentic examples are all but unprocurable in the market. By the end of the same century tables with a developed underframing and fixed legs were usual. The term refectory table is popular jargon, better replaced by long table (Plate 11A) or other suitable description. Dining- or parlour-table is used of less extensive items. Drawing- or draw-table had movable extensions of the top, pushed in below it and drawn when needed. Various kinds of side-table include what is now called occasional table. Some small examples are known, correctly or otherwise, as games- or gaming tables. Certain table-constructions are now reclassified as counter. Billiards tables were known in the sixteenth and seventeenth centuries. As apart from the draw-table, the folding, falling (or flap-) table, its top with one or more hinged sections, was in more or less general usage by the early seventeenth century (Plate 2c). Various forms include bow- and bay-front (also found minus flaps). Flaps were supported by a movable bracket or leg. A development of the principle resulted in the gate- or gate-leg table, with oval or circular top, the developed underframing of legs and stretchers including movable sections or gates. Gate-tables made to fold completely flat are known, but the more usual construction involved a rigid centre-section.

In churches the post-Reformation communion table, replacing the medieval altar, is essentially similar to the domestic long, parlour, or side-table previously mentioned, though some examples have special features.

Table-chair, -bench. Correct term for the absurdly misnamed monk's chair, or -bench. Chair-table is also used. Convertible chair, the back pivoted to form a table-top when dropped across the uprights (Plate 8A). Though the type existed in pre-Reformation times, most surviving examples are so much later in date (say seventeenth century) as to obviate any monastic association in England.

Tarsia. A form of wood inlay or marquetry widely used in Italy but most notably in Lombardy and Tuscany. Tarsia decoration *alla certosina* made up of polygonal tessere of wood, bone, metal, and mother-of-pearl arranged in geometrical patterns was very popular in Lombardy and Venetia in the fifteenth century and much used for the decoration of *cassoni*. The art of pictorial *tarsia* was brought to a high level of excellence at Florence in the fifteenth century by a number of craftsmen, of whom Francesco di Giovanni called il Francione was, according to Vasari, the most highly esteemed. In the fifteenth and subsequent centuries *tarsia* was much used for the decoration of both ecclesiastical and domestic furniture. Panels representing views of real or imaginary architecture were popular on *cassoni* in the late fifteenth and sixteenth centuries, but during the seventeenth century abstract designs seem to have been preferred. In the eighteenth century *tarsia* was applied to tables and chests of drawers, usually in patterns of flowers and ribbons. The last great artist in *tarsia* was the Lombard Giuseppe Maggiolini.

Tavern table. Small, sturdy, rectangular table on four legs, usually braced with stretchers. Generally with a drawer or two in the

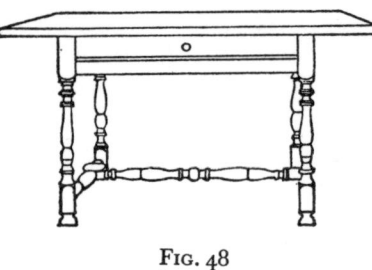

Fig. 48

apron (Fig. 48). Much used in eighteenth-century taverns for serving a customer where he was seated.

Tea-caddy and tea-chest. A small box for storing tea. "Tea-chest" was the common name for this piece from the end of the seventeenth century, when tea-drinking was introduced, until the second half of the eighteenth century, when "caddy", a corruption of "kati", a Malay measure of weight of just over one pound, came into general use. The custom of locking up the family's tea in a box continued long after tea had ceased to be an expensive luxury; caddies, therefore, were invariably provided with locks and were either divided into small compartments or were fitted with canisters (*q.v.*) for the different kinds of tea. A great variety of materials was used in their construction, including woods of all kinds – carved, inlaid, veneered, painted, or decorated with tortoiseshell, ivory, straw-

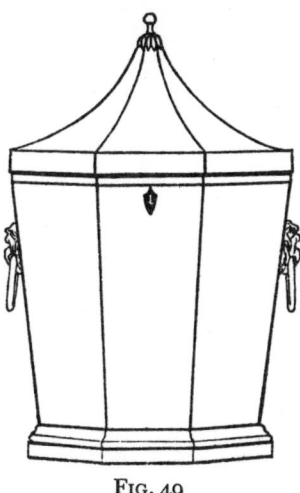

Fig. 49

work (q.v.), Tunbridge ware (q.v.), etc. – metal (silver in the best examples) and papier mâché (q.v.). There was also considerable diversity in shape, from rectangular (Fig. 46)

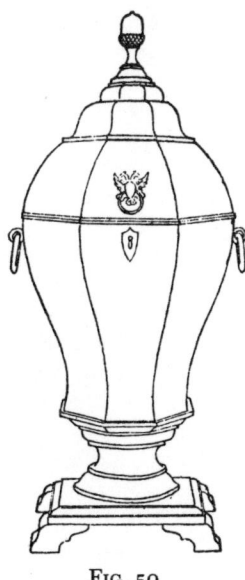

Fig. 50

to square and octagonal (Fig. 49); while vase and pear (Fig. 50) forms were introduced after 1750.

Tea-canister. The container for tea in the caddy (if the latter were not already divided into compartments); made of glass, metal, or earthenware; usually bottle-shaped until c. 1750, and vase-shaped later.

Teapot-stand. See Kettle-stand.

Tear drop. See Drop handle.

Toilet mirror (or **dressing-glass**). A small mirror designed to stand on a table or, in early examples, to hang on the wall. This kind of mirror was a luxury in the medieval and Tudor periods, and did not begin to come into wider use until the late seventeenth century. Post-Restoration mirrors were usually square in shape, and frequently had their frames decorated with stump-work; they stood by means of a strut or hung by a ring. By about 1700 oblong mirrors with arched tops, in narrower moulded frames, veneered or japanned, had begun to replace the square shape. In the eighteenth century several changes occurred. Shortly after 1700 appeared the mirror supported by screws in uprights mounted on a box stand; the box was often in the form of a flap or desk above a drawer which contained the many toilet requisites of the time; the mirror had a pronounced arched heading at first, and the front of the box was sometimes serpentine in form. The older type of strut support, without the box stand, continued to be made, however, and occasionally a stand with small trestle feet was found. By 1750 mahogany was in general use for toilet mirrors, though some in the Chinese style were gilt or japanned. Similar designs were introduced in the neo-classical period; mirror frames, in mahogany or satinwood, were often of oval or shield shape, and the uprights were curved to correspond. The stand was also a simpler arrangement, as toilet articles were now placed in the table on which the mirror stood. At the very end of the century and later, a wide oblong mirror was fashionable, and was usually swung on turned uprights. Mahogany and rosewood, often decorated with stringing, were the chief woods for such mirrors at this time.

Torchère. See Candle-stand.

Toy furniture. Though toy furniture authentically of the Age of Oak exists, it is rare, and there are many copies or imitations. Toy is here used in its sense of knick-knack.

Some such pieces were children's toys, or dolls' furniture, others were made as models to satisfy the adult love of "miniatures". Yet others are said to have been fashioned as trade samples, or as "prentices' pieces" to demonstrate an apprentice's skill. In practice, it is not always possible to differentiate between these various subdivisions.

Tray. For food, tea-things, plates, etc.; also known as a voider (the medieval term for a tray which was still in use in late Georgian times). Tea-trays (or "tea-boards") were introduced in the late seventeenth century, and most of them were japanned; none, however, seems to have survived. Japanned trays were still popular in the middle of the eighteenth century, though by then ornamental mahogany trays with fretted borders were being made. Later, oval trays decorated with fine inlay were in vogue. About 1800 there was a considerable production of trays in japanned metal and papier mâché.

Trail. Undulating band of formalized leaf, berry, or floral pattern. Thus vine-trail (Fig. 51).

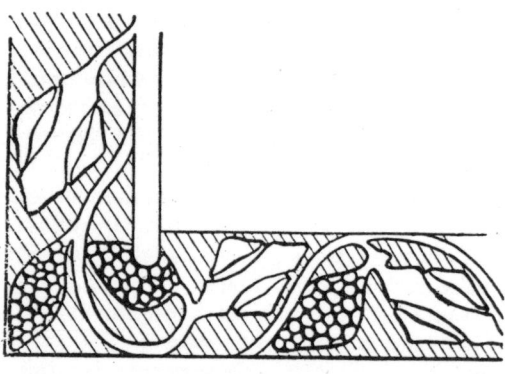

FIG. 51

Treen. Old adjectival form of tree; wooden. Now used of an extensive array of articles, mainly small and of almost any period, such as bowls, Welsh love-spoons, stay-busks, etc., and not excluding furniture.

Trespolo. Elegant three-legged tables known as *trespoli*, usually designed to stand against a wall and to carry a small *objet d'art* or candle-stick, were very popular in the eighteenth century, especially in Venice. Sometimes the supporting column was made in the form of a term figure, but it was more usually carved in a graceful curve (Fig. 52).

FIG. 52. Trespolo; Venetian; mid-eighteenth century

Tricoteuse. A term probably of nineteenth-century origin, applied to a small work-table surrounded by a gallery, part of which can be lowered to contain sewing materials.

Tridarn. *See* Cupboard.

Tuckaway table. A hinged-leaf gate-leg table with cross legs which fold into each other as compactly as if tucked away.

Tudor. The Tudor dynasty reigned from 1485 to 1603; Tudor is loosely used of furniture emerging from the Gothic or not fully developed as characteristic Elizabethan. The periods of Henry VIII (1509–47) and Elizabeth (1558–1603) are usually given their own names.

Tulip-ornament. Formalized ornament of tulip-like form, influenced by the tulipmania in Holland, when huge sums were paid for rare bulbs. On English furniture the vogue for tulip-ornament continued from about the middle to the end of the seventeenth century.

Tulip wood. A soft, light wood used as a secondary wood and in painted furniture; also called tulip poplar.

Tunbridge ware. A special form of inlay which developed at Tunbridge Wells *c.* 1650, employing minute strips of wood, in a great variety of natural colours, to build up geometrical patterns and, later, floral decora-

GLOSSARY

tion, landscape scenes, etc.; used for boxes, trays, desks, tea-caddies, etc.

Turtle-back. A type of ornamental boss, shaped somewhat like a turtle's back, often applied to Jacobean-style cupboards, etc.

Twist-turning. Form of turning derived from the twisted columns of Romanesque via Renaissance architecture. In England its main vogue on furniture was in the mid/latter half of the seventeenth century. R. W. Symonds had differentiated the single-roped twist (Dutch-Flemish type) from the English double-roped or barley-sugar twist (*see English Furniture from Charles II to George II*).

Urn-stand. *See* Kettle-stand.

Veneer. Thin sheets of wood applied to surface for decorative effect or to improve appearance of furniture. Though veneering arrives in the second half of the seventeenth century, at the end of the oak period, it is sometimes found as a limited enhancement of pieces which would be classed as oak by collectors.

Vernis Martin. A term applied generically to all varnishes and lacquers used for furniture and interior decoration in France during the eighteenth century. It derives from the brothers Martin, who in 1730 were granted a monopoly to copy Chinese and Japanese lacquer. They also evolved a special kind of coloured varnish, which was applied in a large number of coats and then rubbed down to give it lustre. It was available in a number of colours, including grey, lilac, yellow, and blue, but the most famous was the green, which was often applied to furniture. Vernis Martin was also used to decorate *boiseries*, carriages, fans, and small boxes. The Martin family were much patronized by the Court and by Madame de Pompadour (*see also under Lacquer*).

Wagon seat. An American double seat, generally with a two-chair back of slat-back or Windsor variety, usable both as a farm porch settee and a wagon seat.

Wainscot. Now mainly used of wall-panelling, but anciently of wider significance, its derivation from MLG. *Wagenschot*, perhaps meaning wagon-boarding, referring rather to the planking itself, and thence to a wall-lining as well as to other forms of woodwork. Bedstead, chair, stool, etc., are frequently listed as being "of wainscot". Though this term in some cases implied that their construction involved a noticeable amount of panelled work, furniture stoutly built of slabs or planks of wood was perhaps "of wainscot", involving various forms of boarded furniture with "slab-ends". As a term, wainscot may have been loosely as well as precisely used (*cf.* definition of coffer).

Wall-lights. A lighting appliance usually of more than one light which can be fixed flat to the surface of a wall. They were very popular in France during the Louis XV and Louis XVI periods, and large numbers were made, usually of ormolu and often in pairs or sets of four to six. The *ciselure* and gilding on many of them are often of very high quality.

Walnut. Finely figured hard wood good for carving, veneering, and turning. Black walnut was used particularly in the William and Mary and Queen Anne periods for elegant furniture, and replaced by mahogany when importations increased. In America it retained popularity in Pennsylvania and the south. White walnut, known better as butternut, grows between New England and Maryland. It is open-grained and light brown, and used mainly in country furniture.

Wardrobes. The wardrobe developed out of the cupboard and the cabinet in the late seventeenth century and was treated monumentally by Boulle and his *atelier*, many being made for the Crown and very sumptuously decorated (*see* Plate 99). From the constructional point of view it consists of a straight, upright cupboard closed by two doors and with one or more shelves on the undecorated interior. It survived into the early Regency, sometimes of plain carved wood, but as rooms became smaller it seems to have disappeared. A number, however, were made in the Boulle technique in the Louis XVI period from earlier designs. Some were also made of plain wood under the Empire.

Washing-stand (or **basin-stand**). Specially adapted for bedroom use after 1750, and of two main kinds. (1) A tripod stand with three uprights, a circular top fitted with a basin, and a central triangular shelf with a drawer (or drawers) and receptacle for soap

(Plate 118D). A four-legged version of this type was also made. (2) A cupboard or chest of drawers on four legs with a basin sunk in the top, the latter covered by a lid or folding flaps.

Water leaf. A carved ornamental motif of narrow leaf with regular horizontal undulations divided by a stem going down the centre. Used in classical style and much favoured by Duncan Phyfe as a leg decoration. In many ways it is the classical style counterpart of the acanthus leaf of the Chippendale period.

Web foot. *See* Duck foot.

What-not. A portable stand with four uprights enclosing shelves, in use after about 1800 for books, ornaments, etc.

Wheat ears. Hepplewhite carved ornament of wheat ears, used in America by McIntire, Phyfe, and others as low-relief decoration on bedposts, chair and sofa backs, etc.

Whorl. Circular ornament on medieval (and later) furniture, the enclosed carving raying from the centre of the circle, or in certain other, including geometrical, dispositions (Fig 53). The general sense of the term seems to approximate whirl. Whorl is freely used, though in doubtful or obviously inapplicable cases roundel is employable.

FIG. 53. Whorl and Roundel

Windsor chair. Developed from the buffet chair, made of turned members with a saddle-seat. Until recently the English Windsor chair was made only around High Wycombe, Bucks. Whether the American Windsor chair was evolved from the English Windsor or the English corner chair, or both, is not yet certain. In any event, the American development is unique. In the American Windsor the back has no splat and is formed entirely of spindles socketed into a top rail. There are two main types – comb-back, in which the top rail is shaped like the head of a comb; and hoop-, or bow, back, the top rail bent like half a hoop (Figs. 54 and 55). Four other

FIG. 54

FIG. 55

types are differentiated – low-back, a semicircular horizontal top rail somewhat like that of a corner chair; New England arm, a simpler form of the hoop-back; fan-back (which some authorities think may have been the side chair to the comb-back arm-chair); and loop- or balloon-back, the top rail loop-shaped. American Windsors have saddle-shaped seats of solid wood or, occasionally, rush seats. The legs, simple turned, are pegged into the seat at a rakish angle, adding a final charm to the stick-and-spindle lines. Windsors were first made in or near Philadelphia about 1725, and were found so comfortable that by 1760 they had become the most popular of all chairs in everyday use. A type fitted with rockers, called the Windsor rocker, is often found.

Wine cistern (or **cooler**). A case for wine bottles, very similar to a cellaret (*q.v.*), but normally larger, without a lid and designed to contain ice or water for cooling the wine. Bowl-shaped wooden cisterns on feet or stand were lined with lead and came into wide use after *c.* 1730; stone and metal (especially silver) cisterns were also found. At the end of the century the tub form, with hoops of brass, was general.

Wing chair. An upholstered chair with high back, stuffed arms, and wing-shaped protectors at head level protruding from the back over the arms (Plate 54A). The chair was known in England during the seventeenth century and was probably introduced in America before 1725.

GLOSSARY

Winthrop desk. A Chippendale slant-top desk mistakenly named for one of the seventeenth-century governors of Massachusetts.

Work-table. The name usually applied to the special table made in the second half of the eighteenth century for ladies' needlework, etc. In Sheraton's time these tables were of several kinds; some, mounted on four tapered and reeded legs or on trestle feet, might include, in addition to a drawer, such fittings as a pouch for the work materials, an adjustable fire-screen, and a writing-board or slide. Another type, the "French work-table", was a tray on trestle feet with a shelf or shelves below.

Worm-hole. Tunnel bored in woodwork by various types of beetle, collectively and popularly called "the worm". Worm-holes are not *per se* evidence of antiquity, though they *have* been artificially simulated. "Worm" is, however, a condition demanding attention to destroy infection. New worm-holes usually show a light-coloured interior, whereas old ones may be discoloured. A simple, though not final, test for possible activity is to tap the suspected piece and watch for a fall of wood-dust. If the mischief is superficial, furniture may be cured by repeated applications of one of the proprietary fluids sold for this purpose; but more heavily infested articles may need expert attention. In some furniture worm may have been extinct for centuries. When worm-holes are laterally exposed to any noticeable extent, it may be inferred (*a*) that the wood has been recut after infestation; or (*b*) that the surface was formerly painted or otherwise covered with some since-vanished substance which formed a side-wall to the channel. Exposed channels occur on some fakes (*q.v.*), but are not *per se* condemnatory, though, in many cases, suspicious.

Writing-cabinet. Fall-front cabinets, enclosing a system of small drawers, became prominent in the latter part of the sixteenth century, especially in Italy and Spain (*see* Bargueño), some of them serving as writing-cabinets. Such cabinets were sometimes furnished with stands, though others were standless, placed on top of a table or chest as needed. Certain of the latter were supplied with stands at a later period.

Such pieces are ancestral to the fall-front scrutoire, secretary, escritoire (*qq.v.*) (from Fr. *secrétaire*) of later times, the slope-front variety being at least in part a development of the writing-desk.

Writing-table. Many varieties of small writing-tables can be found dating from the end of the seventeenth century, when they were first introduced. Early examples were made with turned baluster legs and folding tops, and were frequently used also as side- and card-tables. Gate-legs were usual and some tables were fitted with a drawer. Decoration with marquetry was often found on them. In the early eighteenth century small knee-hole writing-tables were popular, with tiers of narrow drawers on each side of the central recess. Similar tables, it may be noted, were also used as dressing-tables, and it is not always possible to determine their exact purpose. After the introduction of mahogany, when the fashion arose for larger pedestal tables in libraries, many versions of the convenient lighter table continued to be made. It was at the end of the century that perhaps the most elegant kinds of these smaller tables were seen, frequently of satinwood. Some closely resembled contemporary secretaires and cheverets; others were fitted with an adjustable board for writing and with a screen.

LIST OF MUSEUMS

The following list does not seek to be exhaustive and covers only major museums containing furniture and a few provincial ones which contain a certain number of good examples; however, many provincial museums can show one or two good specimens and are usually worth a visit.

GREAT BRITAIN
Castle Museum, York
Collection of Wooden Bygones, Oxley Wood House, Northwood, Mddx
Museum of English Rural Life, University of Reading
Townend, Troutbeck, nr Windermere
State Apartments, Hampton Court Palace, London
State Apartments, Kensington Palace, London
Museum of Welsh Antiquities, Bangor (Welsh furniture)
Bowes Museum, Barnard Castle
Holburne of Menstrie Museum, Bath
Cecil Higgins Museum, Bedford
Aston Hall, Birmingham
Art Gallery and Museum, Brighton
Thomas-Stanford Museum, Brighton
Georgian House, Bristol
The Red Lodge, Bristol
Towneley Hall Museum, Burnley
Astley Hall, Chorley
Valence House Museum, Dagenham, Essex
Burrell Collection, Glasgow
West Yorkshire Fold Museum, Halifax
The Old House, Hereford
Wilberforce Museum, Hull
Christchurch Mansion, Ipswich
Broghton House, Kirkcudbright
Temple Newsam House, Leeds
Anne of Cleves House, Southover, Lewes
Victoria and Albert Museum, London
Courtauld Institute of Art, London
Binning Collection, Fenton House, London
Geffrye Museum, Shoreditch, London
St John's Gate, Clerkenwell, London
Wallace Collection, London
City Art Gallery, Manchester
Heaton Hall, Manchester
Wythenshawe Hall, Manchester
The Lady Lever Art Gallery, Port Sunlight
Ford Green Hall, Stoke-on-Trent
Hall's Croft, Old Town, Stratford
Torre Abbey Art Gallery, Torquay
Oak House, West Bromwich
The Priest House, West Hoathly, Sussex

Victorian Furniture
GREAT BRITAIN
Victoria and Albert Museum, London
London Museum, London
William Morris Gallery, Walthamstow, London
Shipley Art Gallery, Gateshead

French Furniture
GREAT BRITAIN
Bowes Museum, Barnard Castle
Victoria and Albert Museum, London
Wallace Collection, London

EUROPE
Louvre, Paris
Musée des Arts Décoratifs, Paris
Musée Nissim de Camondo, Paris
Musée Marmottan, Paris
Rijksmuseum, Amsterdam
Residenzmuseum, Munich
Nationalmuseum, Stockholm

U.S.A.
Metropolitan Museum of Art, New York
Frick Collection, New York

Seattle Art Museum, Seattle, Washington
Shelburne Museum, Vermont

Italian Furniture
EUROPE
Palazzo Pitti, Florence
Museo Comunale Stibbert, Florence
Museo Horne, Fondazione Horne, Florence
Civici Instituti di Storia e d'Arte, Milan
Museo Civico, Treviso
Palazzo Rezzonico, Venice
Palazzo Reale, Genoa
Palazzo Reale, Turin
Palazzo Quiranale, Rome
Hofburg, Vienna
Osterreichischesmuseum für
   Angewandtekunst, Vienna
Palais Czernin, Vienna
Palais Harrach, Vienna
Palais Schonberg, Vienna
Palais Schwarzenberg, Vienna
Osterreichisches Barockmuseum, Vienna
Horichesmuseum der Stadt, Vienna
Niederösterreichisches Landesmuseum,
   Vienna

Bundesmobiliendepot, Vienna

U.S.A.
Ringling Museum, Sarasota, Florida
Frick Collection, New York

Philadelphia Museum of Art
Cleveland Museum of Art, Cleveland, Ohio

American Furniture
U.S.A.
M. H. de Young Memorial Museum, San
   Francisco
Wadsworte Atheneum, Harford, Conn.
Winterthur Museum, Winterthur, Delaware
Colonial Williamsburg, Virginia
Freer Gallery of Art, Washington
Art Institute of Chicago, Chicago
Boston Museum of Fine Arts, Boston,
   Massachusetts
Detroit Institute of Arts, Detroit, Michigan
Brooklyn Museum, Brooklyn, New York
Metropolitan Museum of Art, New York
Cleveland Institute of Art, Cleveland, Ohio
Philadelphia Museum of Art, Philadelphia

INDEX

OF NAMES AND PLACES

Note: the Glossary on pp 313–355 should be used to supplement this index, which does not contain purely glossarial matter

Abelle, Lawrence, 325
Ackermann, Rudolf, 306
Adam, James, 89
Adam, Robert, 21, 77–78, 82–84, 86–88, 89, 142, 306, 327
Affleck, Thomas, 146
Albertolli, G., 204
Allen, Josiah, 146
Allison, Michael, 146
All Souls, Oxford, 305
Andrewes, Lancelot, 304
Appleton, Nathaniel, 146
Armainvilliers, 306
Aronson, J., 178
Arundell, Lord, 278
Ash, Gilbert, 146
Ash, Thomas, 147, 172
Ashbee, C. R., 115, 116
Atkynson, Robert, 269
Augsburg, 301
Axon, William, 147

Backman, John, 147
Badlam, Stephen, 147
Bagatelle, 306
Bailey's Dictionary, 239, 241, 245, 247, 271
Baillie, Lady Grisell, 239, 241
Bamberg, 302
Bantam, 277
Barker, Robert, 250
Barnsley, Sidney, 115
Barry, Joseph B., 147
Bath Cabinet Makers, 117
Batley, H. W., 113
Bayreuth, 302
Beauvais, 306
Beckford, William, 22 ff, 306
Beket, 271
Belassis, Robert, 250
Bell and Roper, 112
Belter, John, 147
Beman, Reuben, 147
Beneman, Jean-Guillaume, 218

Benson, W. A. S., 114
Bérain, Jean, 205, 208, 216, 306, 318
Berlin, 314
Berry, Duchesse de, 307
Bettridge, Jennens and, 108, 244
Bielefeld, 107
Bilbao, 316
Bird and Hull, 109
Birmingham, 249
Blackheath, 305
Blomfield, Reginald, 115
Bombay, 246
Bonzanigo, G. M., 186, 203, 345
Bosse, Adam, 215
Boulée, 310
Boulle, André Charles, 205, 215, 216, 218, 317, 353
Boulton, Matthew, 249
Bourbon, Duc de, 300
Boyd, Morant, 111
Bradburn, John, 77
Brewster, William, 318
Bridgens, R., 107
Brighton, 311
Bristol Art Gallery, 113
Brown, Ford Madox, 110, 114
Brown, R., 107
Brühl, Schloss, 302
Brünn, 210
Brustolon, A., 184, 203
Buckingham Palace, 310
Burges, William, 109, 110, 111
Burghley House, 280
Burling, Thomas, 147
Burney, Dr, 250
Burnham, Thomas, 147
Burnwood Carving Company, 107
Bute, the Marquis of, 110

Cabinet-Maker's London Book of Price, 346

Cæstius, Caius, 309
Caffiéri, Jean-Jacques, 218
Cairness House, 310
Calder, Alexander, 147
Camera dei Papira, 309
Canina, Luigi, 311
Canterbury, 306
Capodimonte, 203
Cardiff Castle, 110
Carlin, Martin, 235, 342
Carlton House, 310
Carpaccio, 204
Carver, John, 321
Caserta, 203
Castell Coch, 110
Cave, Walter, 115, 116
Caylus, Comte de, 309
Cescinsky, Herbert, 316, 334
Chantrey, Sir Francis, 108
Chapin, Aaron, 147
Chapin, Eliphalet, 147
Charles VI, 205, 207
Charlottenburg Palace, 301
Chatsworth, 43, 280
Cheam, 46
Cheney, Silas E., 147
Chester, 267
Chevalier, S., 302
China, 277, 279
Chippendale, Thomas, 24, 77–78, 80–81, 84–85, 89, 122 ff., 176, 184, 185, 186, 282, 305
Chipping Sodbury, 271
Church Chests of the Twelfth and Thirteenth Centuries in England, 314
Clause, S., 279
Clay, Henry, 341
Clodion, 310
Cobb, John, 77–78
Coccetti, L., 310
Cogswell, John, 147
Colbert, 215, 333
Collcutt, T. E., 111, 112, 113

359

INDEX

Collinson and Lock, 112, 116
Conca, Tomaso, 310
Connelly, Henry, 147
Connoisseur, The, 282, 300
Cooper and Holt, 112
Copland, Henry, 77, 84
Corfe Castle, 247
Coromandel, 277–8
Cotgrave, 241
Courtney, Hercules, 147
Crace, J. G., 109
Cressent, Chas., 235

Dagly, G., 299–301
Dagly, J., 300
Dampier, W., 279
Dance, John, 310
Dance, N., 310
Deffand, Mme du, 306
De Montfaucon, Bernard, 309
Dendera, temple of, 311
Dennis, Thomas, 147, 174
Denon, Baron Vivant, 310, 311
Desmalter, Jacob, 307
Desprez, J.-L., 310
di Giovanni, Francesco, 350
Disbrowe, Nicholas, 147
Downing, A. J., 150 ff.
Downs, Joseph, 324
Dresser, Christopher, 113, 114
Dryden, J., 280
Dubois, Jacques and René, 235
Du Cerceau, 214
Duc, Viollet le, 307
Dunlap, Samuel, II, 147
Du Paquier porcelain factory, 210
Dyer and Watts, 109

Eastlake, C. L., 111, 112, 150, 153, 182
Eaton Hall, 306
Eberts, J. H., 314
Egerton, Matthew, 147
Elfe, Thomas, 147
Elliott, John, 147
English Cottage Furniture, 348
English Furniture from Charles II to George II, 353
Eridge, 245
Étupes, 310
Eugene of Savoy, Prince, 206, 211
Evans, Elder F., 182
Evelyn, John, 45, 250, 280

Ewell, 325

Fabyan's *Chronicles*, 273
Fantastici, Agostino, 311
Fischer v. Erlach, Johann Bernhard, 205
Fischer v. Erlach, Josef Emanuel, 205
Florence, 186, 187, 203, 204, 246, 314, 315, 325, 343
Folwell, John, 147
Fontainebleau, 308
Fonthill Abbey, 22, 23, 306
Forestier, Etienne, 340
Forestier, Etienne Jean, and Pierre Auguste, 235
Forsyth, James, 109
Fox, Thomas, 109
France, William, 78
Franklin, Benjamin, 343
Frederick the Great, 302
Frederick William I, King of Prussia, 300
Frothingham, Benjamin, 147

Gaines, John, 147
Garnier, P., 301
Gaudreau, Antoine Robert, 235
Gauteir, A., 171
Genoa, 325
George, Prince Regent, 282
Ghiberti, 308
Ghirlandaio, 204
Gibbons, Grinling, 49, 54, 58
Gillingham, James, 148
Gillow, 109, 111, 112, 116
Gimson, Ernest, 115
Goa, 246
Gobelins, 215
Goddard, John, 148, 316
Godey's *Lady's Book*, 151
Godwin, E. W., 113, 114
Goodison, Benjamin, 77
Gostelowe, Jonathan, 148
Gouthière, Pierre, 235, 310
Grant, Dr J., 282
Greenough, H., 182
Grendey, Giles, 77, 303
Grünes Gewölbe, 309
Guérin, J., 302

Hadley, Mass., 334
Haines, Ephraim, 148
Hains, Adam, 148
Halfpenny, W. and J., 305

Hall, J., 151
Hamburg, 301
Hampton Court, 274
Hampton Court Palace, 280
Hardman and Cox, 109
Harrison, William, 45, 46
Harrison's Wood Carving Company, 107
Hatfield, 272
Hawkesmore, Nicholas, 305
Heal and Son, 116
Henry, J. S., 117
Hepplewhite, George, 77–78, 79, 82, 84–88, 212
Herstmonceux, 111
Herzog, Anton, 206
Hever, 245
Hewetson and Milner, 112
High Wycombe, 354
Hindley, Charles, 109
Historical Description of the Island of Britain, 45
Hogarth, William, 275
Hohenzollernmuseum, 299
Holland, H., 310
Holland and Sons, 111
Hollingbourne, 304
Holme, Randall, 240, 241
Hooke, R., 57
Hope, T., 78, 143, 311
Hörringer, J., 302
Hortense, Queen, 307
Hosmer, Joseph, 148
Houghton, John, 267, 268
Howard, 109

Isis, 310

Jack, George, 114, 115
Jackson, 107
Jackson and Graham, 113
Jacob, 310
Jacob, Georges, 235
Jefferson, T., 171
Jeneson, William, 250
Jennes & Bettridge, 108, 244
Jephthah, 248
Johnson, 84
Johnston, Philip Mainwaring, 314
Johnstone and Jeanes, 109
Jones, Arthur J., 108
Jones, Owen, 112, 113
Jordan's Patent Wood Carving, 107

360

INDEX

Josef II, 205, 210, 211
Josephine, Empress, 307
Jouquet, A., 116
Journal du Garde Meuble de la Couronne, 334
Juvarra, F., 203, 303

Kansas City, Missouri, 303
Kauffmann, Angelica, 25, 86
Kedleston, 44, 306
Kelso, J., 172
Kent, William, 50, 77, 80, 84–85, 186, 247
Kenton and Company, 115
Kimbolton, 304
King, Thomas, 107
Kléber, J.-B., 307, 310
Kunstindustri Museet, Oslo, 301

Ladatte, F., 203
Ladies' Amusement . . ., The, 282
Lamb, Henry, 109
Langley, Batty, 77, 305
Langley, Thomas, 77
Langlois, père and fils, 300
Lannuier, Charles Honoré, 148
Lansdowne House, 310
Larkin, O. W., 178
Lascelles and Company, 113
Laurent, J.-A., 307
Lawson, John, 267
Lawton, Robert, 148
Leake, 107
Le Brun, Charles, 215
Ledoux, 310
Lee, Ann (Mother), 178
Leeds, 111, 311
Lehman, Benjamin, 148
Leicester, the Earl of, 267, 270
Leleu, Jean François, 236
Lemon, William, 148
Leopold, I, 206
Lethaby, W. R., 115
Liberty's, 114
Linnell, John, 78
Linnell, W., 281, 282
Lock, Matthias, 77, 84
London Bridge, 269
Lorimer, R. S., 115
Lormier, Alfred, 108
Louis XVI, 210, 211, 310
Lucas v. Hildebrandt, Johann, 205, 206
Lucca, 184, 186

Lucraft, 109, 112

Macartney, Mervyn, 115
Mackintosh, Charles Rennie, 116
Mackmurdo, A. H., 115
Madison, James, 343
Madrid, 46
Maggiolini, Guiseppe, 203, 350
Maragliano, A. M., 203
Marchetti, G. B., 310
Maria Theresa, 205
Marie Antoinette, 23, 310
Marketon, Derbyshire, 242
Marlborough, Duke of, 278
Marochetti, Baron, 108
Marot, Daniel, 49
Marsh, Jones and Cribb, 111, 115
Martin, brothers, 353
Martin, E. S., 300
Martin, G., 300
Martin, J., 300
Martin, J. A., 302
Martin, R., 300, 302
Martineau, H., 182
Massia, P., 303
Mazarin, Cardinal, 277
McIntire, Samuel, 148
Meacham, J. (Father), 178 ff.
Meek, C., 150
Mengs, Anton Raphael, 309
Merelaws, 311
Method of Learning to Draw in Perspective, &c, The, 281
Milan, 246
Mills & Deming, 148
Minshen, 242
Misson, M., 302
Montagu, Elizabeth, 281, 282
Montbéliard, Prince de, 307
Monument de Costume, 314
Morris, Marshall, Faulkner & Company, 110
Morris, William, 24, 110, 111, 114, 115
Morrison, Alfred, 113
Mount Vernon, 338
Moxon, 242
Munich, 301, 302

Naples, 186, 203, 270, 325
Napoleon, 186, 307, 308, 310, 311

Newport, 316
Nieuhoff, J., 301
Northampton, Earl of, 277, 278
Notre Dame, 307
Nymphenberg, 302, 306

Oeben, Jean François, 26, 236
Ogden, Henry, 109, 112, 113
Osborne House, 107

Palazzo Braschi, 310
Paris, 333
Parodi, D., 203
Pasquale, Fra, 308
Paston family, 304
Pegge, Richard, 240
Peking, 277
Pepys, Samuel, 241
Percier, 307
Pergolesi, 86
Peterhof, 311
Petit Trianon, 307
Philadelphia, 354
Phyfe, Duncan, 148, 320, 344, 347, 354
Piazza di S. Pietro, 308
Piccadilly, 311
Piffetti, P., 184, 203
Pillement, J., 282
Pimlico, 107
Pimm, John, 148
Pinturicchio, 308
Piranesi, Giovanni Battista, 309, 310
Place Vendôme, 310
Playfair, James, 310
Plymouth, Mass., 318–19
Pompadour, Mme de, 300
Potsdam, 302
Poynter, E. J., 110
Prignot, Eugène, 108
Prince, Samuel, 148
Pugin, A. W. N., 108, 109, 111, 112
Purdie, Bonnar and Carfrae, 109

Racconigi, 307
Ramsey, Sir Thomas, 270
Randolph, Benjamin, 148, 345
Raphael, 308
Rebecca, 248
Riesener, Jean Henri, 23, 26, 218, 236
Rijksmuseum, 299

INDEX

Robinson, P. F., 311
Roe, F. G., 173
Roentgen, David, 237
Rogers, W. G., 108
Rome, 184, 186, 325
Rose, Walter, 324
Rosenborg, 279
Ruskin, John, 112, 182

Saenger, J. J., 301
Sager, E., 278
Salem, Mass., 344
Salisbury Cathedral, 246
Sanderson, Elijah, 148
Sanssouci, 302
Sass, Jacob, 148
Savery, William, 148
Scarron, P., 300
Schnell, M., 301
Schönborn, L. F. von, 301
Scott, M. H. Baillie, 115, 116
Seddon, George, 77
Seddon, Sons, & Shackleton, 243
Sévigné, Mme de, 300
Seymour, John, 148
Shaw, John, 148
Shaw, Norman, 109, 113
Shearer, T., 142
Shelbourne House, 310
Sheraton, Thomas, 25, 49, 77–79, 82–88, 142 ff., 185, 186, 275
Shoolbred, James, 111, 113
Short, Joseph, 148
Simpson, 54
Skillion, John and Simeon, 148
Smee, 112
Smee and Snell, 109
Smith, Edward, 240
Smith, George, 311
Smith, W., 278
Soane, Sir John, 310
Sobry's *Architecture*, 268
Socchi, G., 204
Spa, 299
Spender, A., 302
Spiers & Son, 244
Spooner, Charles, 116
Stalker, J., and Parker, G.:
 Treatise of Japanning and Varnishing, 120

Stitcher & Clemmens, 148
Stobwasser, J. H., 302
Stokes, Samuel, 57
Stowe, 309
Strawberry Hill, 20, 21, 304, 305, 306
Strickley, G., 153
Sullivan, L. H., 183
Symonds, R. W., 353

Talbert, Bruce J., 111, 112
Tarver, E. J., 111
Taskin, P., 301
Taylor, John, 109, 282
Taylor, Warington, 111
Terry, Eli, 341
Théâtre du Marais, 307
Thomas, John, 108
Thomire, Pierre Philippe, 218, 236, 340
Tickell, Thomas, 305
Tiepolo, G., 302
Tiepolo, G. D., 306
Tompion, Thomas, 51
Tonbridge, 245, 249
Toppan, Abner, 149
Tosello, I., 302
Townsend family, 149
Townsend, Job, 149
Townsend, John, 316
Townsend, Stephen, 149
Trapnell, C. and W., 109
Treatise of Japanning and Varnishing, 276, 280, 335
Treviso, 303
Trollope, 109, 112
Trotter, Daniel, 149
Tufft, Thomas, 149
Tunbridge Wells, 352
Turin, 310, 345

Urbino, 46

Van Aelst, P., 305
Vanbrugh, John, 304, 305, 309
Vandale, Ernest, 109
Van Linschoten, 277
Van Risen Burgh, B., 301
Vatican, the, 308, 309
Venice, 210, 246, 268, 302–3,
 316, 321, 324, 325, 328, 336, 337, 343, 352
Verney, E., 280
Verney, Ralph first Earl, 272
Versailles, 279, 300
Vertueuse Athénienne, La, 314
Vicenza, 306
Vien, J. B., 314
Vienna, 185, 205 ff.
Vile, William, 77
Villa Borghese, 309, 311
Village Carpenter, The, 324
Villa Valmarana, 306
Voysey, C. F. A., 115, 116

Walker, Robert, 149
Wallace Collection, 26, 300
Walpole, Horace, 19 ff., 43, 275, 281, 304, 305, 306
Walthamstow, 115
Warwick, 313
Warwick Castle, 108
Washington, 338
Watt, William, 113
Watteau, Antoine, 208
Wayne, Jacob, 149
Weaver, Holmes, 149
Webb, Philip, 110, 114, 115
Weisweiler, Adam, 237, 342
Wells, 333
Wells, S., 180
Whitaker, Henry, 107
White and Parlby, 107
Whytocks, 109
Wickliffe, R., 182
Wilkinson's, 116
Willard, Simon, 315, 336
Willet, Marinus, 149
Windsor Castle, 306
Wollaston, 76
Wood, Edgar, 116
Wornum, 107
Wright and Mansfield, 109, 113
Wyatt, James, 306
Wyatt, Sir Matthew Digby, 111
Wyatville, Sir Jeffry, 306
Wylie and Lockhead, 117

Yarborough, Earl of, 310
Youf, 204